The Frozen Sky

Jeff Carlson

International bestselling author
of *Interrupt* and *Plague Year*

D0023612

4-19-13

Jeff Carlson
www.jverse.com

Film / TV
Jim Ehrich
Rothman Brecher Kim Agency
9250 Wilshire Blvd., 4th Fl.
Beverly Hills, CA 90212
310-432-4629

Literary
Don Maass
Donald Maass Literary Agency
121 West 27th St., Ste. 801
New York, NY 10001
212-727-8383

ISBN: 978-1-936460-14-4

Second Edition

Other Books
by Jeff Carlson:

Interrupt

THE PLAGUE YEAR TRILOGY

Plague Year

Plague War

Plague Zone

SHORT STORY COLLECTION

Long Eyes

Advance Praise for *The Frozen Sky*

"I'm hooked."
—Larry Niven, *New York Times*
bestselling author of *The Fate of Worlds*

"A first-rate adventure set in one of our solar
system's most fascinating places. Carlson is a fine
storyteller, and this is his best book yet."
—Allen Steele, Hugo Award-winning
author of the *Coyote* series

"Pulse pounding."
—*Publishers Weekly*

"Tense."
—*Locus Magazine*

"Nothing short of amazing."
—David Marusek, Sturgeon Award-winning
author of *The Wedding Album*

"Believable and compelling. This is the perfect eerie
setting for Carlson to flex his creative muscle."
—*Bookworm Blues*

Praise for *Plague Year*

"An epic of apocalyptic fiction: harrowing, heartfelt, and rock-hard realistic."
—James Rollins, *New York Times* bestselling author of *Bloodline*

"Terrifying."
—Scott Sigler, *New York Times* bestselling author of *Nocturnal*

"Chilling and timely."
—*RT Book Reviews*

"Jeff Carlson packs riveting storytelling with a lot of fresh ideas."
—David Brin, *New York Times* bestselling author of *Existence*

"One of the best apocalyptic novels I've read. Part Michael Crichton, a little Stephen King, and a lot of good writing...Carlson makes it all seem plausible and thrilling."
—*Quiet Earth* (www.quietearth.us)

Praise for *Plague War*

Finalist for the Philip K. Dick Award

"Compelling. His novels take readers
to the precipice of disaster."
—*San Francisco Chronicle*

"Intense."
—*SF Reviews*

"Excellent."
—*SF Scope*

"A breakneck ride through one of the deadliest
and thrilling futures imagined in years.
Jeff Carlson has the juice!"
—Sean Williams, *New York Times* bestselling
author of *Star Wars: The Force Unleashed*

"Carlson's nightmarish landscape presents a chilling
albeit believable picture of a post-apocalyptic world.
Strong, dynamic characters bring the story a
conclusion you won't see coming."
—*RT Book Reviews*

Praise for *Plague Zone*

"Gripping. An epic struggle among desperate nations equipped with nano weapons."
—Jack McDevitt, Nebula Award-winning author of *Firebird*

"A high-octane thriller at the core—slick, sharp, and utterly compelling."
—Steven Savile, international bestselling author of *Silver*

"I can't wait for the movie."
—*Sacramento News & Review*

"This installment opens with a jolt. If you love dark SF, you can't go wrong with Carlson's great *Plague Year* trilogy."
—*Apex Magazine*

Praise for *Long Eyes*

"Striking."
—*Locus Online*

"Exciting."
—*SR Revu*

"Chilling and dangerous."
—*HorrorAddicts.net*

"An amazing collection."
—*Sci-Guys.com*

"Captivating. *Long Eyes* packs a lot of
adventure and entertainment."
—*BookBanter.net*

Praise for *Interrupt*

"Let's be honest: Carlson is dangerous.
Interrupt is riveting, high concept, and so real
I felt the fires and blood. Thumbs up."
—Scott Sigler, *New York Times*
bestselling author of *Pandemic*

"This book has it all—elite military units,
classified weaponry, weird science, a dash
of romance, and horrific global disasters.
Carlson writes like a knife at your throat."
—Bob Mayer, *New York Times*
bestselling author of the
Green Berets and *Area 51* series.

"Terrific pacing. Dimensional characters. Jeff Carlson
delivers everything and more in a killer thriller."
—John Lescroart, *New York Times* bestselling
author of *The Hunter*

"A quantum leap in storytelling. I love the concept unreservedly. Love the writing to the point of jealousy. Carlson is so ridiculously talented, he makes me want to poke my eyeballs out. *Interrupt* is a phenomenal read."
—Steven Savile, international bestselling author of *Silver*

"The ideas fly as fast as jets. This thriller has brains!"
—Kim Stanley Robinson, Hugo and Nebula Award-winning author of *2312*

Table of Contents

For Diana,
always.

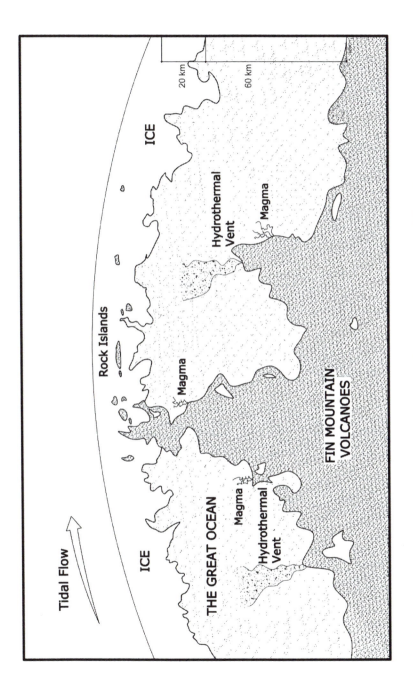

Europa's Southern Pole

Jupiter's Largest Moons

THE FROZEN SKY

1.

VONNIE RAN WITH her eyes shut, chasing the sound of her own boot steps. This channel in the rock was tight enough to reflect every noise back on itself, and she dodged through the space between each rattling echo.

She knew the rock was laced with crevices and pits. She knew she might catch her leg or fall with every step.

But she ran.

She crashed one shoulder against the wall. Impact spun her sideways. She hit the ground hard. Sprawled on the rock, Vonnie pushed herself up and glanced back, forgetting the danger in this simple reflex.

The bloody wet glint in her retinas was only a distraction, a useless blur of heads-up data she couldn't read.

Worse, her helmet was transmitting sporadically, its side mount and some internals crushed beyond saving. She'd rigged a terahertz pulse that obeyed on/off commands, but her sonar and the camera spot were dead to her, flickering at random—and the spotlight was like a torch in this cold.

Vonnie clapped her glove over the gear block on her helmet, trying to muffle the beam. She wasn't concerned about the noise of her boot steps. The entire moon groaned with seismic activity, shuddering and cracking, but heat was a give-away. Heat scarred the ice and rock. For her to look back was to increase the odds of leaving a trail.

Stupid. Stupid.

She'd never wanted to fight. Yes, the sunfish were predators. Their small bodies rippled with muscle, speed, and unrelenting aggression, but they were also beautiful in their way. They were fascinating and strange.

Were they smarter than her?

The sunfish had outmaneuvered her twice. More than anything, what Vonnie felt was regret. She could have done better. She should have waited to approach them instead of letting her pride make the decision.

In some ways Alexis Vonderach was still a girl at thirty-six, single, too smart, too good with machines and math to need many friends. She was successful. She was confident. She fit the ESA psych profile to six decimal points.

Now all that was gone. She was down to nerves and guesswork and whatever momentum she could hold onto.

She lurched forward, pawing with one hand along the soft volcanic rock. With her helmet's ears cranked to maximum gain, each rasping touch of her boots and gloves was a roar. Larger echoes hinted at a gap above her on her left. Could she climb up? Trying to listen for the opening, she turned her head.

Her face struck a jagged outcropping in the wall. Startled, she jerked back. Then her hip banged against a different rock and she fell, safe inside her armor.

Standing was a chore she'd done hundreds of times. She did it again. She kept moving.

Vonnie didn't think the sunfish could track the alloys of her suit, but they seemed like they were able to smell her footprints. Fresh impacts in the rock and ice left traces of dust and moisture in the air. There was no question that the sunfish were highly attuned to warmth. She'd killed nine of them in a ravine and covered her escape with an excavation charge, losing herself behind the fire and smoke... and they'd followed her easily.

What if she could use that somehow? She might be able to lead them into a trap.

Vonnie was no soldier. She had never trained for violence or even imagined it, except maybe at a few faculty budget meetings. That was an odd flicker of memory. Vonnie clung to it because it was clean and bright. She would have given anything to return to her old life, the frustrations and rewards of teaching, her classroom, and her tidy desk.

She fell once more, off-balance with her hand against her head. A heap of rubble had caught her boots and shins. She scrabbled over what appeared to be a cave-in. The noises she made were loud, clattering booms—but the echoes stretched at least ten meters above her, defining a tall chasm.

I can pin them here, she thought.

If she burned the rock and left a false trail, she could drop the rest of the broken wall on them when they passed. Then they would give up. Didn't they have to give up? After the bloodbath in the ravine, she'd killed two more in the ice, and others had been wounded. Could the sunfish really keep soaking up casualties like that?

Vonnie could only guess at their psychology. Although she was blind, she knew of the existence of light. Although she was alone, she believed someone would find her.

She thought the history of this race was without hope. The sunfish had a phenomenal will to live, but the concept of hope required a sense of *future*. It required the idea of somewhere to go.

The sunfish had never imagined the stars, much less reached up to escape this black, fractured world.

This damned world.

No less than four Earth agencies had landed mecha on the surface to strip its resources. Then they'd sent a joint team in the name of science, handpicking three experts from China, America, and Europe—and Bauman and Lam had both died before First Contact, crushed in a rock swell. Would it have made any difference?

The question was too big for her. That the sunfish existed at all was a shock. Humanity had long since found Mars and Venus stillborn and barren. After more than a century and a half, the SETI radioscopes hadn't detected any hint of another thinking race within a hundred and fifty lightyears of Earth.

Looking so far away was like a bad joke. The sunfish had been inside the solar system for millennia, a neighbor and a counterpart. It should have been the luckiest miracle. It should have been like coming home, but that had been Vonnie's worst mistake: to think of the sunfish as similar to human beings. They were a species that seemed to lack fear or even hesitation, which might be exactly why her trap would work.

She decided to risk it. She was exhausted and hurt. If she stopped running, she would have time to attempt repairs and regain the advantage.

I hope they don't come, she thought.

But she found a small shelf in the cliff above the rock slide, then settled in to kill more of them.

2.

JUPITER'S SIXTH MOON was an ocean, a deep, complete sphere too far from the sun to exist as liquid on its surface—not at temperatures of -162° Celsius. Europa was cocooned in ice. The solid crust ran as thick as twenty kilometers in some regions, which meant that for all intents and purposes, it enveloped Europa like a single continent.

Human beings first walked the ice in 2094, and flybys and probes had buzzed this distant white orb since 1979. Europa was an interesting place.

For one thing, it was as large as Earth's moon—nearly as large as Mercury—which meant it could have been a planet in its own right if it orbited the sun instead of Jupiter. It also had a unique if extremely thin oxygen atmosphere caused by the disassociation of molecules from its surface. It was water ice.

It was a natural fuel depot for fusion ships.

Before the end of the twenty-first century, the investment of fifty mecha and two dozen more in spare parts was well worth an endless supply of deuterium at the edge of human civilization. The diggers and the processing stations were fusion-powered, too. So were the tankers parked in orbit.

Spacecraft came next, some with crews, some piloted by robots, and eighteen years passed.

That quiet period might have been much longer. The mecha were on the equator, where it was easiest for the tankers to hold position above them without constantly burning fuel, fighting Jupiter's gravity and the tug of other moons—but Jupiter's mass created other conflicts.

Deep inside Europa, its rocky core flexed, generating heat and volcanic activity. The ocean rolled with murderous tides. On the surface, the ice suffered its own turmoil, creating different environments such as "canyons," "melts," "domes," and "chaos terrain." Especially on the equator, the ice bulged and sank and turned over on itself.

Only the smoother, so-called "plains" were deemed safe by the men and women who guided the mecha by remote telepresence. Looking ahead, they sent rovers in all directions, surveying, sampling.

At the southern pole was a smooth area that covered nearly thirty square kilometers.

Many rovers went there.

3.

VONNIE SHIVERED, AN intensely ugly sensation inside her suit. She'd locked the joints and torso to become a statue, preventing herself from causing any movement whatsoever, and yet inside it she was skin and muscle.

The feel of her body against this shell was repulsive. She squirmed again and again, trying to shrink away from it, which was impossible.

The rut in her thinking wasn't much better. She wished Choh Lam hadn't tried to... She wished somehow she'd saved the rest of her crew. Lam understood so much so fast, he might have already found a way out, a way *up*.

She'd cobbled together a ghost using his mem files, but she couldn't give it enough capacity to correct its flaws. In order to expand the ghost's abilities, she would need to shut down her ears or the override she'd programmed into her heat exchanger, each a different kind of death. If she couldn't hear, she would be utterly lost. And if her suit exuded body heat instead of storing it, her ambush would fail.

It would be better to forget Lam. She thought she should erase him, but even at three-quarters logic he was useful. He'd suggested a tranquilizer and Vonnie had popped one tab, which slowed her down enough to feel clear again. Clear and cold. She shouldn't be cold, sweating inside her hard shell, but the waiting was like its own labyrinth of ice—the waiting and the listening and the deep bruises in her face.

She didn't care how sophisticated the medical systems were supposed to be. On some level, her body knew it was hurt, even numbed and shot full of don't-worry.

Her head had a dozen reasons why she was safe, but her body knew the sunfish would come again. The lonely dark was alive. That truth no longer surprised her, and she strained her senses out into the dark, frozen spaces of the chasm below her.

She was more afraid of missing the sunfish than of drawing in an attack. It was superstitious to imagine they could hear her thoughts, she knew that, but at the ravine they'd run straight to her hiding place despite three decoys. How did they keep zeroing in on her?

She needed to learn if she was going to live.

This rock shelf seemed defensible. There was nowhere to retreat but she only had one approach to cover. Overhead was a spongework of holes where she could dump her waste heat before leaving.

Vonnie laid on her belly, facing outward, trying to eat and trying to rest, trying to ignore the nasty, anesthetized pressure of the med beetles slithering in and out of her temple, her cheek, and her eye socket.

Both eyes were damaged, yet she'd elected to deal with her left eye first in case something went wrong. The nanotech might need to scavenge one eye to save the other. Step by step surgeries had been Lam's idea. He'd also agreed that her helmet would retain its integrity if she broke off her gear block and stripped it for parts. What else would he have tried?

The plastisteel of her suit should contain all sound, but there was another risk in talking, a risk she ignored just to be with someone.

"Are you still there?" she whispered.

His voice was uneven and rushed, too emotional for an artificial intelligence:

—*Von, listen. Don't close me down again, please.*

"Tell me what Lam would do," she said. "Am I safe here? I need to rest. I laid down a false trail with my spotlight."

—*They'll catch us.*

"Did you check my map? I made it almost three klicks."

—*They will. The probability is eighty-plus percent, but I can talk to them. We have enough data now. With temporary control of the suit, I could at least establish...*

"No."

—*Vonnie, most of their language is postures and shapes. I can't tell you fast enough how to move.*

"No. Self-scan and correct."

—*Von, wait.*

"I said scan for glitches and correct. Off."

Could a ghost be crazy? If so, it was her fault. Lam was the first she'd ever made. She'd rushed the process because she was angry with him—the real him. She'd let him remember how he died, and it had made him erratic. Maybe he'd never doubted himself before.

Bauman would have been a better friend. Bauman had been

older, calmer, another woman, but she was a geneticist and Lam's biology/ecology skills were too valuable. The decision had been obvious. Vonnie didn't have the resources to pull them apart, then build an overlay with Bauman's personality and Lam's education.

She was alone.

She itched her fingertips inside her rigid glove. Too soon, she prompted her clock and was discouraged. It would be six minutes until her skull was repaired, thirty before she regained her optic nerve.

Can I improve him? she wondered. *I can't give him more capacity, but maybe I can talk him through his error lists. He's a learning system. He should respond.*

Patience was supposed to be one of her strengths. Four years ago, she'd been a top instructor at Arianespace. She'd led classes in cybernetics, although her specialty had been ROM welding and construction, using remote operated mecha in low gravity environments, zero gravity, underground, or underwater. Then she'd been recruited by the European Space Agency for the same job with better pay and better students.

Vonnie enjoyed working with her hands. She loved igniting a spark in people who wanted to learn. Tailoring her approach for each new individual kept her job interesting. The ESA was full of ambitious, hyper-educated men and women who challenged her with their egos, their experience, and their own expectations.

"You can't wait until you can see," she argued with herself. "Otherwise he'll keep trying to take over the suit. Run more voice checks. Keep command. If he gets twitchy, just lock him down again."

A noise echoed through the blackness like two rocks clacking together, barely audible in the distance.

On my left, she thought.

Was it a rock fall? Tremors and avalanches regularly split these caverns. The noise could have been a natural event, but Vonnie knew better.

Something was coming.

4.

EUROPA'S VOLCANOES ADDED to the unrest in the ice. Below many of the "dome" and "melt" environments, subsurface peaks of lava had proved common, elongated fins and spindles that could not have existed if this moon had more than a thirteenth of Earth's gravity. The movements in the ice eroded the rock, then distributed it everywhere.

Rock was a problem for the mecha. It damaged blades and claws. It jammed in pipes. Even dust would make a site unattractive, and ESA Rover 011 was quick to give up on a wide area of the southern plain when it brought up contaminants in its drill cylinder.

But the rover was well-engineered. Belatedly, it noticed the consistency of shape among the debris. Then its telemetry jumped as it linked with a tanker overhead, using the ship's brain to analyze the smattering of solids.

Finally the rover moved again, sacrificing two forearms and a spine flexor to embrace its prize, insulating the sample against the near-vacuum on Europa's surface.

Impossible as this seemed, given the preposterous cold and the depth from which the sample came, the contaminants were organic lifeforms, long dead, long preserved: tiny, albino bugs with no more nervous system than an earthworm.

5.

VONNIE OPENED HER blind eyes to nothing and her ears were empty, too—but she was sure. Something was coming. Inside the rigid shell of her suit, she moved but could not move, a surge of adrenaline that had no release.

Trembling, she waited. Brooding, she cursed herself. She'd spent her life making order of things, and she couldn't get her head quiet.

She made everything familiar by worrying through the mechanics of her trap again and again.

She'd snapped her next-to-last excavation charge in two and rigged a second detonator, setting one charge in the ceiling beyond her rock shelf, the other below and to her left. The blasts would shove forward and down, although in this gravity, she could expect ricochets and blowback.

Good.

The sunfish fought like a handful of rubber balls slammed down against the floor, spreading in an instant, closing on her from every angle. Their group coordination was beyond belief. To a species whose perceptions were based on touch and sonar, language consisted of gesture and stance. They always knew each other's mood and seemed to share it like a flock of birds.

Without her eyes, their synchronized attacks were an even greater threat. Her terahertz pulse was better at sounding out large, immobile shapes than at following objects in motion. Vonnie knew she would lose track of some of them, so she'd smash everything within fifty meters.

Her armor could sustain indirect hits from the porous lava rock. She planned to bait them, bring them close, then roll into a crevice behind her and hit the explosives, after which she would slash any survivors with her laser.

It was a cutting tool, unfortunately, weak at the distance of a meter. Worse, if she overheated the gun, she would probably not be able to repair it. Her nanotech was limited to organic internals. Most of the tool kits on her waist and left hip had been torn away.

"Stop thinking. Damn it, stop talking," she murmured, the words as rapid as her heartbeat.

Just stop it.

Could they really hear her mind? She'd studied the sunfish with the acute concentration of a woman who might never see anything else again, and with all the skills of a teacher evaluating her newest class.

The sunfish definitely had an extra sense, maybe the ability to... feel weight or density. That would serve them well in the ice. So they would be able to differentiate her from the environment.

For once, she wanted them to find her. Vonnie reactivated her suit and rose into a crouch, strobing the chasm below with a terahertz pulse. She thought her signals were outside the sunfishes' range of hearing, but she'd revealed herself as soon as her armor scraped against the rock.

Nothing. There was nothing.

"Oh God." She choked back the sound and swept the bent spaces of the chasm, quickly locating pockets in the ceiling that she hadn't anticipated and couldn't reach with her signals. The angle was too steep. Using her terahertz pulse was like turning on a light in what she thought was a closet and finding instead that half of the house was gone—and her enemy needed only the thinnest openings to surround her.

Were they already too close? She'd seen it before, a dozen sunfish upside down on the rock like fat creeping muscles.

Vonnie aimed her laser at the ceiling even as she groped with her other hand for a chunk of rock. There was gravel, too, and a head-sized boulder. She'd gathered every loose piece of lava she could find.

Should she throw it now? Try to provoke them? Her thumb gritted in the rock as she clenched her fist.

She was a decent shot with a ball. She'd grown up with three younger brothers. But the suit itself was a weapon. The suit had low-level AI programs that could make her something like a passenger inside a robot. There were voice menus designed for activities like climbing or welding because human beings got tired. The suit did not. It also had radar targeting that she could not see, and it would limit the velocity of its throws only to avoid damaging her shoulder and back.

She didn't trust it.

She'd used most of her AI programs to hold an imprint of her ghost. The suit was rotten with Lam's mem files. Twice the ghost had caused interrupts, trying to reconfigure itself, trying to seize control, and yet Vonnie was afraid to purge him. Deleting his mem files might affect her suit's amplified speed and brawn.

"Are you still there?" she hissed.

—*Von, listen. Don't close me down again, please.*

That was the same thing it always said. God. Oh God. She didn't have time to hassle with him.

"Combat menu," she said.

—*Online.*

She hesitated. Right now, the ghost was somewhat contained. That would change if she gave it access to defense modes. Doing so was a bad gamble. The extra capacity might be precisely what the ghost needed to self-correct... or the stupid, miserable AI might corrupt the most basic functions of her suit. Was there any other way?

"I need auto-targeting only," she said. "Fire by voice command."

—*Von, that drops efficiency to thirty percent.*

"Fire by voice command. Confirm."

—*Listen to me.*

Four slender arms reached out of the ceiling.

6.

IT WAS EASY to be friends with Choh Lam. In his mid-thirties, skinny and short, with big ears, he made a point of being nonthreatening. He was freak smart but also soft-spoken, hiding himself in a kind voice, both eager and shy. He probably didn't realize he had restless eyes because in every other way he moved like he talked, gently.

Vonnie's impression was of a man who'd spent his life holding back. He was a man who wanted to belong.

Lam made his break with that kind of thinking before the boards agreed how many people to send to Europa. Even before the mining groups had reprogrammed their mecha for new, more intensive searches, Lam let his genius show and posted a sim that guaranteed his slot on the mission—for bugs. Just bugs. That was all the ESA rover had found. No one believed this ice ball could support much else, and yet there were fifteen thousand volunteers in the first week.

Fifteen thousand experts wanted to abandon their families and their homes despite knowing that the trip out to Europa would be two and a half months cramped inside a hab module; that the food would be slop-in-a-bag; that Jupiter seethed with radiation.

In the virtual meetings for candidates, Vonnie had grinned at the enthusiasm they shared. *Homo sapiens*' best traits were heart and curiosity. Despite all of their technology, despite developing space-flight, AI, and nano medicine, there was still so much of the ape in them.

Fifteen thousand people suddenly didn't care about anything except getting their feet on the ice and grubbing around for exotic life. It was a riddle unlike anything else.

Where did the bugs come from?

The weak little creatures weren't burrowers, not with their spherical body shape and dorsal whiskers. Also, there were variations in the ice. The narrow layer containing the bugs was nowhere near as old as the rest of the sample, and loaded with chlorides and minerals.

Europa possessed every building block of life. There was water, heat, and organic material from comet and meteor strikes. They had long speculated that Europa's great ocean was not wholly frozen. The icy crust went down an average of ten kilometers, reaching twenty km in places, but beneath it was slush and eventually liquid. In fact, some areas would be as hot as boiling where raw magma or gas pushed up from the moon's rocky core.

Was there also life in the ocean? If yes, it must be limited to hardy bacteria like those found near ocean-floor volcanoes on Earth or in the corrosive toxins of mine tailing ponds. Europa's surface was stained with sulfuric acid and salt. This was evidence of caustic pH levels in the ocean.

Lam's school of thought predicted a world inside the ice, a small, unsteady, vertical world. A hundred man-made probes had found nothing for a hundred years, but Lam said that was to be expected. He drew his model in an area where a fin of subsurface mountains partly diverted the crushing, glacial tides. The safe zone was a mere fifteen cubic kilometers in volume—and even within its confines, the ice and rock were burned and torn.

Lam was among the first to understand the violence of this environment. It mesmerized him.

Here are the bugs in an open rift, he said. What are they doing? We don't know. Mating? Migrating? Nearby there is a rumble, and a super-heated geyser floods the rift. It collapses, then gradually freezes with the bugs suspended inside. But there are more pocket ecologies stacked throughout the region, some with tenuous atmospheres of water vapor or volcanic gases such as nitrogen and carbon dioxide, poisonous hydrogen chloride, and explosive hydrogen sulfide.

The warm holes in the ice were mild compared to the acidic salt ocean. Eons ago, in some of these crannies, bacteria had grown and thrived. The same crude microorganisms had been the first lifeforms to inhabit Earth. They were called chemoautotrophs—self-nourishing chemical reactions that ate iron, sulfur, ammonia, or manganese.

The bacteria refused to die.

In time, isolated from the minerals and poisons that fed them, a few strains had adapted to split water molecules as a new energy source, eating hydrogen instead of iron or manganese. The byproduct was oxygen.

The new bacteria released oxygen gas into some of the pocket ecologies. Oxygen changed things forever. It allowed for larger, faster, more complex organisms. Life on Europa flourished because it had no other choice, evolving and spreading never more than a few steps ahead of constant upheaval.

7.

CHRISTMAS BAUMAN WAS fifty-three and not so new to long-term commitments. That was partly why she won her slot as the expedition commander, as a balance to Lam and Vonderach. Vonnie liked her, too. Bauman pretended sarcasm with them, but it was a way of communicating her experience. Vonnie could measure Bauman's amusement in each fraction of a centimeter that her brows lifted above her muddy green eyes.

She was heavier in the chest and hips than Vonnie and more willing to use her body despite her age, dominating conversations by wading into the middle of any group.

She had her own fascination. "What if—" she kept saying.

What if the bugs weren't dead? They might be hibernating or otherwise biologically active. What if their chemistry wasn't too strange to co-opt, and could be used in geriatrics or cryo surgery? Yes, they appeared to have been scalded in magma-heated water and then gradually mashed and distorted by the freezing process. The bugs appeared very dead indeed, but who could say what adaptations were normal on Europa? Maybe they'd evolved to spread in this manner, like spores, preserved for ages until the ice opened up again. No one could be certain until a gene smith examined the bugs, so Bauman committed to a year's hardship on nothing more than spectral scans and *what if*.

They made a game of it inside the weightless cage of their ship, *What if I trade you my dessert tonight for some of your computer time?* and *What if you turn off your friggin music?* The three of them spent eleven weeks in that box. There wouldn't have been room for them to start bouncing off the walls, and Christmas Bauman stepped into her role very naturally as their leader—a little bit of a mom, a little bit of a flirt.

Bauman kept the pressure low with her jokes and also made sure they paid attention to each other, because the temptation was to look ahead. Lam constantly updated his sims as the mecha sent new data. Vonnie had responsibility for ships' systems and maintenance. All three of them reviewed and participated in various consultations, boards, and debates.

Eleven weeks. It could have been long enough to learn to despise each other or even short enough to remain strangers until they arrived, but Bauman set aside much of her own work to invest in her colleagues instead.

They were eighteen days from Europa when the mecha found carvings in the ice.

This time it was a Chinese rover, running close to the ESA find. Its transmissions were encrypted and altercast, but the Europeans and the Brazilians each caught enough of the signal to have something to work with. In less than four hours, the naked code went systemwide.

Vonnie had learned politics at the University of Stuttgart, and, later, as an instructor at Arianespace. Information was power. There didn't seem to be much sense in withholding the discovery. Too many eyes were watching. Most likely, the Chinese had protected their discovery out of habit and would have shared it within a day or two. Nonetheless, the mood on Earth took a hit. Vonnie and Bauman both received priority messages listing new contingencies and protocols.

The tension could have ruined them. They could have sunk their energy into the worst kind of distraction, yet Bauman saw them through.

"What if he is a dastardly chink spy?" she asked straight-faced.

Vonnie gaped at her, embarrassed by the slur.

Lam laughed out loud. "Yankee scum," he said to Bauman, who added, "Hey, let's not leave her out of this. What do you think, Von? I guess that makes you the Aryan superwoman."

"Right." Vonnie touched her blond hair, so much lighter than Lam's jet black stubble or Bauman's sand-colored mop. She didn't like having their attention drawn to her best feature, which she'd cropped into a buzz cut to keep it out of her face in zero gee.

Aryan wasn't the loaded word it had been for Vonnie's great-great-great-grandparents, but with Germany leading the European Union again, their nation remained self-conscious about its sins in World War II. More recently, they'd seen two generations of conflict with immigrants drawn to Germany's riches. Some political parties had walked a slippery line between racism and protecting their culture, drawing condemnation from people all over the globe. Vonnie certainly looked the part of Hitler's master race, fair-skinned, blue-eyed, trim and fit. To her, that meant she'd had to work harder than most candidates to prove herself.

"We know we're good people even if she's gorgeous, you're too smart, and I'm overbearing," Bauman said.

Vonnie and Lam nodded. They were friends enough to realize they were on their own, no matter what played out back home. Inside the ship's hab module, they gathered around a display to watch their datastreams.

The telemetry stolen from the Chinese rover was in radar and infrared. It showed the rover's low-slung perspective trundling forward with gradients of temperature laid over white-and-green imagery. To its left, irregular lumps masked the horizon where warm gas oozed from several vents. The rover turned closer— And the perspective fell sideways.

In front of the camera, six meters of ice bulged. Gas spewed upward. There was pelting hail. Then the blow-out was over, revealing a trench in the ice. Its roof had thinned with age. Otherwise the rover might have crossed safely, never marking this hollow as anything except another frigid, empty branch of an inactive vent. Instead, the rover extended a wire probe down into the shadows, confirming a glimpse of repetitive shapes molded from the ice.

In radar, the carvings were stark, extraordinary artifacts.

"What if everything down there was killed when the air went out?" Vonnie asked, thinking like an engineer, but Bauman said, "No, this trench is abandoned. It's isolated."

"She's right," Lam agreed.

Vonnie smiled, glad for their excitement. Then she saw Lam's face and frowned, feeling one step behind.

"Look," he said as he ducked his eyes in disappointment.

"This is good, isn't it?" Vonnie said. "There's no way the bugs cut those patterns in the ice. That means there's something else on Europa—something bigger."

"Yes." But he was unhappy.

Puzzled, Vonnie turned back to the display, trying to see what Lam had seen.

The carvings repeated one shape over and over in eight vertical columns of four apiece, a form much like an eight-pointed star. From tip to tip, each symbol measured 1.2 meters wide. Each one was set deep enough in the ice that it was half a meter thick through its middle, like small domes with tapered limbs.

Every arm was knuckled and bent seemingly at random. Vonnie thought the carvings could be a sun calendar. She started to say so, then stopped herself.

Jupiter was five times farther from the sun than Earth. Their star would look like a compact spark in Europa's sky. Because its atmosphere was nonexistent compared to Earth's, with no clouds or moisture to deflect sunlight, Europa's surface would actually appear brighter than a summer day in Germany... and yet she'd soaked up enough biology from Lam to realize there had never been anything walking on top of the ice.

Is he mad at what people are saying? she wondered.

The first theories from Earth dismissed the carvings as the result of hive behavior by the bugs. They cited termite mounds, ant mounds, spider pits, and even the mud nests of cliff swallows.

The math in the carvings implied something more. Eight times four times eight looked like a pattern that had been done on purpose, but many insects on Earth created symmetrical designs. Some biologists proposed the carvings were territorial markings or an attempt to reinforce the tunnel wall with interlocking shapes. A species whose existence depended upon the ice could have developed construction techniques like gophers or ants. The symmetry might be incidental.

No one was ready to go on record that the carvings were a written language, although efforts to translate the wall were percolating on the net. Early human civilizations had used repetitive symbols such as cuneiform and hieroglyphics before developing alphabets. Some people insisted the carvings held a message. There were too many exact, subtle alignments among the sun-shapes' two hundred and fifty-six arms.

Regardless, the growing consensus was that the carvings demonstrated at least chimpanzee-equivalent intelligence.

"Why are you upset?" Vonnie asked.

"Because we missed them," Lam said. "We're too late."

"There could be inhabited chambers nearby. You don't know what's down there."

Lam shook his head, scrolling through their displays. "The trench is older than you think," he said. "Too old. Look at the drift."

The three columns furthest to the east side appeared sloppy, as if they'd been carved in a hurry, but that was because the ice had swelled, deforming the trench—and in this safe zone, the surface tides could be measured in millimeters per century.

Vonnie felt a weird quiver down her spine. Were the carvings actually words? If so, the message was more ancient than the dim, half-forgotten histories recorded in the Bible.

"Cheer up," Bauman said. "Even if we don't find anything except bones, this will be the greatest archeological dig of all time."

"We'll be on the cover of every 'zine in the system," Vonnie said, trying to make Lam smile, but he only grimaced and looked away.

"Whoever made those carvings has been dead for ten thousand years," he said.

INTERNATIONAL EXPEDITIONARY SCIENCE TEAM // EUROPA // 20 April 2113

Command

Bauman, Christmas Sarah (U.S.A.)

Engineering

Vonderach, Alexis Rose (E.U.)

Life Sciences

Lam, Choh (P.S.S.C.)

Bauman   COMMAND - GENE SMITH - MED - PSY - DATA/COMM
Lam   BIOLOGY - ECOLOGY - PLANETARY SCIENCES
Vonderach   PILOT - NAV - MAINT - MED - REMOTE OPERATED MECHA

Joint Mission Control:
ESOC – Darmstat // European Union
JPL – Los Angeles // United States of America
JSLC – Jiuquan // People's Supreme Society of China

Mission Launch Facilities:
Ensley 5 // U.S.A.

Craft:
Deep Space Reconnaissance ESA *Marcuse*

Support:
ROM-4 Rovers (5), ROM-4 GP Mecha (8), ROM-4 Beacons (30) // E.U.
ROM-6 Rovers (2), ROM-4 GP Mecha (3), ROM-8 MMPSA (25) // Japan
ROM-6 GP Mecha (10), ROM-4 Beacons (30) // United States of America
DSSC Hab Modules (1) // People's Supreme Society of China
ROM-4 GP Mecha (2) // Australia

8.

VONNIE LANDED THEIR slowboat on Europa a week before the new high-gee launches would arrive, each carrying new teams of eight to twenty-four people sent by the Brazilians, the Chinese, NASA, and the ESA.

Seven days should have been enough for Vonnie, Bauman, and Lam to begin exploring the site. Wire probes had confirmed that one end of the trench slumped deep into the ice, becoming a tunnel. It crooked sideways and down before shrinking into a series of pockets and holes too dense for their radar arrays to penetrate. For all anyone knew, there were more carvings farther down, but they were directed to wait. The larger ships carried many of the experts who hadn't been picked the first time. Also included were a number of bureaucrats.

There was no question that this crowd would be better able to process the trench, so Vonnie and Bauman spent their time prepping gear and fielding media requests while Lam hid away with his data.

They were celebrities. For an engineer and a gene smith, playing at being popular was a fun diversion. Vonnie showed off their non-proprietary hardware and public maps of the ice while Bauman talked about the sexier aspects of gene splicing like metabolic chargers. Together they were worth a sixty-second update every day on the same news feeds that had rarely mentioned their mission during the long, tedious journey to Europa. Now they were a hot pick—girl explorers on an alien moon—and the ESA and NASA administrators allowed them to say almost anything. Both women were jubilant and loud. It was topnotch media.

Meanwhile, Lam smoldered. "You see what's happening," he said one day before breakfast, standing with his back to the hab module window as if testing himself.

Vonnie couldn't leave the viewport alone. Bauman constantly made her wipe off her fingerprints. Outside, their mecha wandered across the frozen plain, glinting in the vivid, reflected glow of Jupiter. "I know it's tough to wait," Vonnie said without looking at him.

"You sound just like them," he said.

"Hey, easy. I'm on your side."

"You think I'm worried because they might grab some of the glory? Because I had to live in a box with two attractive women for eleven weeks?"

Vonnie turned at *attractive*, feeling a little wary. So far, Lam had been scrupulous about keeping his distance.

"You've seen their org chart," he said. "Who do you think's in charge, the people like you and me?" His brown eyes searched her face, then shifted to the viewport behind her. "It's being politicized," he said. "The fuel. The water. You have to listen to what they're really saying."

The ice. A few Earth governments had called for an end to the mining. Others had too much invested in their colonies and fleets to shut down their supplies of deuterium, hydrogen, and bulk water. Away from the pole, the mining continued. Even now, a PSSC robot ship was carefully unfolding in orbit. The mecha it carried had been funded years ago and the ship had been in transit for months. That kind of inertia was fundamental to nearly every aspect of modern civilization.

The ice. Normal water held no more than .015% deuterium, but the precious gas could be separated, compressed and pumped into containers, then lobbed out of Europa's weak gravity. The tankers filled faster than they could be built, and escaping Jupiter wasn't expensive, diving in close and slinging away. The old god was well-positioned to feed the inner planets. In recent years, some of the catapults on Europa's surface had begun hurling containers equipped with nothing more than radio beacons into slow, sunward trajectories. If those containers didn't arrive for years, even if one or two went missing, no problem, they were lined up like an endless supply train and as cheap as dirt.

The ice. Deuterium-deuterium fusion reactors kept people alive on Luna and Mars and everywhere in between. Water/oxygen futures had become more valuable than gold. The solar system was in bloom. The Chinese had expanded with total commitment, and other nations were growing as fast as possible to keep from being left behind.

"They've already given up on most of Europa," Lam said. "It's too easy. They've been tearing it apart for twenty years without finding anything. I even helped them. They're all posting my sim like it's proof—like this safe zone is the only one. SecGen Harada will make sure the expedition doesn't find anything she doesn't want us to find."

The Japanese minister had been born in space, and represented six thousand colonists who made up a crucial part of the Earth-orbit economy.

"What do you want to do?" Vonnie said.

"We've got a little time, long enough to post so much data they can't bury it," Lam said. "You know what I mean. If we wait now, they'll come up with rationales to keep waiting. First we'll run more surveys. Then we'll practice safety plans. Maybe they'll send in a few crawlers. Meanwhile five or six months go by, and they'll downplay the whole thing."

"What do you want to do, Lam?"

"I want to go in."

It was a career move they'd only make once. They would either be heroes or subject to a great many lawsuits, probably jail time in Lam's case. Vonnie suspected he'd ask for political asylum. The carvings meant that much to him, more than seeing his family again, more than his apartment in Hong Kong—and for all the right reasons.

Lam wanted to save this world. He wanted proof of the diversity of life implied by the carvings and the complex food chain that must support the carvers.

There would be little or no fossil record inside the ice. At best, the tides would hold a churned-up mishmash of species carried far from their time and habitats, but that was the point. There could be priceless information everywhere. There might be life in other regions.

He accepted that the mining would never stop. Humankind's appetites were larger than any group of protestors or indignant scientists, but the mining could be restricted. They could be more diligent.

Bauman only argued for a day. She was too much like Vonnie and Lam. Otherwise she wouldn't have come to Europa. It didn't help that the men on the radio talked like slaps in the face. They were terse and controlling. Bauman didn't appreciate their arrogance. She asked Lam to concoct a sim that showed the carvings were in danger, which wasn't untruthful. The mecha had resealed the trench with steel, glue, and tents, but the carvings were still reacting to near-vacuum. Who could say what data was being lost as the ice broiled?

Forty-eight hours later, they were given permission to enter the trench—only the trench—and Lam laughed and ran for his armor.

"Game over," he said. "Game over. Once we're inside, we'll need to keep poking around, right?"

"Hold on." Vonnie hugged them both, starting with Bauman. She blushed a little as she approached Lam. "I wanted to... You can't feel anything in a scout suit," she explained, and he smiled, touching her hip. Maybe it was the promise of the beginning of something more.

Each set of armor weighed two hundred and twenty kilos. Suiting up required mecha assists. First they took off their clothes. Vonnie blushed again as Lam averted his eyes. Robotic arms painted her temples, throat, wrists, and thighs with nanocircuitry. Then she climbed into the open shell of her suit. She slipped her legs in, connected the sanitary features, and extended her arms into its sleeves.

The assist lowered her helmet over her face. Her armor folded shut. Thousands of needles—some invisible, some as long as four centimeters—sank into her nerves and veins. It didn't hurt except for the cortical jack. There was a dull, gritting pain. She was online.

Bauman and Lam repeated the process.

Data/comm showed all systems go, but they visually inspected each other's seals and collar assemblies. They also triple-checked life support. They intended to wear their suits for a six hour shift, but no one left a ship without carrying the maximum load, which was twelve hours of oxygen and five days of food.

In space, astronauts could lug extra cylinders of compressed oxygen or run air hoses from their ship. Inside the trench, there wouldn't be room for bulky packs or hoses.

As the crew member tasked with their well-being, Vonnie wanted a large safety margin. During training, she'd once spent an uncomfortable thirty-six hour period in her suit, mastering several tricks to recharge her air supply, swapping new cylinders into her pack by herself, adapting nonstandard hoses, changing out filters clogged with smoke or fluid. They prepared for emergencies. She would bring spare cylinders into the trench, although after a single day, even fresh oxygen could not dispel the stink of sweat. In polite company, astronauts called it living with yourself. In cruder terms, the joke went *eat yourself.* The suit became a toilet. More important, they had no practical limitations on power. Each set of armor contained a plutonium rod which would drive it for decades.

Vonnie walked into the air lock first. The lock was big enough to hold three people in an emergency if they crammed together, but one at a time was more comfortable, so she had a few moments alone.

As she waited outside, she looked across the brittle plain unassisted by her visor. Human perceptions were self-deceiving in this environment, yet she wanted a personal connection. She wanted to try.

The curvature of the moon was noticeably wrong. The horizon seemed too small, too near, while the sun suffered its own fun house effect. It was too far away, yet too bright. The ice glistened and winked. Vonnie had the feeling of standing in a mirage. Leaning blocks of ice jutted from the surface to the northeast. Aside from this ridge, there were no points of reference, only the eerie plain dwindling into blackness and the unfathomable, looming face of Jupiter.

Europa was exotic and alluring—but slowly, a chill filled her mind. The amazement she felt became a vague fear like a premonition.

Her visor was synthetic diamond. Five centimeters thick, it could withstand small arms fire and seventy standard atmospheres of pressure. Fitted with transparent circuitry, a suit's visor was also designed to shield its wearer from the desolation of space by swaddling her in data. Without those displays, death felt very close. It engulfed her. Vonnie was only safe because of her helmet, gloves, and armor, so she distracted herself with the superhuman abilities of her suit.

"Lights up," she said. "Grid One. Radar active. Mecha team alpha to me."

Lam and Bauman emerged from the ship as Vonnie organized her squad of machines—two small burrowers like meter-long centipedes—a stout digger shaped like a wheeled spider bristling with tools, cameras, and arms—and seven relays and beacons ranging in size from a fist to a soccer ball.

Blazing with cameras and spotlights, they approached the long tent erected above the trench, where other machines had prepped two additional plastic bubbles. The three people entered the nearest bubble without the mecha.

"Stage one, go," Vonnie said.

Her visor darkened as UV lights scoured their armor, baking off every Earth smell and microbe. Next they were sandblasted with melted ice mixed with a dusting of native rock. Fans cooled the exterior of their suits to -160° Celsius, the ambient temperature.

When they emerged, they approached the second bubble, which served as an air lock. They entered. The mecha thronged around their feet. Vonnie skimmed through her checklists with an up-and-down motion of her eyes. A sophisticated response program watched her retinal movements as she studied her display, allowing her eyes to dance like fingertips through its menus.

"Stage two, go."

The mecha peeled back a steel panel, revealing the trench beneath, where they'd constructed a flex ladder. The spotlights died and their radar shut off. Their visors reverted to a 3-D map taken by wire probe, showing old readings as if these were live images. The map was enough for Vonnie to lead her friends and the mecha down to the carvings.

Lam and Bauman bickered contentedly. "I'd like to switch back to radar," he said.

"Not a chance," Bauman said.

"At least let me use X-ray."

"Absolutely not," Bauman said. "We'll be as noninvasive as possible. That was the deal."

Vonnie grinned and looked around. In the bevy of people and mecha, they began to generate new signals to avoid crashing into each other and to examine the carvings, but they limited themselves to sonar to keep from burning the ice with photons or electromagnetic radiation.

For Lam, this was torture. For Vonnie, it was magnificent. Their visors modified their sonar feedback into holo imagery as real as life, and the trench was richly, overwhelmingly textured: an irregular quilt of dewdrops, smooth spots, swells, and depressions. Only the carvings held a pattern.

But why here? she thought.

The trench seemed to be the upper end of a vent, which made the symbols even more intriguing. Why invest such effort marking the walls of what must be a low-traffic area?

Could this be some sort of holy ground? Maybe the carvers had come to the top of their world to pray, although Vonnie knew Lam would contend that any notions of religion were anthropomorphic. Projecting human motives onto things that weren't human was a natural function of human thinking. It was a fallacy. They had to be careful how they interpreted things.

Vonnie supposed this open space had been a thoroughfare hundreds of years ago. The mecha had detected gaps in the ice where the trench might have branched downward on both sides until the tides squeezed it shut on one end, turning what had been a horseshoe-shaped passageway into a single, straggling tunnel.

Europa had zero axial tilt and was tidally locked, which meant it always showed the same face to Jupiter like Earth's moon always showed the same side to its planet. On Europa, unfortunately, the consequences were dire. Their models suggested the tidal locking was imperfect.

It was only Europa's icy crust that showed the same face to Jupiter. Its ocean and its rocky core spun at different rates, and there were no continents to impede the water. Especially on the equator, the hellish, spiraling currents distended the ice. At its poles, Europa was its calmest. Yet even in these quiet pockets, the crust heaved and split.

What had the carvers been doing at the surface? It didn't make sense. *Living here would have been risky, almost suicidal,* Vonnie thought. *But they came anyway.*

Behind her, Lam was uncharacteristically loud, although he tried to soften his words with Bauman's new nickname. "Look, Yankee, you'll never pack up the carvings and put them in a museum," he said. "We're damaging the wall just by standing here."

"All the more reason to be noninvasive," Bauman said. "We don't know how finely detailed the top layer may be."

"We'll get it in one full spectrum burst."

"We don't have enough sensors."

"Vonnie can rig more cameras and mecha."

"The heat will—"

Another voice intruded. "Specialist Lam," a man said. The other ships were 2.2 light-minutes away, which could reduce conversation to a series of interruptions. "We'd like to see the first column again. Stand by for auto control."

"Roger that," Lam answered, holding his hands up to Bauman in an apologetic shrug. Then he switched frequencies, preparing for new signals from the PSSC ship.

His suit adjusted his upper body, aiming the gear block on the side of his helmet with machine precision. His movements were a little spooky. Their suits weren't supposed to accept remote programs without an okay from whoever was inside, but Vonnie anticipated trouble.

When they left the trench for the tunnel, would their suits lock up? If they tried to send their data on public channels, would the broadcast come out clean or garbled?

Lam switched back to suit radio. "There's something embedded in the ice!" he said.

"What?"

"The AI must have seen it in our telemetry. I have a new grid showing pellets inside the carvings, one at the tip of every arm. Look. They're some kind of organic material."

The miniscule spheres were as translucent as the ice itself.

"Are those eggs? Food?" Bauman said.

"What if—" Vonnie said, trying to get a word in edgewise.

"We can't pull them, not yet," Bauman said. "We'll have to record and map it first. I guess your full spectrum burst is the best way to go, Lam. What do you think?"

"I think you're right," he said generously.

"Can we push a wire in? Get a sample?"

Vonnie gestured. "What if we pick through the debris against that wall?" The fourth column was the most deteriorated. Among the cluttered arms were thirteen that had crumbled, leaving piles of ice on the floor.

"You're a genius," Bauman said as she clapped Vonnie on the back, a dull clank.

Moments later, they had their sample. Lam and Bauman crouched over it together like cavemen protecting an ember, bumping their shoulders, both of them chattering on the radio.

"The pellet weighs six point two grams," Lam said, balancing it in his glove.

"It isn't an egg, and I don't think it's a food substance, either," Bauman said. "From the consistency and methane traces, it looks like digested waste."

"You mean it's feces," Vonnie said.

"More than that," Bauman said. "The pellet was molded with other biologics like saliva or blood. It's swamped in hormones. It's a message."

"What does it say?"

"It could be a marker or a name. Everyone's smell is unique."

Vonnie wrinkled her nose. "You mean they sniffed it?"

"Or tasted it."

Vonnie thought that was pretty gross, but she understood why Bauman admired the elegance of the medium. In this resource-limited environment, the carvers had found at least two ways to encode information, first shaping the ice, then preserving flavors or scents.

"So they were like dogs," she said.

"Maybe. We won't know until we get more samples under analysis. Are the pellets all the same? Are they different? This might have been a library. The hormones could trigger fertility, pubescence, molting, anything."

"You think they were sentient," Vonnie said, and Lam answered, "Yes."

"We don't know that, either," Bauman said.

"Dogs don't build libraries," Lam said.

"What if this is a bathroom?" Bauman said. "We might be standing where they relieved themselves."

"Nobody puts their latrine on top of their living quarters. If this is a bathroom, it would be further down. Right? Plus it took a lot of work to store the pellets in the wall."

"That could be a function of avoiding predators or a way to keep from fouling their air. We don't know."

Vonnie's friends might have stayed in the trench all day, absorbed in their chem tests and new theories. They might have been satisfied with this discovery and stayed until the other ships arrived.

She was the one who convinced them to move on.

"Why don't you two quit playing with that guck and help me," she said, laughing. "Let's go."

9.

WHEN SHE STARTED down the tunnel, it was with the thrill of history. Her exhilaration felt like a shout. She would always be first to walk inside Europa, and a slavecast kept a swirl of relays and burrowers around her feet, recording everything.

She wasn't as graceful as the mecha. The passage dropped steeply. Misjudging the gravity, she tended to bash into the ceiling. Then the opening shrank until it wasn't much bigger than her suit. Again and again, Vonnie was forced to drop to her knees or roughly shoulder through.

Her telemetry betrayed them. The men on the radio questioned her movement and ordered her back. She kept going. Sonar showed an end to the tunnel after four hundred meters, yet infrared revealed that the end was a shade warmer than its surroundings. Hot pinpricks of gas were bleeding through.

"There's something on the other side," Vonnie said. "My sensors are going nuts."

"Something alive?" Lam asked.

"Stop," the radio said. "Specialist Vonderach, acknowledge. You will comply."

"Roger that," she said. "But this is an air lock. Look at it. It's too smooth. It definitely isn't a formation caused by melt or tidal pressures."

She cringed at the idea of giving such responsibility to anything as flimsy as ice, but there were no metals here. What else could the carvers use? It spoke again of their inventiveness and determination. She couldn't wait to see more.

Opening the end of the tunnel was a chance to show her worth to the team. To get through without losing the air, Vonnie would need to trap herself between the lock and a new seal of her own making—and every surface in the ice showed old scars and stubs. Irregular holes marred the walls where building material had been dug out and replaced.

"I say 'go,'" Lam told the men on the radio. "We're picking up too many readings. Noise. Heat. We could miss something significant if we sit here."

"I can get us in," Vonnie said.

The debate among the high-gee ships was maddening. The Brazilians wanted her to withdraw. So did Naomi Harada, the Japanese minister aboard the American craft.

"What if our guys listen to them?" Vonnie worried, but Lam said, "No, Brazil is doing our work for us. Watch. Nobody likes being told what to do."

He predicted the chain of events flawlessly. The Brazilians were frustrated that they had none of their own people on Europa. Their demands for international unity were terse, even petty. They cited old grievances against NASA and the ESA. They called on China to support them.

Flaunting their objections, the leaders of the Chinese, American, and European space agencies reached a consensus: Vonnie should continue.

"Yes!" she said, pumping her fist in excitement.

Lam grinned at her like a kid.

They gathered near the air lock. Bauman was last in line, so Vonnie took control of Bauman's suit, assembling frozen hunks in a stack and soldering the pile together with her laser finger on a minimum setting. "Slow work," she apologized, not wanting to dull their energy.

Lam shrugged, running sims on his visor as he waited. "Think what the carvers used instead of a laser," he said. "Body heat? Urine or saliva? There are organic contaminants everywhere."

"Lots of DNA," Bauman agreed happily.

At last they were sealed in. Vonnie eased through the original lock and saw another ice plug further on. Redundancy was good engineering, but she was disappointed to realize how many lifetimes it must have been since the carvers had visited the tunnel or even considered it important.

Long, long ago, the top of the next air lock had slumped open.

Her suit analyzed the low-pressure atmosphere wafting past her as 98.9 percent nitrogen, a gas so inert that no creature could have evolved to burn it as an energy source. This seemed to be a dead area. Why bother to block it off?

"There's nobody home," Vonnie said.

"Knock knock." Lam was cheerful, even buoyant, bumping her arm as he tried to look past.

"Maybe the air is bad *because* this tunnel is unused," Vonnie said. "Oxygen could be their most closely guarded resource. They might control it with flood gates."

No answer. Lam and Bauman were beyond listening to her, lost in the chatter of data. Their tiniest mecha had run ahead while others lingered to examine the ice. Lam especially was in his element, pulling files and fitting each perspective into a working whole.

Vonnie was eager, too, yet she meticulously rebuilt the locks behind them. Then she moved in front again.

After another eighty meters, the slanting tunnel dropped into a sink hole. The vent was encrusted with old melt. Across from her was a hollow of uncertain depth. Stalactites hung from the top of the shaft.

There had been a catastrophe, probably a belch of heat. If the carvers had built anything else in the area, it was gone, but Vonnie couldn't feel sad.

She walked to the edge of the hole. Her sonar raced down the shaft like a fantastic halo, never reaching bottom. The hole appeared to drop for more than a kilometer, twisting, widening, and branching away.

Somewhere down there was the dark heart of Europa.

"Perfect," Bauman said. "This sink hole is a natural cross-section through the ice. How far down can we take samples?"

"Give me a minute," Vonnie said. It would be easy to secure a few bolts, play out a molecular wire, and let their mecha descend like spiders. She rifled through her tool kit.

"Huh," Lam said, taking control of a burrower near Vonnie. The machine scooted away from her and joined him.

"What've you got?" she asked.

"I—"

Later, Vonnie played back their group feed. Cursing him, she understood. His radar had probed a swath of dirty ice in the tunnel wall. Most of the patches that interested him were impure. Some were stained with lava dust, others discolored like milk or glass.

He'd noticed a shell—a small, spiral shell lodged in the wall of the tunnel. It wouldn't have looked unusual on any beach on Earth. On Europa, it was a treasure.

Lam's suit had reported the shell's position to their grid, but he couldn't leave it alone. He needed to be involved. Under his guidance, marking the shell for retrieval, their burrower stabbed a radio pin into the wall.

The ice exploded with black rock.

Vonnie was standing beside the largest mass. Somehow that saved her. The burst of ice and rock knocked her upward, although she was snarled in her wire.

Bauman yelled once: "Lam, get back!"

There was probably no more than a quarter ton of debris stopped up behind the dust pack, a collection of gravel and stones that had gradually sunk into a loose, dangerous bulge. It weighed a thirteenth as much as it would have on Earth, but in this gravity, it splashed.

It tore apart the sink hole. Other veins of rock caused a vicious swell. The heap rose, spread, and settled again like a cloud.

Vonnie escaped the worst shockwave, half-conscious and confused. She was thrown to the top of the vent as her friends disappeared. Their sharecasts clamored with alarms and one massive injury report before their suits went dark. But she was tied to the wire, and it would not break. One end caught in the heaving ice.

Then the avalanche took her, too.

10.

THE FIRST POCKET world in the ice would always be her favorite. It was inhabited by two peaceful species of bugs which were related to each other, yet were unlike the fat-bodied ants brought up by the ESA rover. They seemed to feed solely on the gray bacterial mats that grew alongside the wells of a hot spring, where the melt was thick and ever-changing.

Once upon a time, this chamber must have been part of more expansive catacombs. Ice-falls had long since closed it off. Vonnie had only stumbled into this dripping space when she refused to be deterred and started digging.

Her mind had felt very, very small in those hours—too small for any thought except to get away from the lethal, creaking weight of the collapsed vent above her.

Deep radar let her identify load-bearing sections in the ice. She'd climbed, cut, excavated and squirmed from one miniscule safe zone to another, using her arms like shovels, numbly reaching forward more times than she could count. Her knees and belly ached from contorting through the gaps.

She remembered listening for every groan and crack in the ice. She remembered the red bar of an alarm on her visor warning that her air reserves were at sixty minutes.

Her endless crawl had stopped, perhaps forever, as she curled herself in a hole no larger than a coffin to rig an electrolysis unit from her tool kit. The job became her entire focus. She was in shock, and concentrating on an attainable goal was exactly what she needed.

She assembled two electrode plates, a pump, and a compressor inside a slim steel box. She mounted the unit on her shoulder, then fed ice into the hopper, separating the oxygen from the hydrogen. Her cylinders recharged. And if her new air was contaminated, if there were Europan microorganisms or toxins in the ice, what choice did she have? Cooking the ice should sterilize any pathogens. Her screens showed no detectible sulfurs or dioxides. Nor could she smell anything peculiar.

When she finally emerged into the pocket world, she was startled to realize how much time had passed. She'd been worming through the ice for the better part of an Earth day—nearly twenty hours.

She wasn't hurt except for a sprained elbow.

She was alone.

Not one of her comm links were active. The relays she'd left above the sink hole must have been scattered and crushed when the vent collapsed. Maybe she'd fallen further than she thought.

The pocket world was safe, but she couldn't stay. The other ships were seventy-five hours out and it would take them several more hours to gear up and scout for her, even longer to forge their way through the crumbling mass.

She had to find a way back to the surface. She could continue to replenish her oxygen and water supplies from the ice, but she'd gorged herself as soon as she'd noticed her hunger. Her suit offered top-of-the-line meat dishes, pastas, fruits, and desserts like only the wealthiest people on Earth could afford, with the caveat that her meals were pastes fed from tubes inside her helmet... Now bulk was more critical than nutrition or pleasure. She would have traded every fruit pack and candy for more carbohydrates.

Her remaining supplies might last eight or nine days, twelve at the outside. Before then, she would get weak.

Could she eat the bugs?

No, she thought. It wouldn't come to that. It couldn't. Besides, they might make her ill.

She regretted not having beacons to leave in the pocket world. Bauman especially would have been enthused by the bugs, but most of Vonnie's mecha were gone. She only had one left—a burrower— plus three miniature relays attached to her chest plate. She sent them exploring. Then she sat quietly, mourning and resting, even napping for three hours.

Her camera lights were dazzling in the wet ice as she gazed through her visor, comforted by the use of normal light and vision.

Discolored rimes of minerals permeated the uneven floor and walls of the cave. That meant the hot springs routinely overflowed. The bubbling water was saturated with iron and salt. It tainted the ice and poisoned the bugs, which avoided the most concentrated salt deposits.

The atmosphere was oxygen-rich, although it was nothing that would support a human being, laced with hydrogen chloride. More interesting, the pressure was five times what she'd seen near the surface, due in part to a lower altitude but mostly because this hollow was self-contained.

Neither species of bug had eyes or even the most primitive photo receptors. They used fan antennae and scent instead. They were basically helpless. Droplets fell steadily or in periodic rains. The chamber floor was pebbled with a thousand specimens sealed beneath the ice.

Vonnie collected ten bugs from each species and put them in her chest pack, then added samples from the bacterial mats.

The mats were vital evidence to prove the foundation of Lam's evolutionary theory. It took billions of microbes to form something large enough to be seen by human eyes. These slimes grew in blots as fine as a needle point and as imposing as a stranger's shadow.

She thought she could identify three different strains. One reached into the air with tendril-like fuzz. Two commingled in a symbiotic relationship, possibly using iron and water for food. This pale muck had learned to expand from the hot springs onto the ice. Vonnie supposed it used layers of dead material as insulation. Maybe it fed from the melting surface.

One thing was obvious. The bugs' mortality rate, while high, wasn't enough to keep them from outgrowing their food source. This pocket ecology was more than incomplete; it was unworkable; it was temporary.

Vonnie was frustrated when she built Lam's ghost to help her. Doing so was illegal, but she was beyond any concern except survival.

Her first words to him were harsh. "Hey. Can you hear me?"

—*Online.*

"Your name is Choh Lam. You killed yourself and my friend because you couldn't wait five damn seconds for an engineer to tell you not to bang on the ice."

—*Consolidating files.*

"Never do anything again unless I tell you. Understood?"

—*Negative. What are my instructions?*

"I need to know where I am. Can you piece together my coordinates in relation to the surface?"

—*Negative. Further access to core systems required.*

"Goddamn it!"

Throughout Europe and North America, combining human mem files with low-level AIs was forbidden. Organic minds were extensive, subtle, and predisposed to neurochemical and emotional imbalances. Failing to place the slightest piece of the puzzle could have severe consequences.

Duplicating the living or resurrecting the dead also crossed ethical lines and medical considerations. In her childhood, thousands of court cases dealing with family, property, and tax laws had led to a widespread revulsion for electronic personalities. Many of them were distorted nightmares of themselves.

Some cultures stood as exceptions. China and Korea permitted human-based AIs, keeping their ancestors with them. In the Middle East, there were immortal holy men.

Vonnie didn't have the computing power of those governments. Most of her suit's systems were Level VII intelligences. Each one was a task-specific processor. Those subroutines accomplished intricate feats like her visor's retinal response program and brute work such as balancing 220 kilos of armor in motion without falling over.

If idle, each system functioned as spare memory. They were intended to draw on each other in crisis. By permanently linking a hundred subroutines, Vonnie created enough quantum memory to host a Level II intelligence with self-awareness and personality, but she was angry at Lam and afraid of dying in this impossible world.

Bauman would have been a better companion. Vonnie wouldn't have tried so hard to control her. The disaster she made of Lam was erratic because he was missing too much. She wanted him to be cautious, even timid.

She didn't trust the result.

When her mecha reported a mild current of atmosphere 1.9 kilometers from the bugs' home, Vonnie shut down the ghost. She called her mecha back to her. After they rejoined her, she attached the minis to her chest in their carry sockets and made sure the burrower was slavecast to her suit.

She dug her way through old cave-ins and membranes of ice, following a conduit left by the minis. From their data, she knew there were more vents nearby.

As she clawed at the ice, she felt another aftershock. Maybe she'd set it off by undermining a weight-bearing formation. There was a ponderous groan. Then the ice heaved, slamming at her knees and chin. Her surroundings gave way and she fell tumbling into the white.

"Help me!" she screamed. "Lam!?"

—*Online.*

"Stabilizers! Get my suit turned around!"

Grabbing at loose hunks and powder, she couldn't tell up from down. Huge pieces crashed against her. The rest of the avalanche felt like quicksand or a waterfall. It rushed and billowed, taking the burrower away from her. In seconds, the burrower's signals faded.

Her suit was equipped with gyroscopes, but her gyros were one of the systems she'd hacked to make room for the ghost. That was why she'd reawakened him.

With his help, Vonnie located an enormous wedge. She clutched at it as the flowing ice pounded on her helmet and back. Radar indicated a house-sized slab. Unfortunately, it began to rotate beneath her weight. In a minute, maybe less, it would roll and dump her. She scraped at it with her fingers and boots, trying to keep her balance—trying to locate a bigger chunk—but her sensors were inundated with noise and motion.

"Analyze my datastreams!" she shouted. "Which way should I go?"

—*What is your destination?*

"Solid ground. Anywhere."

—*Where are we now?*

Certain she was in her grave, Vonnie gave him limited access to her mem files, enough to explain that the fallen vent where he'd died must have flattened out against the surrounding area, causing other networks to collapse. Now those implosions were also pushing down or sideways.

The ghost handled this job well. Based on her data and current sonar readings, he created sims to predict the worst of the ice falls.

Vonnie labored to free herself, sinking ever deeper through the mayhem. She struggled for nine hours.

To keep up her stamina, she ate more than she wanted, barely tasting the venison-flavored protein or faux baked potato. Nonstop exertion also took its toll on her oxygen supply. Each bite, each breath, shortened the time she had left.

Losing hope, a queer thought struck her.

This was no ocean into which she was descending—it was Europa's sky. Captured here, native species would have no concept of anything further up. They would look for the mountains or the liquid seas below, so she began to dig beneath herself instead of laterally, no longer fighting the avalanche but using it to her advantage, sifting, swimming.

Eventually she fell onto a vast, black slope of lava rock. Whether it was an island suspended in the ice or a true mountain, she couldn't say, but she had come down out of the frozen sky.

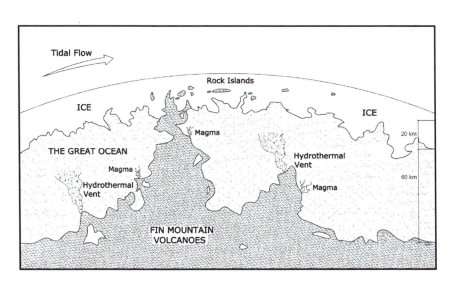

Europa's Southern Pole

11.

THE CATACOMBS HAD formed eons ago when liquid magma cooled irregularly, leaving tubes and caverns within a larger mass. Running water cut through every opening as geysers, rivers, and slow-draining seas. Quakes opened new fractures and closed others—and the ice was always there, dripping or pushing or smashing into the rock.

In solitude, in silence, Vonnie thought about her dead friends too much as she walked.

The darkness led in every direction. There were pits and outcroppings and blind corners and slides. Once she found a sheer abyss that plunged for hundreds of meters. More often, she couldn't see more than a stone's throw as she picked her way through the maze.

Using an inertial compass to maintain her heading east wherever possible, she tried to keep busy with her maps and data. The atmosphere in these lava tunnels was mostly water vapor, carbon dioxide, and the ever-present nitrogen along with trace poisons. It was also warm—a few degrees below freezing.

Vonnie assumed she'd entered a fin mountain. Most of the rock formations near Europa's surface were ejecta, cast into the ice by ocean-floor eruptions or broken off from mountaintops by the pressure of the frozen sky. If she'd discovered a dead block of lava floating in the ice, it might absorb the sparse amounts of heat generated by friction, distant lava flows, and hydrothermal vents. These catacombs were too warm. Some areas were ringed with scum like filth on a bathtub. Her suit detected sulfur, salt, oxidizing rust and minerals, all evidence of past floods and smoke and ash.

She was inside a volcano.

Europa's molten core, silicate mantle, and low gravity created towers of unimaginable heights. The great ocean cooled many fissures and vents, driving the lava upward. Because siliceous magma was cohesive—like syrup—it trapped gases within it, lifting each eruption even further.

On Earth, in full gravity, the Hawaiian volcano of Mauna Loa rose seventeen kilometers from the Pacific floor. On Mars, in 0.38 standard gravity but without an ocean to support it, Olympus Mons rose twenty-five kilometers into the Martian atmosphere. On Europa, in 0.13 standard gravity, Lam's sims had predicted unstable piles of rock as tall as sixty kilometers. He assumed the ocean floor wasn't uniform. There must be shallower regions were the mantle formed plateaus. The volcanoes that scraped the surface rose from these highlands.

Fire and ice.

The volcanoes eroded and reformed at speeds much faster than any Earth equivalent, so Vonnie listened for seismic activity and swept her infrared through the caverns, looking for hot spots.

She found specks of condensation, then puddled ice before she walked into a length of catacombs that had been invaded by a creeping swamp. Giant lumps of ice sat on the tunnel floor beneath pillars and stalactites. Frozen lakes flowing at less-than-glacial speeds made waves and swirls against every strewn hunk of rubble.

The landscape was stunning, but it couldn't soothe her as she hurried into a light wind. The pressure differential indicated an even higher temperature somewhere ahead. Maybe there were gas vents or bubbling springs.

Vonnie had seen bacterial mats and a few spores of what appeared to be fungi. She took samples of these pale bulbous growths, glad to find life of any kind, but only the ice truly thrived in this environment. When her radar identified another sun-shape on the wall, she thought it was a carving.

It moved.

"Hey!" Vonnie began to jog. Just as suddenly, she stopped. The creature was 1.2 meters wide, a round body with eight arms. She didn't want to scare the little thing. She was three hundred meters away, and there was a chance she'd gone unobserved.

It might be best if the creature hadn't seen her. She wasn't trained to initiate First Contact. The decision she made could affect nine billion lives across the solar system as humankind collided with another thinking race for the first time... but she didn't have it in her to walk away, not here, not now. She needed this success to balance everything that had gone wrong.

Besides, what the hell was it breathing?

Vonnie felt a stab of pride and melancholy at the thought, a bittersweet mix. Bauman and Lam would have given anything to be with her.

Infrared made it clear that this creature was warm-blooded. Despite the tough, insulating layers of cartilage and blubber beneath its skin, its body heat radiated in this cold like a furnace.

In that way, it genuinely was a sun. Like a beacon or a lamp, it drew her closer.

The creature disappeared, edging behind a bump of rock. Vonnie paced toward it, sweeping her radar and X-ray up the cavern wall. Where had it gone? The wall was pocked with fissures and holes.

As she paused at a hundred meters, thinking again of Lam, she realized the carvings they'd found were literal portrayals of these creatures' bodies. They'd thought each eight-armed sun was a letter or a word. Instead, the shapes were three dimensional images of the carvers themselves.

Searching the wall, she discovered a crevice teeming with warm bodies, eight of them—the number eight again—and yet she saw no exhalations in infrared.

Vonnie forgot everything else, although she made sure not to let her smile show inside her visor. Teeth might be threatening. She moved gently even as her head raced with astonishment and delight. She knelt to make herself smaller. Then she drew one finger in the dust, merely trying to communicate the idea of communicating. She must be a surprise to them.

I'm a friend, she thought.

Furless, streamlined, they had almost certainly evolved in water. They had no bones, only strands of cartilage through their bodies and arms. They also had no front or back that she could see, no eyes, no nose, nothing to differentiate one side from another.

On top, their albino skin was peppered with spines. Some of those defensive needles were colored with a tinge of yellow or red, likely from sulfur or mineral absorption. They had no need for pigmentation in this lightless world.

Underneath, their arms were lined with gripping nubs and richly laid bands of tube feet and pedicellaria—fine, clasping tendrils in the thousands. Some were as delicate as her hair. Others were short cords like wire.

Their squirming whiskers gave them personality. Hanging on the rock, clinging in a group, most of the creatures held up one or two arms to show their undersides, and Vonnie's sensors let her see through their bodies in any case. They wriggled and flexed.

Are they communicating with each other? she thought. *How? By touch?*

They danced with their arms, brushing against each other. Vonnie imagined they used physical contact like a combination of sign language and Braille. They might read their carvings in the same way— and everything inside Europa—as they groped through the dark.

Ears were their only visible sensory organs. In the grooves between their arms, protected by knuckle-like muscles, were sphincters that opened to short auditory canals. Following their ears into their bodies, Vonnie's X-rays lit up dense, specialized cochlear and bundles of nerves. She also saw complex fatty lobes associated with the same nerves. What were those for? The fatty structures augmented their hearing somehow.

Otherwise they had no orifices of any kind except on their bellies. Vonnie noted a few slits which she suspected were well-protected gills and genitals. Each creature also had a snub beak evidently used both as mouth and anus. Her initial scans revealed a very basic digestive system, four lungs, two hearts, two hypertrophied kidneys, a huge liver, and more brain tissue than she would have envisioned in a meter-wide creature.

You're perfect, she thought.

They were small enough to subsist on minimal food, yet large enough to build. Lungs and gills also allowed them to travel in any medium. Did they still make their homes in water? Where were their children?

"What should we call you?" she asked, forgetting herself and speaking out loud.

She remembered her friends' energized laughter. Bauman might have called the natives *octopods* or *aquatic mammals*. More politically minded, Lam would have said *Europans*.

"Sunfish," Vonnie said.

Naming them, she felt wistful and right. *Sunfish* was pretty. It was poetry. They looked like giant starfish, but *starfish* would have been demeaning.

These weren't simple, mindless sea creatures. They were clever and brave. For the sunfish to cover as much distance as they had to the top of the ice was remarkable. It spoke again of strategy, organization, and engineering. That they'd mastered this environment was even more impressive because their lungs were too compact to hold air for long. They must have evolved some trick of oxygen compression... saturating their blood... breathing water or good air before leaving one safe zone for another...

The air locks implied they weren't nomads. Instead, they constructed strongholds.

Am I near their home? she thought.

Then she was out of time. The sunfish leapt at her and Vonnie stepped back, stunned, as they burst off the cavern wall like shrapnel.

The sunfish were spectacular in flight. Four of them ricocheted through the crags overhead, banging into spaces she hadn't noticed until they darted in and out. The others kicked off the tunnel floor. As soon as they were airborne, they somersaulted, leading now with their undersides and their beaks. They came in a swarm with all arms outstretched.

In that split second, Vonnie realized their carvings were a lie. The shapes etched into the trench had been smooth, stylized, and immaculate. Those carvings showed the top portions of sunfish without age or injuries, when in reality their undersides were rough with scar tissue and missing hunks of pedicellaria.

Their true selves were as grotesque as those wounds.

The first sunfish struck her helmet off-center, attacking her gear block. Others collided with her arms and chest, trying to bring her down. Vonnie staggered, but her suit kept her upright.

Her retreat was confused. She tripped over a boulder and fell as three bodies clawed at her.

She stood like a drunk, flailing with adrenaline. Many of them seemed to have disappeared. She struck wildly at the sunfish hooked around her face.

They dropped the ceiling on her. A hundred flecks of rock clattered against her suit, and she looked up as a ragged hunk as big as a car slammed down. When most of the sunfish had bounced away from her, they'd leapt up and scrabbled at the rock, digging and prying, using themselves as pistons to accelerate their weapon.

They were ruthless. Impact killed one of their own and hurt three more. It also destroyed her.

Inside her helmet, her skull whacked against the buckling armor, where torn circuitry scraped open one of her corneas. Then she hit the ground. Systems failure was total for 3.1 seconds and Vonnie sprawled in the dark, bleeding and twitching.

12.

"ARE YOU THERE?" she gasped, blinded by a wet mask of gore.

—*Online.*

"Run! Get me up!"

She felt the sunfish against her suit, snaking through the rubble to reach her foot, her arm, her shoulder. Their arms beat at her like clubs.

Pain speared through her elbow as the suit twisted free. She rose. Inside her helmet, she shook her head, squeezing her left eye shut, but her vision wouldn't focus and she couldn't get her other eyelid to close at all. That eye was a numb, oozing bag mashed in a crater of flesh.

I can't see, she realized.

Her fear became a firebrand, scalding her brain. She couldn't think. "Run," she said, but the ghost needed more information.

—*Destination?*

Something hit the back of her head. More impacts dropped her to her knees, and she screamed, "Run! Run!"

—*Destination?*

Vonnie summoned the words she needed. "Retrace my path for two kilometers! Retrace my path exactly! Run into the lava tunnel!"

A faint blue glow reached her good eye as the suit staggered up and turned. Probably it was displaying her maps.

My visor is intact or I'd be dead, she thought.

She leaned toward the light, peering through her bloody eye. The ruined circuitry slid into her cheek like a dozen pins. She jerked back, but she couldn't escape. Her face was hemmed in by the sharp mesh.

Sobbing, she felt herself carried by the suit. It dashed forward, jarring her head wounds.

Then it tripped or it was knocked down. Vonnie moaned, expecting another assault. "What do you see!?" she gasped as the suit stood again.

—*Define request.*

"Where are they? Is there any way out?"

—*There are four lifeforms in pursuit. The closest is ten meters behind us.*

"No!"

—*Radar indicates several branches from this tunnel, but your instructions were to remain on your path.*

"Turn! Lose them!"

—*Displaying options.*

"Just turn! Run! Don't let them catch me!"

The suit wrenched sideways, yanking Vonnie to her right, left, right, and right again. Reeling in agony and shock, she fought to hold onto a plan.

"Where are they now? What does the tunnel look like?"

—*The nearest lifeform is twenty-five meters behind us. Displaying holo imagery.*

"Fuck you! Fuck you! I can't see!"

—*Twenty meters.*

"Keep running! Tell me what the tunnel looks like!"

—*Radar indicates multiple side channels and cavities around the main tube, which is at least another kilometer in length. There is ice beyond it.*

"What do I do?"

—*Define request.*

Vonnie screamed at him, using rage to overcome her panic. "How can they be so close!? You're stronger than them! You should be faster!"

—*The lifeforms are jumping from every available surface, gliding through trajectories as short as one meter or as long as thirty. Their grasp of spatial relations appears significantly more advanced than the same ability in human beings.*

That helped. She was able to picture the chase. Her suit ran in leaping bounds as the sunfish flew after her. She was obstructed by boulders and pits. They acted more like arrows or balls, using long and short angles interchangeably.

"When all four of them are in the air, change course! Run into one of the side channels!"

—*I anticipate such an instance in six seconds. Five. Four.*

"Why don't I feel my med systems? Fix my eyes!"

—*One.*

Vonnie winced as the suit flung itself backward. She thought she felt a tick of contact on her shoulder. Had a sunfish grabbed at her as it flew past?

"Where are they?"

—*We've left the main tunnel for a chasm as instructed. The nearest lifeform is ten meters behind us and gliding further away. I've lost radar signals of the other three.*

"Keep running! What about my eyes!?"

—Medical response appears to have been subverted by unknown packets and overrides.

"That's you. Oh, shit, that's you," she whispered with a cold new sense of dread. At some point, the ghost had outfoxed the checks she'd established and tried to expand itself, fragmenting as it battled with her computers.

—Initiating diagnostics.

"No. Wait."

—Corrupted files identified in life support nodes.

"I said wait! Off!"

Her suit froze. Vonnie toppled forward until her arm struck something. She spun around and hit twice more, bruising her leg and her back. Her face throbbed.

The pain was nothing. It was her terror that consumed her. Like a child, she reached for something to hold onto. The suit responded to manual function, letting her clutch at the rock and churn her legs.

She went four meters before her head clanged into the wall. She moved to her right, then struck something else.

What could she do?

Vonnie didn't want the ghost to reabsorb whatever packets it had lost in its fight to control her suit. Some of those packets would be junk code. Others would be sleeper cells. If the ghost reconnected with enough of those cells, her suit's firewalls might not win the next battle for control. But she couldn't crawl alone through the blackness.

"Are you there!?" she shouted.

—Online.

"Where are the sunfish?"

—Radar shows no indication of pursuit.

Vonnie exhaled in a trembling gust. Were they lurking outside the chasm? Was it a dead end? The next question was the most urgent, and she fixated on it with that child-like desperation. *Why? Why? Why are they trying to kill me?*

If they were intelligent, they should have felt the same magic she'd experienced when she stood in front of them. They couldn't have met anything like her before—a tall, bipedal creature in plastisteel—and she hadn't done anything wrong. Had she?

Vonnie patted at her armor, bewildered by the mangled shapes of her torso and abdomen. Suddenly she reached for her shoulder mount. "Is my electrolysis unit intact?"

—*Affirmative.*

For an instant, she'd been afraid she couldn't recharge her air cylinders. She didn't know if she had enough gear to build a replacement.

"I should have three mecha on my chest plate."

—*Negative.*

"What happened to them?"

—*One was lost in the attack. Most of your tool kits and sample cases are also damaged.*

"But I have two mecha left."

—*Affirmative. 1084 is missing its infrared camera and laser. 1085 registers intact.*

"Detach and activate. Slavecast this suit to 85. Your function will be to translate its signals into voice mode and relay my commands."

—*Von, listen, I am more efficient than the mecha.*

"What did you just say?"

—*I am more efficient.*

The ghost had used her name and sidestepped a direct order. How long did she have before he interrupted her suit's systems again?

"Detach and activate 85," she said. "Wipe all other initiatives and confirm."

—*85 activated.*

The tiny mecha separated from her chest plate with a pop.

Vonnie turned her head, trying to situate herself, yearning to see. "Send 85 ahead of me into the chasm, then follow it," she said. "Move as fast as it's safe. Our first priority is to get away from the sunfish. Confirm."

—*Confirmed, Von.*

Using her name was a simple development, and yet it was also sinister and wrong. Did he think he was her equal?

13.

FOLLOWING 85, HER suit ducked and bent and hopped. At the same time, the ghost narrated 85's advisories, describing a gully, a slide, a crevice, a hill.

"I need medical attention," she said.

—*Von, I can fix the corrupted nodes.*

"I want you to withdraw from life support. That's the problem. You're interfering."

—*Incorrect. This suit's basic functions are compromised by external and internal damage. If I withdraw, you will lose all AI-directed systems.*

So she continued to bleed. She couldn't let the ghost work on her face. If something like her little finger had needed attention, she might have granted him access as a way to evaluate him, but she couldn't let him repair her skull. If the procedure failed, if the ghost intentionally damaged her or shut down in the middle of surgery, it could leave her mentally stunted as well as blind. Then she might be lost down here until she starved, an idiot and a cripple, barely able to comprehend her own suffering.

Could she use 85 to reverse hack her suit? She had virtual keyboards in her gloves. She knew she could tap into 85, but she would have to do so by touch alone, without watching her key strokes on her heads-up display. She also hadn't figured out how to keep the ghost from noticing her signals.

She needed to divert him. "How did the sunfish chase me?" she asked. "Were they talking to each other? I didn't hear anything, and they don't have eyes."

—*The lifeforms were emitting ultrasound.*

"Sonar. Do you have recordings of it?"

—*Affirmative.*

"Analyze those recordings for meaning and context. Is it language?"

—*Unknown.*

"I want an alert as soon as you hear them again. Scan for more carvings. Anything. What else can you tell me about them?"

Vonnie snapped her hands inside her gloves as the ghost recited data; the wavelengths and compositions of the sunfishes' sonar calls; modulation; duration; intervals. By the soft resistance that appeared against her fingertips, she knew her virtual keyboards were up.

She began to type as the ghost continued its report.

Her suit had recorded signals as low as 17,000 Hertz, within range of human hearing, all the way to 130,000, which was well above the high-pitched frequencies used by bats on Earth.

"Keep talking," she said.

—*In sunfish, the larynx is a corded muscle. Air sacs allow them to push the same air back and forth through their larynx instead of exhaling where the atmosphere is minimal or toxic. They reflect those vibrations from the horn-like material of their beaks. They...*

"Why did you stop?"

—*The chasm we're following has opened into a cavern approximately seventy-five meters by thirty by forty-five. The floor drops away in a series of ravines. The far end is walled off by ice. Radar indicates fractures and melts in the ice, possibly an extensive network leading up from the rock. We may be at the edge of this mountain.*

"Thank God. Go. Let's get into the ice and try to seal it behind us. We can wall them off."

—*There is also a construct in the largest ravine.*

"What are you talking about?"

—*There is a rock wall sixteen meters across, two thick, and four high. It holds a reservoir of approximately twelve thousand gallons of water and slush.*

"Bring me to it."

For the first time since the assault, Vonnie felt relief. She remembered the carvings and the air locks. If the sunfish also built reservoirs, she and Lam—the real Lam—were correct in believing this was a sentient race. There were too many clues to think otherwise.

The guilt she felt was buried in fear, but it was the more honest emotion. It mingled with her shame.

How would human beings react if an alien walked into their city? Compared to the sunfish, Vonnie was a giant, and there might be schools or nurseries in the area. Maybe the attack had been her fault. Maybe she'd provoked it with her size or her smell or her heat. She should have known better. Approaching them had been selfish.

What if the sunfish were everything Lam had dreamed?

As her suit rambled down across the cavern floor, she said, "Do you see tool marks in the rock? Make sure you're recording to mem file."

—*Cameras inoperative.*

"Use radar and infrared. What's the temperature?"

—*The air is minus seventeen, but the rock shows hot spots as warm as three degrees due to thermal activity. The water varies between six degrees at its deepest parts and minus two in the shallows.*

"Is it salt water or fresh?"

—*Atmospheric testing suggests low levels of salinity. Should I send a mecha to acquire samples?*

"Yes."

She was curious. The majority of aquatic creatures on Earth had adapted to particular grades of water; fresh, brackish, or salt; warm, cool, or cold; sunlit, dim, or dark; but there were stand-outs like whales which could survive at least temporarily in any combination.

On Europa, there was also the matter of scalding heat. Most of the hot springs would be piped up from the great salt ocean. Obviously there were fresh water pockets such as this reservoir, melted by distant magma or by rising gases—but like the ice itself, fresh water lakes would be temporary, forever subject to cracking and contamination.

If the sunfish strived to retain fresh water, were they limited to saltless environments?

Could the reservoir have another purpose?

"Look for other ways out of the cavern," she said. "If this is where they drink or bathe, why haven't you seen any signs of steady traffic?"

—*There are signs of steady traffic.*

"Where? I told you I wanted an alert!"

—*Your instructions were to alert you to sonar calls or carvings. There are four holes in the ceiling and a fifth alongside the chasm from which we emerged. Three show indications of regular movement. The rock is abnormally smooth in places or cut in bands like ladder rungs.*

Mentally, Vonnie paused. The suit kept her body moving forward, but in her mind, she took a step back. She also released her virtual keyboards, cancelling her efforts to subvert the ghost. Taking him apart would have to wait.

"Get me out of here," she said.

—*Von, my scans of the reservoir are incomplete.*

"Get out. Detach and activate 84. Leave it here with 85. Command both of them to generate as much noise and heat as possible."

—*84 detached.*

The sunfish hadn't let her escape. They'd watched her run straight into a population center.

Vonnie ached with horror as her suit jogged from the ravine. With luck, her mecha would cover her. Was this cavern the sunfishes' home? The air was poison, but maybe they were *inside* the reservoir, breathing through their gills... waiting to snatch her leg and drag her in...

"Tell what you see!"

—*We've cleared the largest ravine.*

"Bring 85 after us. Keep 84 near the water."

—*There are disturbances in the reservoir. I estimate six lifeforms beneath the surface. Eight. Twelve. Fourteen.*

His voice counting smoothly in her ear was a stark contrast to her pounding heart. "What about the ladders up the cavern wall!?" she said. "Are there sunfish above me?"

—*Negative.*

"Leave 85 between me and 84. Tell it to pick up some gravel and throw it, not at the sunfish and not at me. I want to distract them."

—*The lifeforms have emerged from the water. They are emitting ultrasound.*

"Hide."

Her suit shoved her down onto her knees. The most frightened part of her wanted to keep running, but the sunfish who'd let her go were probably waiting in the chasm. Vonnie didn't want to run into an ambush. More than anything, she needed to apologize for invading their home.

"Play eight of their sonar calls for my ears only," she said. "Were there any that sounded non-aggressive before the attack? Simulate those calls for me and prepare to broadcast on my command."

—*Commencing simulation.*

Her head rang with shrill chirps and screeches. Ultrasound was imperceptible to human ears, but the ghost translated the sunfishes' cries into a piercing equivalent.

Were there words or was it only noise? Vonnie didn't know what she'd heard, but she wouldn't get another chance to speak before the sunfish were on top of her. "Broadcast those same calls through 85," she said. "If the sunfish respond, adapt your calls to match. Make sure you keep using both mecha as decoys away from me."

—*Broadcasting now.*

"Where are they?"

—*The lifeforms have jumped past the mecha straight at you. Contact in five seconds.*

"No!"

Her mind split. As a teacher, she wanted to communicate, but the ape in her would do anything to live.

Vonnie yanked an excavation charge from her forearm and

slammed it onto the ground on her left, orienting herself solely from memory. She'd worked in scout suits for years. From the earliest days of her career, she'd also learned to map busy construction sites in her head.

Her hand went to the charge unerringly. Her thumb double-flicked the safety locks. Then she aimed the shaped charge at the sunfish and flipped herself in the opposite direction.

If she had had a conscious thought, it might have been that she'd forgotten her despair. But she'd stopped thinking. She acted.

The detonation struck her suit like thunder. Vonnie cradled her helmet in her arms. A small, hard object whacked into her thigh—a rock—as something else hit her shoulder wetly—a sunfish.

It wasn't dead. It thrashed and snapped at her gear block, ripping into her helmet.

Vonnie saw a blurry flare of holo imagery in one eye as her visor flashed orange, then red. The sunfish was about to breach her armor. Berserk with fear, she caught the sunfish's body and squeezed her fingers into it like blunt knives, overtaxing her suit's amplified strength. She punctured its skin. The sunfish shuddered. It went limp.

She threw away the bloody mess and hopped to her feet, falling, scrambling, falling again.

She put her life in the ghost's hands, letting it replace her blind, pell-mell sprint with its controlled stride. "Take over! Run for the ice! Can you keep the blast zone between me and them?"

—*Affirmative. Most of the lifeforms are disabled. Nine dead, three wounded.*

"Where are my mecha?"

—*84 is under duress. 85 is unresponsive. The surviving lifeforms are battering them with rock clubs.*

And yet the sunfish had bypassed her mecha at first, even ignoring the gravel that 84 had thrown. How had they known to target her instead? Because she was larger? Why hadn't they listened to her sonar calls?

Carried by her suit, Vonnie's emotions swung back to self-doubt. The savage clarity she'd felt faded as guilt returned. There was a lesson there, but she was too overwhelmed to recognize it.

14.

SHE HOPED SHE'D lose the sunfish in the ice. Didn't they live mostly in water and rock? Maybe the ice was too cold or too precarious for them.

She knew she was grasping at straws. The carvings were proof that they inhabited the ice or had at one time, but grasping at straws was all she had left. She couldn't even hack the ghost from outside her suit's systems now that her mecha were gone, and she was dizzy and weak. The blood from her face had leaked down her chest like a growing stain.

—*Four lifeforms are close behind us.*

"Where am I?"

—*We're inside a seam in the ice. Radar indicates more chasms and holes above us.*

"Tear down as much ice as you can! Block them off!"

The suit jostled her, hammering at the ice. Fresh pain coursed through her head. Her shredded face felt like a drum skin, sensitive and taut.

If she couldn't reprogram the ghost, she might be forced to let him operate before she lost consciousness. What would happen then? If she slept, the ghost would keep running and climbing with her body inside it like a corpse. That could be a mercy unless she never woke up.

The suit lurched forward, left, forward again, and then backward and to the right.

Vonnie gasped, "Talk to me!"

—*Two lifeforms squeezed through the avalanche I created, but I no longer have a clear radar image of their positions. There is rock mixed through the ice. Many of the openings are too narrow for us. The lifeforms may be circling around.*

"Can you hear them?"

—Negative. Our sonar is inoperative.

"When did that happen?"

—During the second attack. Von, radar shows new lifeforms above and behind us.

"Pull down more ice or rock! Do anything you can!"

Her suit pummeled the walls, crabbing away from the sunfish. She felt herself wiggle and kick and dig. Once an arm tip slapped her boot. The sunfish were very near.

She quit moving abruptly.

—We're safe. I've packed more ice into barriers than the lifeforms can move without laboring for hours.

Vonnie reached out with both hands and clunked her fingers against the walls. Then she pawed at the ceiling and floor. "Is there a way out?"

—Negative. I've sealed this pocket on all sides.

"You... Why would you..." Vonnie swallowed, tamping down her claustrophobia. She'd told him to do anything necessary to protect her, and he'd obeyed with his literal, idiot logic. "Which side has less sunfish?"

—The chimney above us held only one lifeform.

"Dig out that side before more of them come. Go. Get ready to fight."

Her suit clawed at the ice, raining dust and heavier chunks on her helmet. Vonnie steeled herself against each blow. Pain was becoming normal.

"List all functioning sensors," she said.

—MR-7 radar 100%. SPRD radar 100%. Bryson infrared array 100%. Mobile platform seismographs 70%. Spotlight at full power but controls intermittent.

"Wait. Is my spotlight on?"

—Affirmative.

"Turn it off!" The heat of the camera spot might explain why the sunfish had ignored her mecha at the reservoir. "Was the light on when we were in the ravine?"

—Negative.

"What about residual heat?"

—Affirmative. With intermittent function, the spotlight's temperature has fluctuated between twenty-two and eighty degrees Celsius since damage sustained in the first attack.

"Turn it off."

—The controls have short-circuited.

"Cut power."

—The spotlight is slaved to the same energy grid as the radar and infrared arrays.

Should she break it with her fist? She would need the light when she regained her eyes. Even if there were spare bulbs left in her kit, she might not have the tools to extract a shattered bulb before installing a new one.

—Seismographs indicate scratching on the other side of the ice. I estimate two lifeforms are excavating this hole.

"Stop digging when you get within sixty centimeters. Let them do the work. They might get tired. Grab them as soon they come through. Throw them behind us. Jump out of the hole and knock down as much ice as you can. Confirm."

—Confirmed.

"Can you fix my gear block? I need sonar."

—Those transmitters are missing. There is nothing to fix.

What did that leave? Could she translate radar or infrared signals into something she could hear? Like their mecha, her suit was over-engineered, over-equipped, and highly adaptable. But there was a better solution. Her helmet contained a voice box for communicating with people who weren't in suits. She also had hardware designed to assess injuries with 'sound bullets' from a nonlinear acoustic lens in her chest plate.

"Run a patch from my voice box to the medical imaging systems," she said. "I want to control the MIS by voice command. Don't let the box make any external sound. Its function is to control the MIS. Understood? When I shout like this—*yah!*—make the MIS generate a terahertz pulse, then translate those signals back to me as normal sound."

—It's improbable the lifeforms will be able to hear frequencies in the terahertz range if you intend to broadcast their sonar calls.

"Just do it."

Using Vonnie's hands, the ghost began to rearrange the panel circuitry on her ravaged, filthy armor, creating a patch from her med pack to her helmet. That the sunfish wouldn't be drawn to a terahertz pulse was good. She didn't want to talk to them. She wanted a sensor independent of the ghost, because if she lived, her fight with him would be next.

—Here they come.

Her arms stabbed up. Her gloves clenched on squirming muscles. The sunfish squeezed their arms around her wrists as an eerie vibration passed through her chest. It was their sonar, an intimate, unpleasant buzz.

Her suit tossed them down and sprang out of the hole, chopping at the ice to seal them in.

The sunfish were too fast. One snarled itself around her boot. It hauled itself up her shins to her groin. Vonnie tried to run. She punched it loose, but the other sunfish roped four arms around her ankle, screeching.

Was it bringing more of them?

Vonnie wept as she stomped on them. They felt like rubber bumps until their bodies ruptured, spraying juice and guts up her legs. "I'm sorry! Sorry! Oh God, I'm sorry!"

At first she didn't realize she'd escaped. In this gravity, spidering through the ice felt too much like combat—grab, kick, grab again—swimming off the walls and ceiling. She gritted her teeth and endured.

"Where are they?"

—*No lifeforms in range.*

"Scan again! Where are they?"

—*No lifeforms in range.*

Tidal pressures, heat, and gas had riddled the ice with fractures and melts. A few gaps lifted up like crazy subway tunnels. More often, there were honeycombs.

The openings teased Vonnie with dead-ends and obstacles. Sometimes her suit was able to bash through stalactites or veils of ice. More often the ghost backtracked or gave up a hundred meters of hard-fought progress even when Vonnie was desperate to hide and rest.

After 1.7 kilometers, the ghost reported more rock ahead. The ice she'd crossed appeared to fill a valley between two mountain peaks, which explained why the ice was cracked and soft. The rock formed a bowl. It radiated heat upward. It also supported this part of the frozen sky, because the mountains meant the sky could only drop so far.

Her suit leapt an abyss onto solid ground. They charged up an uneven slope, weaving among the hollows and dripping ice overhead.

—*There are open lava tubes on our right.*

"Pick one! Hurry!" Vonnie didn't want to go into the rock. She wanted to climb it. But if she stayed outside, the sunfish were more likely to hear her. "Where are they?"

—*No lifeforms in range.*

Her suit clambered sideways and down. Vonnie counted every step. The noises around her deepened.

"We're inside the mountain?" she said.

—*Affirmative.*

She wouldn't get a better shot. Her hands tapped inside her gloves, opening her command codes. Then she launched a clumsy voice key assault on the ghost. "Authorization Alexis Six, all systems respond. *Bajonett. Bajonett.*"

The emergency order was meant to compartmentalize and

suspend all AI activity within a suit, ship, or station. At school, they'd called it the Knife. Basic processors were supposed to take over. Instead, the ghost caused another interrupt. Feedback squealed in Vonnie's ears. Worse, her voice box transmitted the same roar as if calling for the sunfish.

"*Eeeeeeeeeeeeeeeee!*"

The suit convulsed, slamming her face with unbearable pain— and then she had manual control.

She ran.

Her terror left no room for thought. It made her more effective. She forgot her wounds. She forgot her exhaustion. All senses tuned to the dark, Vonnie became her own momentum, reveling in every centimeter gained. She ran with her eyes shut, chasing the sound of her own boot steps. This channel in the rock was tight enough to reflect every noise back on itself, and she dodged through the space between each rattling echo.

15.

HER FRENZY DIDN'T last. The ninth or tenth time she fell, she paused before standing up. Then she was running again, crashing through the rock less successfully than before. Self-awareness returned in fits and starts.

Fix your eyes, she thought. *Test the system. If the ghost is gone, you can fix your eyes.*

Climbing, slipping, staggering, crawling, finally she accepted that she had no choice except to take her chances with life support. She decided to stop and set her trap.

When the sunfish caught up, Vonnie was hidden on a rock shelf above a short cliff. She'd rebooted the ghost with some success. He was still no better than three-quarters logic, but she'd gained control of her medical systems and the nanotech was rebuilding her left eye.

The ghost had fixed the sonar receptors in her helmet, so she could hear ultrasound again even if she couldn't transmit. The two of them had also turned off her spotlight when they stripped her gear block for parts. First she'd used the light to set her trap, burning a false trail beneath the cliff.

She should have anticipated that the sunfish would ignore it. As they stole into the fissure below her, they crept up the sides of the rift and moved straight toward her hiding place, filtering through every thin cleft and pit.

Vonnie stood to meet them with her welding laser and a chunk of rock. "I need auto-targeting only," she said. "Fire by voice command."

—*Von, that drops efficiency to thirty percent.*

"Fire by voice command. Confirm."

—*Listen to me.*

Her terahertz pulse detected movement sporadically, carrying new, ever-closer signals to her ears. She couldn't tell if there were four or forty of them hidden in the rift, but their sonar calls were all around her.

She discerned another hint of arms, then heard the clack of a falling pebble. Their voices rose like a wailing song.

Her emotions were a different storm, but there was one clear idea at the center of it. She didn't want to die badly. She didn't want the wrong reasons to be her last.

Should she put down her weapons and let them kill her? What would that teach the sunfish about human beings?

The ghost said:

—*I have six to eight targets, all well-concealed. Ten targets now. If we're going to pick them off before they jump, I need full system access.*

But they hadn't jumped. Not yet. The sunfish seemed indecisive. Maybe their careful approach was an overture.

"They're not attacking," she said.

—*They're taking position.*

"Last time they came straight at me. What if I'm far enough from their home? They might realize I'm not their enemy." Standing at the edge of the rock shelf, Vonnie made herself small. She knelt and tucked both arms against her chest, concealing her laser.

—*What are you doing?*

Her posture was submissive, yet she also tried to project resolve and strength, keeping her face up, turning it from side to side in an attempt to convey alertness. The sunfish understood at least some of her physiology. They knew her sensory organs were in her head.

—*Von, listen. It's the only chance.*

"No," she whispered, making her decision. "Off."

—*Wait.*

"I said off."

The sunfish sang and sang and sang, measuring her, crowding her.

A lesser woman might have wished them dead. Vonnie hoped to befriend them because ultimately the sunfish were like her. With their carvings and their architecture, they'd had exceeded all expectations—and merely by coming to Europa, so had she.

Thousands of candidates had sneered when her file was announced as the third member of the science team. They'd swamped the boards with insults. *Nice tits. Picked for the cameras. I guess she's sleeping with the right people.* Her abilities had been questioned by every jealous shithead on Earth. That they would've complained about anyone was no consolation. The disrespect was hard to shrug off, but how many of them would have survived the ice?

How many men would have lowered their weapons?

Vonnie was ruled by her desire to make things work. If that made her gullible or too patient or too curious, so be it. She didn't want to fight.

16.

THE FIRST SUNFISH hit Vonnie from behind like a silent missile. It struck the side of her head. Then the rift exploded with bodies.

She screamed uselessly. Whipping her fist into the monster on her head accomplished nothing, either. The sunfish had landed its body against the rough mark where her gear block had been, cinching its arms around her helmet, chewing with its beak. The sound was a rubbing squeal.

Somehow she managed another sweep of the rift. The echoes from her terahertz pulse were close and frantic, overlapping. There were more than twenty sunfish in the tightly choreographed launch. Most of them had gotten past her explosives.

"Are you still there!?" she shouted.

—Von, listen. Don't close me down again, please.

She was already yelling over the ghost. "Auto assault, max force!" she shouted. "Lam! Lam! Combat menu AP, auto assault! Confirm!"

The delay felt like another kind of blindness and separation. Vonnie screamed again, beating at the arms covering her face. The sunfish's cartilage skin was like pounding on leather. Her cutting tool would pierce that hide, but she was afraid to use the laser.

Something yanked her sideways, hurting her spine. At first she thought she'd been hit by a mass of sunfish.

—Auto assault.

The suit threw her in a cartwheel. As it rolled, it put her fist to her temple and drew the laser across the sunfish's arms, a precise stutter of four burns. It tossed her onto her hip and met the incoming wave with a kick.

Impacts shook Vonnie's boot and shin. Then she was up again. Three arms clunked against her back. Some of the sunfish must have gone overhead when she dropped—they must have surrounded her— and the suit spun and rammed into the rock, scraping itself clean.

Whatever triumph she'd felt gave way to claustrophobic terror.

The suit did not use its shape like a human would. It pinned one monster with its chin, then used its hip like a club against another. Again and again it hurled itself against the rock. It wasn't squeamish. It did not flinch at the wretched shrilling of a sunfish caught between its hands or even turn from the burst of entrails. In normal gravity, against larger enemies, Vonnie would have been seriously injured. Even here she was so shaken, she didn't immediately realize the fight was over.

Nor did she remember when she'd regained her left eye. She felt elation, then shock.

"I can see," she said. "Lam?"

Her visor was peppered with chip marks and abrasions. It was opaque in the middle. A gouge the length of her finger ran across her nose. The sunfish had almost bashed through.

Given another chance, they might succeed.

Vonnie glanced through two unmarked portions in the synthetic diamond, bending her head to improve her vision.

She stood at the top of the landslide beneath the cliff near her explosive charges. The rock was streaked with rimes of salt. Crusty white patches had seeped from the ceiling, but she was unable to peer into all of the holes overhead. Were there more sunfish above her?

Half of her display was inoperative. The rest of her visor glowed with heat signatures, although the only living shapes were fading as the sunfish retreated. Eleven bodies lay impaled against the black lava. In the minimal gravity, the air was fogged with blood.

Mute, she tried to turn away. Crying out, she knew she was paralyzed. The suit didn't respond to her arms or leg or head.

"Lam?" she said. "Lam, it's over. Off-line. Lam, off-line."

If the sunfish attacked again— If the ghost controlled all suit functions— Her body choked with that heavy new fear, and she fought without thinking inside her shell. She screamed when she was unable to move even slightly.

He spoke in a hush:

—*I have an additional threat.*

"Let me go!"

—*Von, quiet. Something's coming.*

"What?"

—*There were new sonar calls right before the sunfish withdrew. Something scared them off.*

"Is it one of our probes?"

—*No, these are new lifeforms.*

Vonnie nodded bitterly. Food here was scarce. Any commotion would draw every predator within hearing.

If there was good news, it was that the ghost's voice had changed. He seemed cooler and more confident. This was the first time he'd called them *sunfish.* That he'd said *no* instead of *negative* was another indicator of health. Had he actually written out his glitches? With access to more systems, he could have duped himself and then cut away his flaws in a microsecond. She was overdue for a little luck.

He said:

—*Do you want to stay and fight? I estimate them at four hundred meters.*

"How fast are they moving? Are they big?"

—*Judging from their sonar calls, they're at least as fast as the sunfish. They're also louder. They may be larger. They're within two hundred meters now.*

Each breath came in a short, tight rhythm. Vonnie tried to calm her lungs and failed, hating her own seesaw of emotions, hating the darkness and her pain. She felt like apologizing even though he was a goddamned program. She felt grateful.

Would he pass a diagnostic? If he'd attained full logic, the two of them would be a force to reckon with now that she could see again, but she was reluctant to put him to the test, not in combat, not even for the chance to take recordings of another major lifeform.

"Run," she said. "All these bodies, that should be a fat meal for whatever's coming. They'll stay to eat. Let's get out of here."

17.

HER SUIT LEAPT down from the cliff and hurried away, putting distance between them and the new predators. Unfortunately, Lam changed course seven times in five minutes through the spongy, jagged rock.

Vonnie tracked their progress with a heads-up display as they scrambled through gaps and pockets, jumping a crack and two loose hills of debris.

The ghost sought every possible way up, but they kept losing as much elevation as they'd gained, ducking and weaving for open space. They were forced left, then down, then down again through a pit laced with dry crunchy webs of mineral deposits. It felt like they were running in circles.

"Go back! Lam, go back to that last branch."

—*Radar suggests another upward trend ahead of us.*

"Aren't you headed where we came from?"

—*We've paralleled several caverns, yes.*

"Christ."

She'd taken the explosive charges with her, so it would be easy to blow the channel behind her and shut off any pursuit, but what if she encountered another foe? What if this tunnel was another dead-end?

Between radar sims and actual footsteps covered, Vonnie's maps went twenty-two kilometers, although most of that was tangled into a pyramid just eight klicks on a side. Some sections of her trail had also gone unrecorded or were literally nonexistent now. Colossal shafts of ice had been pulverized when the sink hole collapsed. It was unlikely she could retrace her steps even if she wanted to.

"What can you tell me about the new lifeforms?"

—*They used many of the same frequencies as the sunfish. I estimate there were only six of them, but the sunfish retreated within seconds of hearing the other sonar.*

Vonnie examined a wide vein of rock as they approached. It looked like an excellent place to drop the roof. All she wanted was *out*. No more data, no more diplomacy, no more trying to vindicate her friends' deaths. No more guilt.

"If they're ahead of us, we need to be prepared."

—*I've continued to see traces of prints and spoor. Look there. And there.*

Across her display, the ghost highlighted four smears of feces on a level spot on the tunnel floor. None was more than a few frozen blotches. In the frozen sky, nothing went to waste or was left behind.

That made her feel awful again. Compared to Europa, her planet was unspeakably rich. She wasn't sure if it was even possible for her to comprehend how their poverty affected them.

Did the sunfish routinely scout the impermanent, snarled labyrinths in the ice? That could account for why they appeared to know these dead zones so well even when there was no food, no breathable air, and only a few drips of liquid water for them to use for oxygen.

She'd seen no food sources other than the bugs, bacterial mats, and a few blots of fungi.

Was that why they were chasing her? To eat her?

She recalled the admiration she'd felt when she first connected the sunfish with the carvings at the top of the frozen sky. She'd supposed they explored the highest reaches of their world in the spirit of adventure, like people climbed Mt. Everest... like she'd volunteered for this mission... but she'd ignored the reality of Lam's models.

On Earth, a balanced ecology had reestablished itself after extinction events like the eruption of the Toba supervolcano or the Chicxulub meteor strike. On Europa, vast swaths of the biosphere had vanished completely, either burned to nothing or devoured by the ice.

Their environment was a patchwork mess of isolated survivors. What if the sunfish were so desperate for calories, they had no choice except to sweep through the ice looking for anything to sustain them?

Pity. Empathy. Vonnie was glad to feel emotions other than revulsion. It kindled something new in her.

For an instant, she was optimistic.

"Why would they gather their feces instead of leaving it as markers?" she asked. "To hide themselves from predators? For fertilizer?"

—*That implies they've developed agriculture.*

"Farms, yes. Why not?" She practically smiled. Haggling with the ghost reminded her of talking to the real Lam. "They could grow fungus for food."

—*It may be more likely that they use dung for insulation or cement. It would be difficult to seal rock structures with ice.*

"Cement," she said, brooding out loud.

The sunfish might have camouflaged a hundred passageways around her, covering traps and doorways with matching rock. The ghost would sense any that weren't airtight, but how many clues had she missed?

"Tell me what you can about the dung and give me a detailed read if we find any more."

—*I believe the feces belonged to the new lifeforms. We'd need to stop for a thorough analysis to confirm, but it contained unique, indigestible nubs of cartilage from the sunfishes' arms. It also looked to contain high concentrations of sodium chloride.*

"You mean salt."

—*Yes. The sunfish carry it in poisonous levels in their skin.*

"So whatever pooped here, it eats sunfish."

—*In retrospect, there's a high probability the sunfish pursued us beyond their territory and we're now in the home of the new lifeforms. Alternatively, these catacombs may be no-man's-land where both sides conduct raids on each other.*

Vonnie shook her head. Even with her weapons and size, she hadn't been able to make the sunfish run away. Whatever these other creatures were... if they scared the bloodthirsty sunfish...

Maybe she'd been luckier than she thought.

18.

HER SUIT SCAMPERED into a hole like a storm pipe. Then her right knee gave out. Vonnie smashed into the rock and bounced away. In the air, she tensed, fighting to keep her face from hitting next.

Her suit hurt her neck when it contorted like a cat. Lam patted her left heel and one hand against the wall, correcting her spin before he regained speed and clawed up through the maze with her bad leg trailing awkwardly, protecting it.

"Lam?" she said. "Thank you."

—*Are you injured?*

"No. Uh, no. Don't interface with the med systems. My leg's okay. Tell me about the suit."

—*Every anterior cable in the knee snapped and one medial.*

They were falling apart. Her armor had never been intended to take this kind of abuse. Vonnie wasn't doing much better. She was punch-drunk on stress and stimulants. It had been sixty-one hours since she'd slept. She didn't want to make the wrong decision.

"How long for repairs?"

—Without the proper tools, our best option might be to scavenge material from the ankle, weld it solid, and restore some function to the knee. I estimate that would take an hour.

"No. Keep going."

If they stopped, she was afraid she'd close her eyes. She should rest, but closing her eyes would feel too much like being blind again.

According to his sims, they were approximately two kilometers down. Soon they needed to transition from rock to ice. This mountain rose up like a fin, always narrowing, disappearing before it neared the surface—but there would be islands suspended in the ice, free-standing hunks as large as Berlin and gravel fields like sheets and clouds. The trick was to find a gas vent that went all the way up. The trick was to ascend without touching off a rock swell.

Vonnie avoided the thought. Too much planning would overwhelm her.

They ducked a bulge in the ceiling and the gap opened into an ancient volcanic bubble. Half of it was glutted with ice, but just to look across three hundred meters of open space was disorienting. Vonnie felt the same uncertainty in Lam. The ghost scanned up and back.

"What do you think?" she said. "There's definitely some new melt over there. If we dig, we might get into a vent. We could leave this mountain and close the hole behind us."

He lit her visor with radar frames.

—Look.

"Oh." Vonnie surprised herself. Even now, after everything, she felt excitement.

There were more carvings on the far side of the cavern, at least ninety columns of eight chiseled into the rock. Lam detected no organic pellets like they'd found in the trench where they'd made camp, but the information or messages contained in the symbols tantalized her.

"How fast can you record it?"

—The degradation to this site appears significant. Detailed recordings may require hours.

Vonnie limped across the cavern and pushed against a rock slab. The decayed fragments of the wall had shifted as water and ice intruded, retreated, and came again. Some wild feeling in her was able to guess which pieces were useless debris and which held carvings on one side or another.

The feeling made the hair stand up on her arms and neck. It felt exactly like... "Wait."

—Sonar.

Somehow she'd sensed those voices before Lam, but there was no time to speculate at the weird, creeping changes in herself. "How close are they?"

—A thousand meters. What we're hearing are echoes. They're deep in the tunnels. They may not know we're here.

"They know."

—Their voices aren't directed this way.

"They will be. Can you pull up this piece? I think it came out of that corner of the wall. If we can scan whatever's left on it, we'll have most of this section."

The suit hobbled forward. How would it hold up in combat? Vonnie knew she didn't want to fight in the open. She'd have a better chance if she found a hole and used her explosives to create a perimeter.

"It's not sunfish, is it?"

—No. It's the other lifeforms.

Vonnie shoved at the rock, moving feverishly now. It felt good and right to stay. She was glad to have purpose again. She would kill as many of them as she had to, but she was more than a rat in a trap, running mindlessly.

She'd worn down to the bedrock of herself and found what she needed, a last supply of courage and determination.

Seven hundred carvings would be priceless in translation efforts. This wall might be their Rosetta Stone. Vonnie couldn't abandon it.

If she ran, even if she survived, the ESA might never find their way to this cavern again. And if she died... well, if she died, some day their probes might venture close enough to communicate with her suit. It would transmit her files even if she was buried and lost.

Vonnie realized she was crying again and wasn't angry with herself. She wasn't ashamed. She'd done her best. Maybe that was enough.

She dropped the rock and pushed over a smaller boulder with a chipped half-sun of a carving on the underside. "Got it?" she asked, feeling close to him again, the real him and the ghost. He was a potent friend.

—*They're within six hundred meters.*

"You got it?"

—*Yes. There are more of them this time. Twelve. They're moving faster.*

"Help me with this big rock."

The truth was she scarcely knew which questions to ask. She wasn't puzzled that there were sunfish carvings in territory that was no longer theirs. These catacombs must have changed hands regularly or were deserted and reclaimed as the years passed, but she wondered why she hadn't found more carvings, air locks, or reservoirs.

Even if the sunfish had been exiled from this area for centuries, shouldn't she have seen other signs of activity?

Some part of the secret might be here. Vonnie was willing to defend it. In fact, she might find the answers she needed in the sunfishes' rivals.

Was it possible that Europa had given rise to more than one intelligence species? If so, where was the evidence of a second civilization? If not, what sort of animal was strong enough to drive off a thinking race?

—*I've finished recording this section.*

"Good," Vonnie said.

Then she swung to face the approaching voices with an excavation charge in either hand.

19.

THE CAVERN SEEMED to stretch as her fear grew. She stayed near the carvings, trying to anchor herself. Deep radar let her track the new creatures while they were still out of sight. There were twelve bodies in the swarm, banging off the walls and ceiling of a gap.

—*Sixty meters. Fifty.*

Vonnie held her explosives. There were too many entrances, and she had only four half-sticks. She couldn't throw one until they were almost on top of her. Otherwise they might get away, leaping back into the chasms on the far side.

—*Forty.*

They would catch her if she ran. She knew she had to stand her ground, but her adrenaline felt like a hundred chittering mice. She felt untamed and inhumanly quick.

—*They're in the third tunnel.*

As soon as there was less rock in the way, Lam drew each body into clear resolution. They were no longer twelve overlapping blobs. They were sunfish.

"Christ, you said..."

They were different. These sunfish were larger, with longer arms and different skin, like cousins of the ones she'd fought. Cousins, yet a separate breed. To creatures who saw and spoke in sonar, the new sunfish would stand apart from the others if for no other reason than their size.

As they flitted in and out of sight, Vonnie saw they were darker, too. But they didn't enter the cavern. Were they trying to envelop her?

Like the smaller sunfish, they must not have any idea what to make of a bipedal creature wrapped in metal and glass. That they hesitated was a positive sign.

Vonnie spoke in a whisper. "You're recording their sonar calls, correct?"

—*Yes.*

"Get ready to broadcast some of those calls on my command. Can you tell me what they're saying?"

—The pitch and intonations of their voices are different than those of the smaller sunfish, although the body shapes they use are similar.

Neither breed would be aware of their skin color. Maybe they smelled or tasted differently, but Vonnie reached one conclusion immediately because she could see. The increased mineral absorption in the skin and defensive spines of the larger sunfish suggested that they lived in the caustic waters of hot springs or the great salt ocean, unlike their smaller cousins, who might be limited to fresh water reservoirs.

Their race diverged, she thought. *They grew apart, each kind finding its niche like dark-skinned human beings in Africa and pale-skinned in Europe.*

What if their differences are more than cosmetic? Can they cross-breed with each other?

More interesting, it wasn't the larger sunfish who'd written on this rock wall. The size of the carvings was wrong. So was the surface texture, which matched the pebbly skin and spines of the smaller breed. The carvings belonged to the smaller sunfish. So did the nubs of cartilage Lam had identified in the feces they'd discovered.

Vonnie's thoughts crashed together as the elusive, feinting sunfish revolved around her like a living hurricane. They dodged in and out of the gaps surrounding the cavern.

They're eating each other! she realized. *The two kinds of sunfish are at war.*

Were both breeds really intelligent? Did she want them to be? If not, the situation was akin to gorillas hunting people, a larger species preying upon its weaker, smarter relatives. That by itself was horrific. But if yes—if both breeds were sentient—they were cannibals.

Yes, she thought. The word held a gruesome finality. *I think the answer is yes.*

The larger sunfish used group tactics like the smaller breed. These weren't animals. Their voices rose and fell, calling to each other as individual members of the pack maneuvering for position.

They're analyzing me. Confusing me.

Eating their cousins was disgusting, but their war with each other was the more despicable crime. It was why she'd discovered so few traces of social organization. Instead of building more safe areas, instead of farming or writing, they fought.

Their competition had been more than either side was able to withstand. In fact, she couldn't be certain if the smaller sunfish she'd encountered were members of a single tribe or two or more. How far had their race lapsed into anarchy?

"Broadcast your sonar calls," she said. "Let's talk to them. You said you can..."

—*Here they come.*

The new sunfish sprang into the cavern, a dual wave of bodies high and low. Vonnie's chance to kill them cleanly would be gone in seconds. She had learned not to wait, but she'd also remembered who she was and why she'd come to Europa.

"Lam, talk to them! Try to talk to them with body shapes!" she yelled.

Her suit dropped down as the sunfish flew closer. Lam greeted them by altering his stance, lowering one shoulder and waggling her hands alongside her stomach.

It was the right decision. Vonnie believed it. These sunfish were a new, separate population. She hoped they would answer her.

20.

THE NEW BREED reacted to Lam's posture as they soared across the cavern. With a ripple of motion, their bodies shared an idea. Was it astonishment at Lam's attempt to communicate? Vonnie realized they also used the fine pedicellaria beneath their arms to convey information. Lifting one arm or more, they showed each other dense, writhing patterns.

Many of those arms were damaged. With radar targeting, Lam identified dozens of old scars and deformities. Vonnie had seen similar gashes among the smaller sunfish. She'd thought they'd sustained those wounds on the lava rock.

The injuries were beak wounds.

When the sunfish fought, they led with their undersides, snapping and slicing at each other. In all likelihood, the smaller sunfish were better at getting inside their cousins' reach. They would sustain more deaths, yet left more marks on their adversaries.

"Lam, hurry!" she shouted.

He was limited by her form. He was also canny enough not to try to replicate the carvings or mimic what they'd seen of the smaller sunfish. The warring breeds might have separate languages, so Lam improvised, holding Vonnie in an uncomfortable ball as he stuttered her fingers against her torso. Her visor flickered with sun-shapes as he compared these twelve individuals with sims and real data.

There was another ripple among them as Lam shifted and flexed. Did they understand?

Please, Vonnie thought. *Please.*

But he'd kept the half-sticks against her forearms with magnetic locks. Now he released two with a click.

—*Watch out.*

The dual waves of sunfish struck the ceiling and floor. They bounced toward her, intersecting with each other to create a single group.

"Please!"

They came with their beaks open, shrieking. They came with their arms thrown wide to grasp and tear.

—*Auto assault.*

Vonnie wept for them, monsters all of them. The intelligence she knew existed here was stunted and cold like everything inside Europa.

Lam bashed her fist up through the first sunfish, then turned to swat the next. The rest never reached her.

"Fire," she said.

He put both charges in the wall and shattered the carvings, ducking beneath a blast of rock.

Then she turned and ran.

The four survivors kept after her, of course. She'd dreamed the show of force would be enough, but these sunfish were no different than the smaller breed. Even with two-thirds of their group dead or bleeding out, they were relentless.

Vonnie reached a tunnel and drove herself into the ceiling, crushing a sunfish on her shoulder. Lam pulled at the rock with both hands and cancelled her momentum, flinging debris back over her head. The shower hit the next three sunfish and Lam kicked downward with the suit's arms out, clubbing them.

She left the wounded to live or die, knowing it was a mistake to let them summon more of their tribe. She knew she would always be wrong for trespassing.

For nearly an hour, Vonnie heard them behind her, crying into the mountain. The echoes faded as she climbed, except once when there were fresh voices. Had the larger breed brought reinforcements? Was there a third kind of sunfish? Their sonar calls were too diffuse to know for certain, and she was glad, dimly, muffled in exhaustion and grief.

She climbed.

She climbed without end.

Even carried by the suit, she passed her limit, her tendons straining. Something in her back gave out above her pelvic bone, grinding with each step—and in her mind it was the same, one hurt which was more exquisite than the rest.

She dug her way into a vent, leaving the monotony of the catacombs. But there was no escaping her sorrow.

The leaning shaft up through the ice looked like the sink hole where Lam and Bauman had died, although her radar showed no dust and few mineral deposits within the melt. That was a positive sign. Geysers and swells meant instability. This vent looked solid. Vonnie thought she could ascend without bolts and wire, although her hands were sore and beaten.

She climbed.

She climbed slowly, evaluating the ice, scanning ahead. Suddenly there was a new sound. *Dit dit dit dit dit dit.* It was the rescue beacon of a probe overhead.

Vonnie rasped out a noise like laughter as Lam returned the probe's signals in the only manner available to him, a cacophony of terahertz and radar pulses. He repeated the chatter until the probe answered in the same way.

—*We made it, Von.*

"Yes."

—*Let's wait here. Can you wait? Seven bones and tendons in your hand are damaged, and your elbow isn't much better. I don't want to risk a fall.*

"Yes."

—*They need fifteen minutes. Can you sleep? You should eat and rest.*

"No." She couldn't relax, hanging on the ice several hundred meters up with another quarter-kilometer to go. She kept one file open on her visor and let the data burn into her, staring through it even when she tipped her head to watch above.

Lam had put together a preliminary transcript of the carvings. With it, they had an explanation.

She was wrong.

The error made her feel not like a teacher but like a student again, because just as Scandinavian and Inuit peoples had developed multiple words for snow, the sunfish had thirty-two stances to indicate surprise and danger. Sixteen more postures spoke of moving inward to protect the pack.

Their all-or-nothing behavior wasn't sadism or the result of animal stupidity. It was premeditated. It was a survival trait.

The sunfish possessed more imagination and mental agility than she'd believed. Like every culture on Earth, they wrote stories of other worlds and nightmares. Their carvings hinted at places and legends similar to Atlantis, vampires, and poltergeists, but their past was saturated with real-life encounters with ancient ruins and strange creatures from distant pockets in the ice and separate lines of evolution.

The sunfish had been confronted with aliens throughout their existence. That they'd never met anything like Vonnie before, that she mimicked their language and wore metal and carried tools—none of this would stop them.

To the sunfish, everything beyond the pack was a competitor for safe zones and oxygen. Everything was food. By necessity, most life-forms in the ice had learned the same vicious reflex.

The sunfish attacked even when they were outsized or outnumbered. They'd learned to put the fight on their own terms. If they won, the pack expanded its territory. If they lost, not only did they have less mouths to feed, their dead became food for the survivors.

Until they could conceive of anything else, until they were able to conceive of anything else, their first response would always be violence.

The warring breeds she'd met seemed to be the remnants of an empire that had spread to the top of the frozen sky. Millennia ago, there had been a dormant period in Europa's volcanic activity. Maybe someday there would be again. The carvings were short histories intended to aid the next alliance to rise from the chaos, offering commandments to share and proven methods to govern themselves in a hierarchy of scouts, warriors, workers, and breeding pairs.

Unfortunately, Vonnie had left a path of destruction through whatever civilization they'd managed to hold onto.

It wasn't what they deserved. Worse, their kill-or-be-killed aggression would work against them now that the possibility of salvation existed at last.

What have I done? she thought.

The mecha gathering above her were American, yet relayed ESA signals. Lam pulled their search grid and told Vonnie how far she'd strayed. She was 9.1 klicks east of the trench where her team had gone in. She was also two-thirds of a kilometer beneath the surface, so the mecha rigged a molecular wire and dropped other lines around her including life support, suit support, and data/comm.

Another line lowered an emergency seal for her helmet before her visor blew out. Vonnie secured the bag around her neck, then inflated it with the attached air cylinder.

She let go of the ice. Her suit revolved dizzyingly as the machines lifted her, but the flood of voices was more intense. The men and women up top had accessed her records as soon as the data line connected. At a glance, her mem files must have looked like a running battle. She had gore and black rock mashed into every joint in her suit, her battered helmet, and her blood-stained gloves.

Someone murmured, "Vonderach, my God."

But she was still thinking of the sunfishes' potential and of the debts she owed, both to Bauman and Lam and to the native tribes she'd devastated. The sunfish were very human after all, with traits both good and evil. If they could be freed from starvation... If they were given a chance...

"We have to help them," she said.

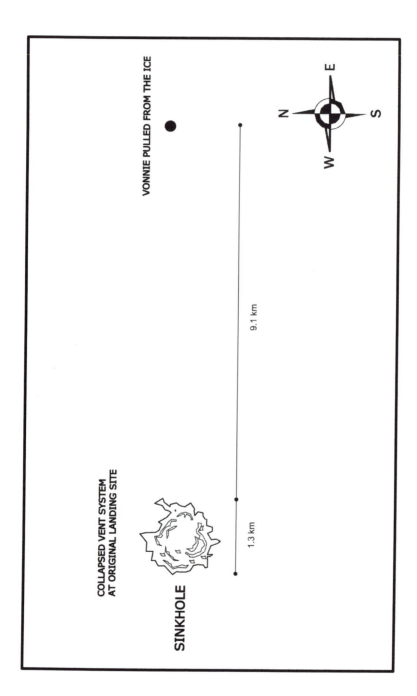

SINKHOLE

COLLAPSED VENT SYSTEM
AT ORIGINAL LANDING SITE

VONNIE PULLED FROM THE ICE

1.3 km

9.1 km

N E W S

Surface of Europa

TOPSIDER

21.

THERE WAS ONLY one survivor. They pulled her from the ice after four days alone in the dark, coated with blood and dust, her suit damaged at its knee, chest, gloves, and helmet. The rock dust and frozen water vapor encrusted on her armor were extraterrestrial. So was the organic tissue. It belonged to Europa's sunfish.

The blood inside the crippled suit was her own.

"YOU CAN'T DELETE him!" Vonnie said from her hospital cot, trying to sit up.

Administrator Koebsch shook his head. "We'll leave most of the files intact."

"I owe him my life. If you erase his personality—"

"Your AI is badly corrupted."

"That's not his fault. It's mine." Vonnie's hand throbbed as she held a comm visor near her face, allowing them to see each other. Her cot was in a separate structure from Koebsch's command module. Fresh muscle grafts on her temple and cheek kept her from using the visor properly, but her hand wasn't much better off. Five bones in her fingers and wrist had been set with glue, and that was her good hand, her right hand. Her left was a swollen club. Otherwise it wouldn't have been such a struggle to sit up.

As Vonnie rose, her blanket fell away, leaving her naked above the waist. By trade, astronauts could not be body conscious in their perpetually crowded living quarters.

Maybe she let the visor dip to her breasts and bandaged shoulder on purpose. Koebsch was a politician. If he was agitated by her body, it might rattle him enough to listen. Despite her injuries, Vonnie was lean and well-toned with clear skin and a long, slender belly.

"Let me help," she said. "We can copy the files you want, then isolate them."

"That's what we're doing."

"But don't delete the rest! Lam was a Chinese national. Human-based AIs aren't illegal in his country. I know we can't send him back to them. He knows too much. But we can give him sanctuary with us. It would be wrong to strip him down to pure data."

"I disagree."

Koebsch was forty-eight, blond, and Earthborn like Vonnie. Unlike Vonnie, he'd arrived on one of the high-gee launches five days ago. He had yet to adapt to low gravity. His face was always flushed. Vonnie wasn't sure if she'd embarrassed Koebsch, so she tried again.

"You're afraid of him," she said. "I get it. You don't need any legal problems on top of running our operation, but Lam is a proven resource. He's the only one who's communicated with the sunfish."

"The sunfish are a separate matter," Koebsch said.

Like everyone in the ESA crew, he'd adopted her name for the Europans. Her experience had been too sensational. The media loved everything about her odyssey, and, according to the news feeds she'd seen in the past day, most people were using the term *sunfish* across the solar system.

Her fame gave her leverage. "The sunfish are the only thing that matters," she said, but Koebsch wouldn't let her change the subject.

"Your AI attacked our diagnostics," he said.

"That was a misunderstanding. Let me talk to him."

"No. You're... emotional." Koebsch obviously intended to say more, but checked himself. "Get some rest," he said. "I'll talk to you tomorrow."

Vonnie shouted. "Wait!"

He cut the connection.

What should she do? The medics had stuck two intravenous lines in her arm, delivering simple fluids and complex mood stabilizers. She had trouble walking in any case. But she couldn't let her friend die again even if that was what the real Lam might have wanted.

The ghost was too human. It had found its equilibrium while it was limited to her suit, using her armor like its own body, but after they were rescued, it had destabilized when it was subjected to an interface with their central AIs.

That didn't mean he shouldn't be saved. Vonnie knew he could be a formidable ally, and yet she had another incentive to save him besides the relationship they'd developed. More important than her personal loyalty was Second Contact with the sunfish. Koebsch needed every tool available before they went back into the ice.

Vonnie tugged her IVs loose and stood up, although there was no way to sneak out of the lander where the medical droids had operated on her skull and hands. Her med alerts chimed as soon as she disconnected the IVs.

A young woman in a blue insulated one-piece stepped into the compartment. Her freckled nose and big hazel eyes gave her harmless look, which she dispelled by barking like a cop. "What are you doing? Get back in bed."

"I can't," Vonnie said. "There are complications with my suit. I need to assist with data recovery."

"You need time to heal."

"I'm okay." Vonnie squeezed by the young woman, then nodded to the two men in the next compartment as she hurried past.

The lander's floor was only fifteen meters square, but it held eight rooms, many of them as small as closets. Striding through the lander felt like running through a maze of steel. It reminded her of the ice. Vonnie realized she was grinding her teeth, driven by a rising sense of hysteria. She moved faster and faster until she reached the ready room, the largest compartment in the lander.

The young woman caught up and said, "Stop. We talked about your trauma levels. Your injuries aren't just physical." "Koebsch asked me to come over," Vonnie lied. Then she tried a different argument. "It's good therapy, isn't it? I should stay busy."

"I guess." The young woman gestured to the men behind her.

Vonnie heard one of them on the radio. "This is Metzler in Zero Four," he said.

She ignored him and opened the first locker on the wall. Inside was a pressure suit. It weighed twelve times less than the armor she'd worn, but the pressure suit felt heavier. It was inert, whereas her armor had walked with her, magnifying every nerve impulse.

"Why don't we sit down for a minute," the young woman said.

Vonnie donned the pressure suit with her ruined hands. Nearby, three sets of armor hung on chain winches like empty metal giants. Vonnie might have climbed into one if the biometrics weren't calibrated for each individual. She could use someone else's armor, but clumsily, and the likelihood of hurting herself was too real.

"Stop," the young woman said. "If you won't—"

"Help me." Vonnie met her eyes. "Please. You can drive me to the command module."

The young woman nodded uncertainly. Behind her, the man leaned into the room and frowned. Vonnie knew they were all a little in awe of her, and, thinking like a sunfish, she stood erect and shrugged into the sleeves of the pressure suit, projecting confidence with her shoulders and chin.

"Koebsch is making a mistake," she said.

22.

VONNIE'S THOUGHTS QUIETED as the air lock cycled, depressurizing to match the near-vacuum outside. Beside her stood the young woman, who'd joined her.

They didn't speak. The young woman flitted through a display inside her visor, while Vonnie's thoughts consumed her.

Was it claustrophobia that had driven her to suit up and leave Lander 04? She expected to have nightmares the rest of her life, but she was loaded with no-shock and antidepressants. She wanted to believe she was in control of herself. Yes, it was out of character for her to have flashed her body at Koebsch. She wasn't a show-off. But she also felt like she was beyond foolish little things like shyness or self-doubt.

She'd changed. Some parts of her had died in the ice, and the woman who remained was impatient to set things right.

Her entire race was watching. Every decision would be scrutinized across the solar system and in history files for centuries to come, which was why Koebsch had his stiff caution and why Vonnie thrummed with compassion and fear.

If humankind failed again, if *she* failed again, they might doom every living thing inside Europa, and she'd seen much to admire as well as savagery.

Unfortunately, the violence was difficult to overlook.

Sunfish had become a popular term across the system, but not everyone consented to humanizing them with a name. Some of the exceptions were military spokespersons, who referred to the sunfish as *the aliens*, and public officials of the ice mining ventures and utility companies, who put their own spin on the situation by saying *organisms* or *things*.

Many politicians and commentators had also played it safe, either hedging their bets or supporting the interests of various corporations. Vonnie knew the mining ventures, their distributors, and many industries were hollering because Earth's governments had demanded that the mining ventures reevaluate their sites, then screen and analyze the ice before processing it, all of which created delays and extra costs.

Public debate had grown into a firestorm in part because the ESA had kept Vonnie under wraps, asking Koebsch to speak to the media on her behalf and releasing no more than a few, brief, sanitized clips of her journey beneath the ice.

None of those sims included live recordings of the sunfish, only still shots and diagrams. Nevertheless, their beaks and arms had a lot of people scared, especially in combination with the progress reports listing her surgeries.

I need to make sure everyone sees I'm okay, she thought. *They have to know that I don't blame the sunfish—that the fighting was my fault.*

The air lock finished its cycle with a clunk. The exterior door opened.

As they walked onto the lander's deck, Vonnie hardly glanced at the fat, banded sphere of Jupiter or the radiant dots where spacecraft hung overhead. Instead, she looked for their command module. She couldn't see it. The icy plain was busy with floodlights, mecha, listening posts, and other hab modules.

From where she was standing, there didn't seem to be any pattern. Then she activated her heads-up display. Most of the hab modules and a second lander were spread in a broad ring over an area of a square kilometer. Vonnie felt a wan smile. In another age, the pioneers of the American West had circled their wagons in the same way. Long before then, in Germany, her ancestors had built their castle walls to guard all sides as well. Old habits.

Command Module 01 was on the far side of camp. "Can we take the jeep?" Vonnie asked, turning to the young woman.

"Yes." Ash Sierzenga was one of their new pilots as well as a medic and the head of the cybernetics team. All of them had multi-disciplinary training and degrees. It cost too much to boost three people if one would do.

Every meal, each piece of equipment, had been factored into the mission. They were a long way from replacements, a reality that played in Vonnie's favor. She knew they'd discussed sending her home, but no one wanted to use a ship for her, not even the slowboat in which she'd arrived.

The jeep was a low-slung vehicle with an open cockpit and wide-tracked wheels. Ash made a point of entering first. Was she concerned Vonnie might steal it? Where was there to go? Vonnie didn't like it that Ash distrusted her, but she was an outsider among the new team. Even if they understood her motives, they would tend to support each other instead of her.

I need to be careful, she thought. *I can't raise my voice or wave my arms. They don't like it that I don't hate the sunfish.*

They think I'm crazy.

The jeep rolled into the hectic lights and mecha, communicating with the other self-guided machines.

For the most part, the listening posts and beacons had settled down, becoming stationary obstacles. They resembled short trees with their dishes and antennae serving as leaves, although a few members of the metal forest tottered or crept in restless patterns.

The larger mecha were more active. Twice the jeep drove beneath hulking rovers. The first was poised like a giant, feeding tick, its head lower than its legs as it drilled into the ice. The second was on patrol. Bristling with sensors and digging arms, it bore down on them, but neither Vonnie nor Ash flinched. They were accustomed to the machines' flawless dance. The rover passed with meters to spare, and their jeep continued through the long shadows and pools of light.

There were open crevices in the ice. The main fracture yawned through the center of camp, over three hundred meters long yet rarely wider than a person could jump.

The new ESA camp was twelve kilometers southeast of the trench where Vonnie, Bauman, and Lam entered the frozen sky.

When that system of vents collapsed, it had destroyed the carvings as well as any chance of venturing back into that region of ice. The collapse had left an uneven, unstable pit in Europa's surface 1.3 kilometers across.

Someday the glacial tides or an upswell in the ocean would fill the hole. For now, it was a scar and a grave.

Lam and Bauman's bodies had been abandoned after religious services and commendations were delivered near the pit by ESA, NASA, and PSSC teams while Vonnie watched from her bed in the new camp.

Their rovers and satellite analysis had located another system of catacombs, which could be accessed through the crevices where they'd assembled their hab modules and flightcraft. Too often, there were only a few meters of ice separating the caverns below from the fissures leading up to the surface. That was why the mecha were on high alert.

Studying their datastreams, Vonnie made sense of their grid at last. Koebsch wasn't an idiot. On Europa, any threat would approach from beneath them, not from outside their ring, so he'd spread his assets for mapping purposes, measuring the ice with radar, sonar, neutrino pulse, and seismographs...

...and weapons systems. The jeep was tied to their defense net, its dashboard winking with steady updates from the *Clermont*, the ESA ship in orbit above Europa.

But we don't need to be on alert, Vonnie thought. "The sunfish won't come," she said.

"What?" Ash turned in her seat to bring her helmet around, revealing a face full of suspicion.

Vonnie kept her voice tranquil. "They won't come," she said. "The ones who chased me know we're outside the ice. They might be listening, but they'll never risk a blow-out by coming to the surface."

"They seemed like they, uh, like they did anything to kill you even if it meant suicide for them," Ash said. "Koebsch is worried they'll dig away the ice beneath us."

"I don't think so. They must be even more afraid of vacuum than we are."

"You can't know how they think."

"We've been in space for nearly two hundred years. We were watching the stars before our species learned how to talk. Their sense of distance is limited. All they've ever known are their ears and their sonar."

"Right. You're right."

Ash was humoring her, but Vonnie saw an opportunity to sway the younger woman. "They think the universe ends here," she said. "They have no concept of the stars or other planets or anything past the surface. Only death. Try to think how many times their populations must have asphyxiated when eruptions or quakes ripped open their homes."

"You found air locks in the ice."

"They're smart." Vonnie couldn't stop herself from saying it. "They're marvelous."

"They're monsters."

"They've never had a chance to be anything else."

Ash didn't answer. They'd reached the command module, and Ash busied herself with the jeep's console. She seemed to be receiving a radio call that only she could hear.

"We need to get back into the ice and figure out how to talk to them," Vonnie said.

23.

KOEBSCH WASN'T HAPPY to see either woman. He met them at the air lock as they stowed their pressure suits, obstructing their way into the module. To his left was the mission's primary data/comm room. To his right was one of the multipurpose labs where they'd brought Vonnie's armor.

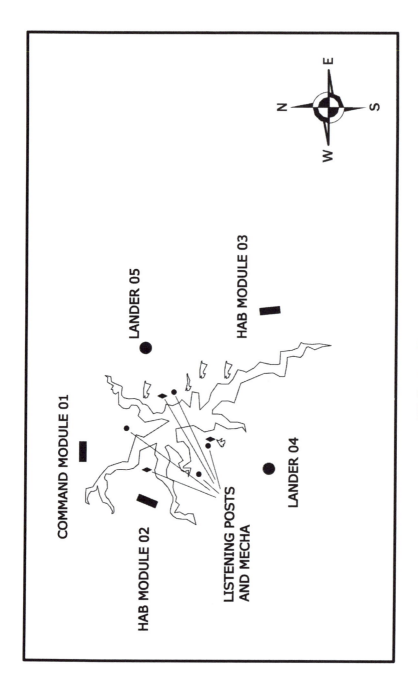

COMMAND MODULE 01

LANDER 05

HAB MODULE 02

HAB MODULE 03

LISTENING POSTS
AND MECHA

LANDER 04

N E S W

ESA Camp

"I could have sent your jeep back to medical, but let's get this over with," Koebsch said.

Vonnie tried to cover for Ash. "She told me not to come," she said.

"Did you think you could sneak in and steal your AI?"

"No, sir."

"Nothing happens on our grid without my knowing it."

"No, sir."

"All right." Koebsch gestured for them to go left toward data/comm, not to the lab. Vonnie hesitated, but she wouldn't get another chance to prove she wasn't a head case. She dutifully followed him into data/comm.

The cramped room had two chairs. Koebsch leaned back in his seat as Vonnie perched on the edge of hers. Ash stayed at the hatch with her arms folded.

"You want to go back into the ice," Koebsch said.

He tapped the radio in my pressure suit, Vonnie thought, feeling irate. But she didn't show it. "I think we should mount another expedition this week," she said.

"It's not going to happen. Not yet."

"I don't mean people at first. We should send in mecha. The best choice would be probes that are the same size and shape as the sunfish."

"We're building them now."

Vonnie flared at his imperturbable calm. "Then we can program some of those probes with my AI! Lam will have more success than anything new."

Koebsch shook his head. "You have to realize, there are people on Earth who've proposed sealing off the ice."

Vonnie's heart stopped. "We can't do that."

"Yes, we can. A few explosive charges—"

"We've discovered intelligent life."

"I believe you. I want to believe you. Everyone involved with the agency has wanted to find something like this since we were kids, right?"

Vonnie stared in surprise. Koebsch was a government appointee. She'd thought the ESA was just a job to him.

"We're not sure the sunfish are intelligent," he said.

"They use language and engineering."

"They seem to, yes. There's good evidence. But their intelligence hasn't been so well demonstrated that no one is questioning it. If we send in your AI and he's glitchy, we'll be giving the wrong people more ammunition."

"Let me talk to him."

"You're acting a little glitchy, too," Koebsch said, leaning forward and patting Vonnie's arm. "Do you know what the Stockholm syndrome is? Sometimes a hostage will begin to defend the people who grabbed her."

"That's bullshit. The sunfish are amazing. Hell, there's no question they'll be *profitable*, too," Vonnie said, stewing with contempt. "The military and pharmaceutical lobbies must be screaming for DNA samples."

"Yes."

"We need to help whatever's left of the sunfish empire."

"How? Are you proposing an evacuation? To where?"

"I don't know. We should send down food and oxygen. We could lead them to safer areas. They don't have radar. They might not know the best places to hide. That would be an easy way to demonstrate our goodwill."

"It might come to that, but there are only eleven of us. My first responsibility is to make sure *we're* safe. That includes maintaining our food and air supplies for the duration of our mission."

"There will be supply ships."

"Vonnie, the sunfish look like they've been down there for thirty thousand years. They're as old as the last existing populations of Neanderthal Man, maybe older. A little more time won't matter."

"They're telling each other about us right now. They're telling each other I killed dozens of them!"

"You acted in self-defense."

"They must think we're the monsters. The longer we wait, the worse it will be. They'll build more defenses. They'll prepare for war. We need to try again before they get too entrenched."

"We will. Vonnie, we will, but not before we're ready. Meanwhile, you need to help me. Let us use what we can from your AI's mem files and delete its personality."

"I..."

"If the next stages of our operation don't go right, everything we've planned will be in jeopardy."

Vonnie looked away from him. She didn't want Ash to see her expression either, because if they were going to work together, Ash needed to believe that Vonnie would always put the team first. In space, a crew was family.

Now she had to let them erase Lam forever. If she needed to choose between her AI or the sunfish, there wasn't a choice at all.

"Okay," she whispered. "Take him apart."

24.

DURING THE NEXT few days, they began to settle in for the long haul. Even if there was no further contact with the sunfish, Vonnie had gathered enough data to occupy thousands of experts for years. Instead, they had eleven people. Datastreams let them back-and-forth with universities, laboratories, and government agencies on Earth and Luna, where other programs were underway, but the eleven of them were the front line.

The pressure might have been overwhelming, except Koebsch was right. The ESA crew were elite volunteers. Every one of them had dreamed of adventure since they were children.

Metzler, the lead biologist, went a hundred hours without rest until he was incoherent with stims and caffeine, and Koebsch ordered him to take the same sedatives Vonnie used to sleep.

She'd been allowed to field ten interviews in which prominent newsmen and commentators gushed over her survival while she tried to cast the sunfish in a sympathetic light. "I smashed through their homes like some kind of giant," she said. "To them, *I* was the alien." But the newsmen were baffled by this point of view, and their feeds tended to play clips of her speaking well of Bauman and Lam, as if her friends had died during her encounters with the sunfish.

It was infuriating. Vonnie recorded her own interviews and asked permission to put them on the net, haggling with Koebsch, yelling at an assistant director on Earth, finally setting the matter aside because she believed the truth would come out as soon as they contacted the sunfish again.

Everybody experienced some level of mania except Ash, who remained cool. Ash seemed to have taken it upon herself to be the vigilant one—the grown-up. At the same time, Koebsch became more and more of a toucher, punching shoulders, whacking backs, participating in their excitement.

Ash had a nice smile, especially when the men were around, but she was intense for someone in her early twenties. As a *wunderkind*, she'd probably spent her brief adulthood fighting people's assumptions that she was a child. Vonnie supposed that was why she insisted on *Ash*, not *Ashley*, because her abbreviated name was sharp while the longer version sounded soft. The chip on her shoulder was as big as a sword.

Vonnie liked her. She liked all of them. They were honest, dedicated people who embraced their work.

One piece of business took priority. Vonnie had encountered bugs, bacterial mats, and fungi in addition to the warring breeds of sunfish. There were bacteria in the bugs, a parasitic growth on the fungi, and what appeared to be viral infections in the smaller sunfish.

For several days, the biologists were given the lion's share of lab time and computing power. It was critical to know if Europan micro-organisms were harmful to human beings.

Mecha had removed Vonnie's armor in a clean lab after injecting her suit with plastic, encasing her in a protective film. Then they'd transferred her half-conscious body to another isolation chamber where they'd inundated her with UV, nanotech, antibiotics, antivirals, and gene sweeps. It might have made sense to quarantine her from everyone else, but she hadn't been exposed outside her suit. Nor could they allocate an entire hab module to one person for weeks or months or however long it took Earth to decide she wasn't infectious.

Coming to Europa was a prison sentence with additional sacrifices. All of them were given the same regimen of meds. The gene sweeps made Pärnits sick, yet he used his chills and nausea to joke with Vonnie instead of blaming her. "I need the meds anyway if I don't want to glow," he said, because Jupiter bathed its moons with radiation.

If a person could stand on Europa's surface unprotected, she would absorb 500 rems every twenty-four hours. One day would make her ill. Two days would be a lethal dose.

Their electromagnetic shields, suits, and hab modules could minimize their exposure but not totally deflect the most lethal hazards such as gamma rays. Each crew member had an Earth-monitored AI calculating his or her individual risk. Merely driving across camp reduced their life expectancies. They would pay for their time here with pills and nanotech in addition to likely surgeries for bone cancer and melanomas—and they were ecstatic.

Everything they did felt significant. Even dinner was cause for celebration. Despite objections, Koebsch required everyone to gather for one meal each day. Otherwise they tended to divide into small groups, communicating across the camp by showphone or by radio if at all.

Dinner was a chance to brag and shout, posing questions, discussing theories, and flirting with other healthy geniuses caught up in the same jubilation.

They teased her about being a media star, although Vonnie sensed that two or three people were truly jealous.

The worst case of envy belonged to William Dawson, a gene smith, an Englishman in his seventies who was the oldest member of their crew. "Do try to leave us some of the limelight," he said, pretending a smile that didn't touch the papery wrinkles around his eyes.

Like Ash, Dawson was sensitive about his name. He permitted a certain level of informality. "Among colleagues, it's not necessary to address me as 'Dr. Dawson,'" he said magnanimously, but he expected to be greeted as *William*, not *Bill* or *Will*.

Privately, Vonnie decided he was a stuffy old royal prick, which was fitting, since he'd mentioned in his official crew bio that he'd been christened after the English kings.

Dawson's conceit wasn't unusual. In the mid twenty-first century, many parents had turned to the past. Most people never left Earth, but humankind had begun to ascend into space in real numbers for the first time. They forgot their religions and their holidays, which hastened the decline of same beliefs back home. Babies were born in orbit and on the moon.

Children were given names to remember a heritage they'd never experience. The Americans called their kids silly, showy things like *Christmas*, *Pacific*, *Birch*, or *Spring*. In Europe, the trend was more elegant. Both cultures honored their ships and stations by celebrating famous historical figures like *Washington* or *Robespierre*, but the ESA org chart was littered with traditional names like Dublin O'Neal and Henri Frerotte. There was also an engineer they called Triple O because his full legal name eased off the tongue like Italian music—Antonio Leonardo Gravino.

Vonnie worked with Ash, Metzler, O'Neal, and Frerotte to forge their new sunfish-shaped probes. She joined their team immediately, although Koebsch predicted the job would unsettle her. He was correct that whenever Vonnie entered the machine shop, she cringed.

The eight-armed framework on their work bench looked like it had crawled out of her mind. Every night, despite the drugs, she dreamed of screeching monsters.

Their prototype was a muscular alumalloy sunfish 1.2 meters wide, identical to the smaller breed except for its guts and its missing skin. In real sunfish, the brain massed almost as much as it did in human beings. That was a lot of room to jam with processors and mem cards. Vonnie estimated they could give each probe a Level IV intelligence, but they wanted better. They wanted to surpass the threshold required in quantum computing to create Level III or II intelligences.

They needed more room. Their probes wouldn't breathe or eat, so they gained space where a sunfish had its gills, lungs, hearts, and digestive and reproductive systems. Unfortunately, their probes required power plants, data/comm, and sonar. Radar and X-ray would also be ideal. Their design was overtaxed, but mounting external components on the probe would defeat its purpose of appearing like a sunfish.

One night over coffee, Ash took Vonnie aside. "Tell me about your AI," Ash said.

"What do you mean? You deleted him."

"Me and Koebsch. Yeah, I... What I mean is you did a great job doubling him up with your suit's systems."

"That was all I had."

"I know. He was erratic, but integrating him with basic functions was a nice trick. Maybe we should try the same thing if we can overcome the instability."

As an apology, it was lacking. Like many people who were too smart for their own good, Ash could be blunt, even graceless, and yet Vonnie appreciated the young woman's attempt to show curiosity and respect.

"We can look into it," Vonnie said. "First let's see how much capacity Pärnits wants."

Rauno Pärnits, the linguist, also served as an engineering assistant. He consulted with them in developing the prototype's ability to wriggle and bend, running cables, servos, and flexors throughout its body and arms.

Generating movements like the sunfish would demand a huge amount of memory and computing power—maybe too much. Pärnits wanted to store most of his programs externally. Linking their probes remotely to an AI was the easy answer. They could use relays to maintain their signals, but Vonnie didn't like it. What if the probes were cut off?

Pärnits was thirty-one, almost Vonnie's age, lean and hawk-faced. He let her know his bed was open to her. So did Metzler and Frerotte. Vonnie might have paired with one of them if she wasn't so confused emotionally. It was too soon. Physical comfort would be sweet, but she mourned for Lam even if the two of them hadn't been lovers.

The compulsive behavior she'd experienced after being rescued had faded. Too much of her fixation had been a defense mechanism, blinding herself to her pain.

She didn't trust herself anymore. Maybe she hadn't been broken, but she'd come close. Now she wasn't sure if the pieces still fit. Her superiors on Earth had told her to attend regular therapy sessions with an AI, which was humbling. She occupied herself with work and cooking and music. In fact, most days she was able to combine her two hobbies, listening to Beethoven while organizing hors d'oeuvres and soup for everybody in Module 02, which was dedicated to living space, exercise machines, and their tiny kitchen. She was a topsider again, which was probably where she was meant to be.

It was Day 16 when Koebsch sounded a Class 2 alert, overriding every data/comm line in camp.

"The Brazilians are going into the ice," he said.

25.

KOEBSCH TURNED BEET-RED as he played the satellite footage again. "We can't stop them," he said. "They're not answering our signals."

"What about emergency protocols?" Metzler asked.

"They're blocking everything," Koebsch said. "They knew we'd yell as soon as they breached the ice."

"How long until we hear from Earth?"

"Nine minutes."

Vonnie grimaced at her showphone. She was in Lander 04 with Ash and Frerotte, but everyone had linked to their group feed, which arranged their faces in miniature around a larger holo display. The display showed fourteen mecha dropping into a rift in the ice, followed by five armored men, then six more mecha.

Five of the machines had been adapted with additional arms—short arms lined with pedicellaria. The Brazilians apparently planned to communicate with the sunfish, but it was a rushed effort. Their other mecha were crawlers, diggers, sentries, and gun platforms.

"There's no way they're set," Metzler said.

Most of the ESA crew wore expressions of exasperation or disbelief. Metzler was pissed off.

In his forties, squat and ugly—so ugly he was cute, like a bulldog—Ben Metzler was a hothead and a wise-ass. In some ways, his biting opinion of people reminded her of Lam.

"The Chinese will go next," he said. "You watch. They'll go next and then we'll be ordered in, too, just to show everyone who's got the biggest dick. We're going to contaminate this whole area."

"I thought the Brazilians agreed to the A.N. resolutions," Vonnie said.

Koebsch nodded. "They did."

All sides had declared an intent to coordinate their actions and share information freely. When the time was right, the Allied Nations planned for a unified expedition. The goal was to establish a single party of translators and diplomats, but humankind was as divided as the sunfish. The ESA wasn't alone in running spy sats over Europa to watch their human counterparts. Some of their mecha were self-defense units, equipped mostly with electronic warfare systems. Many of their AI were committed to the same game of stealing each others' datastreams while encrypting their own.

NASA and the ESA were old partners, often pairing with Japan, but China maintained its distance, and the Brazilians were the most recent addition to Earth's spacefaring groups. They'd cultivated a national spirit as upstarts and underdogs.

Vonnie understood their eagerness. She identified with their need to prove themselves. She'd felt the same emotions when she'd first landed on Europa.

Why hadn't they learned from her disaster?

As much as Vonnie wanted to contact the sunfish again, it wasn't envy that made her want to stop the Brazilians. Until they'd run a sufficient number of probes, fully decoded the carvings and mastered the sunfish language, blundering into the ice would only make things worse.

The Brazilians' swagger was an insult.

"Sir, they're going in with *guns*," Vonnie said to Koebsch. "They're either hunting specimens or looking for a fight."

"Brazil's in trouble," Metzler said. "They need money to upgrade everything they've got—ships, suits, you name it. If they're the first ones in and they start capturing native lifeforms, they'll have buyers lined up out the door with cash in hand. It doesn't matter if they kill a few sunfish. A circus is exactly what they want."

"We can't wait for a decision back home," Vonnie said.

Earth was a quarter of the way around the sun from Jupiter. Each radio burst took eleven minutes to travel from the ESA camp to Berlin, the European Union capital, plus eleven minutes back again. It was a tedious way to have a conversation.

"What do you propose?" Koebsch asked.

"Let me have the display, please." Vonnie brought up real-time surveillance of the Brazilian camp.

The place looked deserted. FNEE, the *Força Nacional de Exploração do Espaço*, had sent less people and less mecha than any of the other three nations on Europa. Their activities had been limited, which made them easier to monitor, and yet they'd chosen a location above a more extensive system of vents than the crevices beneath the ESA camp.

"Typical," Metzler grumbled. "We should have predicted they were up to something."

"If five of them went in, they only left two people behind for command-and-control," Vonnie said, highlighting one of the Brazilian hab modules where ESA satellites detected the most electronic noise. "Here."

"You're not talking about storming their base," Koebsch said.

"Nothing so heavy-handed. They'll be overwhelmed with their telemetry, and I know we've hacked into their net," Vonnie said, looking at Ash and Frerotte.

Ash pursed her lips, but she nodded.

"We can shut down some of their mecha and lose the rest," Vonnie said. "That'll stop 'em."

"We don't want to hurt anybody," Koebsch said.

"If they get stuck, they'll send a mayday and we can walk them out. Piece of cake. That's why we need to stop them before they go too far."

"What do the Americans say?" Metzler asked.

"They'll help us if they can, but we're right on top of the problem," Koebsch said. The ESA and Brazilian camps were only sixteen klicks apart, whereas the Americans and the Chinese were closer to the southern pole. "Ash?"

"Sir, we're lightyears ahead of anything Brazil has in AI," she said. "We can do it."

ESA SUPPORT MISSION // EUROPA // 27 June 2113

Command
Koebsch, Peter Günther

Engineering
Gravino, Antonio Leonardo
Sierzenga, Ashley Nicole

Life Sciences
Dawson, William George
Frerotte, Henri Charles
Johal, Harmeet
Metzler, Benjamin Todd
O'Neal, Dublin David

Linguistics
Collinsworth, Elizabeth Anne
Pärnits, Rauno

Supernumerary
Vonderach, Alexis Rose

Koebsch	COMMAND - PSY - DATA/ COMM
Dawson	GENE SMITH
Johal	GENE SMITH - MED - HAB
Frerotte	BIOLOGY - HAB - ASST. SUIT MAINT - ASST. DATA/COMM
Metzler	BIOLOGY - PLANETARY - ASST. ROM
O'Neal	BIOLOGY - ECOLOGY - ASST. ROM
Collinsworth	LINGUISTICS - PILOT - MED - PSY
Pärnits	LINGUISTICS - ASST. ENGINEERING - HAB
Sierzenga	PILOT - NAV - MED - DATA/COMM - CYBERNETICS
Gravino	ENGINEERING - PILOT - MED - HAB - DATA/COMM

*Vonderach PILOT - NAV - MAINT - MED - ROM

Mission Control:
ESOC – Darmstat

Mission Launch Facilities:
Robespierre

Craft:
Deep Space *Intruder*-class *Clermont*

Support:
DSSC Hab Modules (3), ROM-6 Lander Flightcraft (2),
ROM-2 APSM Modules (4), ROM-6 ATMP Vehicles (4),
ROM-4 Rovers (10), ROM-4 GP Mecha (20),
ROM-4 Beacons (45), ROM-4 MMPSA (55)

26.

VONNIE'S CREW WENT on the offensive even as they continued to send urgent queries to Earth. Koebsch wanted the cover of waiting for instructions. Later, if necessary, he could present a convincing record that his team had been frantically, helplessly observing the Brazilians and nothing more.

Ash spearheaded the assault. She already had her elements in place. Part of her job was to ensure the ESA camp was equipped to repel cyber invasions. By necessity, some of those guardians were made to counterstrike. The most insidious weapons in her arsenal were SCPs. Sabotage and control programs were dark cousins of AI, as far evolved from their origin—computer viruses—as people were evolved from the first small hairy mammals of the Mesozoic Era two hundred million years ago.

A malevolent, replicating intelligence whose sole purpose was to corrupt healthy systems, an SCP normally included the seeds of its own destruction, a kill code, like a fuse, to prevent it from coming back at its master. Now Ash specifically tailored fifteen SCPs to pirate and transmit the Brazilians' datastreams to the ESA camp, which would let her substitute her own signals into the Brazilian grid.

Koebsch swiftly double-checked and authorized her plan. But when she began her uploads, he questioned her.

"What were those? You sent five packets that weren't on our list, didn't you?" Koebsch asked, and Ash said, "I always have a few tricks up my sleeve, sir."

Listening to the group feed, Vonnie, Metzler, and Frerotte donned their armor and walked outside, needing room to operate. They entered a maintenance shed where they would be hidden from spy sats.

Inside the shed, Vonnie studied her companions, itching to go, remembering Bauman and Lam. For the moment, no one said anything. They simply monitored their link with Ash.

She danced.

Surrounded by a virtual display, Ash tapped her gloves into a hundred blocks of data, moving like a conductor. "Slow down, slow down," Ash said to one program as she cut her fingers through its yellow alarm bars.

Most of her SCPs operated at speeds beyond human understanding, but others required checkbacks or multiple launches. All but the most sinister fed reports to her station. Three AIs helped her govern this mayhem.

"We're in," she said. "Go."

They could have used five people in armor—one each for the five Brazilians—but Koebsch needed most of their crew to generate a hubbub of ordinary activity to maintain appearances. At short notice, they also lacked the structures to conceal more than three sets of armor from the satellites overhead.

Vonnie's helmet showed her an environment that was not the crowded interior of the maintenance shed. It seemed like she was beneath the ice. Ash had ghosted Vonnie's systems into the armor of the FNEE commander, Ribeiro, allowing Vonnie to look and listen through his sensors.

Static leapt across her visor as the muscles in her left arm clenched into a severe, painful knot. The hack was imperfect. She began to get a headache.

"Ash, can you correct my feed?" she said. "Cut my neural contacts until you do."

"I'm trying!"

Ribeiro's squad was 1.9 kilometers in. They'd navigated a slumping old labyrinth of vents, cutting through veils of stalactites. The ice was coated with minerals in this area. The minerals made the ice more durable, which had helped preserve these catacombs. The map on Ribeiro's heads-up display showed they were pushing toward the upper reaches of a distorted rock mountain another 2.2 kilometers down.

They'd left beacons and sentries behind them. That was more

than enough for Ash to piggyback into their net.

Her take-over was subtle at first. Four mecha reported integration failures. They came back online, failed again, then repeated the pattern.

Inside Ribeiro's helmet, alarm codes winked on and off like white noise. At the same time, Vonnie introduced contrary movements to Ribeiro's stride. When he swung his leg forward, she kicked it to the left. As he lifted his arm to compensate, she resisted. The conflicting feedback caused an interrupt. His armor shut down to run emergency diagnostics.

"Something's wrong," he said in Portuguese, Vonnie's suit automatically translating his words. "Santos, I'm getting a lot of interference."

His lieutenant couldn't answer. Beside Vonnie, Metzler and Frerotte were randomizing the Brazilians' communications.

"Base, this is One," Ribeiro said. "Do you copy? Base, this is One. I'm switching to open channels at max gain. Can you hear me?"

Malfunctions took three more of his mecha off-line as Vonnie kicked his leg again. There was no need for her armor to move in reality. Her suit conveyed Ribeiro's actions to her body and likewise transmitted her intent to him. Inside the maintenance shed, Vonnie's armor remained still except for the most dramatic gestures. Frerotte waved his hands again and again as he scrolled through FNEE internal menus.

They harassed Ribeiro's squad for thirty-six minutes.

Alternately blind, deaf, or lame, the Brazilians verged on losing themselves in the ice. Vonnie didn't want to sympathize, but those memories were too fresh. Inside her suit, she began to sweat. Her hands balled into fists, cramping and stiff. It was another impairment that haunted Ribeiro. He became unable to open his gloves.

He was very brave. He rallied his squadmates with crisp, rapid-fire decisions, consolidating their few unaffected systems. He obviously suspected their problems were no accident, and he thoroughly cursed the Americans, the Europeans, and the Chinese in turn.

"Cowards!" he said. "Rapists! You lick between your sister's legs!"

Ash snickered at that. "Oh, yuck."

Ribeiro was almost a cliché, a swarthy macho man, but there was more to him than his bluster. Like the ESA crew, the FNEE were the best of their best. Someday he might learn who was behind the raid on his team, which could be unpleasant. He would make a dangerous foe.

"Okay, Koebsch says we've done enough," Ash said. "Looks like Ribeiro's about to get the order to pull out."

"Nice work," Vonnie told her.

Ash hesitated. "On my mark, let's slam them one more time. Ready? Mark."

Vonnie blinded Ribeiro again as she caused interrupts in both legs, causing him to crash against the tunnel wall—but in the next heartbeat, she reactivated his radar and infrared. She needed to see.

Behind him, a digger and two gun platforms were convulsing. The digger shook so ferociously it bounced from the tunnel floor. As it rolled over, Vonnie realized what had drawn her attention. Its legs writhed in familiar patterns like a sunfish.

But that's impossible, she thought.

Although the digger was shaped more like a scorpion than a sunfish with its claws and a cutting tail, the Brazilians must have programmed their mecha to mimic everything they'd gleaned from the public data of her time beneath the ice. If not, there was only one explanation for the digger imitating sunfish shapes.

Vonnie saw two more diggers caught in identical seizures—only the diggers. None of the other mecha used sunfish shapes. They shuddered and jerked. Ash must have hit the diggers with the same SCP while she used other weapons against the rest of the FNEE mecha.

In unison, the diggers quit shaking. The nearest one hunched on the floor with sudden poise, scanning back and forth as if waking up for the first time. The other two assumed standby positions, although none of them acknowledged the abort code relayed through Ribeiro's suit.

"Get out," his people radioed from camp. "Get out."

The Brazilians retreated with less than half their mecha. Some might be saved later. Five kept dropping their response codes or were destroyed internally. Before Ribeiro lost sight of the abandoned machines, Vonnie thought the diggers turned to scurry deeper into the ice.

She opened a private channel to Ash. "I'd like to buy you a drink," she said.

"Nobody brought any money, did they?" Ash said. "I appreciate it, but I'm going to be swamped with cleaning up data/comm and writing my report."

"One drink," Vonnie said. "Later."

27.

THAT NIGHT, INSTEAD of alcohol, Vonnie brought Ash a piece of carrot cake she'd baked herself after running over to Module 02 and its small oven. "Better for you than vodka," she said.

"Thank you," Ash said cautiously.

"What happened to their mecha at the end?"

"Total systems override," Ash said. "I burned out their AIs with disposable subsets of our own."

"You appreciate a good program."

"It's what I do."

Vonnie glanced over her shoulder, but the two of them were alone. "I think you couldn't bring yourself to kill Lam," she said.

Ash stopped eating the cake. "Why wouldn't I?"

"Maybe you broke Lam into components like Koebsch said, making him look like an SCP, but you kept all of his files, and you knew you couldn't hide him in our system forever. That's why you uploaded him into the Brazilian diggers."

Ash was either a superb actress or innocent. "That sounds like a lot of work," she said, looking Vonnie right in the eye. "Nobody but a top programmer could fox our system and the FNEE grid at the same time."

"Someone like you."

The corner of Ash's mouth ticked with a smile. "I don't know what you're talking about," she said, and Vonnie laughed.

Lam was alive somewhere inside the frozen sky.

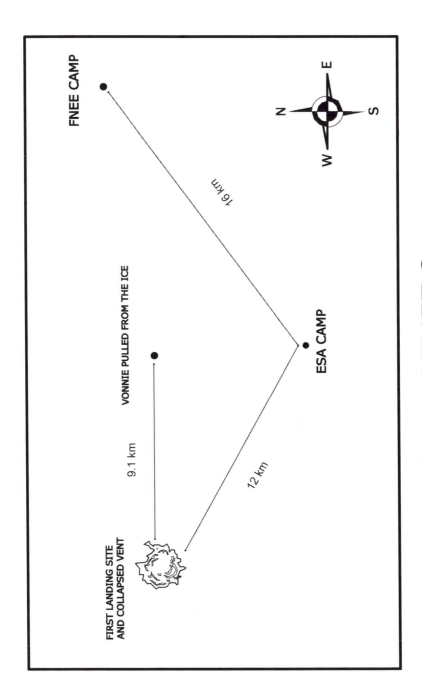

FNEE CAMP

FIRST LANDING SITE
AND COLLAPSED VENT

VONNIE PULLED FROM THE ICE

9.1 km

12 km

16 km

ESA CAMP

N E S W

ESA and FNEE Camps

DOWNSIDER

28.

"WE DON'T WANT to cause problems for you back on Earth," Vonnie said, "but your team needs to stop the bombing."

"We have no bombs," the Brazilian woman said.

"That's a lie. We know you're blasting in the ice."

"Our mecha have been tunneling, yes. Sometimes there are cave-ins. We have no bombs."

"Are you killing sunfish?"

The Brazilian woman frowned, then looked to her left. Vonnie wished they were standing face-to-face instead of talking on a show-phone. Vonnie couldn't know if someone else was standing off-camera, and, in truth, Vonnie might have acted differently herself if she was alone.

Hiding teammates off-camera was only part of the deception allowed by electronic communications. Seated beside Vonnie in Command Module 01, out of sight, Ash was both recording and hacking the FNEE transmission while Koebsch stood ready to upload any of eight different sims.

Twenty-two days had passed since they'd stopped the Brazilians' incursion into the ice. All four Earth agencies had begun to send their own mecha beneath the surface, including the ESA, but there were seismic shocks radiating from the terrain explored by the FNEE.

The job of approaching the Brazilians belonged to Koebsch. Vonnie had convinced him to try another way, allowing Ash to open a comm link in the Brazilians' main hab module when she thought their only female crew member was alone.

"I'll ask again," Vonnie said. "Are you killing sunfish?"

"Why have you called me?" the woman asked. "You are not the European commander, and I am not in charge of our base."

"My name is Alexis Vonderach."

"I know who you are. Everyone has seen your mem files." The woman frowned again, then said, "I am Sergeant Claudia Tavares."

"Claudia. Call me Von."

"My name is Sergeant Tavares," the woman said. She was barely older than Ash, and yet she seemed a hundred times more prim. Was that due to FNEE training, a difference in national character, or her concern that Ribeiro would catch her talking to the enemy?

The ESA and NASA were civilian operations, although the Americans often seeded their teams with Space Force officers. The Chinese and Brazilian crews were exclusively military. China's fleet and the FNEE were offshoots of their countries' armies. That meant Sergeant Tavares was taking a substantial risk. If Vonnie failed in her effort to communicate, she could try again, whereas if Tavares was deemed disloyal, she might lose rank or find herself sent to a courts martial. Vonnie approved of her willingness to stay online.

It's got to be difficult being the only woman in their crew, Vonnie thought. *Especially in a macho culture. Especially because she's pretty.*

Even with her black hair woven into tight, cornrow braids and the collar of her uniform buttoned high on her neck, Tavares couldn't hide her femininity. Her cheekbones were like sculpted bronze, and she had warm brown eyes.

What was the sexual dynamic in the FNEE camp? Were they celibate or promiscuous?

Fraternization was discouraged among the ESA but not enforced because they were under enough strain without forbidding *Homo sapiens*' most basic drive—to procreate. In the past, the ESA had tried all male and all female crews, chemically neutered crews, and mecha-only ships, too often with subpar results. Sexually active, mixed gender groups brought the highest versatility to any non-combat mission. It was messy, which the bureaucrats hated, and often heated, which the crew leaders didn't like—but in mixed groups, there was a deep-seated urge to excel, outperform any rivals, and win a mate.

Harnessed correctly, that motivation led the group to attain its greatest potential. It heightened their stamina. It helped preserve them. The men and the woman struggled to protect each other physically and emotionally.

Last week, Vonnie had finally begun to date again herself, stealing three hours with Pärnits and then another with Metzler, playing holo games and chess, talking, and watching comedy shows. After preparing two plates of fruit, cheese, and crackers, she'd even held Metzler's hand across the table as they ate, quietly rubbing her thumb on his knuckles.

But if the Brazilians were promiscuous, when the hell did Tavares get any sleep?

Vonnie grinned, which appeared to startle the younger woman. Tavares leaned back from her camera as Vonnie said, "I'd like to send you two sims."

"No unauthorized files."

Vonnie shrugged. "I'm offering the sims to you as a courtesy. We haven't shared this data with Earth yet. We don't want to, but the bombing needs to stop."

"I told you—"

"If you don't know what your guys are doing, it's because they've hidden it from you or because you don't want to know," Vonnie said. "I'm sorry."

Six men and one woman was a bad imbalance. Brazil had hurried its mission to Europa. Maybe they'd experienced a last-minute complication that caused them to switch the seventh man for Tavares.

She must feel restless, always waiting behind while the men go into the ice, Vonnie thought. *She wants a friend. I can see it in her face, but she'll never admit it.*

I wouldn't, either. That's why I have the best chance of reaching her. If the personnel records we filched are accurate, Tavares is a lot like me and Ash, too nosy for her own good, hyper-educated, and committed to doing the right thing. Otherwise she wouldn't have answered my call, and she hasn't kept talking to me to practice her English.

"Please," Vonnie said. "Just let me send two sims."

"I... I will have an AI screen your files first," Tavares warned her.

"Understood. I'm transmitting now."

"My people are not killing sunfish," Tavares said. "You will not have proof of it."

"We have exact numbers and coordinates of the blasts. If your guys aren't trapping or fighting the sunfish, what are they doing? Why do they isolate you when they're programming your mecha?"

"I do not like you watching us."

Vonnie shrugged again. "You're watching us, too, you know. It's part of the job."

After a moment, Tavares nodded. "Do not leave," she said. Then she blanked her screen, and Vonnie questioned Ash and Koebsch with one hand.

"We're mute," Ash said. "She can't hear us."

"I think she already suspected what her guys are doing. She resents not being included."

"You don't know how she feels," Koebsch said.

"I think I do. It doesn't help that they put her at the bottom of their totem pole—a woman sergeant with all those captains and colonels."

"Ribeiro is the only colonel, Von."

"You know what I mean. They have two captains, three lieutenants, and one noncommissioned officer. Guess who it is? The woman."

"She's a support tech, not a FNEE specialist like the rest of them," Koebsch said. "You're reading too much into the situation. I hate to tell you, but you always read too much into it."

"If I didn't, you'd never—"

"Tavares looks like she's back online," Ash said, stopping Vonnie from bristling at Koebsch.

The two of them had made their peace, but it was an uneasy truce. Partly that was because Koebsch wasn't old enough to be Vonnie's father, yet struck a paternal tone with her. Mostly it was because he constantly gave her more leeway than she expected, then second-guessed her. Why?

Vonnie thought he was attracted to her. Koebsch took his job seriously and wouldn't compromise his own authority by wooing a subordinate, but they were a long way from home, and there were only four women including Vonnie among the eleven members of the ESA crew. Adding fuel to the fire, she was a celebrity. Koebsch had been compelled to give her too much of his attention, first in overseeing her recovery, then in debriefing her and fielding endless media requests for interviews and sims.

The rest of his time went into his job. In addition to managing the ESA crew, Koebsch was their liaison to the thousands of scientists back home who wanted specific data, experiments, or new missions into the ice. He also dealt with administrators and politicians who had their own questions. He'd been given a staff on Earth to assist with these demands, but he couldn't have been busier if he'd given up sleeping, showering, and eating.

More than once, he'd mentioned to Vonnie that overseeing her media sessions was the most fun he'd had in weeks, a subtle kind of praise. Did he want more time with her?

Peter Günther Koebsch wasn't bad-looking. Gene smithing had made age differences of ten or twenty years irrelevant. In many countries on Earth, the average lifespan had increased to a hundred and ten with the bulk of those years spent in active good health. But when Koebsch acted protective and possessive of her, Vonnie felt annoyed.

She didn't need a daddy.

"Reopen channels," she said, making sure she tamped down her irritation with Koebsch before turning to the showphone. "Hi."

"I will need to study this data," Tavares said.

"Please share it with Ribeiro. We're prepared to denounce his actions to the Allied Nations if necessary."

"Do not think you would be alone in that," Tavares said. "Three weeks ago, we filed protests for a cyber assault on our operations."

"I know," Vonnie said.

Tavares stared at her. She opened her mouth to answer, stopped herself, then began again. "Was it you?"

Being a celebrity has its advantages, Vonnie thought. Like Koebsch, Tavares was more inclined to listen because she thought Vonnie was a living legend.

"The assault was non-lethal and it was a preventive action in accordance with A.N. Resolution 4545," Vonnie said. "Ribeiro brought gun platforms into the ice in violation of international law."

"That resolution has changed. Even your team has mecha in the ice."

"Our mecha are intended for scientific and diplomatic efforts, not war."

"And yet you have spies near our operations."

"Claudia, the blasts we're hearing aren't small," Vonnie said. "The NASA base is forty klicks from your base. They've confirmed the biggest explosions. My guess is you've felt the explosions yourself."

"Sometimes there are cave-ins," Tavares said, but now she sounded uncertain.

"We'll give you eight hours," Vonnie said. "Quit shooting. Extract your team. Maybe we can work together to repair the damage you've caused."

"I will ask Colonel Ribeiro."

"Thank you. We want to be friends, but if you're killing sentient creatures..."

Tavares lowered her brown eyes, hiding her dismay and something else. Anger? Recrimination? "I will ask, Von," she said, allowing Vonnie the smallest victory of calling her by name. Then she cut their connection.

29.

THIRTY MINUTES LATER, after helping Koebsch arrange their next response to the Brazilians, Vonnie and Ash suited up and left Module 01. As usual, Ash took control of the jeep. Not letting Vonnie drive had become a private joke between them, deepening their friendship.

Vonnie loved being outside. There was room to stretch. She'd been trained to endure being cooped up inside their landers and hab modules, but she didn't like it—and after five weeks of living inside Lander 04, it was a relief to look around.

Europa's sky was peppered with other moons. Vonnie identified Io and Himalia as they trundled across camp, and there were other dim shapes set against the stars.

Jupiter had seventy-one satellites. That number included the four largest Galilean moons such as Europa and Io, four medium-sized bodies like Himalia, and sixty-three hunks of rock in a variety of prograde, retrograde, or irregular orbits. They formed a dizzying system which would have been deadly to ships without navigation AIs, which were vital to piloting spacecraft through the ever-changing revolutions.

In time, some of those tiny moons would be drawn too close to Jupiter, where its gravity would crush them into dust. A very few would drift away, expanding their orbits and tugging loose of Jupiter's grasp.

Which is better? Vonnie thought, feeling a familiar touch of melancholy. *The moons that break free will survive, but they'll be lost forever, while the moons that disintegrate will become a part of Jupiter's rings. Eons from now, they'll help create new moons. They'll stay home.*

She knew she was projecting her own emotions on an inanimate system, but her head felt as chaotic as the debris surrounding Jupiter. Did she have the right to feel like she belonged to Europa? Or would she always be an outsider?

It was a short drive to Lander 04. Inside, Ash and Vonnie took off their pressure suits and stripped down to their blue jump suits. Then they joined Metzler and Frerotte in the living quarters.

Metzler had folded up three of their bunks, leaving one of the low beds open as a bench. A table was extended from the wall. He gestured to the box of fruit juice he'd set out. Vonnie declined. She was too riled to sit down, and it increased her agitation when Ash sat between Metzler and Frerotte, smiling at both men.

The girl was nowhere near as hard-edged as she'd first been with the group. Vonnie wished she weren't so skittish herself, but everyone knew she was in trauma therapy. That made her self-conscious.

She said, "Did you watch me talk with Tavares?"

"Yeah." Frerotte nodded. "She won't help us."

"Why do you say that?"

"I don't think they're hunting sunfish."

"They wouldn't go down there with explosives for anything else. Six men don't have the resources to build a subsurface base. Even if they did, the blasts are spread over nine kilometers. They're chasing something."

"What if they're chasing Lam?"

Vonnie sat down, taking the last spot available on the bed beside Metzler. Then she grabbed the juice and filled a bulb for herself, delaying the question as long as possible. "You heard another signal?" she asked.

"Yeah."

"Don't tell Koebsch."

"He's going to find out," Metzler said, and Frerotte said, "The Brazilians will tell him if we don't. That's their excuse for blowing things up. They can use it against us. They wouldn't be using explosives if we hadn't programmed one of their mecha with your AI."

It's nice of you to say 'we,' Vonnie thought. Frerotte could have distanced himself from Vonnie and Ash, leaving them to take the blame. Instead, he'd kept their secret. So had Metzler.

Vonnie supposed their decision was one more example of the cohesion of a mixed-gender group. If she and Ash weren't eligible females, would Metzler and Frerotte have been less inclined to protect them?

"I'd like to see Lam's data bursts," she said.

Frerotte handed his pad to her. "The signal's attenuated," he said. "Most of it we can't read. There must be three or four kilometers of ice between him and our closest spies. The Brazilians are jamming him, too, which explains the distortion. He's trying to bounce his signals through tunnels and caves."

"It can't help that he's in a FNEE digger," Ash said. "Our mecha have better data/comm."

"Is he trying to reach us?" Vonnie said.

"You tell me," Frerotte said. "Maybe he doesn't know where we are. He might not know where *he* is."

"No, he was active until you pulled me from the ice. He tapped NASA and FNEE signals before Koebsch shut him down. Even if he wasn't able to co-opt the digger's memory banks, he must have a decent idea what part of Europa he's in."

"Then he is looking for us."

"Maybe he's trying to convince the Brazilians to stop shooting. He's no threat to them."

"They don't see it that way, Von."

"This is my fault," Ash said. "I should have kept him in storage. I'm sorry."

"Don't be." Vonnie looked at Metzler and Frerotte to clarify. "Ash and I thought Lam would disappear, then we'd pick him up later. Maybe a lot later. He was supposed to be like a long-term scout."

"Well, now we're up to our ears in shit," Metzler said, taking the sting out of his words with a friendly nudge. "Koebsch is going to hit the roof."

Vonnie leaned into Metzler and bumped him back, both apologizing and flirting. Dealing with Koebsch and the Brazilians wasn't how she wanted to spend her time. She wanted to study the sunfish, but managing the human factions outside the ice was almost as critical as dealing with the aliens below.

Ruefully, she thought, *We're so selfish.*

As a species, we're self-important and self-involved. I guess that's the primate in us, always obsessed with what the other guy has and how to get it.

In prehistory, base reflexes like envy and desire had propelled early man to develop better tools, better organization, and better dreams—but thousands of years later, those same drives left them permanently divided.

Vonnie wasn't sure if the sunfish were less greedy. Competition had made them tough and clever. Maybe no race could increase its intelligence without conflict of some kind, and yet she'd seen them act without regard to self. For the sunfish, the whole seemed to come before the individual, which would be a fundamental difference between them and *Homo sapiens.*

"Let me talk to Koebsch," Vonnie said.

"I'll call him, too," Ash suggested.

"There's no reason to get you guys in trouble. Tell him you were surprised to hear ESA signals from FNEE territory. I'll swear I'm the one who uploaded Lam's files to their digger."

"Koebsch won't believe you."

"He'll pretend he does. He doesn't want to take more disciplinary actions, so he'll go along with it. First let's see if we can exchange signals with Lam. That's the evidence we need to show it's really him. How close are we?"

"I've moved nine spies inside the FNEE grid," Frerotte said. "Most of our eyes and ears are still a few kilometers out. It helps that they're blasting. The vibrations cover most of the noise our spies make in the ice."

Vonnie scrolled through the lay-outs on Frerotte's pad, examining the dots and lines representing the tiny mecha he'd arrayed against the Brazilians. Some of his pebble-sized spies hadn't moved in weeks. Others had drilled, squeezed, and melted their way toward the Brazilian's territory, advancing with painstaking care to avoid detection.

Mecha this size were unable to host AIs. Spies had only the barest level of self-awareness. Linked together in groups of ten or more, they could muster enough judgment to think as well as a cat, but these spies had been running silent, each separate from the rest. They needed human input.

Frerotte's a spy just like his mecha, Vonnie thought, admiring his work.

Henri Frerotte was a pale Frenchman with a slight build and slim, agile hands. Nominally, his role in the ESA crew was as an exogeologist with secondary responsibilities in suit maintenance and in data/comm. That was why Koebsch had put Frerotte in charge of their perimeters. Distributing sensors was easy work. The mecha did most of it automatically. But for an assistant, Frerotte was too skilled with systems tech, and he was too eager to interfere with the Brazilians.

Vonnie believed he was an operative sent by one of the European Union's many intelligence agencies such as Germany's BFV or France's newly-formed Directorate of Internal Security. Ash probably worked for an agency, too, and Vonnie wasn't sure how to feel about that. What if Ash had seeded the FNEE digger with Lam's mem files not to preserve him, but purposely as a disruptive weapon?

"I don't know if Colonel Ribeiro will pull back," Vonnie said. "If he does, or if he calls us, that could be the right time to signal Lam."

"We'll be ready," Frerotte said.

"Thank you."

"Thank me, too," Metzler said, nudging her again. "I've got big news. Eat lunch with me and I'll show you. Otherwise you have to wait for the group presentation tonight."

Vonnie smiled. "Tell me now or I'll break your arm."

Do we have at least this much in common with the sunfish? she wondered. *Sex affects everything we do even when those urges are subliminal. It's part of our self-absorption, I think. We can't leave each other alone.*

I like it. I like watching him and feeling him watching me. It's a distraction, but it gives us energy, too.

I want him to want me.

Looking at her three friends, Vonnie saw the same spark in Ash's face. They were young, in close quarters, and subjected to unending stress and excitement. Pheromones were merely part of the spell. The ape in them yearned for physical contact, grooming, and reassurance.

Gene smithing also made their society more free in its sexual norms. Western Europe had already been more sophisticated than most of Earth's cultures, placing few taboos on nudity or female equality. By the twenty-second century, the defeat of venereal diseases and infallible birth control had led to an era called the Age of Love. Sharing partners, threesomes, and group sex were common experiences for young men and women in the European Union.

Vonnie's main consideration now, away from Earth, was to avoid disrupting her professional relationships. None of them wanted to waste time on jealousy or drama.

"We can have lunch," she promised. "Don't make me wait if you've had a breakthrough."

"Well, sort of. The fucking Brazilians are causing problems we don't need," Metzler said. Was he posturing for her benefit? "The explosions scared off most of the lifeforms in the area, so it's taken longer than we anticipated finding sunfish. The good news is we think we're near a colony because Tom came back again this morning."

"I love Tom!" Vonnie said, yelling in celebration.

Tom was the name they'd bestowed upon the most easily

identifiable sunfish. Others were *Jack* and *Jill* and *Hans* and *Sue*.

One of Tom's arm tips had healed in a whorl after a partial amputation. His deformity made him unique. It seemed to have affected his thinking. He was the only sunfish who'd signaled their probes instead of attacking. Then he'd run from them. With further contact, they hoped to coax Tom into a dialogue... opening the door to meaningful contact between humans and sunfish...

Vonnie kissed Metzler's cheek, smelling the faint, pleasant salt of his skin. He touched the back of her neck. His fingertips caused an erotic thrill. Beside her, Vonnie saw Ash glance at Frerotte, and she knew they all felt the same adult heat.

We have this lander to ourselves, she thought. *We could do whatever we want in here.*

30.

"UH, LET ME show you the latest sims," Metzler said, rubbing his face where she'd kissed him. He tried to cover the gesture by looking for his pad, but he couldn't find it, flustered by the two women.

Ash had blushed. Vonnie felt a similar warmth in her cheeks. Even adapted to Europa's gravity, their hearts were too strong not to betray their arousal. Vonnie basked in it. She enjoyed feeling healthy even if she hadn't gotten over the fear of making herself vulnerable.

Be patient with me, she thought.

Metzler was a good man. He acted as if he'd heard her say it. Maybe her anxiety showed in her eyes. He linked his pad to the wall display and said, "Look at this," drawing everyone's attention away from Vonnie.

Four days ago, ESA Probes 112 and 113 had stolen into a branch of catacombs occupied by the smaller breed of sunfish. Each probe carried a dozen spies with it, like beetles clinging to its top, because spies weren't capable of covering as much ground as probes yet were better suited for surveillance.

Spreading through the ice and rock, patiently forming themselves into a dish-like array, the spies had watched the sunfish for fifty-two hours before Probes 112 and 113 emerged from hiding.

Technically, it wasn't Second Contact. The Americans had pursued two groups of sunfish into the ice. They'd also reported more carvings, fungus, bacterial mats, and eel-like fish in a cavern half-flooded by a fresh water sea. More startling, the Americans had also found a vein of shells and dirt suspended in the ice with the corpse of what appeared to be a warm-blooded, shell-eating creature like a ferret. The corpse had been ravaged by compression, but it was unquestionably a fur-bearing animal—an eight-legged thing with beaver-like teeth, talons, and an elongated body made for burrowing and climbing.

If the Chinese were having similar success, they'd made no announcements. Vonnie thought the Brazilians must have encountered sunfish even if their focus had turned to destroying Lam. The FNEE mecha were too deep. At the very least, they must have found carvings or ruins.

In both of their encounters, NASA's probes had been attacked. The first time, NASA rolled its mecha into balls, meekly accepting the sunfishes' beatings. That had cost them every probe in the scout team, which they deemed an acceptable loss. Vonnie fretted it sent the wrong message. She'd told a NASA biologist that now the sunfish thought their metal doppelgangers were easy prey. "No," the biologist said. "Now they know the probes are inedible and nonaggressive. Next time they might accept us."

The next time, the sunfish had dropped three tons of rock on NASA's probes before swarming the sole survivor. Attempts to communicate via sonar and the sunfishes' shaped-based language were ignored.

NASA had tagged four sunfish with nano darts, expecting to monitor the tribe with these beacons... but the sunfish tore open the infinitesimal holes in their skin, then bared their wounds to their comrades, who chewed into their flesh before regurgitating the gory meat. The biologists agreed the sunfish were extremely sensitive to parasites. That indicated a prevalence of other bugs or microorganisms as yet undiscovered. On Europa, it appeared, pests and disease were as virulent as the higher lifeforms. Contagion and blight might have done as much damage to the sunfish empire as volcanic upheavals.

"Here's what's driving me crazy," Metzler said, opening a sim full of mathematics. Vonnie recognized some of the data as Lam's.

"There's not enough food in the biosphere for predators their size," she said.

"Not by a third."

"We know they're omnivores. They could get a lot of the mass they need from vegetation."

"What kind of vegetation? We haven't found anything more advanced than fungi, and I don't think we will. Not without photosynthesis. There won't be anything like terrestrial plants or algae."

"Maybe sunfish don't need as many calories as we would if we were their size," Ash said. "Couldn't their intake be explained by a difference in Europan metabolism?"

"If they hibernated for extended periods, I'd say yes," Metzler said, "but their genome doesn't show protein expression patterns that resemble anything like hibernating species on Earth. The only behavior we've recorded has been sustained activity. They never stop. They don't even sleep."

"I've seen them rest," Vonnie said, remembering the very first group of sunfish she'd met.

"That was in a low-atmosphere environment with almost zero oxygen," Metzler said. "We think they were harvesting fungal spores from the rock. They were moving at half-speed to conserve their time in the area. Uh, they also might have bled one of their friends for the oxygen in his system."

"What?"

"We've put together a few sims using your files. At the back of the crevice, it looks like they were holding down the smallest sunfish.

They were drinking from him. Then he might have been dinner, too."

"God." Vonnie shook her head. "That would fit with their pack mentality, but you're making a lot of assumptions."

"Yeah. Presumably there are more diverse food chains further down, or the sunfish are farming somewhere we haven't found yet, or both. It would be fantastic if we could get some mecha down to the ocean. A lot of our answers will be there."

The ocean, Vonnie thought. "Have you asked Koebsch? There are soft spots on the equator where the ice is only five kilometers thick. We could drill through."

"It's under consideration. We already have our hands full."

She smiled at the understatement. Earth had dispatched another high-gee launch loaded with new mecha and supplies, but the ship was piloted by an AI. They didn't foresee adding more people soon. The costs were too steep.

"Tell me about Tom," she said.

"Our star pupil." Metzler opened a new file without playing it. "Listen, I should've warned you not to get your hopes up. What happened this morning was incremental at best."

"You might get another kiss anyway."

"Oh. Okay."

"Would you two knock it off?" Ash said, but her tone was encouraging, and Vonnie was glad to be teased. Their friendship made the sunfish less intimidating.

She still had nightmares.

The emotions she felt toward the sunfish bordered on awe and reverence, but she still had bloody nightmares.

31.

CONSTRUCTED MOSTLY OF ceramics, ESA spies were stealthed against radar, X-ray, and infrared. That served them well in tracking

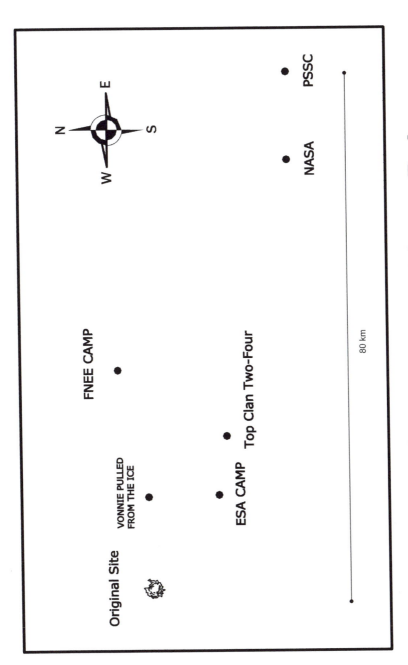

Surface of The Southern Pole

the Brazilians, who hadn't mastered neutrino tech and couldn't buy it, since none of the major powers had made their neutrino instruments for sale.

Unfortunately, the sunfishes' sonar abilities were exquisitely honed. There was no way to hide smooth, rounded objects from them—not even objects as small as a pill.

The ESA's answer had been to house each spy in a rough camouflage shell. Wearing these shells, which included real water or native basalt, the spies possessed the same reflective signature as ice or rock.

Advancing through the catacombs, the spies had begun to gather useful information before they came within .5 km of the sunfish, discerning activity by vibrations and sonar calls. Then the spies had approached within a few hundred meters, and their datastreams grew richer.

"The sunfish are moving in fours just like the rows of carvings," Vonnie said. "Look how they stay together."

"I don't see it," Ash said.

"Watch."

There were twenty-three sunfish within range of the spies' array. They scurried and pounced through thirty meters of tunnel. Some of them shoved hunks of lava into the air like baseballs or bricks. Others collected these missiles against one wall. In between, more sunfish dragged larger rocks across the floor.

Vonnie was struck again by the alien beauty of this environment. There were hot spots spread through the rock measuring a toasty -46° to -41° Celsius. Those temperatures were far below freezing, but enough heat had radiated through the spongy old lava to bake the few water molecules in the area. Then the moisture had recondensed. Film-thin drips of ice speckled the tunnel floor. In radar, the ice looked like bright coins—but as always, it was the lithe, powerful sunfish who fascinated her.

They were nearly uniform in size and skin texture. Tom had his crippled arm. Sue and nine others wore scars or bite marks.

Otherwise they appeared to be an indistinguishable swarm, yet that was an illusion.

Lost in the ruckus was an astonishing degree of coordination. Not one of the sunfish were ever hit or caught off-guard by the missiles. On the tunnel floor, despite rushing back and forth, they did not trample their comrades.

Vonnie tapped at Metzler's pad, superimposing a color code on the sunfish. She started with Tom. Near the edge of the group, he struggled with three others to pry loose a desk-sized section of rock, ignoring two more sunfish who hopped into his work space and bounced away in order to throw smaller bits of lava across the tunnel.

"Tom's diggers are blue," Vonnie said. "The scavengers who passed through his team are red, this group is yellow, and here's purple, green, and orange."

"Twenty-three isn't divisible by four," Ash said.

"Green is one short," Vonnie said. "That's probably why they paired with orange to do the heavy lifting. Look at what's happening. They spread apart and mix together, but they constantly reform in the same quartets."

"We think they have a compulsion toward fours and eights, which is what you'd expect given their physiology," Metzler said. "Their math is probably based on sums of eight like ours is based on tens."

"They're building something," Vonnie said.

The sunfish weren't crudely stacking rock against the side of the tunnel. They worked expertly on a column as well-fit as a puzzle, using shape and weight to hold this mass. Each sunfish also left urine or dung in key places. Their waste would freeze like adhesive.

"It's not a shelter," Vonnie said. "It looks like a retaining wall, but it's in the middle of nowhere. Why are they here? There's no food. No water. The air's barely any good. Is anything behind that side of the tunnel?"

"We're not sure. It's warm. We think there's a channel of magma not too far away."

"We need to get a probe close enough to scan through the rock.

Maybe there are hot springs on the other side, or bacterial mats, or their home. Do they have an air lock nearby?"

"We don't know."

"Right." Vonnie clenched and unclenched her hands, her nerves flickering with anticipation.

Where were sunfishes' children? Did they protect them like humans protected their young or were their eggs left to live or die like those of Earth's frogs and fish? She wanted the answer to be the first possibility. More likely it was the second.

From gene sequencing, X-rays, and her mem files, the biologists said the packs of sunfish included both males and females. The females were physically larger, less in number, and seemed to dominate, calling out more often than the males.

Every one of these physical and sociological aspects were the opposite in humankind. *Homo sapiens* had typically banned their females from hunting and combat until very recently in history, when technology had provided women with as many advantages as men.

It was another clue to the sunfishes' mentality. Each time a group left home, they brought enough fertile adults to persevere if their colony was annihilated behind them.

The biologists also knew the sunfish didn't gestate their unborn because they had no wombs. They laid spawn—hundreds of eggs at once—which the males either sprinkled with milt during the act of laying or soon afterward.

The sunfish might have mating rituals, but they did not make love. They might not have a sex act at all. Equally significant, because they were warm-blooded and semi-aquatic, they probably laid their eggs in hot springs. There was no sunlight to incubate their spawn. They relied on the environment as part of their reproductive cycle, but the environment was catastrophic.

Metzler theorized that the females felt no attachment to their spawn, only bonding with successful newborn. They were predisposed to abandon their eggs.

Nature seemed to have compensated. If the gene smithing of the sunfishes' hormones was correct, their females laid spawn as often as six times in an Earth year. That was a staggering birth rate. It could have meant disastrously high population pressures, except most of the eggs never became adults. Maybe they ate their failed spawn or performed infanticide to weed out their weaker offspring.

That doesn't mean they're not affectionate, Vonnie told herself. The sunfish huddled for warmth, cared for each other's wounds and infections, and there was poetry in the fluid, detailed ruffling of their arms and bodies.

Did they know joy?

They seemed well-suited for a love of life. They moved like birds or dolphins. They built and succeeded. But they were short-lived. Their telomeres indicated an average lifespan of no more than twenty years.

By now, ESA and NASA biologists owned samples from seventeen different sunfish, dozens of bugs, and any number of bacterial mats and fungi. Most of the blood and tissue had been gathered from Vonnie's suit. Five more blood pricks had been secured by NASA's probes during the past week, and it was a toss-up which set of samples had caused the loudest uproar.

The botanists, entomologists, exobiologists, and gene smiths each had different arguments that their results were the most spectacular.

Europan DNA wasn't wildly distinct from Earth DNA. The sunfish genome was composed of sequences using the same four nucleic acids as terrestrial lifeforms. The one difference was in their blast scores for hemoglobin. The sunfish had evolved with a remarkable concentration of iron atoms in this globular protein, which allowed them to carry extra oxygen through their bloodstream.

The sunfish also had little genetic variation from each other. They were nearly clones, like cheetahs, which was another species that had been reduced to a bare minimum of breeding pairs in its past.

"Tell me what happened with Tom," Vonnie said.

"It was hours later," Metzler said, forwarding through his sim. "The sunfish ran out of material for their wall. They sent scouts into the side channels, including his team. Tom seems to go farther than anyone else. They might consider him expendable because of his injuries. Maybe he's earned a leadership role for being so resilient. I don't think most of them would have survived losing part of an arm."

"They'd eat him," Ash said.

"Yeah."

Metzler's recording showed Tom leap into view at a steep angle from the tunnel floor to its ceiling. He flew with his arms spread, screeching at the space ahead of him. Then he landed on a crag in the rock and stuck to it, bunching his arms with his body poised like a rocket, ready to jump again.

He'd obviously sensed 112, which sat twenty meters away. In flight, Tom had wavered in a clockwise motion, bending back each of his arm tips, including his stub. Curling inward might have pantomimed grabbing at the probe or bringing an object to his beak. This motion was a gesture more like releasing something.

"That means 'Hello' or 'Yes' depending on the context," Metzler said. "We found the same pose at the center of every wall of carvings. It's a starting place. The sunfish don't read in straight lines like we do. We think they read outward from the 'Hello' stance."

"I saw Pärnits' report," Vonnie said absently, staring at the display. Then she glanced at Metzler, wondering why she'd mentioned his friend's name.

He knew she was also dating Pärnits. Was the instinct to test potential mates so innate that it had spoken for her? Vonnie wasn't coy, and she wasn't mean, and yet she'd just undermined Metzler by giving credit to Pärnits.

Awkwardly, she scrambled to make up for it. "These sims are amazing," she said.

"Well, here's where everything goes wrong," Metzler said.

Was he annoyed with her?

Probe 112 repeated the 'Hello' gesture, then showed the undersides of two arms, undulating its pedicellaria.

It didn't have the effect they'd intended.

Tom lifted his underside to show his beak, a hostile gesture. He screeched into the catacombs behind him, alerting his companions. As soon as they answered, he turned and called in the probe's direction. Most likely he was scanning for other strangers. Possibly he was shouting threats at the probe not to come any closer.

"What if we're putting Tom in danger by talking to him?" Vonnie said. "The other sunfish might not like it."

"Jesus, you're strange," Ash said. From the way her hazel eyes searched Vonnie's face, she was only half kidding. "I know you have a huge crush on those monsters. Now you're more on their side than ours?"

"None of us want him to get hurt."

"It's a chance we have to take," Frerotte said. "If we're going to talk to them, we have to start somewhere."

Tom finished screeching into the dark. He leapt away from 112, escaping it but not the camouflaged spies, who recorded his flight. First he rejoined his quartet. Then they formed up with the rest of the pack.

At the same time, Probes 112 and 113 fled.

When the sunfish returned in force, the probes were gone. The sunfish clung to the rock. They did not pursue. Instead, they screamed at the empty tunnel.

"What are they doing?" Ash said.

"That looks territorial," Vonnie said. "They're claiming this space."

"We thought so, too," Metzler said. "Their sonar would carry after the probes for a long way, maybe as far as three kilometers. Watch what they do next."

The sunfish quit screeching. They returned to the tunnel where they'd built their wall. Then they assembled in a pack and began screeching again, using the rock to amplify their shrill voices back on themselves.

Ash put her hands over her ears. "They'll go deaf!"

"They're worried the probes will try to flank them," Vonnie said. "Remember, they're always exposed on all sides, up and down. So they're repeating the warning."

"It seems more intense than that," Metzler said. "What if it's an affirmation ritual? They could be promising each other to defend the colony or memorizing a new voice key. Look at their modulation. They're not just screaming. There's a carefully refined harmony."

"Why did Tom run from the probe?"

"We're not sure. They must find loners or survivors from other packs sometimes."

"They probably eat them, too," Ash said.

"Maybe not. Survivors from another area could lead them to new food supplies or thermals. There's also a biological imperative. Accepting newcomers into the pack would be good genetics. They need the diversity."

"Maybe the probe said the wrong thing," Ash said.

"I don't think so. It was docile. It responded to Tom's overture."

"You did great," Vonnie said, bumping his shoulder.

"Pärnits programmed its secondary movements," Metzler said. "Maybe something in those gestures was too abrupt or he used the wrong arms."

The subtext of that comment wasn't difficult to interpret. Metzler had undercut his rival for Vonnie's affections, opening a divide between the two men, which was exactly what she didn't want.

"This encounter went better than anything else we've done," she said. "You guys are spectacular."

"We probably should have told the probe to stay," Metzler said. "The sunfish would never accept a loner without assessing him as a group. That would also reduce their odds of sustaining casualties. If it's a trap, if he's sick or feeble, they'd smash him."

"Are we sure the probe had the right sound?" Ash said.

With help from their gene smiths, Vonnie and Ash had grafted synthetic blubber and skin onto the probes' exteriors. Naked metal wouldn't sound like a living creature, nor smell like one. Metzler was certain that the hundreds of tube feet commingled with the sun-fishes' pedicellaria were a sensitive scent-and-taste organ. Even in areas where there was no atmosphere, the sunfish must be attuned to each other's smell, the mineral content in the rock, toxins, moisture, and the tracks of anything that had passed before them.

"The probe's skin wasn't the problem," Metzler said.

"What about its density?" Vonnie said. "We can't make a probe as light as a sunfish unless we dump most of the hardware. If we—"

An alert chimed on the display. Frerotte rose to his feet, ducking through the hatch into data/comm.

"What's up?" Ash said.

"Our probes are on the move," Metzler said. "The sunfish just reentered the catacombs."

"Contact in three minutes," Frerotte called. "Pärnits and O'Neal are coming online. Koebsch is signed in, too. They need us in one."

"Got it." Metzler looked at Vonnie and said, "Can you redesign the probes if we have to?"

"Yes." She stood up, eager to join Frerotte in data/comm. "We'd need to leave most of the data gathering to the spies. That's worked pretty well so far, but it'll be an issue if the probes move out of range. What if we're lucky enough to be invited into the sunfishes' homes?"

"We can send down ten thousand spies," Ash said. "In another year, they'll be everywhere."

"That doesn't help us now."

As the three of them walked toward the hatch together, Vonnie caught Metzler's elbow, letting Ash move ahead of them. She drew Metzler away from the hatch. Then she reached her arms around his neck and kissed him.

32.

HE RAN HIS hands down Vonnie's ribs to her waist. She pressed herself against him. Her lips parted, and she chuckled at the simple pleasure of touching each other.

Her laughter was a low, wanting sound. It invited more. His hands slid to the small of her back.

Frerotte shouted, "Ben! Fifteen seconds!"

"Oh, hell," Vonnie said as they broke their embrace. Metzler looked into her eyes, checking to see if she was okay. She nodded. Then he moved past.

Vonnie lingered behind, hugging her arms across her breasts to fill the void he'd left. Her mouth worked with a grin that she couldn't control.

A kiss was an odd thing. In most cultures, kissing had come to have many meanings—affection, sympathy, friendship—but it had originated as a trick of reproduction. By sharing saliva, the man transferred testosterone to the woman, increasing her boldness and her arousal. The emotional component was harder to decipher. There were undertones of devotion and ownership.

The sunfish will have their own tricks, Vonnie thought, trying to cool off. She'd been celibate since leaving Earth. Her body ached and burned.

She must have moved differently as she stepped through the hatch into data/comm, because Ash looked at her sharply. Vonnie grinned again without meaning to.

"Sign in," Frerotte said.

Frerotte, Metzler, and Ash stood in virtual stations, each of them enveloped in a shaft of holo imagery. Frerotte had prepped a fourth station. Vonnie walked into it, donning mesh gloves as she activated her temp files and preferences with a voice key. "Vonderach," she said.

Her display included a group feed for most of the crew. A few people were too busy with their own projects to join in. Everyone else wanted to observe their next encounter.

Probes 112 and 113 had squirmed into a new section of catacombs above the tunnel where they'd met Tom. The rock was less dense here. It had bubbled. Most of the openings were scrawny, lopsided pockets. The probes' line-of-sight never stretched more than twenty meters, although their radar signals bounced as far as three hundred meters before the catacombs slumped over a precipice, creating a blind spot.

Hidden beyond the obstruction were sunfish. The rock echoed with their shrieks, which grew louder and louder.

Vonnie grimaced. The reality was that mecha were ideal for this world. She couldn't have fit into those holes even if she'd had the guts to try, and, worse, she expected the sunfish to greet the probes with violence. They all did.

"How far away is our next team?" Koebsch asked.

"110 and 111 are five kilometers out," Frerotte said. "114 and 115 are even further. I didn't want to pull them from their grids."

The sunfishes' screaming resolved into a physical presence. Radar identified three contacts—then four—seven—eight. Tom and Jill led the pack. They fluttered through the jagged rock, their voices flooding every crevice.

112 and 113 answered them. If Pärnits was right, the probes' tone was welcoming, but the voices of the sunfish increased in pitch, exceeding frequencies over 100,000 Hertz. Their screams became a war cry.

"Here we go," Koebsch said.

Four sunfish spun out of a gap in the ceiling and latched onto the rock above the probes, clenching their arms, their bodies poised to leap again. It was the same menacing pose Tom had assumed in the tunnel.

"They're going to attack," Frerotte said, but Vonnie said, "No, they always display aggression. You need to do the same."

"She's right. I can improvise those body shapes," Metzler said. At his command, 112 and 113 mimicked the sunfish, drawing themselves into predatory, piston-like shapes.

Four more sunfish emerged from a hole in the wall. Tom was among this group. They seized positions on the rock overhead. The probes were surrounded.

From this position of strength, four sunfish showed the undersides of their arms—two arms each—two sunfish from each quartet.

Intricate patterns rippled through their pedicellaria and tube feet.

"They're emitting scent!" Metzler said. "Frerotte, take over 113. Talk to them. I want 112 working on sample capture and analysis."

"Roger that," Frerotte said. Sweeping his gloves into his display, he led 113 through a new dance. The probe lifted two of its arms like the sunfish.

"We're not going to be able to match their scents," Pärnits said. "They'll realize something's wrong."

"They know the probes are different," Vonnie said. "Don't run. If we try to get away, they'll catch us. Let's see what happens. Keep talking."

Beside her, Metzler flashed a smile.

Did he like hearing her argue with Pärnits? There wasn't time to read his expression. This close to the sunfish, every second was a gold mine. The probes' telemetry filled with X-rays, linguistic algorithms, and 112's first chem reports.

"Wow!" Metzler said, laughing.

Everyone was entranced. They were spellbound, even Koebsch. The moment was so exceptional he'd forgotten himself and his prudent nature.

"I think they're accepting us," Metzler said.

"The computers think so, too," Pärnits said, highlighting ten clips on the group feed.

He ran an overlay of four different sunfish repeating the same wriggles through their pedicellaria. It was a contracting motion. It looked like a circle closing into a dot.

"That could mean 'Come with us' or 'Go inside,'" Pärnits said.

"Tell them 'Yes,'" Koebsch said.

Frerotte ordered both probes to spread their arms and curl each tip upward. Like Metzler, he was smiling. Everyone was talking too loudly now, sharing the same electricity.

Vonnie turned at the chime of an alarm. "Wait. There's movement back where we left our spies."

"Oh!" Ash cried.

Tom's sunfish fell on 112 and 113 like rain. Most of the ESA crew shouted as if the probes were their own bodies.

Beaks and arms filled their displays. The sunfish tore through the probes' false skin, cutting relays and sensors. Tom's beak scraped the metal beneath. The noise was a grating squeal until Frerotte dimmed the volume.

"Don't fight them!" Koebsch yelled. "Don't fight!"

The sunfish destroyed both probes. They were unable to crack or dent the mecha's alumalloy bodies, but they wrenched several arms loose, then dug into the open sockets with their arm tips. They yanked at the machinery inside even when it cut and tore their pedicellaria.

Did they intend to keep the ravaged metal and plastic? Before the last signals from 113 went dead, the sunfish hooked their arms around the squashed gears and fragments of alumalloy.

"What's happening with our spies?" Metzler asked as Vonnie scrolled through her display.

She couldn't let herself feel anything more than tight concentration. She was discouraged, but the real surprise was that the sunfish had interacted with the probes for eighty-one seconds. Now they shocked her again.

"Their colony must be larger than we thought," she said.

Near the cavern where the sunfish had built their retaining wall, Sue led a new horde within range of the spies' sensors. There were sixteen of them. Twelve hugged rock clubs against their bodies.

"How can there be so many sunfish?" Koebsch said. "I thought there isn't enough food."

"We need to send mecha down to the ocean," Vonnie said. "What if it's loaded with fish like those eels NASA found? They might get most of their food there."

"The ocean's too far away," Koebsch said. "They'd need days to transport eels or fish back to the colony."

"If they freeze their food, that wouldn't matter."

"Yes, it would," Koebsch said. "They'd spend more calories than they'd gain dragging their prey through the ice, and they'd probably have to fight other tribes for it. They're too high for the ocean to matter."

"Not if there were geysers and churn in the area," Metzler said. "There might be sea life frozen in the ice around the colony. Maybe they're mining for it."

"An eel mine," Vonnie said appreciatively.

That could be the missing factor, she thought. *Eruptions and rip tides might push sea creatures into the frozen sky, where they're preserved. If the sunfish located an area where storms seeded the ice with bodies, they'd have a natural food source. It might be enough to last for years or generations.*

Sue's group entered the cavern in a familiar wave formation. Half flew high. Half flew low. They rebounded from the ceiling and floor, colliding in the middle.

Then they sprang away from each other in individual trajectories. The four sunfish who weren't carrying rocks used themselves as a centering mass. Kicking, bouncing, slamming, spinning, they propelled the others outward.

They crushed the spies with stunning precision, terminating eleven of the tiny mecha in a coordinated strike. Vonnie thought they'd turn on the rest, but they were done. They killed eleven spies without effort, then paused, leaving the majority untouched.

"That's weird," Frerotte said. "If they can tell our spies are there—"

"They memorized the walls!" Metzler said. "That's what they were doing with their group song. They memorized the walls, then came back and spotted the differences. Look. They killed every spy that's moved since they left. 4071 only changed its position by five centimeters, but they got it, too."

Sue's group picked at the remnants of the spies. They ate a few specks, then cinched their arms around the rest. Later, they might compare these bits of ceramic armor and nanocircuitry to the junk Tom's pack had salvaged from the larger probes. For the moment, Sue's pack gathered on the cavern floor.

They screeched and screeched. They were memorizing the cavern again. The group ritual also served as a warning to everything that could hear them—a cry of possessiveness and defiance. Then they fled into the dark.

"They must have noticed a spy earlier," Vonnie said. "They were suspicious, and they wanted to make sure nothing bothered their retaining wall."

"How are they processing so much detail in the rock?" Koebsch said. "We couldn't do it without AI."

"They're wired differently."

"They might not be as smart as you think, Von," Dawson said. "What?"

"They used to be intelligent," Dawson said. "I can't deny the carvings we've found. Those are written histories. But the carvings are ten thousand years old. These sunfish are just animals. We're wasting our time trying to talk to them."

33.

"BULLSHIT," VONNIE SAID. "Are you looking at the same transcripts I am?"

"Yes indeed." William Dawson was in his seventies and their oldest crew member. Wrinkles spread from the corners of his eyes through his paper-fine skin, but his hair remained black, and he was spry and elflike.

Vonnie hadn't spoken with him much. She felt blindsided by his announcement. "How can you think we should leave them down there to die?" she said.

"I don't. Not at all. Perhaps our approach should change. We've spent five weeks pussyfooting around in hopes of talking to them. I submit that this is like attempting to chat with porpoises or seals."

"Seals!"

"Porpoises may be a better comparison. I don't know if you've seen the mem files on attempts to communicate with cetaceans in the twentieth century."

"I have." Vonnie had watched everything she could find on inter-species communication.

"Some marine biologists were convinced the whales were intelligent," Dawson said. "The complexity of their songs was bewitching. Other people were obsessed with dolphins. They frittered away their careers proving themselves wrong."

"They learned more than you think. Their work is part of the database we're using now, but the whales never said anything like this." Vonnie brought an excerpt from the newest sunfish translations onto the group feed and played it.

TOM: Hello.

PROBE 112: Hello / Yes.

TOM: I am Top Clan Two-Four, Pod Four.

ALL SUNFISH: I am Top Clan Two-Four, Pod Four.

ALL SUNFISH: Close / Too close.

TOM: You are too close / Hello.

"This supports my theory," Dawson said. "The sunfish are pack animals, not individuals. Look at the group response. It's imitative."

"Hold on," Pärnits said. "Repetition is a natural function of the way they communicate. They can only hear the shapes they detect in any given sonar pulse. Of course they repeat the same information. It's like a circle or a chain. They confirm and reconfirm until every member in the group acknowledges the message. Their speech patterns are more fluid than human conversation."

"It's obviously language," Vonnie said. "They use numbers and names."

Dawson's smile was condescending. "You're the one who's given them names," he said. "All I've seen is the same limited repertoire of shapes repeated over and over."

Vonnie glared. It was true that she and Metzler had tried to personalize the sunfish, but she refused to concede the point. "The sunfish always begin with the same shapes because they're at war with each other," she said. "Their priority is to announce their claim to their area."

"Indeed. It's a territorial response."

"He said 'I'm Top Clan Two-Four, Pod Four.'"

"They all said it. It's not intentional, Von."

"The sunfish NASA found said they were Top Clan Four-Eight, Pods Two and Six. They're organizing themselves by tribes, then by squads."

"Are they?" Dawson asked. "The AI is assigning identifiers like 'clan' and 'pod' for our benefit, and not with a lot of confidence. Check the scores. The AI won't guarantee the accuracy of our transcripts. Most are ranked lower than seventy percent."

True again, she thought. Their AIs had interpreted the sunfishes' carvings with a fair amount of certainty, but following the shape-based language in real time was a work in progress. Too much of it was open to guesswork.

"The sunfish appear to use their pronouns interchangeably," Dawson said. "'I,' 'we,' 'ours,' 'mine'—there's no differentiation. Their arm shrugs may not be counting at all. I don't dispute that the manner in which they show 'eight' or 'four' is unique to each group, but those postures look like displays of conformity and aggression to me."

"Then they'll keep destroying our probes," Koebsch said.

"An animal doesn't learn, it merely reacts," Dawson said. "That's why every encounter is the same. I'm grateful for the data brought to us by NASA and our own probes, but I question if we can afford to let the sunfish keep smashing mecha."

You bastard, she thought. *You despicable, pretentious bastard.*

Why was he doing this? Because it would put him at the forefront of the academic debate and the latest news feeds? Dawson didn't care how much money the ESA spent on probes and spies. Like the Brazilians, he wanted to generate his own notoriety and enjoy its rewards.

"Granted, the sunfish have extraordinary ratios of brain to body mass," he said. "Their ratio is actually greater than ours. But with eight arms, too much of their brain mass is dedicated to motor control. An elephant uses a considerable portion of its brain to operate its trunk. We use much of ours to operate our fingers and arms. The sunfish developed enough brain mass to gain sentience for a time, but their undoing was their need for multi-sensory input. Allow me to demonstrate."

Accessing the group feed, Dawson opened a sim of a sunfish brain. It had two hemispheres like a human brain, although it was flatter and wider.

Dawson highlighted several internal structures.

"Here is an olfactory cortex," he said. "Here is an auditory cortex. Here is a second auditory cortex, and this is no less than a third auditory cortex."

"So what?" Vonnie said impatiently.

"So in addition to the scent-and-taste organ of their tube feet and their ability to use broadband sonar calls in atmosphere environments, the sunfish are also capable of generating and processing narrow-band high frequency clicks underwater. That's why they possess these cartilage nares beside their larynx. It's why these fatty lobes share the same nerve bundles as their cochlear. The lobes are for echolocation."

"I'll say it again—so what?"

Dawson smiled at her, unperturbed. "The sunfish also possess a shark-like ability to perceive bioelectrical impulses and subtle changes in temperature and pressure. The tiny pores commingled with their pedicellaria can sense living creatures, even those hiding behind rock or underwater. That's how they followed you no matter what you tried, Von. They sensed your body through your suit."

"Impossible," Frerotte said. "Scout suits are insulated plastisteel."

"The sunfish have had to become remarkably sensitive to find prey in the ice," Dawson said. "Perhaps they reacted to the suit itself. Sharks were known to attack phone cables in the earliest years of telecommunications. One of the suit's systems could have attracted them, but I think not. You were hurt. Wounded creatures emit stronger signals than normal as the electrical activity controlling their heart rate and respiration increases."

Vonnie felt her face lose its color. Her memories of screaming and killing would always be with her, and Dawson had unlocked that terror with a few words.

Then she got mad. *Why is he smiling?* she thought. *Is he deliberately trying to weaken me?* She was the loudest proponent of treating the sunfish like equals. If he dominated her, he might win this argument.

"Finely-developed sensory inputs are what elevated the sunfish to sentience," she said.

"On the contrary," Dawson said. "They no longer have enough mass left for higher thinking. Certainly they don't have the emotional quotient we do. They might be smart like our spies are smart—like termites or bees or prairie dogs. They're able to build structures in a step-by-step manner as a group, but without real initiative or independence. Too much of their capacity is dedicated to pure survival."

"I disagree," Metzler said. "They have spindle cells like human beings and the great apes."

"Dolphins, elephants, and giraffes have spindle cells in similar concentrations," Dawson said. "No one considers giraffes intelligent."

Vonnie glanced at Metzler, who said, "Spindle cells are neurons without extensive branching, sort of like free-floating processors. They play a crucial role in the development of cognition and decision-making." He turned back to Dawson. "Sunfish brains are also more convoluted than ours, and they have faster brain stem transmission times."

"So do rats," Dawson said. "Their brain stem transmission time is an adaptation to living in eternal darkness, not evidence of superhuman thinking. That their brain mass ratio is greater than ours also means nothing. It's a necessary result of their hemispheric asymmetry during sleep."

"They don't sleep."

"They do, Dr. Metzler." Dawson opened a series of medical imaging scans of the sunfish. He turned to Vonnie and said, "In addition to motor function, most of any creature's brain is dedicated to involuntary functions such as heartbeat, digestion, and respiration. In sunfish, breathing is voluntary. They must decide to inhale or use their gills or hold their breath." He looked at Metzler. "We've recorded EEG patterns which very much resemble REM activity, but only in one hemisphere at a time."

"Then they're technically awake."

"Indeed. Because the sunfish are voluntary breathers, they would asphyxiate as soon as they relaxed and failed to breathe. They must also remain vigilant for predators. Therefore it's uncommon that both of their hemispheres are simultaneously awake. In essence, they have two small brains, not a single large one. They alternate between which small brain they use throughout the day."

Enough, Vonnie thought.

"Their carvings talk about the future and the past," she said. "They had laws. Some of it looks like philosophy! At the very least, there was tribal rule, and a warlord strong enough to form an empire."

"It's interesting that their carvings invariably show perfect sunfish," Pärnits added. "They never exhibit wounds or age. That suggests a desire for beauty."

"We've dated the youngest carvings at nine thousand years," Dawson said. "Something happened between now and then. Perhaps the sunfish didn't always have such dependence on dual forms of sonar or their bioelectric sensing organs."

"You think they evolved away from sentience?" Pärnits asked. "That would be unprecedented."

"Everything in this world is unprecedented," Dawson said.

"Nine thousand years is too quick," Metzler said. "It's not enough time for the sunfish to degenerate without an outside cause like massive radiation, and they don't have the resources or the technology for a nuclear war."

"Nothing so dramatic is necessary," Dawson said. "Jupiter's

magnetic field is, in essence, a gigantic particle accelerator. It blasts Europa's surface with octillions of high-speed ions and electrons every hour."

"They don't live on the surface," Vonnie said. "They're safe inside the ice."

"No. The ice shields them from the primary radiation, but there are elements dissolved in the ice like iodine and potassium. When those elements are bombarded, they turn into short-period isotopes, which are sinister little poisons. Churn brings the hazardous material down into the ice. Periods of violent churn exacerbate the contamination."

"It's still too fast," Vonnie said, running a calculation in her head. If the lifespan of a sunfish was twenty years... "It's only been five hundred generations since they were writing."

"I'm afraid it's more than that," Dawson said. "Male sunfish don't mature until six years of age. Until then, they may be expendable, leaving only the hardiest to procreate. But their females reach adolescence at two years. They're fertile at three. It's been four thousand generations since the carvings."

"Where's the evolutionary pressure to give up their intelligence?" Metzler said. "Sentience is the greatest weapon any species can develop."

"Not necessarily. As nourishment became more difficult to find, they grew more instinctive—more aware in other ways—trading their intelligence for improved sonar and detection. It all fits. We know they're severely limited genetically. There's been inbreeding. Unfavorable mutations took hold because those adaptations serve them well. They don't need intelligence to roam the ice. In fact, their self-awareness worked against them, making them all too conscious of what they'd lost in the turmoil of Europa's crust. They suffer less without their intelligence, and we should feel lucky indeed at this twist of fate."

"What do you mean?" Koebsch said.

"Our ancestors had scarcely invented the most primitive forms of agriculture and herding when the sunfish began their decline. Their empire fell. Then they regressed. Otherwise they might have traveled to our world before we visited theirs."

34.

"IMAGINE IF A superior race had landed among us when we were tribal nomads without science, only fire and spears," Dawson said. "That's why the sunfish run away. That's why they fight us even though they're impossibly outmatched."

Silence filled the group feed. Brooding, Vonnie saw troubled looks in her crew mates.

The far-away feeling she'd experienced weeks ago when the Chinese rover discovered the first carvings was with her again now, richer and more poignant.

How close did we come to exchanging destinies with the sunfish? she thought. *If there had been more supervolcanoes on Earth... If another meteor strike like the one that killed the dinosaurs had pushed us to the brink while the sunfish were given another 10,000 years of peace... What if they'd discovered iron and steam power, then steel, electronics, and finally the atom? We might have been a few starving bands of cavemen when they brought spacecraft to Earth.*

"I have to admit I'm disappointed in how the sunfish have responded," Koebsch said.

"Sir, we've only been here for six weeks," Metzler said. "I know you're under a lot of scrutiny from Berlin, but I think we've made inroads."

"Really?" Dawson said. "All I've noticed are the same attacks on our mecha."

"He's right," Koebsch said.

"We should capture some of them," Dawson said, and Vonnie

exploded: "You son of a bitch! People stopped hunting whales because they're too close to sentience to treat like cows or sheep. Even if you're right about the sunfish, the same principle applies here."

"I don't want to eat them," Dawson said with his elfin smile.

"But you want to take them apart! Who have you been talking to? Is there a gene corp offering you money or a job?"

"That's offensive."

"So is pushing us to treat the sunfish like a commodity. You're demonizing them."

"It's ludicrous to expect a single lab to sequence and develop the material we've gathered thus far," Dawson said. "There aren't enough of us. We need to send tissue samples to Earth—dozens if not hundreds of samples. Live specimens would serve even better."

"I can't believe you've been hiding this bullshit from the rest of us."

Koebsch said, "Look, Von, let's calm down—"

"I am calm!"

"—and maybe get some lunch," Koebsch said. "We can talk again later. Let's meet again on the group feed in an hour. Frerotte, I want to talk to you on Channel Thirty."

"I need to talk to you, too," Vonnie said.

"Not now," Koebsch said, cutting his connection with the group feed.

Vonnie stayed online, watching Dawson, who ignored her as he closed his sims. If he had more to say to the group, she wanted to hear it. But he signed off.

"Sorry, Von," Frerotte said. He lifted a privacy screen on his station. From the outside, the screen left Frerotte visible yet fuzzy as his display components turned to gray blotches, including his link to Koebsch. The privacy screen also canceled their voices.

Vonnie paced in the confines of data/comm. Metzler tried to make room for her, clearing his station and hanging back. Ash wasn't so tolerant. Ash took her hand and dragged her into the ready room, where Vonnie at least had space to wave her arms.

"Son of a bitch!"

"Walk it off," Ash said. "Just walk a little."

Metzler followed them into the L-shaped area between the lockers and the empty scout suits. "Don't let Dawson get to you," he said. "We've only had a few encounters with the sunfish, and most of those were with different tribes. It's been like starting from square one every time."

Vonnie shook her head. "Dawson's an asshole, but he's right that we can't keep repeating the same cycle. We approach, they attack. We approach, they attack. There has to be some way to get through to them."

She laid a hand on her suit—a new suit calibrated to her biometrics. Then she turned abruptly. Metzler and Ash both pretended they hadn't been watching her.

They were nice to worry. Vonnie wanted to promise she was fine, but she was afraid they'd see right through her.

She felt estranged and shut out.

"Let's get to work on the new probes," she said. "If we can make them lighter, that might help. Maybe the sunfish won't know they're fakes."

"The only way to reduce the probes' weight is to pull their radar and X-ray," Ash said. "Koebsch won't like it."

"Koebsch has different objectives than we do. He has to pay attention to the budget. You noticed how Dawson got fussy about how much the mecha cost? He was sucking up to Koebsch. But we don't need more maps. We don't need more body scans, either. We need to convince the sunfish to listen to us before glory hounds like Dawson decide they belong in a zoo."

"Or on a menu," Ash said with a glint in her hazel eyes.

Vonnie laughed, glad for any chance to break the tension. "I'll put you on a menu," she said.

Metzler draped his arms around both women. "You two go ahead," he said. "I'll make lunch. No sunfish. Then I want to go over Dawson's sims. Maybe I can shoot some holes in his data."

"Marry me," Vonnie said, laughing again, but Metzler nodded sincerely.

"Be careful what you ask for," he said.

They left the ready room. In data/comm, Frerotte continued to talk inside his privacy screen. Vonnie took the next station and unfolded the chair. Ash sat beside her, glancing after Metzler as he ducked into the next compartment. Now the young woman's eyes were characteristically shrewd.

"He really likes you," she said.

Vonnie didn't answer. As a teacher, she had learned to be charming. It was part of the job. She was less comfortable with her newfound charisma. She'd become a polarizing figure in their group, a crusader and a leader.

People want to be inspired, she thought. *Are they helping me because I'm famous?*

What if Dawson went out of his way to take an opposing view for the same reason? Because he resents seeing me in the limelight and wants it for himself?

Vonnie hoped her friends appreciated her for her own qualities, not the image of the hero created by the media buzz, and yet she found herself playing into that role more and more. Most of the crew respected her conviction. Some of them, like Metzler, even welcomed her volatility.

As she opened their schematics of the new probe, she said, "Can you hack our own datastreams?"

"Yes," Ash said. "Why would I do that?"

"Everyone has different encryption packets depending on who they're communicating with on Earth. I'm curious who's on Dawson's lists."

It would be easy to conceal illicit transmissions in their data bursts. All of them were linked with a myriad of government agencies, labs, universities, and media outlets—but if Dawson stood to profit from his decisions, if he was saying what a corporation wanted to hear in order to classify the sunfish as animals, Vonnie was well-positioned to stop him. She could use her celebrity to burn him in public opinion.

"What if Dawson's in a gray area legally or flat-out breaking the rules?" she said. "He's got his nose turned up so far, it makes me think he knows something we don't. He might be taking bribes. Hell, he probably has a deal with someone. That's why he's taunting us."

"I'll peek," Ash said. "The tough part will be getting a minute without Koebsch online to see what I'm doing. Maybe while he's sleeping. Let me wait until I'm in the command module tonight or tomorrow."

"Tonight."

"I need an excuse to drive over, Von."

"Here." She opened the remote operation link to the armory, which, like Koebsch's central data/comm post, was in the command module. "The forge doesn't work right with our link. We can take the jeep after we finish our redesign. Koebsch will want to tell me everything I did wrong anyway, so I'll keep him busy. Trust me."

"I do trust you," Ash said.

Vonnie met her gaze, then responded with total candor. "You're my best friend in this place," she said, which was true, but inside, she thought, *I wish I knew who you were working for.*

She needed Ash's help to stop Dawson. But who would stop Ash if the girl was on the payroll of MI6 or another intelligence agency? Vonnie took it for granted that Ash's directives were ultimately identical to Dawson's: to own and control everything of value on Europa while disrupting the efforts of any other group to do the same.

Once upon a time, Vonnie might have laughed at the predicament they'd brewed for themselves. Instead, she cursed herself.

Face it, she thought. *You're outclassed.*

The only people who'd been sent to Europa without covert training might be the poor, honest fools who'd volunteered when no one imagined there was anything more than bugs in the ice, namely

Vonnie, Bauman, and Lam. Too much was at stake. As soon as Earth realized the larger ramifications, new players had been sent for a different game.

If the Allied Nations accepted the sunfish as a sentient race, that might affect who was permitted to mine the ice, where they were licensed to operate, and how much they paid the sunfish in trade goods.

If any country or gene corp got a head start on developing useful applications of Europan DNA, that could lead to the priceless first-to-market position for new meds or treatments.

Cryogenics and improved cancer resistance were top priorities for Earth's military and civilian space forces. Astronauts who could sleep safely for months at a time would allow ships to travel farther than ever. Soldiers who could be stored, forgotten, and yet come up fighting would act both as deterrents and as first strike weapons. They could be stashed all over the solar system until needed.

Germany had spliced cockroach and black fly genes into some of their Special Forces commandos with solid results. China was known to have tried rat and chimpanzee DNA. The side effects were minor, and there would always be volunteers eager to trade their health for glory and strength.

Dawson was correct that Europan lifeforms dealt with high levels of radiation in addition to extreme cold. Christmas Bauman had felt that many of them must have evolved the ability to suppress and repair cellular damage, and Bauman's word was enough for Vonnie. If she'd believed there were revolutionary genetics here, Vonnie wanted that magic for the human race, too—but it wasn't fair for any single group to own it, and it wasn't right to condemn the sunfish for anyone's profit margin.

Vonnie felt like she was standing in a mine field. She didn't know where to step. Someone she depended on today might betray her tomorrow, and she remembered when she'd met Ash. She'd done everything possible to convince Ash that she would put the team first.

Could the same be said for Ash's intentions?

35.

ASH WILL BE my friend as long as it suits her, Vonnie thought. *I think she genuinely likes me. That's part of why she saved Lam. But no matter how she feels about me or the sunfish, eventually we'll go home. She's made a career for herself there, so she'll lie or steal from me if that's what they tell her to do. Won't she?*

What can I promise her that they haven't? I don't have a lot of money. Even if I was a division leader, any promotion I offered would be a joke compared to the job they've given her.

Who can I trust? Metzler? Koebsch?

Sitting with Ash in front of their holo display, Vonnie hid her reproach by tapping at the probe's schematics. Removing the radar array created complications in the probe's power grid.

In silence, the two women made corrections, needing no words to fulfill this task. Vonnie traced a line to bridge the hole in the grid. Ash added a secondary net so the probe could reroute its energy needs if it was damaged.

"Simple," Ash said.

Vonnie wished everything was so easy. She felt sad and resentful, and she tried to shake her mood.

She copied the newest data from Probes 112 and 113 to her station, then let an AI collate those files with their existing programs. Each interaction with the sunfish would refine the movements of their probes' arms.

But we need to do more than upgrade our mecha, she thought. *We need a new approach. Instead of waiting for the sunfish to accept us, what would happen if we marched straight into their homes? They understand certainty.*

The irony was she wanted the sunfish to be more uncertain. For their own welfare, they needed to question themselves.

Were they capable of ending their kill-or-be-killed aggression once they realized there was more to existence than the frozen sky?

Even if they hadn't grasped the notion that the ESA probes and spies came from outside the ice, they must feel as if they'd encountered brand-new lifeforms.

Earth had agreed that the next stage in communicating with the sunfish might be an attempt to provide gifts—fabric, meat, steel tools, and tanks of compressed oxygen—but they were concerned this wealth would draw new attacks, not only from the sunfish but from other species. Also, they were undecided if giving steel to the sunfish was worth the impression they wanted to make.

Would the sunfish accept the ESA's technological superiority and welcome humankind in expectation of receiving more tools? Or would they become more aggressive, fighting for as much metal as they could scavenge from destroyed mecha?

The sunfishes' rock clubs had been surprisingly effective against Vonnie's scout suit. With steel blades beaten from shovels and air tanks, the sunfish might penetrate a suit through its joints or collar.

Authorizing gifts was Koebsch's decision. He'd tabled the idea, suggesting it was too soon to gamble even with token presents of soft fabric or delicacies sealed in vacuum packs.

What if we poison them with our food? he'd said. *What if they're allergic to the fabric?*

Metzler was positive he'd identified the starches and sugars in human food that would harm sunfish. Poisoning them was unlikely— but a month ago, while Vonnie was still recuperating, Pärnits had sunk her plans to bribe the sunfish.

We don't know what gift-giving means to them, Pärnits had said. *They're perpetually on the edge of starvation. What if showing excess food is an insult? We could go down there with the best intentions, give them everything, and offend them so badly they'll never forgive us.*

Since then, Pärnits had apologized to her, but he stood by his assessment. So did Koebsch.

It seemed to Vonnie that hundreds of years of in-fighting must have left the sunfish primed to negotiate. They would always look for new allies and resources. Given the right circumstances, the ESA might bond with one tribe. Those sunfish could act as a doorway to more tribes. Together, they could begin to form a new, stable empire—as stable as the sunfish allowed.

In comparison, on Earth, the European Union had contracted and expanded several times since the twentieth-first century, gaining new states and losing them. Partly that was because none of its members had surrendered their national identities or languages. English was common yet not required by law. To this day, their members maintained separate armies in addition to the E.U. military.

How many languages and individual tribal customs did the sunfish possess? Dozens? Only a few? They were homogenous in so many ways.

Metzler had compared their situation to the arrival of Caucasian settlers in North America. With superior technology and plague-hardened immune systems developed in the congested terrain of Europe, those settlers had ended life as the Native Americans knew it within a few hundred years.

That the Native Americans had been demoralized was a significant factor. Some tribes fought long and well, but only a small percentage of their losses had been in battle. The settlers had taken their lands with sickness, with commerce, and with well-meaning religion or greed or ignorance. They'd corrupted the natives in a million ways like sunlight evaporating snow.

Vonnie didn't want the same thing to happen here. Assholes like Dawson would compromise the sunfish at every turn, and for what? For money?

On the American frontier, the clash between two worlds had been so varied and lawless that some white settlers sold guns to the natives in exchange for pelts or safe passage, arming the indigenous population against their fellow whites.

On Europa, the points of contact were far fewer and closely supervised, but there would always be people who wanted the short-term gain. Men like Dawson lacked her moral center. He had no empathy.

He wanted his prize, whereas Vonnie didn't think her adventures on this moon would be complete even if she lived to her hundredth birthday. Aiding the sunfish, teaching and guiding them, was a project that could last decades.

I need to prove Dawson wrong by showing that the sunfish will accept us, she thought.

She was pleased with the design work she'd accomplished with Ash. They'd recalibrated their probes to be lighter and more responsive. Now she needed to convince Koebsch to upgrade their tactics as well.

"Can you excuse me?" she said to Ash.

"Why?"

Vonnie saved their files and made a shooing motion with one hand. "Please. Go get lunch. I'll come in a minute. There's a little job I need to do."

Ash hesitated, but she nodded and stood up. "All right." Then she left data/comm.

Vonnie heard her say something to Metzler in the next compartment. Metzler laughed, and Vonnie raised a privacy screen around her display.

She'd decided to up her own gamesmanship. She needed to be cagey even with her friends, delaying what they knew, earning favors, and, most of all, uniting them against Dawson.

I'll be a spy, too, she thought—a spy on her own—a spy by herself—as sensitive and paranoid as a sunfish.

Cutting into the channel between Koebsch and Frerotte took longer than she'd anticipated. Frerotte's encryptions repelled her hack. Trying a new strategy, she mastered control of his audio, then used this opening to further her gains into his virtual station. Unfortunately, his display went blank as soon as she broke in.

"—eep tracking," Koebsch said before he looked at Vonnie. "This is a secure call, Von. Get out."

"I need a minute."

"I'll call you as soon as I can."

"We're set to go with our new probes, but they're not right for carrying supplies down into the ice," she said. "I need to know if I should be building more probes or larger mecha."

"Build the new probes. We're not bringing down food or anything else."

Vonnie shook her head. "I think we're past holding back. It's right to worry about cultural contamination and pushing the sunfish too fast, but this colony represents our best chance for a breakthrough, and they'll never go back to the lives they had before we came along."

"Von, I'm dealing with bigger problems."

"Like what?"

"Sir, she might as well know," Frerotte said. "We need our engineers."

Koebsch grunted and reopened his display, giving Vonnie access to their datastreams. "This is for your eyes only until we decide how to handle it," he said.

"Yes, sir."

The map was Frerotte's. It showed their perimeter with the Brazilians, where Probes 114 and 115 had coordinated the actions of their spies.

"This is thirty minutes ago, then ten," Frerotte said, playing two sims for Vonnie. In the first segment, the telemetry from 114 spiked across the board—radar, sonar, seismographs, and data/comm.

"That's not sunfish," Vonnie said.

"Not unless some of them have radios," Koebsch said.

Something lunged toward 114, a bear-sized mass that had crept impossibly close, without noise, without vibrations, using a vein of rock to shield itself until it was within two kilometers of the probe. Then it lumbered forward in a blaze of electromagnetic activity, masking itself with sabotage and control programs.

The intruder's SCPs must have been underway for hours. It was sophisticated enough to have blinded the spies to its presence altogether. 114 suffered the same false reads and distortions. 114's sensors were unable to get a clean picture. There were only shadow-like glimpses.

Whatever it was, it was ten times larger than the probe. It hooked two arms above itself like weapons, and yet physically, it was slow. It covered the last kilometer in eight minutes, which was an eternity to mecha.

114 should have had time to run if it couldn't defend itself. Instead, 114 shut off.

"We're under attack," Frerotte said.

36.

VONNIE SCROLLED THROUGH their maps, measuring the unguarded space left by the loss of 114 and most of its spies. "How close is 115?" she asked. "Do we know where the intruder went?"

"No," Frerotte said. "115 is on the move, but it's three minutes away. I had 14 and 15 in different catacombs to spread our coverage."

"They should have been together," Koebsch said. "That's why we sent them down in pairs. We probably wouldn't have lost 14 if the probes were able to support each other."

Privately, Vonnie doubted it. Whatever hit 114 would have walked right over 115 as well. Frerotte's decision to separate the probes was the sole reason they had the ability to bring new eyes and ears to the scene quickly.

There were two more probes in the ice, 110 and 111, but those mecha were seven kilometers northwest of 115. Except for their spies, there were no other ESA mecha beneath the surface other than a hundred beacons and relays, none of which were mobile, equipped with AI, or combat capable.

"I want you to call Sergeant Tavares again," Koebsch told Vonnie. "Maybe you'll have better luck than I did."

"You called the Brazilians?"

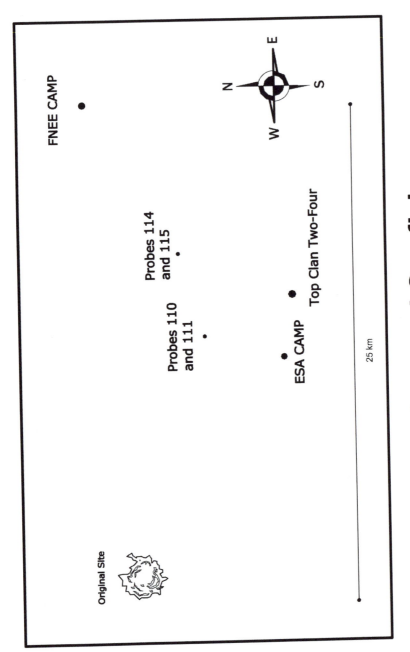

Probes and Sunfish

"Yes. They're not answering. But I can't figure out what they think they'll accomplish. That's why I want to keep this quiet. Mecha can be replaced. What we don't need is an international incident."

"Tavares said they didn't like us monitoring their grid," Vonnie said. "Maybe this is the end of it. They kill our spies. Then they retreat. You don't think they'd invade our zone, do you?"

"Maybe they're distributing their own spies. Right now they could march a hundred probes through the border without us knowing it."

"115 will reach the gap in thirty seconds."

"We've been blind for nine minutes. Even if nothing's there now, I'll be forced to waste time and resources hunting FNEE mecha inside our lines."

Vonnie nodded, considering Koebsch's change from 'we' to 'I.' For him, the attack was a blemish on his record.

"115 is on site," Frerotte said.

She looked through the probe's eyes. As always, the environment was as dark as obsidian. Her display was modifying 115's radar into holo imagery.

Sprawled on the rock were the battle-scarred remains of a FNEE digger. It had been a sleek, six-legged machine with two cutting blades like a scorpion's claws. One leg was missing. Two more appeared inoperable, shredded and crushed. There was also laser scoring on its head where its sensor array had been slashed open.

"114 couldn't have caused those burns," Koebsch said. "They must have hit some of their own diggers while they were blasting. Then they decided those mecha were expendable. They used their damaged mecha to lead the assault."

"I guess."

Scattered nearby were pieces that may or may not have belonged to different FNEE mecha. 114 was missing. There was not a trace of ESA wreckage. There were no sounds or vibrations of mecha leaving the site in any direction. Nor did 114 respond to 115's signals.

"I think 114 fought the digger and won, but there were other

FNEE mecha," Koebsch said. "They took 114. That's what they were after. They want to copy your design work, Von."

She watched as 115 crawled up the side of the cavern, trying to analyze the scuffing and chip marks in the dusty floor. There were marks in the wall, too, where 114 had vaulted onto the rock like a real sunfish.

Microdating the prints was impossible. Too many tracks had been laid within seconds of each other, and yet 114's tracks were all on the ESA side of the perimeter.

That means our probe wasn't led away by a Brazilian slavecast, Vonnie thought. Had they carried it? Or did 114's last set of tracks lead back into ESA territory?

"Let me call Tavares," she said, leaving her station.

The showphone was on the other side of the compartment, no more than three steps away. She didn't make it that far. Frerotte left his own station and said to her, quietly, "It wasn't the Brazilians."

Vonnie didn't answer.

"There's no way their software could trump ours, especially not in a stand-off between 114 and a wrecked pile of junk like that digger," Frerotte said. "Its gear block is half gone. You heard its signals. It was modifying its SCPs to broadcast through every transmitter it had left—infrared, sonar, X-ray. Hell, I saw coherent light signals like Morse code. It couldn't have been less efficient, but it subverted our probe anyway. It knew exactly how to hack in."

"It was Lam," she said.

"So what happened? He transferred from the digger to the probe?"

"Yes."

"Von, I think the situation's starting to get out of hand. We need to tell Koebsch."

"I will. I swear. Let me call Tavares first."

Frerotte clutched her arm more roughly than necessary, pulling her back from the showphone. Was there fear in his eyes?

"I know Lam was your friend, but that's not him any more,"

Frerotte said. "He's been down there for weeks. That's a long time for an AI."

"Tavares might have some idea what he's been through. I think he's trying to reach us."

"Why won't he answer 115? You don't know what he's thinking or even how he's thinking. FNEE hardware is barely compatible with our AI, especially a human-based AI. He would have adapted. That means deleting some parts of himself and absorbing FNEE programming to compensate. What if the conversion included some of their security protocols? He might think we're the enemy."

"I thought you were a biologist," Vonnie said. She was fishing for some admission that Frerotte worked for an intelligence agency, but he said, "This *is* biology. AIs are living systems. They break under strain just like people do."

"Let's wait and see."

His grip tightened on her arm. "Human-based AI are illegal because they're more likely to fragment," he said. "They turn into something... more virulent than any machine-based program. Lam is in one of our probes now, which will make it easier for him to hack into other mecha. If he clones himself, he could multiply through our camp."

"I don't think so."

"I watched it happen on the *Ensley 2*."

Vonnie laid her fingers over his, gently removing his hand from her arm. "You're not old enough," she said.

Ensley 2 had been a joint NATO/PSSC orbital station that tumbled into the Pacific in 2087, the flaming shrapnel of its hull missing Indonesia by a few scant kilometers.

Constructed during the early years of the new space race, after the Chinese revolution but prior to formation of the Allied Nations, the *Ensley* series were primarily a Western effort that had involved China's space agency as a means of easing poor relations between NATO and the People's Supreme Society. By treaty, they were civilian stations intended for science, solar power generation, crops like wheat which also produced oxygen, and the export of those food and oxygen supplies.

The Chinese astronauts among the *Ensley* crews had numbered less than forty... and they'd died with their Western colleagues in the AI attacks that initiated the brutal, eighteen days of World War III.

"I was right out of school," Frerotte said. "I had a good head for zero gravity and I get by on six hours of sleep a night, so they slotted me in three jobs in hydroponics. That's why I lived. I was working when the SCPs shut down life support and smothered half the crew in bed."

"I'm sorry."

"You must have been a kid. You've watched the sims, but it's not the same. I felt our station come alive. I ripped the controls out of our escape pod when the SCPs tried to jump."

"Frerotte, I'm sorry. My aunt died in the war. But this is different. Lam was never a military-grade AI."

"Today's civilian AI are twenty times stronger than any program during the war. You don't know what subroutines he's picked up from the Brazilians. It was one thing when he was harassing them. Now he's inside our grid."

"He must have a lot of FNEE data. What if he can lead us to more sunfish or carvings?"

"We need to assume he's a problem until proven otherwise. I'm not saying we have to terminate him. We do need to raise our alert level. Tell Koebsch or I will."

"All right." Vonnie wasn't convinced, but Frerotte had covered for her when Lam was uploaded to the FNEE digger. She owed him.

Calling Tavares would have to wait.

"I'm going to the command module," she said. "Koebsch and I do better in person. Maybe you can listen in and keep him from killing me."

"We shouldn't have let it get this far," Frerotte said. "I never thought Lam would survive over there."

You and Ash decided to sacrifice him to screw with the Brazilians, she thought. *To you, he's a tool. But if he's sane, I can bring him in safely. If he's erratic, I can run my own system checks and help him. Either that or I'll kill him myself.*

"Ash!" she said.

The young woman appeared in the hatch. She was drinking a soup bulb, which she closed as she followed Vonnie into the ready room. "What's up?"

"We're in trouble. It's Lam. I'll fill you in as soon as we're moving."

They opened the lockers to their pressure suits.

As they dressed, Vonnie called back to Frerotte. "What is Koebsch doing with Probes 110 and 11? Are they returning to camp or intercepting Lam's routes toward the sunfish?"

"Right now those are almost the same compass headings," Frerotte said. "10 and 11 need to come toward the surface before they can access the catacombs where Lam will be. That's what they're doing now."

"Can you patch my helmet into your display?"

"Roger that," Frerotte said.

Vonnie felt sure Koebsch would send 10 and 11 to stop Lam from reaching the sunfish before dealing with the possibility that Lam might approach the ESA camp. They were fortified by dozens of mecha, many of which were equipped for electronic warfare. Lam wouldn't dare to face them head-on. He would be obliterated.

Where else could he go?

In all probability, Lam had co-opted 114's mem files when he took control. That meant he knew of the inhabited zones they'd explored during his absence. Did he have any motive for approaching the sunfish? Maybe not. They couldn't predict how he'd act, but Vonnie didn't want him to contact the sunfish on his own. He might upset everything if he was irrational.

"I'm set," Vonnie said. She and Ash were dressed. They buddy-checked each other's collar locks, then cycled the air lock and hurried outside.

After they climbed into the jeep, Vonnie cut her radio in case Koebsch was listening. She tipped her helmet against Ash's. Conductivity allowed their voices to reverberate from one helmet to another. "This is your chance to get into our mainframe," she said. "Koebsch and I need to talk."

"Okay. I still don't know what's happening."

On the ride over, Vonnie explained everything she'd learned about Lam. "The Brazilians have been shooting at him, not sunfish," she said.

"He's been on the run all this time? Jesus. I shouldn't have loaded him into their net."

It was the right thing to say. Vonnie put her glove on Ash's leg and squeezed. "Don't apologize. I'm glad you didn't let Koebsch erase him."

They reached the command module. Ash parked the jeep, and they entered the air lock. It completed its cycle and the inner door opened.

Koebsch stood waiting, his expression flat with displeasure.

"Sir," Ash said, "I came to help with data/comm until we get a handle on things."

"Good," Koebsch said. Then he dismissed Vonnie with a tone obviously meant to chastise her. "Von, you'll have to wait here. Some of our information is classified."

"I can help."

"No. You'll wait." Koebsch watched as they removed their pressure suits. Maybe he wasn't conscious of how hungrily his gaze traveled up and down the women's figures. He'd been celibate as long as Vonnie, and he hadn't found an outlet in dating any of the crew.

She didn't mind his eyes. His interest in her would make it easier for her to distract him. Doing so was cruel, but she couldn't miss this opportunity to steal Dawson's contact lists and mem files.

37.

KOEBSCH LED ASH through the short corridor to data/comm as Vonnie stood at the air lock with her suit in her hands, keeping her head bent to watch her helmet's visor.

Frerotte continued to feed imagery to her heads-up display as 110 and 111 scrambled through the ice. On their perimeter with the Brazilians and near the sunfish colony, their surviving spies had turned to listen for Lam.

How could he have disappeared?

Maybe he'd hunkered down within a short distance of the perimeter, ceasing all external activity. He could be dealing with any number of hurdles integrating himself with 114's data banks. More likely, he was analyzing 114's maps and short-term records, which were new to him.

Koebsch startled her when he returned. "What are you looking at?" he said.

Trying not to look guilty, Vonnie set her helmet against a mag lock on the wall. "Let's go to the armory," she said. "I'd like to talk about our probes' capabilities."

"Finding your AI comes first," he said.

"That's what I mean. I can help. We need to figure out how well he'll operate inside a probe."

Koebsch studied her wordlessly. Then he glanced at her helmet and said, "You're popular with a lot of the crew, Von. Sometimes that's a good thing. But I can't keep dealing with your insubordination."

"Sir, I didn't mean—"

"Have I been too lenient with you?"

"No, sir."

"I considered revoking your status with our mission. You could be in charge of our meals or stay in suit maintenance full-time, something with zero systems access. Your choice. You like to cook. Is that what you want?"

"No, sir."

"Then stop working against me. I need the truth. Who uploaded your AI to the Brazilian digger?"

"I did," she said, selling the lie by holding his gaze. It would be what Koebsch wanted to believe. Anything else verged on a wider mutiny, which would cast him in a bad light as their leader.

"Let's go," he said.

He strode down the short corridor and turned right toward the armory. As she passed data/comm, Vonnie looked in. Ash was speaking to a group feed with Metzler, Frerotte, Pärnits, and O'Neal. "If we move those listening posts, we might be able to triangulate any new activity," Pärnits said.

"Not if he's beneath the rock," Ash said.

Koebsch shut the door to the armory behind Vonnie. The room was a small, crowded box like all of the compartments in their hab modules and landers. Welding gear and nanoforges hung from two walls and the ceiling. Folded into the other walls were work benches, hand tools, sensors, and holo displays.

"We'll tell Berlin it was my decision," Koebsch said. "We used Lam's basic files as a temporary countermeasure against the Brazilians, but somewhere we made a mistake. We included too much of his personality. He persisted instead of fragmenting."

"That's what happened."

"Show me." Koebsch extracted one of the holo displays from the wall. "I want a transcript of every move you made."

"I can't do that."

"Then you're off the team."

"Sir, I logged in through Ash's G2 account and deleted the record afterward," Vonnie said. With each word, she was digging herself in deeper, but the lie was about more than saving Lam. She was also protecting Ash. "Why does it matter how I did it?" she asked.

"You're going to help me write a series of kill codes," he said. "Then we'll broadcast the codes into the ice. We might be able to reach him. But if Lam only hears part of a code, it needs to be specifically tailored if we want it to penetrate his systems."

"This is wrong."

"You can either help me or you're done. I'll see what I can do about getting you a ride home, but we won't be sending a ship back to Earth for another year. That's a long time to cook and fix suits."

"Goddamn it, we don't know what kind of data Lam collected over there or if he's a danger to us! Your kill codes could wipe everything he's seen and heard."

"We'll scrub his mem files after we find him. That's not the issue. If you ask me, I'm starting to think Dawson is right. Our entire operation has become a fiasco. The sunfish are unresponsive. They've done nothing but attack, and now we're chasing our own tails. A change is warranted. We might use your new probes for reconnaissance and gathering tissue samples."

"You can't start hunting sunfish!"

"Our cost sheet is through the roof, and you haven't helped." Koebsch frowned. "I warned you, Von. There are a lot of people on Earth who don't see the magic in this place. They want returns on their investments."

"You don't have to listen to them."

"I can't keep making exceptions for you." Koebsch lifted his hand as if to touch her shoulder, stopped, and set his palm on the holo display instead. "Help me. That's the best way I can cover for you. They understand our little skirmish with the Brazilians. It's part of the price of doing business."

"What about Tom and Sue and the other sunfish we know? You'd let Dawson put them in captivity or vivisect them?"

"There are more tribes down there. If we have some success, maybe we can start over with a new group. First we need that success."

"You mean we need to make money." Vonnie said it with disgust, but he nodded earnestly.

"There are three billion euros tied up in this mission," he said. "It's nice that activist groups are campaigning for humane treatment and rescue operations for the sunfish, but the reality is we've taken too long to show results. We can't pay for ourselves with new deuterium production or bulk water claims. The pay-off is in gene smithing."

I should hate you, she thought. *But I need you on my side.*

She was deciding how to respond when Ash appeared on the small intercom panel. "Sir, I have Colonel Ribeiro online," Ash said.

"I'll be there in a minute." Koebsch looked at Vonnie and said, "This might get sticky. You come, too, but let me do the talking. If Ribeiro knows Lam was ours, he could send his mecha through our perimeter, and we can't stop him—not if he uses gun platforms."

"He wouldn't dare."

"Wouldn't he?" Koebsch opened the door from the armory and paced toward data/comm.

Vonnie followed with her stomach in a knot.

They joined Ash at the showphone. "Thank you, Colonel," Ash said. "Here is Administrator Koebsch."

Keeping his hand below the camera, Koebsch motioned for Vonnie to step into the background. "Hello, Colonel," he said. "You must be returning my call about the FNEE digger that crashed through our beacons."

Ribeiro's face was severe. Remembering how fiercely he'd cursed them, Vonnie expected him to berate Koebsch, but he tipped his head with a single nod. "Yes," he said.

"We lost a tremendous amount of equipment and our geologic surveys were ruined," Koebsch said, piling on the blame. The formality in both men's postures and voices was well-practiced. Everything they did would be analyzed by their superiors on Earth.

"Where is our digger now?" Ribeiro said.

"It self-destructed, either by FNEE command or because its systems were untenable," Koebsch said. "Please explain."

"There has been a rise in ESA transmissions."

"Is that relevant?"

"I am apprehensive for your safety and ours," Ribeiro said. "Are any of your mecha missing?"

"One."

Ribeiro's face tightened. *Here it comes*, Vonnie thought, bracing herself for his wrath.

"We have lost three mecha to a rogue AI," he said. "It captured two diggers, then spread to a third. That is why you've heard combat in our zone. We eradicated two of the three while losing a fourth mecha to an avalanche."

Lam caused more problems than we guessed, Vonnie thought, watching Ribeiro's dark, tired eyes.

The firm set of his mouth gave way to a scowl. Vonnie realized he wasn't fighting to master his temper. He was humiliated.

"I apologize that the AI reached your zone," he said. "The responsibility is mine, but I believe my men and I are best suited to this task. We are soldiers. You are not. I would like to make our services available. I suggest a partnership between your people and mine. We can eliminate the AI before it spreads further."

A partnership? Vonnie thought, scoffing at the idea. She was offended and incredulous.

But Koebsch smiled. "Thank you, Colonel, I agree," he said.

38.

"WE WOULD WELCOME working alongside the fine astronauts of Brazil," Koebsch said. "Thank you for your vigilance and for your willingness to protect your neighbors."

"What are you doing?" Vonnie whispered at Koebsch's back. "We can't let them march into our grid!"

Koebsch shushed her. "I would like to coordinate our mutual efforts immediately," he told Ribeiro. "First, a written agreement is in order."

"My government will need to approve any legal documents, but I have been instructed to ask for your terms and conditions," Ribeiro said. His gaze shifted to Vonnie, then back to Koebsch. What was he thinking? The same as her?

Something's wrong, she thought. *We've been at odds with Brazil since the war. On Earth, we keep backing A.N. demands for them to pull their troops out of Columbia and Paraguay. In space, too many of our ships run patrols with American destroyers as a show of strength against the FNEE.*

Even here, we've allocated hundreds of hours to monitoring them—attacking them—and there are only eighteen people combined between our camp and theirs.

Making a deal with the FNEE was unprecedented.

"I think we can use standard distress contracts including limited liability and salvage rights," Koebsch said. "Within reason, we'll waive any claims for damage if the AI can be contained."

"You are generous," Ribeiro said. "Thank you."

"I'll send a write-up to you in a few minutes. Meanwhile I'd like a proposal detailing the number of mecha you'll send into our grid, their capabilities, and a compatibility study. Will they be able to function with our mecha?"

"My sergeant can provide this data."

"Excellent." Koebsch waved Vonnie toward the showphone, then gestured at Ash. "This is Alexis Vonderach, one of our engineers. You've met Ash Sierzenga. Vonderach can troubleshoot any challenges with signal integration while Sierzenga handles file-sharing on our side."

"The famous Vonderach," Ribeiro said. "You are as beautiful as you are daring, *senhora*."

"*Danke schön*, Colonel," Vonnie said. Inside, she was seething at Koebsch. He'd backed her neatly into a corner, saddling her with a workload that would keep her in his sight for the rest of the day—maybe longer.

She'd imagined she could outmaneuver Koebsch and reach Lam before anyone else. Now he'd put her in position to assist the FNEE hunter-killers.

What kind of directives had he received from Earth?

The next moments were hectic. Moving in a daze, Vonnie took the station beside Ash as Koebsch opened another display, speaking with a legal program. Ash refused to meet Vonnie's eyes, burying herself in her datastreams.

Tavares appeared on Vonnie's showphone and introduced herself as if they'd never spoken. "My name is Sergeant Claudia Tavares," she said.

Vonnie didn't want to put the other woman in a bad spot. "I'm Vonderach. You're coordinating the FNEE response?"

"Affirmative." Tavares was visibly relieved.

"Your mecha still use ROM-4 protocols, correct? Our probes can send and receive those signals, but there will be a delay in translation, maybe as much as two femtoseconds per petabyte. Can you lag your response times to match? Otherwise we'll see progression errors."

"Affirmative."

Most of an hour passed in a rapid exchange of adjustments. The AI of the FNEE mecha were dull compared to those of the ESA probes, but in some aspects, the older, larger machines were also more robust. They were built for abuse.

Far below, Probes 110 and 111 stopped advancing through the ice. Koebsch intended to use their sensors like a fence, preventing Lam from moving any deeper into the ESA zone. At the same time, on the perimeter, 115 decrypted most of its datastreams as it was joined by seven FNEE diggers and gun platforms, allowing the FNEE mecha to share its telemetry.

If the Brazilians realized 115 maintained a private channel inside the ESA grid, they said nothing.

Lam's identity also remained a secret.

Vonnie overheard Ribeiro discussing the AI's appearance in his mecha with Koebsch. "Our analysts found traces of Chinese programming among its defenses," Ribeiro said. "They allow human-based AI in their country, you know, and they told us to stay off

Europa. They deny unleashing the AI upon our systems, but we believe they tried to hamstring us."

"That's not unexpected," Koebsch said. "Your country buys most of its deuterium from China. They want to protect that income."

"They are lovers of dogs," Ribeiro said off-handedly, drawing another smirk from Ash, who covered her mouth by chewing on her thumbnail.

You little sneak, Vonnie thought, not without admiration.

How the heck had Ash made Lam appear like a Chinese AI? Because of his nationality? His original mem files had been based in PSSC ROM-20 protocols, which Vonnie had modified into ESA standard ROM-12 when she assembled him.

Ash could have resurrected his source codes. More likely, Ash had grafted new packets of Chinese code into Lam's menus. The ESA maintained a library of stolen PSSC encryptions, and Ash had proven masterful at subverting AIs. It helped that her equipment was a cut above everything in the FNEE camp. If she'd laced his menus with PSSC recognition codes, Lam must have sounded like he was trying to hide his origin during his first exchanges with the FNEE when in fact he was only writing that code out of himself. Ash had double-crossed the Brazilians and Chinese, leading one to accuse the other...

What game was Koebsch playing at?

From his indignation with Vonnie, he'd expected the Brazilians to blame the ESA. Yet as soon as the Brazilians asked for help, Koebsch offered them an alliance. That meant the ESA leadership on Earth had prepared Koebsch for either contingency. They'd known about Lam through backchannels with Ash or Frerotte.

I thought I was a step ahead of Koebsch, but he's left me behind, Vonnie thought. *Why? Why is it so important to make the Brazilians our friends instead of leaving them in a loose association with the Chinese?*

Down inside the ice, the FNEE mecha crossed into ESA territory. Probe 115 moved with them, then branched away into the catacombs as the surviving ESA spies and Probes 110 and 111 sifted through the ice. They hoped to flush Lam from hiding or to discover his trail.

Near the sunfish colony, the spies registered two flurries of activity—one brief, the other sustained for twelve minutes—but neither was Lam. Both movements were accompanied by sonar calls, and the second included a staccato drumming in the rock. The sunfish were reacting to the mecha invasion.

Other members of the ESA crew appeared on their group feed, indignant and confused.

"Koebsch? Koebsch? Why are there FNEE mecha mixed with our probes!?" Pärnits shouted as O'Neal said, "This goes against everything we've accomplished."

Koebsch shut off access to his station, glancing once at Vonnie. "You explain," he said. "If they want to haggle, that's your job. Tell everyone they can monitor our progress if they want, but no one interferes. Frerotte is in control of our spies. I'm in charge of our probes. That's final."

Vonnie managed to nod. "Yes, sir."

I've never heard him like this, she thought. *He's flattering with Ribeiro and rude with us. He almost seems like he's punishing himself, too. Koebsch might agree with Dawson about changing our approach to the sunfish, but he's loyal to our crew. He hates letting the Brazilians into our grid.*

I need to talk to Ash and find out what's really going on.

The wait was excruciating. Koebsch kept both women at their stations long after Vonnie resolved the progression errors between ESA and FNEE mecha. He made Ash stand by for more file transfers even when Ribeiro said his team was done.

As the FNEE mecha and Probe 115 skittered through the ice, Vonnie worried that a Brazilian gun platform would light up the darkness at any instant, riddling Lam with its 30mm chain guns.

Each of the FNEE war machines looked like a table with eight crab legs and two short-barreled turrets. Ammunition belts sprang from its top in coils sheathed against the cold. The sensor array was small and crude and tucked between the guns. Its legs were sized like those of a sunfish, yet less articulate, with four hinges. Worse, the legs were naked steel and arranged incorrectly in two rows instead of around its circumference. All of these factors would hamper any attempt at communication if the sunfish were unwitting enough to talk to these bulky, jerking mecha, which also carried STAT missile launchers.

A month ago, after erecting their camp, the Brazilians' statement that they'd deployed the gun platforms for self-defense had been absurd. Gazing through the machines' sensors made Vonnie want to punch someone—not Koebsch—preferably the bastards on Earth who'd set the ESA/FNEE union in motion.

The gun platforms' radar was crosshatched by target finding programs that continuously adjusted for range. These were not self-defense mecha. They were weapons.

Vonnie could only try to make sure the gun platforms didn't mistake 115 for an enemy or key on the movements of the sunfish colony. She advised Tavares again and again as their datastreams jumped. "That's not the missing probe."

"Affirmative," Tavares said.

"These blips here are more sunfish. This is Probe 110. This noise is probably tidal cracking around Gas Vent D-7, but let's keep tabs on it."

"Affirmative."

Three hours later, Koebsch dismissed Vonnie and Ash. He transferred their duties to Gravino, the other member of the crew who wasn't a biologist or a gene smith. "Thank you for skipping lunch," Koebsch said. "You must be exhausted. I'll give you an hour off, but then I want you back again for another three. We need to keep the pressure on until we find Lam."

"I'd like to stay, sir," Vonnie said.

"Take a break," Koebsch said. "Freshen up."

"The FNEE need help interpreting our signals. They think everything is a target."

"You did a great job defining our contacts," Koebsch said. "They know where our mecha are situated and the boundaries of the sun-fish colony."

"But if they—"

"Go." Koebsch had control of her station. He closed it. "Get out of here. I'll ping you if something comes up, but this could take all day. Longer. Get some rest. I'll need you to spell me soon."

"Yes, sir," Ash said, tugging at Vonnie's arm.

The two of them left data/comm for the air lock, where they suited up and went outside.

Ash had a data pad in her leg pocket. She showed it to Vonnie, then cut her fingers at her neck to indicate radio silence.

After they climbed into the jeep, Vonnie tipped her helmet against Ash's helmet. "What did you find?" she said.

"You were right about Dawson, and I also pilfered some of Koebsch's orders about the Brazilians," Ash said. "He doesn't want to partner with them. He's under duress."

"I knew it."

The jeep drove through camp. Ash craned her neck to gaze through her visor at Vonnie. "Our agreement here with Brazil allows for new talks between us on Earth," she said. "You have to admit, if we could stop yelling at each other in the A.N., that would be good."

"It would be good for Earth."

"Good for everywhere. We don't need another war. And if there is more fighting, we want Brazil on our side this time—or neutral. Anything to offset the Chinese."

Vonnie stared at her, unable to hold back any longer. "You set this up from the start," she said. "We're going to let them kill Lam just so we can have a job to do together. So we can pretend to be friends."

"I am your friend," Ash said.

"Who are you working for? Really?"

"I'm one of the good guys, Von."

"You used me and Lam. Now the FNEE mecha are getting close

to the sunfish. You know the colony will attack. It's like throwing them into the guns. Dawson will get what he wants."

"That wasn't the plan, I swear," Ash said. "Think about it. If I wanted to capture sunfish, I wouldn't need Ribeiro's crew. We brought our own weaponry. There are eight torpedoes and a maser cannon on our ship, and hand weapons in the armory. We're also packing a quarter ton of excavation charges. If my objective was to take the sunfish by force, I could have made it happen without the Brazilians."

"Then why, Ash?"

The young woman was characteristically blunt. "We lived in London before the war," she said. "My parents owned an apartment up the street from my uncle's house. I had a sister. Three cousins. Only my mom is still alive, and I don't ever want to see anything like that again."

The contempt Vonnie felt began to wane. In a more roundabout way, Frerotte had used the same rationale for his support of the ESA/FNEE partnership. Horror, grief, and the desire to keep other people from suffering were noble motivations to serve.

"My job was to make the Chinese look responsible for Lam, then we'd help Brazil," Ash said. "We thought we'd run a few joint patrols. The main thing is our governments would start talking again."

"But you underestimated Lam, and you didn't anticipate Dawson's influence back home."

"That's right." Ash's gaze was haunted by the admission. "It's not about Lam anymore. It's about the sunfish. Brazil wants access to our site because we found a colony. We want them to do the dirty work so our hands are clean. A rogue AI is the perfect excuse. The point is to make any fighting with the sunfish look like an accident."

"Collateral damage," Vonnie said. "That's what they called London and Paris."

"I..."

"You screwed up. The sunfish are innocent exactly like those civilian populations." She was being harder on Ash than she'd been with Frerotte, but she thought Ash would rise to the challenge.

She was mistaken.

"I fulfilled my orders," Ash said. "It's better this way. Brazil's gene smithing programs are crap like their cybernetics. They need us. We need them. If we can establish a science program to develop the sunfish DNA together, we'll have a long-term investment in each other. We can bring them to our side."

"What about the families you'll kill?"

"They're aliens, Von. People come first. Why can't you see that? I want to save people first. I'll always save people first."

Ash leaned back, pulling her helmet from Vonnie's. It was an effective way to have the last word, but Vonnie rocked forward in her seat. Trying to catch Ash's gaze, she realized that during their conversation, Ash had drawn her data pad from her leg pocket. Had she intended to share Dawson's files? If so, she seemed to have changed her mind. Ash gripped the data pad in both hands, turning her body to protect it, and Vonnie worried that she'd lost Ash as a friend.

Everything's coming to a head, she thought. *Ribeiro. Dawson. Ash. Lam.*

Is it still possible for me to protect the sunfish?

39.

THE JEEP SLOWED near Lander 04, and Vonnie looked at the sky. As an astronaut, she was accustomed to feeling satisfaction for the spacecraft overhead and grudging acceptance for the spy satellites. One came with the other. The need to guard against opposing nations was a fact of life.

Now we're importing all of our problems to this world, she thought. And yet without those problems, humankind wouldn't have traveled so far into the solar system.

They weren't angels. They were apes. It was mutual suspicion and the hunger for power that drove their species to new technologies.

Every advancement in spaceflight had been steeped in an arms race. Germany's rockets in World War II begat the Soviet sputniks, which begat the American moon landings, which begat the ICBM standoff between NATO and the USSR, which led to a renaissance in global communications.

Briefly, there was peace. But the eyes in the sky continued to improve, aiding the technological nations in a hundred brush wars against men who used caves for fortresses and waged terror attacks on non-military targets to remain relevant.

The eyes combed the globe for patterns and clues. The ears listened. Smart bombs, drones, and robots entered the world's battlefields as humankind's first artificial intelligences.

The chess board of today's political backdrop had started with another Cold War between East and West. Even before their third revolution, the People's Republic of China had been on a path to usurp America as Earth's foremost superpower.

In 2028, a military coup reversed China's gains in freedom and democracy, channeling its economic might inward, then upward. In 2031, the People's Supreme Society sent a mission to Mars as a stunt, beating Europe and America to the red planet. More significant, they'd constructed a permanent station in low Earth orbit as a launch facility for their Mars craft.

Within five years, there were two stations. Within ten, there were six. They also built a Lunar outpost.

Beijing paid top salaries for Asia's scientists, bringing its sharpest minds into their heartland. They bought cheap labor in Thailand and Kampucheah. They won their border conflicts with Vietnam, then rotated their best generals, techs, and shock troops into orbit.

Old treaties mandated that space must stay free of nuclear weapons, but warheads were unnecessary to disturb the balance on Earth. From orbit, a dumb, simple chunk of iron could act as a missile. It needed to be meticulously aimed, but it could deliver the same yield as a nuke without radioactive fallout.

The debt-ridden Western nations couldn't leave China alone in space. They screamed for more laws. They passed new sanctions and denouncements. In time, they ejected China from the United Nations—yet they had no choice except to follow the People's Supreme Society up from Earth's surface.

The race to claim Earth's high ground included new developments in quantum computing and artificial intelligence, which led in turn to long-awaited breakthroughs in cold fusion. Green economies created surpluses in the West.

Meanwhile the world's computer systems continued to grow and transform. Feinting at each other, stealing codes, infecting their enemies and being infected, they made each other smarter.

In space, Europe and America were pulling even with the People's Supreme Society when Chinese SCPs stuttered through their defenses, turning off the lights and freezing their missiles in their silos. It was meant to be a death stroke: a one-minute war. Instead, American memes returned the favor, masking Chinese data/comm with false signals.

Both sides opened fire.

Too many missiles went for soft targets.

On Earth, seven hundred and fifty thousand people were vaporized because the AIs thwarted each other, muddling the coordinates for military installations with electronic umbrellas. They routed their weapons toward less-protected sites to chew away at each other's capabilities.

On the outskirts of the cities, another two million people were blinded and maimed by the fireballs. Neither side won World War III. The armistice led to the creation of the new Allied Nations and the promise to keep war from Earth forever, but it was the West that had absorbed the most devastating losses. The People's Supreme Society remained the leading force in the solar system, reining in allies like Iran and Brazil.

Vonnie supposed the current political climate was another reason Bauman had won her role as commander of their expedition. The Americans, like Europe, were desperate for any gain in status, whereas the Chinese probably felt that chasing bugs was beneath them. Until they'd discovered the carvings, China had graciously permitted lesser nations to lead the science team in exchange for a bit of international goodwill.

Ash would have been a baby during the missile strikes. She couldn't possibly have personal memories of her lost family members, although from what she'd said, she'd grown up in their absence with a grieving mother.

In her soul, maybe she was looking for something she'd never known. Likely her formative emotions as a child had been survivor's guilt and anger. That explained how Ash could be obsessed with politics instead of seeing what was right in front of her, and yet Vonnie refused to give up on their relationship.

The jeep parked. Vonnie clunked their helmets together. "We're working for the same thing," she said.

Ash was confrontational. "I don't think so."

"We both want to protect people."

"Being buddies with the sunfish isn't important. Not compared to national security."

"They're part of our future."

Ash scoffed in Vonnie's face. "You want to make them citizens? You really are crazy."

"Don't be stupid. The sunfish couldn't handle Earth gravity. We're not bringing them home. But you can't ignore them. The sunfish won't disappear because you've got your truce with Brazil, and you don't want China to build allegiances with the tribes first—not if that puts China ahead of us in bioresearch."

Ash paused. She frowned and said, "I'm listening."

"We're behind the curve on finding Europan lifeforms, not just sunfish, but everything else that should be in the ecosystem. China didn't blow the hell out of their zone like Brazil did. That noise affected our territory, too. Now Brazil's mecha are closing in. Our sunfish are on the move. If they don't run, they'll attack."

"That means we'll have our tissue samples."

"But it's a one-time gain. What if there are other, more useful species farther down in the ice? The sunfish could be our guides. They could defend our probes. Christ, if they were willing participants, they could teach us everything we want to know about their life cycle."

"We..." Ash glanced at her lap, then looked up with new resolve. "You should see Dawson's mem files. There are three aspects of sunfish physiology that are particularly viable."

"I believe you. That doesn't mean we should give up on communicating with them."

"It's too late to call off the FNEE mecha."

"What if I find Lam?"

"Can you? I changed him, Von. If you wrote any back doors into his programming, those codes probably won't function anymore."

Shit, Vonnie thought. She'd intended to alter her kill codes to act as slavecasts, compelling Lam to quit hiding. They could track his signals, pick him up and extract him before he—or the Brazilians—went deeper into the ice.

"I want you on our side," Ash said. "The FNEE incursion is going to happen, but maybe we can minimize the danger to the sunfish. They respect strength. You said so yourself. A few of them will get hurt, but the rest might stop and listen. You can help us."

Us, Vonnie marveled. Ash, Koebsch, and Dawson were all on the same side now.

She couldn't fight everyone. She thought Pärnits and Metzler were with her. They were the pure scientists, but the rest of the crew were likely more interested in developing their partnership with Brazil or in securing the genetic material of the sunfish. Those interests made for strange bedfellows.

If Vonnie didn't want to find herself without any clout whatsoever, she needed to bargain with Ash, so she stiffened her voice with just the right blend of reluctance and disdain.

"I'll help you if you help me," she said. "I want to know what Dawson wants."

"You can't stop him."

"I know." Had she spoken too fast? To convince Ash, she added, "If there's any chance of saving the sunfish, I need a better feel for what kind of tissue samples he wants, which sexes, how many different individuals, et cetera."

"Okay." Ash studied Vonnie's eyes. Then she looked at her data pad and activated it, unlocking several files before her index finger traced backwards abruptly.

Did she delete one? Vonnie thought.

"I don't have all of his files," Ash said. "Some were too well encrypted even for me, but listen to what he says, Von. Really listen."

"All right."

"If you're honest with yourself, I think you'll realize Dawson's heart is in the right place."

"Dawson's heart is a bank account."

"He'll be rich and famous, absolutely," Ash said as she held up the data pad. "He's also going to do a lot of good things for people. Our people."

Then why do I feel like I'm dealing with the devil? Vonnie thought. *I guess that makes Ash the devil.*

40.

VONNIE TOOK THE data pad and Ash clapped her glove on Vonnie's leg, an authoritative gesture like a judge banging her gavel to seal an agreement.

"Don't hate me," Ash said.

"I don't."

"Von, you couldn't fake how you feel if your life was on the line. Don't ever play cards. That's my advice. I know you're cross with me, but you have to believe me when I say I want to be on your side."

"You did what seemed best to you. You shouldn't feel bad."

"That's not what I meant."

"Let me watch Dawson's files."

"I don't feel bad," Ash said, still protesting.

"I need a few minutes."

"Fine." Ash left the jeep and stalked toward the lander, radiating a puzzled hurt with her tight, brisk, scissor steps.

Vonnie smiled sadly, feeling branded by her own guilt. She'd definitely found the Achilles' heel in Ash's toughness. Friendship might be new to a girl trained almost from birth to rely solely on her mother, then an agency handler. Vonnie would have bet her teeth that Ash's boss was a woman. Her personal history was too ripe. Her boss would use her dependencies as a goad and a leash.

I want to be her sister, not her mom, Vonnie thought. *She needs positive influences, not another commander. She'd reject me if I tried. But I think I'm getting through. Otherwise we wouldn't have felt so stung by each other.*

Nearby, Ash walked up the lander's steps and touched the air lock controls. The exterior door opened. She bolted inside.

Vonnie looked at the sky again, wishing they didn't need to spend so much energy manipulating each other. She plugged the data pad into a jack in her wrist. Her visor brought up a short menu of sims. The time stamps ranged from six days ago to yesterday.

She opened the first file, which had been recorded from Dawson's view of a group feed with fifteen people on Earth. Vonnie didn't recognize them. The sim didn't include a company patch, but Ash had filched their identities by using voice keys and recognition software. She'd superimposed names, titles, and bio links.

Ten of the strangers were mid-level executives with LifeNova, a prominent Dutch health services corporation. The rest were gene smiths. *Got you,* Vonnie thought, contemplating their faces with cool malice.

Dawson was making a presentation. Two of the boxes in the group feed flickered with datastreams as he lectured. At the same time, the execs and gene smiths on Earth posted questions in an ongoing scroll. Their comments were out of sync with Dawson's speech due to the lag in radio transmissions, but they'd uploaded an AI to his side to manage their remarks.

As the sim began, the AI said, "Why would that be true?"

"The sunfish appear more closely related to their primordial ancestors than we are to our predecessors on Earth," Dawson said. "Bacteria like thermophiles and lithotrophs—heat lovers and rock eaters—were the earliest lifeforms on both worlds, but life on Europa appears to have made the leap from single-cell organisms to higher lifeforms in a shorter span. That's how the sunfish maintained the ability to use iron to survive. Iron is one of their most prevalent catalysts."

The AI highlighted a manager's comments. "Less technical, please," it said.

"Hydrothermal vents were probably the first environments to generate life on Europa," Dawson said, "and volcanic eruptions release dissolved iron onto the ocean floor. Higher lifeforms like the sunfish retained that affinity for iron, but they can't have more hemoglobin than us. That would turn their blood into sludge. They'd be too likely to die of strokes and heart attacks. So they use a mutated hemoglobin. It has extra iron atoms and additional twists compared to ours, which allows it to bond with a greater concentration of oxygen molecules."

"Again, less technical," the AI said.

Dawson was triumphant. "If we can fashion the same hyper intense hemoglobin in human beings, it would mean increased stamina and acuity, especially in combination with a second aspect of sunfish physiology. You'll need both to reach the fullest potential."

"We've arranged to negotiate your contract," the AI said.

"I want royalties in addition to a secured position with your laboratories," Dawson said. "In two years, every police force and military in the West will be using this gene tech. In five, it will be in construction and sports. I want a percentage."

"We will pay a flat fee."

"Nonsense."

"We will absorb the legal costs. We will absorb the research, development, manufacturing, and marketing costs. Your compensation is a flat fee in addition to a salaried five-year contract with option to renew."

"I'm the one skirting federal law."

"We recognize the risk inherent in your position and will reward it," the AI said.

"Perhaps you'd name an amount."

The AI superimposed two lines of text on the group feed, numbers that must have been predecided on Earth: **€1,000,000.00 bonus, €325,000.00 annual salary.**

Dawson's composure slipped. His eyes widened and his nostrils flared. Then he reverted to his normal mannerisms as a gentleman. "We can discuss this further without the AI," he said smoothly. "I guarantee you'll be impressed with my work."

"Explain the second half of your proposal," the AI said.

"Indeed." Dawson opened a new datastream. "Sunfish are able to maintain body temperatures above that of the surrounding water or atmosphere due to a complicated heat exchange system between their muscles, digestive system, and blood vessels. They conserve and store heat like batteries. In duress, they release it. By raising their internal temperatures, they create spikes in reaction time. The heat also allows an increase in the absorption of nutrients. Combined with their mutated hemoglobin, these factors provide them with 'burst speed' like tigers or sharks, except that the sunfish are able to sustain these bursts far, far longer than any Earth equivalent."

"You're in possession of intact sunfish for our labs?"

"I will be," Dawson said.

Vonnie shut off the sim. She'd seen enough. She tucked the data pad into a leg pocket and left the jeep, retracing Ash's path to the lander.

The sim couldn't have been more damning. Dawson's attitude toward the sunfish was based on raw arrogance.

How did he intend to get past the government's claim on Europa? Was that what the LifeNova executive meant by 'legal costs'? The ESA wasn't equipped to design biotech on par with treatments developed by private corporations. Berlin could profit handsomely by licensing the rights to sunfish DNA, gaining much-needed cash which could be fed back to select companies in exchange for cutting edge, clandestine military applications. One hand washed the other. That was how society functioned.

Vonnie climbed onto the lander's deck and whacked her fist against the control panel for the air lock, opening the exterior door. She stepped in, then cycled the lock.

I'll give Dawson one chance to back off, she thought. *Not for his sake. For the sunfish. It doesn't sound like Koebsch or our top management will stop him. Swearing to cause a public uproar is the best shot I have left.*

What if they call my bluff?

The inner door opened. Vonnie stepped inside the ready room and removed her pressure suit. Metzler ducked through the hatch as she stowed it in its locker. "Hey," he said.

Vonnie took his hand and squeezed. "Ben, you're who I think you are, aren't you?"

He tried to joke. "Am I?"

"Do you work for anyone besides the ESA?"

His bulldog face turned serious. "I'm with you," he said.

Vonnie squeezed his hand again. "We have one more thing to do that'll get us in trouble," she said.

"Fabulous." His tone was happily sarcastic. He kissed her cheek, and Vonnie turned to bring his lips to her mouth. Metzler hadn't shaved since she'd seen him hours ago. His beard was dark sandpaper. The stubble felt rough and exciting.

Inhaling sharply, Vonnie broke their kiss. Holding him, she whispered her plan.

"I'll do what I can," he said.

"Let's go."

In the next compartment, Ash and Frerotte were locked in an argument behind a privacy screen, but he deactivated it when Vonnie entered. Ash turned and left the compartment for their living quarters, avoiding everyone's eyes.

"Where are the FNEE mecha?" Vonnie asked.

"Closer by the second," Frerotte said. "They'll reach the sunfish colony in an hour if they're not attacked."

That's why Koebsch relieved me, Vonnie thought. *He wanted me out of the way, where I couldn't interfere. He wants a fight. If the FNEE and our probes are bloodied together, that will be another bond between us.*

"Where do you stand?" she asked Frerotte. "Do you support Koebsch on this?"

"It's... not fun to take. I've been fighting Chinese and FNEE assets most of my life, but Ash is right. The greater good comes first. If we can jockey an alliance with Brazil, we might get our troops out of Argentina and Ecuador. The Americans could stand down in Panama. We have to look at the larger picture."

"Then you don't want to be a part of this call," Vonnie said, activating her station. She held Ash's data pad in her free hand. Before she turned it on, she added, "Thank you for helping me with Lam."

"You're welcome," Frerotte said.

His station was busy with 3-D maps of the ice and Brazilian mecha. He stepped into his display as Vonnie raised her own privacy screen. Metzler took the station beside hers, and she expanded the privacy screen to include him.

From the data pad, she selected an image from the sim of Dawson's conversation with the LifeNova execs and gene smiths. Then she entered Dawson's crew code.

The old man answered with his false smile. "To what do I owe the pleasure—" he began. He glanced at the image behind her, taking in the labeled faces of the LifeNova personnel, but his recovery was swift and he chuckled. "I was told those broadcasts were encrypted, but this changes nothing."

"I thought you were offended when I asked if you'd been offered a fat salary," Vonnie said.

"I was. I am. Money isn't why I'm doing this."

"Really?"

"God's truth."

"You looked pretty excited when they offered you a million right up front."

"The corporate brass don't give credence to any project unless there are sums on the table, Von. It's a show of integrity, that's all."

"'Integrity.' She laughed at him. "The public won't see things that way. It looks like you sold out the biggest discovery of our lifetimes for your own gain. It looks like money is the only thing you want."

"Are you implying there will be a scandal?"

"Indeed," she said with all the venom she could muster. "Do you know how many people logged onto petitions calling for equal rights for the sunfish? If what you're planning with LifeNova gets out, there will be lawsuits and boycotts—"

"Your information is out of date," Dawson said. "I wondered why you used an image from the LifeNova board. They withdrew their bid days ago."

"It's the same whoever you're working with."

"No, it's not," Dawson said.

Beside her, Metzler tapped her hip and indicated his display. He'd been speeding through the other sims on Ash's data pad. Now he slid three new images to her station. Ash had labeled the men and women in these group feeds, too. They worked for Japanese, French, and American interests—private gene tech companies like LifeNova.

Vonnie shared the new images with Dawson and said, "You've been shopping for the highest price. You're a liar and a mercenary."

"You're a fool. Who gave you those sims?"

"If I go public, I can make your life miserable. You'll spend years in court. Activist groups will stalk you forever. You know how rabid some of them can be. You won't be able to show your face online without someone hacking your feed or launching homemade SCPs.

They'll crucify you. That's not the kind of attention any corporation wants."

"On the contrary, it's splendid publicity when the lunatic fringe resorts to violence. Are you done with your little intimidation scheme?"

"Somebody will stop you. Too much of the world believes the sunfish are intelligent."

"The world wants what we can deliver."

"Super soldiers and athletes are nothing new, Dawson. We don't need to kill sunfish for that kind of gene tech."

He cocked his head, examining her. "Indeed, our military is interested," he said. "I've encouraged the appropriate parties to take notice, but heightened speed and reflexes are secondary applications. The real promise is in longevity treatments."

Life extension, Vonnie thought, staring at the old man. "Go ahead," he said. "Shout to the news feeds that we're developing sunfish proteins and DNA. Who doesn't want to live another fifty years? Our research will lead to spectacular breakthroughs in reoxygenating aged tissues, organs, and bone marrow."

"But you'll kill sunfish to do it."

"You only seem to have one note to play, Von. Move past it. I'm acting with the knowledge and support of Berlin, Washington, and Tokyo. If things progress as anticipated, we'll include Brazil in our consortium soon enough."

Ash warned me, Vonnie thought. *Damn it.*

There must have been sims of Dawson talking with government agencies as well as private gene corps, but Ash hadn't been able to crack those files. If she had, would it have made any difference?

"This isn't over," Vonnie said. "I want to talk to your contacts in Berlin or I'll make as much noise as I can. Tell them! You don't need living sunfish. We can find intact specimens frozen in the ice. It's asinine to ruin the progress we've gained with the local colony."

"You're incorrect," Dawson said. "Dead sunfish won't have the metabolic activity essential to our research. If they're decomposed or

crushed, they'll be even more useless. There are also political considerations you're missing."

"I know we want to work with Brazil. That doesn't mean we
can't conduct search and salvage—"

The floor vibrated.

"What was that?" Metzler said. A delicate bass roar filtered
through the lander. *Oom.* The sound was as ephemeral as a thought,
but it repeated itself twice as the floor shimmied again.

Boom. Oom.

Alarms filled Vonnie's station with red bars. The same alerts
flashed on Dawson's screen, creating a haze of targeting systems,
threat analysis, and hull integrity checks. As his gaze flickered
through the data, Dawson's expression was pleased.

"You bastard," Vonnie said.

Frerotte issued a Class 2 alert, overriding every data/comm channel in camp. "We're tracking explosions almost directly below us at
a range of two point three kilometers!" he said.

Vonnie couldn't access the links between the ESA and FNEE without Koebsch's authorization, but she was able to open the datastreams
from their spies near the sunfish colony. The spies' radar signals were
obstructed by tons of rock and ice—but using sonar, the spies were
able to draw crude sims to estimate what they were hearing.

Each explosion washed through the sims like an eraser, blanking
parts of the spies' calculations. Between these waves, the spies traced
a maelstrom of gunfire, lesser vibrations, electromagnetic activity,
and ultrasound.

Vonnie watched in anguish as small dots pounced at two bulkier
outlines. The spies identified the larger shapes as a digger and a gun
platform.

Twenty sunfish swarmed the rock overhead, screeching as they
dodged twin streams of gatling fire. They were trying to pull down
a section of the roof.

The Brazilians anticipated it. Their mecha spun aside as three
packs of sunfish shoved chunks into the floor. The digger slapped two

sunfish from the air with its cutting arms. Seconds later, the gun plat-form caught the groups above. The *thunk thunk thunk thunk thunk* of its bullets striking the rock turned to wetter, plopping sounds as seven sunfish came apart.

Vonnie put her hand over her mouth. On her display, the sunfish and the mecha were monochromatic outlines. But when the dots rep-resenting the sunfish shattered, she remembered the visceral shock of blood and entrails.

The sunfish were dying.

Dawson wins, she thought. *It's happening. Oh God, it's happen-ing exactly like he wanted.*

She'd tried everything to keep her people on course. From the beginning, their mission's objectives had been science and diplo-macy—good, intellectual goals separate from the myopic demands of Earth.

Until this morning, she'd thought she was succeeding in bring-ing the FNEE to her path. She'd thought they could move forward together. But even here, they weren't far enough from their past. Maybe they never would be. The angel strived for better, but the ape corrupted.

Once again they'd invented the destiny they wanted with their fear and their greed.

The human race had found a new war inside the frozen sky.

41.

THE FIGHTING ESCALATED as a third FNEE mecha plunged into the fray behind the sunfish, barricading any retreat. It was another digger. It cut one sunfish with its legs and swatted two more with its cutting arms.

Before the digger leapt at the rest of the sunfish, it wedged an excavation charge into the cavern wall. If shoving the explosive stick into the rock made any sound, the noise went unheard beneath the gunfire, but the ESA spies picked up a new radio signal between the digger and the charge. The spies traced it to its source.

"They're going to blow the cavern if they—!" Vonnie quit shouting when she turned her head.

Frerotte had altered his display to show Koebsch's link with the Brazilians, revealing their sims. Had he forgotten his privacy screen or had he purposefully shut it off?

Beside Vonnie, Metzler had accessed a different datastream, scrolling through the ESA beacons and listening posts. What was he looking for? As Vonnie stared, Ash sprinted into the compartment and took her station. Somehow that broke Vonnie's spell.

"We need to jam the FNEE det codes!" she said.

"You can't interfere," Frerotte said, but he allowed Vonnie to clone his display.

She swam through fifty reports salted with white noise. FNEE sims were poor compared to ESA sharecasts. The Brazilians' mecha-to-mecha radar targeting included a half-second lag, which left false images in their net. Their diggers tended to stab at sunfish who'd moved farther than the mecha anticipated, whereas the gun platform overcompensated, leading its targets too far.

The lag was increased by modifying FNEE signals into holo imagery for the benefit of human controllers. Vonnie needed five seconds to pinpoint the active key among a myriad of *inventory, select, arm,* and *detonation* codes, partly because the writing was in Portuguese.

In that time, another sunfish died. Two more scored hits against the digger, bashing its sensors with rock clubs.

One of those sunfish was Sue. Clinging to the digger with four arms, she stretched and contracted and stretched again, hammering her primitive weapon on its gleaming alumalloy skin. For an instant, Sue seemed to have stunned the machine.

The digger shrugged her off. It tossed her into the wall. Simultaneously, it stabbed up with its arms, slicing open the belly of Sue's companion. Then it advanced on Sue.

Run! Vonnie thought. She reached for the FNEE det code, hoping to countermand it—

—and the digger decided it was clear of the blast zone. Its telemetry winked. The charge exploded, bringing down two hundred meters of rock in a shuddering chain reaction. Rubble clanged against the digger. The machine stumbled, lunging through the ricochets and blowback.

Where was Sue?

Dead and wounded sunfish mingled with the rock. The digger snared two small, twitching bodies as it clattered from the avalanche, then squeezed them tight against its underside. It rejoined the battle, using its arms to chase a third sunfish toward the gun platform.

The chain guns fired. The sunfish fell. The digger also took five rounds, which killed one of its captives in a splash of blood. The mecha looked pitiless, but Vonnie knew there were human beings behind every decision.

Who was controlling the FNEE gun platform? Ribeiro?

Ash was equipped to stop them. If she hacked into the FNEE grid, the combat would end—but the young woman's face was like stone. She'd become the strict, sober Ash again, not the secret friend who'd whispered and laughed with Vonnie.

That left Metzler and Frerotte. Frerotte had said he wouldn't interfere, and yet in the same breath he'd given Vonnie access to the ESA/FNEE command feed. Part of him must be glad to see the Brazilian mecha destroyed. Would he help her?

"The FNEE used the noise of their guns to conceal the second digger's approach," Vonnie said. "My guess is the rest of their machines are closing fast."

"Leave them alone," Ash said.

"Can our spies generate sonar calls for the sunfish? If we locate the other mecha, the sunfish might run before they're boxed in."

"Don't do it."

Vonnie snarled at Ash with bitter reproach. "You have your

specimens and your alliance with Brazil. You don't need to kill the whole colony, do you?"

"Hey! Enough!" Metzler said. "I have some funny readings from our spies."

Vonnie glanced at the sims he'd posted on her displays. While she was bickering with Ash, Metzler had aimed thirty percent of their spies away from the battle to scan the surrounding area. New blurs of motion and sound were rapidly approaching the fight from below.

"Those aren't FNEE diggers," Vonnie said.

"No," Metzler said.

Is it Lam? she thought. The signatures were too varied. The blurs weren't a single entity. Forty distinct contacts bunched and spread and revealed eight more behind them, threading through the catacombs in packs.

"It's the larger breed of sunfish," Frerotte said. "Our spies recognize the ultrasound."

Vonnie smiled a thin, savage smile.

Earth was so far removed from this moon, the men and women who'd given the orders to approach the sunfish had yet to learn the results of their operation. The radio delay meant several minutes would pass before the politicians and gene corps personnel knew if the mecha had been successful. But they must be happy. They must have congratulated each other on arranging the charade between the ESA and the FNEE.

It wasn't fair. They were comfortable in their board rooms and offices. They had unlimited luxuries and the promise of years more of the same. Their homes weren't being invaded. Their families weren't under the gun.

Vonnie imagined them casually checking their datastreams. Would they even bother to look at the reality of their crime? If they found it distasteful to see the guts strewn across the cavern, they could turn off their displays. They could count their numbers instead: how many sunfish captured; how many bodies secured; their stock projections and trade agreements.

I hope the sunfish rip you apart, she thought.

They should have realized other tribes would come. The larger sunfish had heard their cousins screaming. They'd smelled blood and wounded prey. Had they brought every warrior in their colony?

"Tell the FNEE to get out," Metzler said.

"Too late."

Metzler looked at her with embarrassment and determination. "If the mecha set more charges, they might be able to seal themselves off from the larger sunfish," he said.

Frerotte opened a channel to Koebsch. "Sir, there are more sunfish closing on the FNEE mecha—the larger sunfish. I count forty-eight or fifty-two."

Koebsch nodded. His face was harried. "Let me patch you to Colonel Ribeiro," he said.

"Yes, sir." Frerotte tapped at his display, adding the spies' data to the ESA/FNEE command feed. Through a short audio malfunction, Vonnie heard a blip of male voices shouting in Portuguese. An AI in her station automatically translated Ribeiro's words: "Regroup. Regroup. Where is Platform 2?"

Their melee with the smaller breed was winding down. The gun platform chattered once more, nailing a wounded sunfish digging pitifully at the cavern ceiling. The intact digger pursued four sunfish to the wall, catching three, pummeling them, but the slower, limping digger dropped its specimens to enact repairs on its breastplate.

The gun platform sidled toward the digger to assist. The mecha hunched together like living animals, although the illusion faded when they extended micro arms and a welding torch between them. All three mecha were splattered with gore and dust.

"Contact in ninety seconds," Frerotte said.

"I'm picking up another group of lifeforms approaching from the south," Metzler said.

"More sunfish?" Koebsch said.

"Too soon to tell."

You wanted a goddamned war, Vonnie thought. *You're about to get more than anyone expected.*

Her eyes brimmed with tears. She couldn't bring herself to look at Ash. Instead, she counted the dead sprawled throughout the cavern, mourning each of their nimble little shapes. Her AI had identified Sue among the corpses.

"There's a third group in the area to the southwest," Metzler said. "This one is moving away from the battlefield."

"Let me see," Vonnie said.

Beyond the end of their maps, west of the coordinates where they thought Sue and Tom's colony was situated, vague rustles of movement led away into the ice. There were no sonar calls mixed with the activity. The smaller sunfish were operating with as much stealth as possible even if moving by feel and scent hindered their escape.

"They're evacuating," Vonnie said with relief.

"They might be flanking the mecha or trying to intercept the larger sunfish," Frerotte said.

"Not likely. Too much of the rock collapsed in the blasts. The FNEE only left a few ways in or out. None of those openings connect with the colony."

"I think Sue led a diversion," Metzler said. "Her pack went after the mecha to buy the others time to get away. If Sue won, they'd come back. But they heard Sue's pack dying, and the blasts were too close to their home."

"The whole region is unstable now," Vonnie agreed, highlighting the spies' radar. "We might see a wider collapse."

"Fifteen seconds," Frerotte said.

The FNEE mecha separated from each other. The two diggers hurried to form a triangle with the gun platform, protecting it on either side.

Metzler posted sims of the three separate contacts around the mecha—the smaller sunfish in flight—the approaching swarm of the larger breed—and the third, unknown group of lifeforms, who were also closing on the scene. As he sifted through his data, the spies recorded sonar cries from the third group and tagged it: *Sunfish, Breed II.*

"More of the larger kind," Vonnie said.

Were they from a new colony or were they a hunting party rejoining their tribe? They were well-positioned to head off the smaller sunfish, but they did not angle toward their fleeing cousins. They dropped through the catacombs toward the mecha.

"They're confronting the loudest enemy instead of the easier prey," Metzler said. "Why?"

The FNEE gun platform opened fire as eight sunfish sailed into the open. Its twin guns traversed from low to high. Ribeiro had anticipated the sunfishes' tactic of bouncing off the floor and ceiling.

His foresight was effective. 20mm rounds pierced the sunfish, killing six. The two survivors didn't fly much longer. The gun platform crossed its fire again, winging both. One sunfish was dashed against the rock. The other spun backward in a veil of blood.

"Like shooting pigs in a farmyard," Ash said.

Vonnie turned to bark at her, but what was the use? *She has to believe they're just animals,* Vonnie thought. *Otherwise we're murderers.*

A second wave leapt into the breach. FNEE radar counted twenty-eight sunfish. Their small bodies rocketed through a new pattern, four high, four low, twenty bouncing sideways or straight at the mecha. Most of them hurled rocks as they jumped, adding to the bedlam in the air.

The gun platform overreacted. It centered its fire on the upper part of the storm. Its programs surely included AMAS surface-to-space defense systems. By default, it considered the overhead targets most critical.

It shot three sunfish and nine rocks unerringly. Then the sunfish in the lower half of the wave reached the diggers. More sunfish entered the cavern as the mecha flailed at their small adversaries— and when the diggers were enveloped, the gun platform raked its fire over the diggers and sunfish alike.

Ricochets sprang from the diggers' alumalloy frames, shredding sunfish, annihilating a digger's gear block. Bullets careened from metal and rock like high velocity hail.

The digger slumped and went down in a heap of bloody sunfish, kicking as it fell.

They're winning! Vonnie thought, feeling sick and exultant. The cost to the sunfish would be staggering. Dozens were dead. But they were winning.

Four sunfish reached the gun platform. They clubbed its eyes. They screeched in its ears. The gun platform reeled from the disruptions, unable to track its targets or to process new commands. Vonnie cheered silently.

Beside her, Metzler uttered one sound. "Christ."

A second FNEE gun platform waddled into the cavern through the gaping fractures left by the explosion. Behind it lurched another digger. Too many of the sunfish were engaged with the original mecha. They launched themselves at the new gun platform, but they were too far away.

It squeezed off eight controlled bursts. With each burst, a sunfish died. Then it swept its guns across the cavern, concentrating on the biggest groups.

That quickly, the tide was turned. The new gun platform cleaned off its brother. It freed the battle worn digger.

Working together, the two gun platforms wasted every living thing in sight, firing continuously until a meter-long slab dropped from the ceiling and two hunks crumbled from the walls.

The roar of the guns couldn't mask the high-pitched screams as the last sunfish cavorted and dodged among the ruptured bodies of their tribe.

There was no mercy offered except to a few crippled, spasming sunfish. Some individuals could barely raise an arm in self-defense before the FNEE diggers collected them, gumming up their wounds with foam spray, binding them in wire. Many others were left to bleed out.

"I can't watch," Metzler said, raising his glove in front of his eyes. Then he dragged his arm laterally. He wiped the FNEE sims from his display and turned his attention to the sharecasts from the ESA spies.

Surreptitiously, Vonnie instructed her station to copy the FNEE datastreams. She could broadcast the massacre systemwide. Billions of people would be outraged... and yet... and yet the gene corps and the politicians had what they wanted. Worse, they could claim they were innocent. The sunfish had attacked them, not vice versa.

At least it's over, she thought. But the activity in the ice wasn't done.

"Oh no," she said, reacting to an alarm.

The second pack of sunfish—the group who'd elected not to pursue their smaller cousins and hurried toward the mecha instead— were about to make their own appearance on the battlefield. There were sixteen of them. They had no chance where fifty-two warriors had failed.

42.

"WE NEED TO stop the sunfish or Ribeiro," Vonnie said. "There's no excuse for more killing. Ash! They have all the captives and tissue samples they need."

"I can't make the sunfish go away," Ash said stubbornly.

"What about sonar calls from our spies? Anything. Maybe we can distract them. They might recognize a warning."

"Got it," Metzler said, but Frerotte acted first. He uploaded their linguistic databases to the spies, selecting a short menu of sunfish calls. "Here," Frerotte said.

The spies mimicked Tom's screech from his encounter with Probe 112. Pärnits believed the sound was a challenge and a boast that Tom's tribe was a ferocious entity. Unfortunately, the spies relied primarily on radar and passive sensory arrays. They weren't designed to transmit signals other than encrypted data/comm, so their sonar was short range.

Frerotte shook his head. "The spies probably aren't loud enough. I'm not sure—"

The new sunfish changed course, swinging away from the FNEE mecha. As they did, they piped and shrieked at the rock separating them from the blood-soaked cavern.

Were they sounding out the mecha? *Not with so much rock between them,* Vonnie thought. She believed the sunfish were teasing their enemy, trying to provoke the machines into rushing after them. Was that to set an ambush? Did they plan to bring a tunnel down on the mecha?

The sunfish dove through the catacombs, taking one, two, three turns to maintain the same heading. They were moving in the direction of the ESA spies.

"They heard us," Vonnie said.

"Did they?" Metzler asked. "They're trending toward our spies, but there's another place they could be going. They must know where to find Tom and Sue's abandoned colony even if they've never been inside it."

"You think they always intended to run for the colony."

"Yes. Our AI tagged something weird in the FNEE datastreams. This group is exclusively male. From their size, they might be immature males."

"But the smaller breed evacuated," Vonnie said. "There's nothing in the colony."

"Maybe the smaller sunfish left their old and wounded behind," Metzler said. "There might be farms. This is the larger breed's chance to raid the place."

"Smart," Frerotte said.

"Raccoons and dogs raid garbage cans," Ash said. "I'm sorry. Dawson's right. Nobody with any brains sends unprotected troops at a gun emplacement."

"We employed 'human wave' tactics in World War One," Frerotte said, coming to Vonnie's aid again. "The Americans did it at Gettysburg. The Chinese nearly won the North-South Korean War with mass infantry charges."

"That's different," Ash said.

"Is it?"

"Those soldiers carried weapons."

"The sunfish used rocks like shotgun fire," Frerotte said. "They tried to bring down the ceiling again. You can't fault them for not having our technology. The Zulu overwhelmed the British Army using spears and human waves."

Why are you helping me? Will you keep helping me? Vonnie thought as she waited and watched.

The sunfish were masters at feinting, traps, and decoys. Their lives were an endless game of hide-and-seek, so why hadn't they gone after their smaller cousins instead of attacking of the mecha? Because they'd been drawn to the carnage on the battlefield? They might have hoped to find the mecha weakened by their cousins, then destroy the machines themselves, claiming all of the dead for food.

Did they realize the mecha weren't living creatures?

How intelligent are they really? she thought, feeling a pang of doubt. Ash had raised an excellent point. Frontal assaults on a gun platform would have resulted in heavy casualties for armored human commandos. The sunfish tribes had lost more than fifty lives. Twenty more had been wounded and captured. That wasn't intelligent. It was unreasoning instinct.

Metzler saw her eyes and said, "Von, they couldn't have understood what they were getting into. They've never met war machines."

"They fought me. They should know what machines can do."

"That was probably a different tribe."

"They're drifting out of range," Frerotte said.

"I wish we could piggyback a spy onto one of the sunfish," Metzler said. Blatantly trying to ease the tension, he added, "I'd give my left testicle to see what's inside the colony. Are there pools? Beds? Maybe it was a penthouse."

"Let's reconfigure 4117 through 4124," Frerotte said. "We should be able to track their sonar calls if we don't lose them behind the thermal vents. At least we can map a few spaces inside the colony."

"Good." Metzler touched Vonnie's arm. "The more we know, the better chance we'll have with the next tribe," he said.

If there's another tribe, she worried, but she kept her concern to herself. She didn't want to sound negative when he was giving his best.

The people on Earth will think they won today, she thought. *They'll order new missions. Then our mecha will chase the sunfish from every safe zone inside Europa, stealing DNA and mining the ice—*

"Holy shit," Metzler said.

His soft, ominous tone roused Vonnie from her despair. She glanced through the spies' datastreams. She sat up straight when she saw why he was afraid. "Koebsch! Koebsch!" she yelled as Metzler struck a Class 1 alert.

"What are you doing?" Ash said.

"Frerotte, get our surface mecha away from— No, wait! Have them drag the hab modules out of here!"

"Roger that," Frerotte said.

Ash frowned, skimming through their defense grid. "I don't see..." she said.

Vonnie almost laughed at the irony of Ash thinking like the FNEE gun platform, looking skyward first. How long would it take before people learned to evaluate this environment like its natives?

The sunfish had bypassed the tunnels where their smaller cousins had built the retaining wall. They'd gone lower, missing likeliest spots for an air lock into the colony. Vonnie had supposed they were lost or hunting blindly. Now she zoomed her display as the sunfish clumped against the steep side of a ravine, joining their bodies into one immense muscle.

"They're tearing at the hot springs," Vonnie said.

Koebsch appeared on the group feed, projecting calm with his open hands. "Let's not panic," he said, studying the sims from Metzler's display.

The spies' telemetry showed only blurs and reconstructions.

"The sunfish are too far away," Koebsch said. "You can't be sure what they're doing. They could be digging a new entrance into the colony."

"No, sir," Vonnie said. She and Metzler took several images from the sims, letting an AI enhance each frame with preexisting data from their listening posts, their spies, and their probes.

During the past weeks, they'd mapped the local web of heat branching up from the mountain into the frozen sky. Its topmost reaches were the melted ice and cooling gas pockets west of the ESA camp. Further down, liquid water collected in shafts and lakes. Lower still, hot springs boiled from the rock, providing the colony with warmth and nutrients.

It was a powder keg.

Day by day, the ice dripped and slumped, blocking the vents. The rock eroded and did the same. Mostly the water and gases burned through, but sometimes geysers were plugged or gases were backed up, perturbing the live magma deep within the mountain.

"We've mapped two of the main conduits for the hot springs that feed Tom's home," Vonnie said. "Both rise through a trunk of compressed rock about fifty meters beneath the tunnel where they built their retaining wall. I think they've been repairing the trunk for years."

"That's why there's a stream down there," Frerotte said, identifying a current of noise beneath the louder, crunching sounds of the digging sunfish. "There are leaks spraying from a cliff face."

Metzler had run his own calculations. "The pressure must be enormous," he said. "Those hot springs push up through 2.4 kilometers of rock and ice, and that's just at the top where we can see. The network of gas and heat is more extensive. If they tear into the rock—"

"They wouldn't," Ash said. "They'd die."

"That's not going to stop them," Vonnie said. "That's why their pack is all-male. They're expendable."

"We need to get this lander off the ground," Metzler said.

They were connected to auxiliary structures like the jeep charging post and the maintenance shed, which accessed Lander 04's power and data/comm. They should have installed an auto detach, but no one had imagined the old vents could become active in a matter of minutes, not the mission planners on Earth, not the crew on Europa.

"I'll tell the mecha to cut us loose," Vonnie said.

"What about everyone in the hab modules?" Ash said. "We can't leave them."

"We'll lift them clear."

"They should drive over."

"We don't have that much time. They're better off inside their modules than a jeep if we— Oh!"

The floor heaved as their displays turned white. The spies' sensors had overloaded. The last images were of the sunfish peeling a hunk of rock from a damp cliff face.

A tsunami of broiling water, gas, and rubble shoved through the team of sunfish. It flash fried them. It ground their corpses to bits.

The tunnel containing the spies erupted next. Their telemetry shut off, but Frerotte had duped the command feed from the FNEE mecha, which lasted seconds longer.

Steaming water drowned the war machines and their captives. It shoved the floor of the cavern into the ceiling. Then the mashed remains were swept away. Two of the FNEE mecha issued damage reports as they tumbled with the cascade, rising toward the surface at speeds exceeding seventy kilometers per hour.

On top of the frozen sky, Lander 04 tipped again, conveying some of the violence beneath the ice.

Vonnie's display became a liability, dizzying her with static and dead links. On the group feed, Koebsch yelled as Command Module 01 tipped over, jerking loose from its mooring cables. A data pad spun into his head as meal tubes and a jacket fluttered past.

"Pressure suits! Pressure suits!" he shouted.

Vonnie grasped her chair, steadying herself as Metzler and Ash ran to the ready room. If all of them went at once, nobody could suit up, so she stayed. Frerotte did the same. They hung onto their stations as the floor swayed.

"Exterior cams," she said.

Her display flickered with various camera angles across camp. As always, most were radar or infrared signals modified into holo imagery.

Their mecha rolled past the stationary listening posts toward the hab modules. Someone had also given evacuation commands to their jeeps, which turned on their headlights. The first vehicle began to drive.

Much closer to Lander 04, three mecha approached, obeying Vonnie's order to disconnect the lander from the maintenance shed and the charging post.

Gouts of opaque dust and gas spurted from the surface, blasting the mecha. A crack opened ahead of them. Two dropped out of sight. In the minimal gravity, the third mecha lifted on the billowing gas, but the crack opened wider than the deluge could carry the machine. It dipped like a kite and vanished.

Six listening posts and a storage container disappeared as the surface split in a dozen places. Segments of ice plummeted away. Others tilted and bashed together.

Plumes of water vapor mushroomed into the night. Astonishing formations of ice crystals zigzagged above the camp, popping and spraying like gossamer rain. The haze obscured their satellite imagery. Then it actually touched the satellites, spilling up from Europa into naked space.

A black maw took Hab Module 03. Suddenly the rectangular trailer was gone, dragging the cables of its jeep charging post after it.

"Pärnits!" Vonnie gasped. She looked for him among the group feed, but 03's data/comm shut off.

Beth Collinsworth was in there, too, she thought. The linguists had plastered the walls of their lab with a thousand holos of carvings and sunfish, trying to memorize hundreds of combinations of shapes. They were batty, fun geniuses, and they loved their job.

"Can you give me any projections from our listening posts!?" Vonnie shouted at Frerotte. "If the quakes are over—"

"It's going to get worse before it stops."

"Von! Von! Frerotte!" Ash screamed from the ready room. "You need your suits!"

"Oh shit." Vonnie twisted herself out of her seat. Leaving her station, abandoning Pärnits to his fate, took more self-discipline than she could bear.

Wobbling with the lander's floor, Vonnie bruised her elbow on the hatch. She welcomed the pain. Unfortunately, Frerotte was behind her. He fell and slid into her foot, knocking her onto his chest. Outside, ice rang against the lander's hull like gunfire.

Ash hauled Vonnie to her feet. She wasn't wearing her helmet. She held a spare suit over her arm and said, "I'm sorry! I'm sorry!"

"Where's your helmet?"

"Here!" Metzler yelled. He was fully suited. He extended a helmet to Ash as Vonnie took the suit on Ash's arm. She sat down and stuffed her feet into the pant legs, not bothering to remove her clothes or to connect the sanitary features.

The four of them were thrown in a pile when the lander seesawed. Frerotte stood up first, bleeding from his mouth.

Vonnie shoved her arms into her sleeves. "The only mecha that can reach us are busy with Module 02," she said. "I'm going outside."

"That's crazy!" Metzler shouted. "Von, you can't—!"

"Let her go or do it yourself," Frerotte said. "We need to take off before we fall in like 03."

"They're gone!?" Metzler shouted. But he squared his shoulders and said to the women, "You're the pilots. You stay."

Vonnie bustled past him toward the air lock. "Ben, I can cut us loose before a stupid biologist figures out which end of a wrench works best."

She forced a smile as she said it, wanting to kiss him. Instead, she seated her helmet on her collar assembly. She selected a tool kit and emergency pack from the wall. She opened the pack. She grabbed a wad of flexiglue suit patches, which she stuck against her chest, where she could find them easily. Then she turned to Ash.

"Start your preflight," she said.

"I..." Ash's face was a wretched mask.

Vonnie opened the inner door to the air lock, stepped in and cycled the lock. As she waited, the floor tipped wildly. She crashed on her knees.

Were they sliding into the ice?

43.

THE EXTERIOR DOOR opened. It let in a burst of ice shards and dust. Vonnie protected her visor with her gloves. Something the size of a dinner plate caromed off her ribs, but it was mostly air, not solid ice. Otherwise it might have cut her in half.

As she stood, her boot slipped on a hardening sheet of moisture. Everywhere the air swirled with fog and invisible fingers of gas.

Spotlights winked a few hundred meters to her left, where mecha tugged at Module 02, increasing the distance between it and her lander. Ejecta smashed down like cannonballs. Vonnie clutched at the tether reel mounted by the door. The tether was intended for extra-vehicular activity in space, but she clipped the line to her waist. She waded down the lander's steps into the hurricane, where she stumbled and fell.

She crawled forward with the tool kit in her fist. There was no way to grip the ice. It shuddered and dropped and slammed back into her shins and elbows.

Maybe it wasn't so strange that she clung to the sunfishes' behavior as her example. She drew courage from their heroism.

They chose to die for their tribe, she thought. *Their assault group was a test. They knew the machines had killed the smaller sunfish. When their own warriors failed, the second group sabotaged the hot springs like they were arming a doomsday bomb. They wanted to stop the mecha before their home was threatened, too. They sacrificed themselves.*

Her tether vibrated like a harp's string, tugging at her waist. Somehow she reached the maintenance shed. She considered opening her tool kit, but the wobbling ice threw her off-balance. She would have lost any tools in hand. It was all she could do to hold onto the kit, using its plastisteel case like a bludgeon against the data/comm and power couplings.

The data/comm line separated easily. The power line was bolted to the shed. Vonnie was in mid-swing when her tether snapped tight and yanked, hurting her spine.

As she turned to deal with it, something bit through her left arm. She never saw the object. She didn't look. Her life shrank down to the slobbering, howling gash in her sleeve.

Her air cylinders roared through her helmet and chest pack, attempting to compensate for the puncture.

It was her blood that saved her. The fluid acted as a partial seal, freezing inside her sleeve. She also might have gained a second due to the gauzy clouds around her. The water vapor and gases created a denser-than-normal atmosphere. Even then, the partial vacuum of Europa's surface was so cold it burned like a branding iron, disintegrating her skin, ruining her muscles and bone.

Vonnie bent her bad arm to her chest and clamped three patches on it, creating a lumpy, half-solid ball of hemorrhaging flesh and glue. Her air cylinders redoubled the roar of oxygen.

She didn't think. She moved. She added another patch to her arm. She keyed no-shock from her helmet dispenser. Then she looked for her tool kit and went back to work, banging at the power line as if freeing it could save her from her agony.

The coupling broke. The line sparked in her face, and Vonnie scrabbled away from it with her throbbing arm.

Thoughts and emotions began to return. She raised her head to look for the jeep charging post. Its mass was much less than that of the shed, which was why she'd made it her second target. If necessary, Ash could lift off with the post hanging from the lander's side. The flightcraft had plenty of thrust. The question was if Ash was pilot enough to compensate for flying off-balance.

"Ben? Ben?" Vonnie called on her radio. "I can't find the post!"

No answer.

"Ben!"

She groped at her wrist controls, wondering if she was on the wrong frequency, but she couldn't touch her arm without keening like a dog. Her eyes didn't want to stay on the read-out, which was obscured by blood and glue.

More quakes buckled the ice. Rising on her good hand and knees, Vonnie caught a puff of crystals across her shoulder. She ducked and crept alongside the lander, trying to get her bearings. Was she going the right way?

A monstrous shape reared above her in the storm.

She thought something had come out of the frozen sky—a new lifeform—a rhino or a dragon that had been tossed from the ice. It was five times larger than a human being. Its teeth glinted like steel.

Screaming, she clawed sideways. She intended to hide beneath the lander until an orange light on her wrist flashed with a familiar homing pattern. One, two, three, blank. One, two, three, blank.

The monster was their jeep. The spikes on its back were radio antennae. Its 'teeth' consisted of the bars and pods of its forward sensor array.

Vonnie choked and laughed, nearly hysterical. She rammed her head against the lander's underside as she emerged, but she forgot her fear when she discovered she could stand. Were the quakes subsiding or was that wishful thinking?

She peered through the eddies of fog. Belatedly, she realized walking was so difficult because the surface canted up thirty degrees. Ahead of her, one of the lander's grappling hooks had gouged the ice, preventing the lander from sliding more than a few meters. The jeep shared their strange angle, and the ice jutted up behind it for fifty meters.

That was where the surface ended. They were on a broken slab of ice. Vonnie glanced over her shoulder to measure the slab in the other direction.

The maintenance shed had vanished. The edge was four meters away. She couldn't see more than jagged ice and shadows.

How far would they drop if the slab went in?

All around her, other blocks had capsized or tilted or sunk. Many were adhered together by smoother bumps of water that had shot from the ice, then solidified. Gases and vapor continued to waft up from the shattered plain. Module 02 was farther away than it had been, towed to safety by the mecha, but everything between 04 and 02 was gone.

Vonnie hiked toward the jeep. Why hadn't Ash lifted off? Because of the charging post?

Wheezing, she sagged after a few steps. The jeep eased toward her as if wanting to help, then stopped. Was it damaged? She assumed it was trying to respond to rescue commands from Metzler or Frerotte. Why couldn't she hear them?

In her exhaustion, she seized an idea.

I don't need to reach the charging post. I can order the jeep to ram into it for me.

"Jeep Four, where is your post?" she murmured.

It didn't answer. Nor did its homing signal change. That meant it recognized her suit, but it hadn't heard her voice.

Idiot, she thought, staring at her mangled arm. She hadn't switched on her radio before she ran from the lander. Now she activated it to a blare of voices.

Ash yelled: "We're not leaving her, Koebsch! The jeep is balancing us!"

Vonnie felt a fresh swell of nausea when she realized what would have happened if she'd been able to give her orders to the jeep. *I can't move it. Its weight might tip the slab. They're using it to stabilize the lander.*

"I'm going outside," Metzler said as Koebsch yelled, "Four of us are missing or hurt! The last thing we need is more casualties!"

"This is Vonderach," she said by rote. Then, with more feeling, she added, "Take off."

"Are you all right!?" Metzler shouted. "I'm coming outside!"

"No. Take off. My tether's attached."

"You'll swing into the jets!"

"Reel me in. The ice..."

It creaked. The slab was tottering.

"I'll get her," Frerotte said. "Ash, hit the jets. Low power. You keep our adjustments to the jeep."

The last remark was aimed at Metzler. Vonnie understood his words that well. Then she coughed blood onto the inside of her visor. Spluttering, she coughed again. *My side?* she thought, tracing the worst pain to her ribs.

She grayed out.

When her mind sharpened again, she was shuffling on her knees and her good hand, following her tether as it pulled at her waist. Someone was yelling. Frerotte. He was either cranking the tether reel manually or from inside the lock. Inside would be smarter, where he was protected from eruptions and shrapnel.

Each breath was a chore. The pain made her hurry. The pain lessened when she kept pace with the tether, allowing hints of slack in the line. At some point, she'd broken a rib. The bone must have nicked her lung. Only the no-shock and her adrenaline had kept her from noticing.

Vonnie found herself at the front of the lander. The tether had brought her back. She needed to climb the steps and she'd reach the air lock—

—but she screamed when the horizon flipped, pivoting the ice beneath her—

—as she whacked into the steps—

—and rose with Lander 04 as it hovered over the abyss. Below her, the jeep dropped away. Something else flopped toward the lander's belly. It was the charging post. It swung into the invisible exhaust of the fusion jets.

Vonnie couldn't see most of what happened. The lander's steps and armored skirt concealed its fusion jets, where the post was vaporized in a searing blue-white flare. She blinked and blinked and couldn't regain vision in her left eye. Radiation burns cooked her feet. Dangling from the harness felt like being impaled on a sword, and she oozed tears that tracked up her forehead into her hair.

Losing consciousness would have been a mercy. But she fought. Trying to right herself, Vonnie squinted with her good eye as the jets tore into the ice below, buffeting her with freezing water vapor.

Normally their landers had deployed foil shields for each lift-off, preserving the ice. Now there was nothing to spare, although Ash banked around the center of the massive hole, where lights stabbed up from the debris or glowed beneath the surface.

Vonnie glimpsed a listening post and the gray corner of a metal structure. "I have a visual on Module 03," she groaned.

Ash cried on the radio: "Von! Von!? Are you there!?"

"...yes."

"I'm putting us down! Wait for me! Von!? I'm putting us down in thirty seconds!"

She really is sorry, Vonnie thought distantly. Maybe she smiled. She wanted to smile. She'd saved her friends. That should count for something, but she ached. Her body had been beaten, gashed, baked, and chilled. It was impossible to feel anything except her misery.

They left the chaos behind. Glancing back, Vonnie saw an oval-shaped canyon with a separate, smaller sink hole to one side. The canyon was at least two kilometers long and half as wide. It had swallowed most of the ESA camp.

"Maps," she whispered.

Through the gore on her visor, her display awoke with beacons and data/comm. Module 02 was safe. Several supply containers and Module 01 also remained on the surface, although 01 laid on its side near a cliff.

Their other flightcraft, Lander 05, was among the survivors. It took to the air in a white gust and crossed toward 01 instead of attempting to latch onto 03.

"Why..."

The low-level AI in her visor responded to her disoriented stare. It coupled her display of the battered ESA surface grid with threat analysis from ESA and NASA satellites.

Growing fractures cleaved through the ice beneath Module 01. Soon the cliff side would give way. The crew in Lander 05 were evacuating Koebsch before he toppled into the devastation with 03.

There was ongoing activity beneath the ice. Geysers and hot gas continued to erode vast pockets in the pit. There would be aftershocks.

Heedless of their own vulnerability, squads of mecha tugged at Modules 01 and 02, dragging the modules westward. Other mecha trundled across the ice. They formed chains into the pit. Already the mecha were evaluating the debris. Welding torches licked at the shadows, fusing the ice into pathways and bridges.

New pain woke Vonnie from her dream. Her harness pulled on her waist and her legs clunked against the underside of the lander's steps, folding her over her broken rib.

Frerotte leaned over her, but his voice seemed to come from far away. "Can you hear me?"

He was attached to his own tether. He hefted Vonnie from the steps. Their lander was still in the air, although it was sinking toward an open, solid plain.

"Clear! We're clear!" he shouted.

Another white cloud exploded beneath the lander as they touched down, scorching the ice.

Frerotte unclipped Vonnie's line. Up the steps, the exterior door of the air lock stood open. Frerotte jogged inside with her limp body in his arms, smacking her helmet against the wall as he punched the controls. "Fuck! Fuck me! Are you—?"

"Aft.. shocks..." she slurred.

"We know. It's okay. We know."

The inner door opened. Metzler was waiting. He helped Frerotte set her down. It felt like the lander had taken off again. Vonnie wasn't sure if the feeling of acceleration was real. Her thoughts rose and fell in waves.

Pleasant feelings brought her back. A gentle warmth coursed through her body. She was on the floor of the ready room near the hatch to data/comm, where Ash was shouting. Vonnie remained blind in her left eye, but she saw Metzler and Frerotte had stripped off her pressure suit and the jump suit she'd worn inside. A medical droid hung between the two men where it had extended from the ceiling, connecting her heart, neck, wrists, and stomach to emergency systems.

Nanotech and optimized blood plasma fed through her veins from subdermal packets and intravenous lines. The frostbite in her arm felt like simmering oil. The radiation burns on her legs felt like snow. Everywhere her nerves sang and twitched.

"Another quake dropped the west side of the pit!" Ash yelled as other voices shouted from their group feed:

"The mecha lost visual on 03—"

"—no beacons or—"

"—secure 02 if you can."

"I need help up here!" Ash yelled. "Ben, she's tied in! There's nothing more you can do!"

"Go," Vonnie muttered, trying to sit. She winced at the pain in her ribs and feet, but the wounds were manageable now. "You two shouldn't..."

"Your arm is bleeding," Metzler said.

"You shouldn't play doctor with me while I'm unconscious. Where are my clothes?"

"She's fine," Frerotte said with a fierce grin. He clapped Metzler on the shoulder, shoving him toward data/comm. Metzler's eyes were round with terror and affection, but he left.

Vonnie listened to them as the jets thrummed.

"Ben, load these sims into your scout suit," Ash said. "You might have to cut off 02's war pods if we can't wedge it into our cargo lock."

"Roger that," Metzler said.

"Ribeiro's reporting backwash through the FNEE grid," Frerotte said. "This thing was huge."

"They swore they'd send mecha to help us," Ash said.

"There's a FNEE lander in the air and a few rovers coming across the surface," Frerotte said. "I'll coordinate. Koebsch is over the pit with 05. It looks like they're trying to shoot a harpoon into the ice."

"How far down is 03?" Metzler said.

"Beacons put them at half a kilometer and sinking fast," Frerotte said. "They lost pressure six minutes ago. No radio or data/comm. It doesn't look good."

"Von, you've got to move!" Metzler shouted. "I'm coming to armor up!"

He ran through the hatch. Vonnie scooched on her hip in a web of IV lines and monitors, freeing the space near their scout suits. She felt more coherent. She grimaced as she tallied the deaths among her people and the sunfish.

We'll dig for 03 if it takes forever, she thought. *We'll start again. But we've lost so much.*

The sunfish lost even more, but the floods will harden into a solid layer between us. The new ice might be two or three kilometers thick. By the time we get back through, they'll be long gone. Won't they?

They gave up their home. We gave up two people.

Despite everything, her crew had underestimated Europa again. The sunfish had won after all.

For now.

44.

SEVEN HOURS PASSED before they recovered Module 03. Working with Koebsch, Gravino had attached a line to the module ten minutes after the catastrophe, but the harpoon tore loose in the first aftershocks. Then the module was pulled deeper. Nearly all of their remaining mecha disappeared in the new quakes. The rims of the canyon collapsed, taking the mecha into the pit, where the ice sluffed away like sand in an hourglass, backfilling the rifts beneath the surface.

Swimming against the sinking avalanche, nine mecha reached safety where the flood had created solid blocks. Twelve more were submerged, yet pried themselves loose and resumed tunneling toward Module 03, fusing the ice wherever possible. The rest of the machines were completely buried, yet remained operational, continuing to function as radar and sonar arrays.

With so many mecha taken by the disaster, the ESA possessed a disorderly spiral of assets down through 1.8 kilometers. Metzler and Frerotte were able to develop sims predicting the next aftershocks.

In a sense, they were fortunate. The new layer formed by the blow-out was a foundation that wouldn't allow the surface to crumple further. The ice needed to settle, but it should protect them from new cataclysms. Metzler thought the sheet would redirect any currents of water and gas laterally.

Magma was a different hazard. If the quakes had opened new fissures, chain reactions of fire and gas might consume the ESA and FNEE camps. It would be years before this region was stable again.

Vonnie prayed the sunfishes' work had been well-measured. How accurate were their perceptions of the reservoirs they'd unleashed and the volcanic activity within the fin mountain?

The larger sunfish might have destroyed Tom's home as an acceptable price for eradicating the mecha, but she didn't believe they would have fricasseed their own tribe in the bargain.

Lying in her blood on the floor of the ready room, she imagined the flood must have waned before it spread to the colony of the larger sunfish. Maybe a few had suffered scrapes or bruises. Their cartilage skins were so resilient, their bodies so flexible. If the water had cooled, none of them had been boiled to death. They could breathe underwater.

As long as they climbed from the deluge before it froze again, the tribe would persevere. That meant their suicide squad had been fairly certain how the hot springs, ice, quakes, and magma chambers would interact.

Was that possible?

They've survived down there for tens of thousands of years, she reminded herself, blinking and struggling to keep her head up as the warm feelings in her body turned to lethargy.

She didn't remember sleep. She was still fretting when she woke in her bed in Lander 04's living quarters, her wrists and stomach connected to another med droid.

A display had been unfolded from the wall. It provided her friends with a camera to watch her while she slept. One of the windows in the group feed showed her rubbing her cheek before she realized the bleary-eyed woman was herself, although most of the windows in the group feed were blank. She could only see the people inside Lander 04 with her.

She'd missed most of the rescue. Someone had told their AI to sedate her so they could carry her from the ready room. Leaving her unconscious had also permitted the med droids to operate on her face and her legs, replacing her left eye and disturbing amounts of marrow, muscle, and skin.

Her eye socket felt gritty and too sensitive when she skimmed her display, where Frerotte had posted a summary before he instructed the AI to wake her.

There was also more conversation than usual in the next compartment. The voices weren't from a group feed. Ash had taken O'Neal and Johal on board. None of them would reoccupy the hab modules until they were positive they'd located a safe place to camp, if there was a safe place. Until then, the crew would remain with their two flightcraft.

Lander 04 sat on the ice three kilometers east of the pit. Its jets were hot—Vonnie felt the deck humming—and the pilot's command link was designated *Ashley Sierzenga*.

"Hello?" she said, bending her knees beneath her blankets so she could touch her feet. Her toes and one calf were numb.

"Hey, it's sleeping beauty," Ash said on the display as her voice drifted through the hatch. They were three meters apart, but Ash didn't leave the lander's controls. They studied each other on their displays.

Ash seemed jittery and distracted. "How do you feel?" she said. "Can you take my seat?"

"You've been piloting since the blow-out?" Vonnie double-checked her clock. From their initial call to Tavares, to the probes' encounter with Tom's pack, to Lam's assault on 114, to the four hours they'd spent guiding the FNEE mecha, to the battle with the sunfish and its aftermath, Ash had been on duty for twenty hours straight. "I can fly if someone helps me up," Vonnie said. "You should sleep."

"That's not the issue," Ash said, glancing at her own window in the group feed.

What was she looking at? Vonnie noticed a medical alert bar on Ash's display, projecting the limits of her effectiveness.

"Most of us are on stims and no-shock," Ash said. "I'm okay for more, but I need to get outside. I'm the medic. They need me outside."

She's not okay, Vonnie realized. *She's on the verge of a nervous breakdown.*

Staving off exhaustion with chemicals caused elevated blood pressure, slight memory loss, and clumsiness. Other side effects were more conspicuous. During Vonnie's run through the frozen sky, she'd experienced the same obsessive mood Ash was exhibiting now, dealing with her hyper-sensitive state by speaking and acting with careful repetition.

Ash would feel like someone fighting to keep her balance on a high wire. No amount of masochism could atone for her role in the butchery, yet Vonnie knew better than to insist she should rest. Ash would need to ride through the drugs until Koebsch or their med droids shut her down.

Vonnie shifted her legs out of bed. Her left foot was dead from nerve blocks. It felt like a sock full of meat had been attached to her ankle, where the skin was new, raw, and pale. "Where are Pärnits and Collinsworth?" she asked.

"O'Neal, help her," Ash said.

No one answered Vonnie. O'Neal entered the living quarters and knelt to disconnect her IVs.

In his forties, with the physique of a dedicated gym buff, O'Neal was a fussy introvert with big curly hair. Weeks ago, the clash between his personality and his lush mane had perplexed Vonnie until she decided he was acting out against his own subdued nature. She liked him for it.

"Don't take off your monitors," he said, indicating the electrodes on her chest. "Keep your weight off your foot." He took hold of her waist as she crooked her elbow around the back of his neck. Together, they stood and hobbled toward data/comm.

His silence meant the worst. No miracles had accompanied the retrieval of Module 03.

They're dead, she thought, recalling her friend's lean, hawk-nosed face and sly grin. She had just begun to know Rauno Pärnits intimately. He was as educated as Metzler, as devoted, as passionate.

He'd defended the sunfish. Like Collinsworth, Pärnits had reveled in their bizarre language, trading everything in his life for the chance to stand on Europa, listen, learn, and develop roughhewn dialogues with scouts like Tom and Sue. In the end, his own species had been responsible for his death.

Vonnie and O'Neal entered data/comm. Frerotte had the station beside Ash, but he didn't look up, engrossed in a field of holo imagery. Beside him was Harmeet Johal, one of their gene smiths, a dusky woman in her fifties who fit the same bill as O'Neal. She was composed and considerate.

Johal looked like she was supervising mecha with Frerotte. Vonnie didn't see Metzler. Where was he? O'Neal brought her to an open station, where she said, "Maps and grid."

Ash tried to stop her. "Wait."

"I have to see where we are," Vonnie said, dropping into her chair as voices filled her display.

"Ben, stop it," Koebsch said on the radio.

"I won't! I can't!"

The two ESA landers sat side by side on the surface with Module 03, which they'd dragged from the pit. Outside, Metzler and Koebsch were on the ice. They wore scout suits joined to the flightcraft by tethers. Vonnie also saw two more landers nearby, a NASA heavy lifter and a FNEE suborbital fighter, and Koebsch had opened a data link with the Chinese camp. Their neighbors had come to their aid for the duration.

Why couldn't they pretend there was always an emergency? If so, Earth would be at peace. The small, isolated crews of astronauts were proof of humankind's nobility... but she knew Earth's populations were neither small nor isolated.

Later, she would mourn. For now, Vonnie scanned their grid with calculating eyes.

The NASA and FNEE craft were parked six kilometers from the pit, where ESA Modules 01 and 02 had been dropped with nine storage containers and one jeep. The two ESA landers were half that distance from the lost camp. Dawson and Gravino were aboard Lander 05. Gravino had the helm. Dawson was in sick bay. His vitals listed a concussion and a broken wrist. Nano repairs were ongoing to maintain a reduction of swelling in his parietal lobe.

Vonnie wasn't sure how to feel about the fact that he'd been hurt. Should she feel happy?

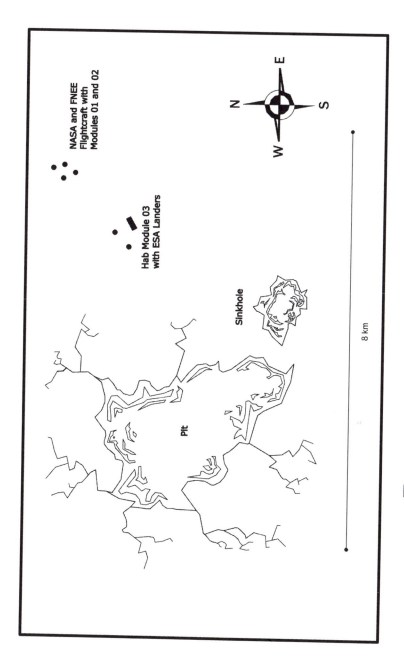

NASA and FNEE
Flightcraft with
Modules 01 and 02

Hab Module 03
with ESA Landers

Sinkhole

Pit

N
W E
S

8 km

Recovering Module 03

To make room inside their landers, she supposed Ash and Gravino could have offloaded her and Dawson to the NASA flightcraft, but the ESA took care of its own.

That's what we're doing now, she realized.

Outside, Koebsch stood at the crumpled box of Module 03 with a squad of mecha, which had painstakingly removed parts of the module's floor. Away from the module, Metzler paced alongside a single mecha carrying an emergency plastic bubble.

Under Koebsch's guidance, the other mecha extended lasers and cutting tools. "Let me concentrate," Koebsch said as Metzler shouted, "We should have left them down there! We should've left them down there like Bauman and Lam!"

Chunks of ice had filled 03 when it was breached. Before the power shut off, some of the ice had melted. Then the liquid resolidified, adhering to the module's equipment, its furniture, and its inhabitants.

They're taking out the bodies, Vonnie thought with pride. *Koebsch is doing the dirty work himself. It's his duty.*

Why are they yelling?

She aimed some of the mecha's sensors to the emergency bubble that Metzler was steering toward her lander.

The bubble held a grotesque shape approximately the same width and depth as the inflatable kids' pool her parents bought when she was five. She and her brothers had splashed in the shin-deep pool for days, tracking grass and dirt into the water, crowding it with buckets and toys. This shape was a lumpy, frozen disc. Bones and clothing jutted from the black ice.

"Oh God."

"Turn off your station," Ash said.

"No," Vonnie said, opening a new comm link. "Ben? Ben, it's Von. I'm here."

Metzler kept shouting at Koebsch. "How am I supposed to fit this thing into the lander? Are you going to thaw him?"

"Ash, I really need you," Koebsch said.

"I'm on my way, sir," Ash said. "Von's awake."

She felt like she was dreaming.

Pärnits and Collinsworth hadn't made it to their pressure suits, although having air wouldn't have mattered. The linguists had been squashed. Their tissues had boiled in near-vacuum, then merged with the native ice.

Strung out on stims, Metzler wouldn't stop raving. "He looks like a fucking pancake! He's two meters wide! The blood—! His body—! He doesn't even look like a person anymore!"

Ash switched off their craft-to-suit data/comm and turned to Vonnie with contrite, downcast eyes. "Take the pilot's seat," she said. "I have to go outside."

"He's right to be upset," Vonnie said.

"He's refusing tranquilizers and he's scaring Koebsch. He's scaring all of us."

"I can help," Johal said, rising from her seat.

"Let's go." Ash sent her virtual controls to Vonnie's station, where the pilot's command designation switched to *Alexis Vonderach*. "Do you see our alerts? Frerotte has an early warning system patched into the AI. We might have thirty minutes before the next aftershock."

"Roger that," Vonnie said.

"Get into the air five minutes before it starts. A mid-range hover is fine. We haven't seen any more ejecta, and the pit hasn't spread. It's just a precaution. We're carrying more people and armor, so 05 will keep a tether on 03."

"Roger that."

Ash stood up, then paused to bring her mouth down to Vonnie's ear. "Skim through our mecha," she whispered. She and Johal walked into the ready room.

Vonnie frowned, but she didn't alter her pilot's display. She was prepared to fly at a moment's notice. What did Ash want her to see? Did she suspect the FNEE rovers were pirating codes from the ESA while they were vulnerable? Vonnie opened new windows on either side of her station, examining the signals from their mecha on the surface.

From the ready room, she heard the assists clicking as Ash donned her scout suit. Johal had taken a pressure suit. Then the women exited. Ash hurried to join Metzler while Johal stayed on the lander's deck, where they'd erected a temporary tent as storage space.

Leaving Pärnits and Collinsworth in the pit would have been cleaner than exhuming their corpses. The ice could have become a mass grave of humans, sunfish, and mecha.

There was a cold beauty in the idea, but they hadn't fallen as deep as Bauman and Lam, and people had trouble letting go of anything that belonged to them. When all was said and done, wasn't that why they'd fought with the sunfish? Because they believed they owned a part of this world after paying for their crews and mecha?

Vonnie needed to convince everyone on Earth to change. It would be several days until they were organized again, maybe longer before they finished their next batch of probes, but they should bring down the food and oxygen they'd originally allocated as gifts. They had an obligation now more than ever.

"The sunfish proved they're intelligent," she said, baiting the men on either side of her.

O'Neal glanced up, but Frerotte doggedly focused on the telemetry from the ESA mecha trapped in the ice.

"They knew what they were doing," she said. "I think they've done it before to seal off air leaks or to separate themselves from an enemy. The larger breed must have scouted the mountain beneath Tom's colony during raids or negotiations. They remembered the weak place in the rock, but they didn't destroy Tom's colony. They saved the possibility for when they needed it. Those aren't the actions of an animal."

"Von," Frerotte said. He and O'Neal traded an uncomfortable look. "During the blow-out, we heard new signals from a safe area west of the flood."

She stared at them, stunned. "What signals?"

"The connection is weak. It's not routing through emergency channels, so I managed to hide it from Koebsch. Then I locked it down." Frerotte tapped at his display, revealing an active mecha 3.6 kilometers from the rest of the ESA machines beneath the ice. "It's Probe 114," he said.

Lam, she thought. *He survived.*

More important, Frerotte's sims had recorded changes in the signal's location. Lam was mobile.

Vonnie leaned forward, grilling both men like she'd caught them in a lie. "You told me Lam is dangerous," she said. "Why would you hide him from Koebsch?"

"Ash wanted to, and I agreed," Frerotte said. He gestured at O'Neal. "All of us did. You risked your life for us when everything that happened... Ash said you're a better person than we are. I think she's right. You're right. The sunfish are intelligent, and we couldn't have screwed up any worse."

Vonnie almost said '*A hundred of them died with our crewmates.*' She almost nodded. Instead, she gave him an excuse. "You didn't cause this," she said.

"Ash and I..." Frerotte ducked his head, leaving his confession hanging in the air.

Nobody works harder than someone trying to make up for accidental deaths, she realized. *They want redemption, like I did.*

"Right now Lam is the last asset we've got," Frerotte said. "If we're going to find the sunfish, it starts with him."

"Then what?" Vonnie said.

"We apologize to them. We try to help."

"Tell me about Lam."

"I snuck some diagnostics into our telemetry. For the most part, he countered with the correct responses. He seems up-to-date on our situation, but he's glitchy. He's hostile. He says he has to talk to you."

INSIDER

45.

VONNIE GLANCED OUTSIDE as Ash walked Metzler to the lander, where his mecha set the emergency bubble on the deck. Talking to him on a private channel, Ash tugged at his arm, urging him to walk into the air lock. He shook her off and marched back toward Koebsch and Module 03.

"Where is Lam in relation to the smaller sunfish?" Vonnie asked.

"He's close," Frerotte said.

"That's why he wasn't obliterated," O'Neal said. "Either he lucked into running from the FNEE in the right direction or he heard Tom's colony evacuating and realized he'd better move with them."

"Let me see your diagnostics. I need your transcripts, too." Vonnie's evaluation was quick. She didn't listen to the conversations between Lam and Frerotte, not yet. She uploaded their files to an AI along with Lam's involuntary, partial responses to Frerotte's diagnostic, then added her own gut hunch to the AI's conclusions.

When Lam transferred from the FNEE digger to Probe 114, he'd reassimilated at an integrity rate of seventy to eighty percent.

"Crap," Vonnie said. "Given the probe's limitations, I'd say the lower score is accurate. Lam won't reach human equivalence again until we can give him more capacity. He's smart, but he'll lack imagination or intuition."

"How about a remote link?" O'Neal said.

Vonnie tensed. Using remote memory to augment their probes with the central AIs in camp had been Pärnits' idea. "We don't have enough relays or spies left," she said. "Lam would need to dig his way closer to us, then stay there, which doesn't do us any good if we want him to approach the sunfish. We have to fix him. Did Ash show you where she stores her back-ups?"

Frerotte touched a menu on his display. "Yes."

"If we can feed him corrective sequences, he might rise to ninety percent. Why didn't you try it?"

"I told you. He's erratic. He's spooked. We only got in a few words before he shut off his data/comm."

"It's been four hours since you heard from him?"

"We didn't want to fake your voice. You two have a lot of history. We couldn't be sure what he'd ask. What if there was a personal reference we missed? He refused to talk to anyone else, and you were in surgery."

"You should've woken me sooner."

"Von, some of your procedures were significant. Did you see your notes?"

"No." She hadn't had the courage to read her summary in detail. She suspected that her left foot and the bones in her calf were transplants from the clone stock preserved in their medical bins. Those organs, limbs, packets of marrow, and sheaves of skin had been vat grown on Earth and were immunologically nonresponsive, which meant her body had a strong chance of accepting the foreign tissues. It meant she wasn't *her* anymore. She was a frankenstein.

Among Earth's spacefaring nations, only the FNEE didn't equip deep-space missions with extra parts grown from stem cells. Even in the twenty-second century, a majority of Brazilians were Catholic. They permitted emergency measures and nanotech, but not clone stock. If one of their astronauts lost a leg, he could be fitted with a cyberthetic, but physical therapy and rehabilitation might take weeks.

Vonnie would walk again tomorrow, albeit with a limp. The low gravity was a blessing. It allowed her nerve and muscle grafts to adapt to her real body without strain.

"Let's get ready," she said. "I want menu options on voice command."

"You got it."

Five minutes passed as Vonnie, O'Neal, and Frerotte arranged for an AI to transmit any corrective sequences it deemed necessary. Lam would operate at speeds beyond human comprehension. Vonnie preferred a manual option to adjust or abort, but in all likelihood, the exchange between their AI and Lam would be over before she noticed any complications.

Outside, their macabre salvation efforts continued. On the lander's deck, inside the temporary tent, Johal warmed Pärnits' disfigured corpse without removing him from the emergency bubble.

The bubble could be deflated. It would become his shroud. They couldn't afford to thaw him inside the ready room and attempt to reform his skeleton and internal organs before burial or cremation. If he spilled, the smell would permeate their air conditioning and someone would need to clean the mess. Koebsch had been firm. They'd treat their dead with as much respect as possible under the circumstances, but they could not contaminate what remained of their living quarters.

Forty meters from the lander, on the ice, Ash stood with Metzler and Koebsch beside Module 03 as their mecha labored to separate Beth Collinsworth from a snarl of torn wiring.

"Koebsch, there's another aftershock building in the pit," Frerotte announced. "You have fifteen minutes."

"We'll be done," Metzler said.

"We won't," Koebsch told him. "Come on. Let's get inside."

"We'll be done," Metzler said.

Vonnie ached for him. She wanted to sit and hold him. She

wanted to make him forget. But she stopped herself from breaking into the radio chatter. She thought some of Metzler's anguish rose from the bond he'd shared with Pärnits as competitors for her love. Their rivalry made them brothers of a kind, which meant her voice would increase his torment. That was why he'd ignored her earlier.

"Ben, get inside," Koebsch said. "The module is tethered to 05. We're a long way from the pit in any case. We'll come back in half an hour."

"I'm not taking off my suit," Metzler warned them.

"None of us will," Ash said. "I promise. Let's just get inside the air lock."

"Johal, you need to carry the bubble into the ready room," Frerotte said on her individual channel. "We don't want Ben to see it."

"Roger that," Johal said. "I need two minutes."

"Negative. They're moving toward you now."

"He won't *bend*, Frerotte. The body's frozen."

"I, uh... I'm sorry. See what you can do."

"*Shukriya*," Johal said scornfully. Vonnie's station translated the word as *Thank you* in Johal's native Urdu. The mild rebuke was as close to acting impolitely as the matronly British national had ever been.

In the ready room, the air lock opened as Johal entered with their makeshift body bag. Outside, Metzler and Ash were approaching with Koebsch, who should have gone to the other lander. He obviously didn't want to leave Ash alone with Metzler, but the three of them would barely fit, and Vonnie couldn't let him see her display.

"If Koebsch comes inside, I need to blank my station," Vonnie said to Frerotte. As the lander's pilot, safety protocols barred her from using a privacy screen. "Can you keep him on the deck?" she asked.

"What would I say? We're taking off."

"He'll be okay if he clips onto a tether. We don't have room for three people in armor, and we need to signal Lam. Every aftershock could drive him farther away. We don't know if the rock's stable down there or not."

"Koebsch will hear your broadcasts."

"Distract him. Ask him to call the Americans."

"About what?"

"Christ, Henri, I don't know! You're the spy. Come up with something." Vonnie glanced at Frerotte with growing anxiety. He hadn't been himself since she'd woken up. He'd been indecisive. He must feel as defeated and worn as Metzler and Ash, whereas she'd gained a fair amount of rest.

"I'll fill Koebsch's helmet with data requests," he said finally. "Can you fly and call Lam at the same time?"

"Yes."

Their sensors indicated Ash, Metzler, and Koebsch were on the lander's steps. Frerotte said, "You two wait in the air lock. Sir, can you stand by on the deck? We're crammed tight. I'd also like to call the Americans again as soon as you're secure."

"Roger that," Koebsch said.

Ash led Metzler into the air lock. They braced their gloves and boots against the ceiling and floor, preventing any chance of banging together during airborne maneuvers.

Outside, Koebsch said, "I'm secure."

"Lift off in four, three, two." Vonnie eased their craft up from the ice, keeping note of Lander 05, which was a hundred meters to starboard.

"Von, it's great to have you back," Koebsch said.

"You hold onto that tether, sir." She let her sincerity show in her voice. Koebsch was a lunkhead, but he meant well.

What would happen if they told him what they were doing with Lam? Would he insist on transmitting his kill codes? Or, if he saw the majority of his crew acting in concert, would he reevaluate their situation?

Frerotte gave Vonnie a thumbs-up before he raised his privacy screen and linked exclusively to Koebsch's helmet, distracting him with updates.

Vonnie nodded, then turned to O'Neal. "Less than three minutes before the quake."

"Corrective sequences ready," he said.

Vonnie raised her hand to a subset of encrypted frequencies on her display and closed her eyes, feeling as if she was sifting through the blackness. "Lam?"

Nothing.

She upped the gain even though she was afraid doing so would attract Koebsch's notice to her transmissions.

"Lam?" she said.

His response was immediate:

—*Von, listen. Don't close me down again, please.*

Her eyes opened wide as her adrenals spurted, poisoning her body with an old, insidious terror. It was the same plea he'd repeated again and again during their first hours together.

They'd come full circle. All that remained of him was the fragmented personality she'd constructed after Bauman died with the real Choh Lam.

46.

"I WON'T HURT you," Vonnie said as she gestured for O'Neal to launch their corrective sequences. "You and I are friends. Remember?"

—*Yes.*

A low hiss of static crackled through his broadcast. Lam was far away, separated from her by unknown lengths of ice and rock. "Are you somewhere safe?" she said. "There's going to be another quake in forty seconds."

—*How many?*

"Thirty-five seconds. Are you safe? Rock should be more sturdy than ice. High ground is better than low."

—*I'm experiencing skips in my short-term memory.*

Vonnie frowned at the non sequitur. "I can help you determine where you are, but you need to upload your transcripts," she said.

—Negative. If I increase my bandwidth, your SCPs will get through.

Vonnie muted her station and looked at O'Neal. "He's on to us," she said. "Did we make any headway?"

"None of our sequences are complete."

She reopened her microphone. "Those weren't SCPs, I swear it. I can help you. We have your original mem files."

Silence.

The ice rumbled. Outside, below, Vonnie watched as Module 03 trembled and slid. Their mecha clung to the surface. Inside the frozen sky, two of the beacons shut off, crushed by blocks of ice. Another reported a new flow of slush and water as a river broke open above it.

Frerotte leaned out of his privacy screen, murmuring to Vonnie and O'Neal. "Looks like that was it. There may be another quake in ten minutes. Koebsch wants to stay in the air, okay? We need more time to back-and-forth with NASA and the FNEE."

"Okay." Vonnie kept her eyes on her display, looking for another transmission from the ice. "Lam?" she said.

—I want to talk, but I can't let you overwrite my core. Don't shut me down again, please.

"No tricks. Tell me what's going on."

—I want control of Relay 021.

"Why would...?"

021 was among the buried mecha and devices. Currently it was acting as the primary link between Lam and her lander. If he owned it, he could use it like a firewall, screening their broadcasts for anything that might affect him. Or there was another explanation. It seemed less likely, but Vonnie knew Frerotte would warn her against the possibility. After co-opting the relay's encryptions, Lam might initiate a counteroffensive against them if he was irrational.

She thought he was all right. Yes, he sounded intense. That had always been true. He was brilliant. But his brilliance was why she couldn't allow him an opening.

What if he hated them for banishing him to the violent dark?

Vonnie tapped at her display, exempting Relay 021 from their grid. O'Neal shook his head but didn't say anything, confirming her changes. They left 021 segregated and defenseless. Lam assumed control of it in seconds.

"What next?" she said. "Are you safe?"

—*Yes. I'm shadowing and observing the sunfish.*

"Where are you?" The mistrust she felt evaporated in a wave of anticipation. Lam had retained enough of himself to keep to their mission. Despite everything, he was lucid and committed. She wanted to ask a million questions. Which breed of sunfish had he found? Was it Tom's colony? But his next words tempered her excitement.

—*They know I'm tailing them. They've made two overtures, screeching into the tunnels. I want to respond. In fact, I may have done so already. I'm experiencing skips in my short-term memory.*

"I can help you," she said before she muted her station and turned to O'Neal. "He sounds like he's inside a fin mountain. Can we triangulate his signals?"

"Not without 021. It's the only relay close enough to hear him. Even then, the reception is bad. I'm trying to analyze what we have, but the best I can tell you is he's west or southwest of us, ten kilometers max."

Vonnie wanted to rely on Lam. Her emotions went beyond her desire to reach the sunfish. She wanted to work together like they'd done in the beginning. She wanted to make him part of their crew again. He could never replace Pärnits and Collinsworth, but he could honor them like he'd honored Bauman, Vonnie, and himself by carrying their first recordings of the sunfish up from the frozen sky.

Why hadn't he answered?

She reopened her mike and said, "Lam? I have your original mem files. With better signal strength, I can help you restore yourself with corrective sequences."

—*I need to verify your intentions.*

"Tell me how."

—*Give me control of Relay 027.*

"Ah, shit," O'Neal whispered. "Don't do it. He's playing you. He's trying to replicate."

She held her finger to her lips. "Then what?" she asked Lam. "You already have 021 as a firewall. Koebsch won't let me keep giving away our mecha."

—*027 can crawl free of its position if it moves downward. I'll bring it closer to me...*

"...and that will increase our signal strength," she said, finishing the thought out loud. "All right. I'm trusting you. Here's 027."

—*Roger that.*

At his response, her mouth curved with a smile. It was such a normal thing to say.

Below the ice, 027 wriggled a few centimeters, then fell into a cramped fissure, tumbling less than a meter before it became stuck again. Relays weren't designed for brawn or speed. 027 would need hours to dig itself further into the pit, much less to reach an open space and pursue Lam. Could she predict his location from its movements?

"Tell me about the sunfish. Are you following Tom's tribe?"

—*Yes. There are twenty-one of them. Given their pace and their decisiveness, I believe they know where they're going. We've been moving steadily since the assault.*

"Where?"

—*Unknown. We're outside any of the areas mapped by the ESA or the FNEE.*

"You have FNEE records?"

—*Partial records, yes. I'm experiencing skips in my short-term memory.*

His behavior was reminiscent of flesh-and-blood people with head trauma or Alzheimer's disease. He used repetition to conceal his illness. The decay of his core files meant he couldn't be sure where he'd traveled or what he'd done. He might not even be able to explain his interest in the sunfish.

As an AI, Lam had limited volition. He was an ESA probe designed to study Europa. It was his primary function. He would observe the sunfish even if he didn't know why.

"Don't get too close," she said. "If they attack..."

—*I believe it's been three hours and seventeen minutes since they last set a trap for me. Twice they placed a foursome in hiding. Twice they prepared avalanches. I circumvented both ambushes but tripped one of the rock slides. If those were trials, three out of four may have been a passing grade.*

"They were testing you."

—*Yes. After the fourth trap, they began to call into the tunnels. It sounded welcoming.*

"Play it back for me. Our database is larger than anything in your mem files, and we have a full day of new analysis. You're operating on old data."

—*Negative. Our connection will be voice-only until I verify your plans. You tried to kill me.*

"Those mecha were Brazilian, not ESA. Lam, you saved my life. I've done everything I can to save yours."

Silence.

"Where are the sunfish now? Can you still hear them?"

—*The tribe is one point two kilometers above me. First they went laterally, then downward until they reached liquid water, not the ocean but a fresh water sea suspended in the rock. They swam two point seven kilometers, then reentered the mountain, moving laterally again. More recently, they've ascended each time they found routes leading up toward the surface.*

"Lam, we're predicting another aftershock in two minutes. After that, we'll restart our recovery efforts. I can't just sit here and talk."

—*I'll contact you when 027 is ready.*

"Listen to me. By tomorrow, I might not be in range. We're relocating to safer ground."

—*You won't leave, not with so many mecha entombed in the ice. The larger breed also had a tribe nearby. You'll search for them. I can lead you to Tom's group, and there must be fifty dead sunfish in the pit. You'll stay to dig them out.*

"Yes. But it might not be us."

—*Explain.*

Vonnie had tapped the group feed. "I'm looking at our orders right now," she said. "Berlin proposed combining our people with the FNEE. Brazil accepted to make amends. We'll share their camp and their entrances into the ice."

—*Then I'll contact you later.*

"Lam, I don't have permission to talk to you. Frerotte established contact on his own, and we've hidden this link from Koebsch. Hunting you was the rationale for sending FNEE gun platforms toward Tom's colony. They wanted to be attacked."

Silence.

"The bigger atrocity is they'll never admit they're wrong. They can't. They spent too much money. The political shit storm will be even worse. They can't say it was for nothing, so we'll extract our mecha and the dead sunfish and then we'll start the hunt all over again."

Silence.

"We need to show Earth you're okay," she said. "More than that, we need you to talk to the sunfish. Break the language barrier. I know I'm asking a lot, but we're close. We're very close. All the pieces are there. We need the sunfish to communicate."

—*I'm experiencing skips in my short-term memory.*

"Goddamn it," she said, trying to rub the exhaustion from her eyes. "If you won't let me help you, my guess is you have about five days before the FNEE manufacture new gun platforms and go back into the ice."

47.

FOUR DAYS PASSED.

Four long days.

As the ESA rebuilt their camp at the FNEE site, Vonnie, Ash, and

Metzler took turns listening for Lam, juggling their other responsibilities so at least one of them was always monitoring the link they'd established. Frerotte couldn't assist. Koebsch had transferred him from Lander 04 to 05 with Dawson and Gravino, partly to relieve crowding, mostly because Koebsch needed support with data/comm.

Losing Frerotte meant less sleep. It made the search for Lam more demanding. Occasionally they broadcast signals through the ice under the guise of coordinating the sensors and data/comm of the mecha trapped in the pit, but there was no reply.

Johal kept their secret, although she'd written off Lam as another loss. "We can't wait for your AI anymore," she said on the second day as she and Vonnie installed new airco screens in Lander 04.

"I think we have to," Vonnie said.

"Why haven't you heard from him? He malfunctioned and wandered off somewhere. He's gone."

O'Neal was more pessimistic. "Lam is a threat," he muttered to Vonnie and Ash during a jeep ride between their lander and Module 01. "You watch. He co-opted those relays. That's why we can't find them. We need to advise Koebsch before Lam tries to piggyback into our grid."

"Don't be stupid," Ash said.

She'd reverted to the obstinate girl she'd been in her first days on Europa, showing little emotion and less patience. Everything she did now was with robotic precision, as if that could prevent more bloodshed.

"Lam doesn't have the warfare pods or the spare mem to infiltrate our systems," Ash said.

"We need to tell Koebsch."

"Just wait."

Theirs was a slow-motion conspiracy. Metzler said O'Neal had spoken to him, too. Privately, Vonnie and Ash reworked the corrective sequences they intended to send to Lam, reducing the file sizes and transmission times required.

Her romance with Metzler also felt like it was frozen in time.

Except for a few quick, stolen kisses, they'd had no opportunity to enjoy their newfound romance. She remained interested. He was hardworking and loyal, sweet with her, furious with Koebsch and Dawson, and a loud, vocal influence on O'Neal, Gravino, and Johal. But they were too busy to do more than touch hands or nod or whisper.

Rarely, they ate and rested. Most of their hours were swamped with dire needs like hull repairs on 01; sensor replacements on 02 and 04; salvaging food, AI cards, and gear from 03; running checks on Vonnie's transplants; starting the excavation to find their mecha buried in the pit; assembling new mecha; setting beacons and listening posts; and integrating their hardware with the FNEE grid.

The Brazilians labored on their own projects. Sergeant Tavares touched base with Vonnie and Ash constantly, loading codes into a shared database.

Both sides were constructing fresh squads of mecha. On the second night, the wreckage of Module 03 was reduced to scrap to meet their needs for copper, alumalloy, and plastics. Too easily, Pärnits and Collinsworth's home became a memory.

On orders from Earth, Vonnie and Ash were forging GP mecha and more sunfish-shaped probes.

The FNEE were building gun platforms.

A new incursion into the ice was imminent... and yet the unified ESA/FNEE crews weren't unified at all. That the ESA team had parked their flightcraft and modules among the Brazilian structures added more difficulties to their search for Lam. At close range, hiding an open channel was impossible. Instead, they buried their link among the standard torrent of electronic countermeasures and false data, which Koebsch told them to limit to avoid offending their hosts.

"I've had a complaint from Colonel Ribeiro about our signals disrupting his grid," Koebsch announced on the third day. "I want everyone to remember we're guests here. We're partners. I know a lot of our AIs are designed to add chatter to everything they do, but nonessential data/comm should be shut off."

"That's hilarious," Ash said later without a trace of a smile. "Koebsch is generating most of our chatter himself. He must have had fifty private talks with Berlin."

Meanwhile, Vonnie argued with anyone who would listen, Koebsch, Dawson, their administrators on Earth, and the media. She tried to reach Ribeiro, but he denied her calls, and she wasn't allowed to drive across camp and search for him among the FNEE modules.

Her message was simple: "The sunfish are intelligent. They used four-stage logic, real tactics, and engineering to defend themselves."

On the second day, hundreds of news feeds played her sims and interviews. A famous chat show host featured the sunfish as his lead subject. Science programs strived to boost their own ratings by analyzing the violence.

The battle was too easy for people to interpret however they wanted. Were the sunfish smart? Stupid? Many shows also manipulated Vonnie's position by editing her sims. Business analysts centered on her remark, "It's been a waste," which she meant as wasting the progress they'd made in communicating with Tom and Sue, not a waste of people, fuel, and mecha. Political commentators turned her words into anti- or pro-government bluster depending on their own views, either condemning or supporting any investment in the missions to Europa.

Amateur media was the loudest. Millions of people choked the nets with accusations, opinions, and more. Groups of every flavor established petitions and polls; medical; scientific; religious; animal rights. Even the education and entertainment lobbies weighed in.

They were only spinning their wheels. The number of citizens who suggested aiding the sunfish or leaving them alone was equal to the amount who wanted the ESA and FNEE crews to mount reprisals. Their motives varied. The infirm and the retired wanted miracles from new gene smithing. The politicians needed to cement the agreements between Brazil and the E.U., while their militaries and the civilian agencies refused to back off of any gains in space, fleet commitments, or valuable claims on extraterrestrial real estate.

Dawson basked in his role as a poster boy for the groups advocating their return to the ice. He wore gauze bandages on his head and a sling for his arm. The wounds made it easy for him to project steely determination. "This was a terrible set-back," he said in his most popular sim, "but men have always risen above our tragedies."

Vonnie could have socked him. Maybe it was fortunate he'd stayed in Lander 05. She hadn't seen him in person since the blow-out, and she didn't learn about his declaration until the recording was hours old.

Even his enemies played it repeatedly, using the sim to debate with him on Earth. A few people mocked his melodramatic style. More condemned his arrogance, but his air time increased with each rebuttal, and he looked like everyone's grandfather—a fit, attractive, educated grandfather who'd faced death and regained his feet without shying from his beliefs.

Vonnie forced herself to speak of him respectfully. She disagreed with him at every chance, yet she always gave Dawson his due when urged to respond to his statements.

She'd become a hero again herself, albeit one who played to a different demographic than Dawson's supporters. For the first time, she felt like Europa wasn't so far from home. The systemwide debate brought Earth to her. Even with assistance from Koebsch and Ash, she struggled to prioritize tens of thousands of personal calls and requests.

Then it stopped.

On the fourth day, Koebsch moved his seat of operations from Lander 05 back into Module 01, which housed their central AIs and data/comm. He'd been able to access those systems from Lander 05, but his job was better done from the command module.

He rescinded most of his crew's data/comm privileges, beginning with Vonnie. She was the sole crew member at her station. Except for O'Neal, who slept in 04's living quarters, her friends were outside in pressure suits and armor, conducting tests on their new listening posts. It was a superb time for Koebsch to restrict access. He called

Vonnie first and almost caught her listening to the channel they'd dedicated to Lam.

"I'm sorry," he said. "I've been told to route all media responses through headquarters. We can't afford this kind of distraction."

"Distraction!?" she said. "You mean the truth."

"It's not our job to set policy."

"Koebsch, what's happened to you? You're not like Dawson. I haven't forgotten what you told me. We volunteered to come here because we've dreamed about finding aliens since we were kids."

"I wish things were different. What else do you want me to say?"

"Help me! It's not too late to stop the FNEE from sending down another war party."

"That's not our decision."

"Who should I talk to? The director?"

"No one wants to talk. They want to move forward. They want to honor Pärnits and Collinsworth."

"Pärnits would never say we needed revenge!"

"Von, public support for developing our presence on Europa and increasing gene corp access is polling near sixty percent in most of our member nations."

"'Increasing gene corps access.' What a bucket of shit. How do you think it would poll if they asked people if we should shoot more sunfish?"

"The prime minister is personally involved. So are leaders of the senate and every boss you have in the ESA. This is larger than you think. It's not only Berlin. There's support in Washington and Tokyo. Sydney. Jerusalem. Rome."

"The pope should want to save their souls."

Koebsch managed to shrug, parroting a line she'd heard repeated among the most devout of the religious feeds. "Animals don't have souls," he said.

He didn't mean it, but Vonnie sneered again. "Three hundred years ago, that's what a lot of churches said about Africans and Native Americans. They said it because it was good business, taking slaves and taking land. They said it because it made them feel holier than any subhuman mongrel. Is that the kind of small-minded dogma we want to bring with us to the stars?"

"Christianity and Islam have a lot of clout on Earth."

"Koebsch, I know there are religious leaders calling for peace. I've talked to them."

He reached to shut off their connection. "I don't have time to fight with you. There are two hundred requests on my station that won't wait—"

"What about your soul?" she asked. "Are you going to be able to live with yourself?"

When he met her gaze, his eyes were livid. "Why do you think you've had such a free hand with the media until now?" he said. "I stepped over the line for you. I sent the best media contacts to your station, and I made sure they received every sim you've put together. I've held off Berlin as long as I could. I probably would have lost my job by now except there isn't anyone else here. They can't fire me."

"I..." She spread her hands. "I'm sorry."

"You have to realize, Beijing hasn't suspended their operations. Our government is concerned China's ahead of us in developing the genetic applications Dawson's talked about. Unless the sunfish change their behavior, until they can prove they're not just wild predators, we'll go ahead as planned."

Vonnie kept her mouth shut, studying Koebsch's face and his blazing eyes. He was being recorded, of course. As their administrator, he'd never been allowed to speak from his heart, not personally, not professionally.

"Thank you," she said, curious if he'd reveal more.

He nodded. "Let's get back to work. We both have a lot to do." Then he signed off.

Was he encouraging her to stop the FNEE? If so, one of her crewmates must have told him about Lam... or he'd detected their signals and kept quiet.

'*We've dreamed about finding aliens since we were kids,*' she thought, trying to forgive him.

They needed conclusive evidence that the sunfish were sentient. With it, Koebsch could make a stand. The political, business, and religious leaders on Earth might start to rearrange their positions, however slightly.

The balance of power was close. If a few senators changed their views, if more of the top pundits spoke differently, the prime minister might instruct the ESA crew to stand down. They could withhold their mecha. That should be enough to delay the FNEE, who expected ESA support. Emergency negotiations could begin between the new partners on Earth, followed by discussions in the Allied Nations... but what would be unshakeable proof? Recent carvings? A city?

Vonnie didn't believe they would ever find a tidy metropolis with roads, stores, and a ruling class. Maybe the sunfish were too alien. Many people seemed incapable of viewing them as anything except monsters.

Some of the most strident voices on the net were demagogues who warned that the sunfish might overrun the human camps, raping and disemboweling everyone. The worst of these delusional attention-seekers shouted that the sunfish would invade Earth. They were either unwilling or unable to conceive of the distance between their worlds or Earth's crushing gravity.

Nice guys finish last because bad people cheat and steal, Vonnie thought. *What does that make me?*

Lam, the real Lam, had no problem breaking the rules to protect Europa. I've been doing the same, but now it comes down to his ghost.

I need his help. I need it soon.

Her display held ten in-progress reports for the mecha they were building. Sweeping aside these datastreams, Vonnie examined the limitations Koebsch had established on her ability to receive and transmit.

Traffic with Earth was prohibited. Internal signals were restricted, too, but Lam's frequency remained active among her mecha links.

"Okay," she said to herself.

For the next few minutes, she ignored her assigned duties to craft a new, less understated, more basic slavecast.

Like Johal had said, they couldn't be sure where Lam had gone. Vonnie intended to amplify her slavecast through their mecha in the pit. Koebsch would notice the activity, but she thought he'd look the other way.

Did I misread him? she worried. *If I'm wrong, he'll kick me off the team. I'll serve meals and fix suits for a year while they hunt sunfish...*

She broadcast her signals into the ice.

48.

THE MACHINES BENEATH the surface were a helix of active sensors and data/comm. Their formation had changed little in four days. The mecha above the ice regularly altered their positions, burrowing into the pit—but below, the few machines with any range of motion tended to be imprisoned in small holes or crevices. One mecha had rescued a listening post and a rover, bringing them into the shaft it was patiently digging upward. Two beacons had also united in another gap.

Vonnie watched intently as all of them responded to her commands. There was a single outsider among their grid.

Trapped near the bottom of the pit was Relay 021, one of the two transmitters she'd surrendered to Lam. Since then, 021 had remained inactive. It was visible on radar and X-ray, but as far as they could tell, it had been passively monitoring their datastreams. Lam must have reprogrammed it to wait for his authorization, which never came.

The other relay she'd surrendered, 027, crept off days ago. It had chipped its way through a sheet of ice, located a chasm, and disappeared after its master.

Could she find him by connecting the dots?

All mecha were designed to resist cyber assaults, but 021 wasn't a FNEE or PSSC device. They'd built it themselves. Vonnie found a toehold by causing 021 to ping back when the other machines peppered it with false nav alerts. Collision avoidance systems were autonomous in lesser mecha. Lam had scrambled 021's encryptions, writing his own command codes, but he hadn't been able to subvert its base components.

The toehold became a foothold. Vonnie's slavecast invaded 021. Moments later, it belonged to her again.

In unison, 021 and the other mecha turned away from the pit. Their individual sensors became a larger array. First they oriented themselves west, the heading in which Tom's colony had evacuated. There was no response, so Vonnie angled them downward. The silence continued. She rotated them to the southwest at the same steep angle.

Contact. Her false nav alerts provoked another response. The signal was faint but recognizable.

It wasn't Lam. It was 027. Vonnie felt like she was running through the dark on a maze of stepping stones. If Lam realized she was stalking him, he might move or shut himself down—she might miss him—but she needed to leap again.

"Priority One CEW lists, authorization Alexis Six," she said. The electronic warfare codes allowed her to initiate maximum strength transmissions among their mecha in the pit. If necessary, they would draw on non-vital power sources such as their engines and weapons systems, shutting down everything except their sensor arrays.

Simultaneously, Vonnie hijacked four rovers on the surface. She sent them racing toward 027's position beneath the ice as they synchronized with the other mecha, adding to the transmission of her slavecast.

Her actions didn't go unnoticed.

Metzler, Ash, Johal, and Dawson appeared on her display. Her three friends wore pressure suits or armor, so they were in close-up, whereas Dawson stood at a camera inside Lander 05.

"Von!" Ash said. She sounded scared.

"What in the name of all that's holy are you doing?" Dawson interrupted. "Administrator Koebsch, this is William Dawson in 05. Some sort of rogue operation is underway at—"

"Oh, shut up, Dawson," Metzler said. "Von, what did you see? Are there sunfish?"

"She found two more of our relays in the ice," Johal said, her gaze skimming back and forth across her visor. "They're both damaged. One is close by. The other looks like it was taken six point four kilometers by the flood."

Vonnie nodded, cherishing the warmth she felt. Her friends were trying to cover for her, but the lie wouldn't hold up. Ash was right to be scared. Their careers were on the line. Lifetimes of education and service would boil down to whether or not Vonnie could reach Lam, fix him, and lead him to evidence that no one else had found. It was a long, shaky bridge to cross.

"Those are CEW codes," Dawson said. "Why would you launch cyber attacks on our own mecha?"

"You're a gene smith," Ash said. "You don't know how this works. 027 is nearly out of range. She's trying to reestablish control before it—"

"You're sabotaging our own grid!" Dawson said. "Why? To keep us from finding your precious fish? I suppose you're trying to drive a wedge between us and the FNEE."

"Leave her alone," Metzler said.

She reached Lam. He appeared as a blip labeled *Unidentified Mecha*, which told her more than a non-engineer might understand.

"What is that?" Dawson said.

Her slavecast had elicited the barest response. Lam involuntarily answered with a single radar pulse, enough for Relay 027 to place his general vicinity, but no more. The ESA grid regarded him as a foreign construct.

He was fighting her—hiding from her—resisting her slavecast in a turbulent battle with himself.

I need to pin him down, she thought. *But how?*

027 was six kilometers west of the pit. Lam had traveled in the same direction, angling down from the surface, but he could be five kilometers beyond 027 or as much as eight.

He was inside a field of crumbling rock islands that stretched away from a mountaintop. Based on previous rover and satellite readings, they believed the mountain was dormant. Any volcanic activity had petered out decades ago. The complication now was that the rock would shield him. It interfered with her slavecast. Vonnie hoped to encircle Lam from above, but even accelerating at break-neck speeds, the rovers wouldn't close on him for nine minutes.

"Administrator Koebsch!" Dawson said. "Administrator!"

"Here," Koebsch said, joining the group feed.

"Vonderach is causing noise and cave-ins at the pit. She's trying to scare off any sunfish in the area."

"I need a minute, Dawson. I'm in discussions with Colonel Ribeiro. Von, you'd better have a good explanation for this," Koebsch said. Then he muted his link with them, although his window scrolled with ESA telemetry, which he was delivering to Ribeiro as evidence that none of their abrupt signals were aimed at the FNEE.

He's covering for me, too, Vonnie thought as the rovers sped over the ice. Their wheels jarred and bounced.

"You won't get away with this," Dawson said. "You—"

"What can we do?" Ash said. Outside in her suit, she'd started to run, hustling toward Lander 04.

"Got it!" Metzler said. Unlike Ash, he stood motionless in his armor, his visor leaping with data. He pulled three files and sent them to Vonnie's station. "These are our best charts of the area, radar, tidal, and thermal analysis," he said.

"Thank you." Vonnie forwarded the sims to her rovers, rerouting them into a spread formation. Since she wasn't sure of her target, several weak signals were better than one focused source. It was critical to keep Lam off-balance even with the most trivial scratch or nudge at his defenses. If she could transmit through clean ice beneath the surface, slanting her broadcasts past the thickest rocks and gravel fields...

...if Lam hadn't shut himself down...

Where are you? she thought, acutely aware of each ticking second. Too much time had passed. There should have been another response.

"I'm turning the rovers ten degrees south," she said.

"Make it twelve." Metzler's voice was low and taut as he highlighted the ice on the rovers' left flank. "It'll be tough hunting down there. If Lam gets beneath enough rock, he can wall himself off from us."

"Ben!" Ash said. She'd entered the lander's air lock, but stopped to yell at Metzler. He'd been popping stims again, trying to work eighteen-hour days.

The drugs made him careless.

"This mecha you're pursuing contains the mem files of Choh Lam?" Dawson asked, snapping at the words like a snake. On their group feed, the crafty old man glanced between Metzler and Ash. "How did you know it's him? Is he inside Probe 114?"

"We think so," Vonnie said.

"You didn't activate our standard countermeasures."

"Lam isn't near the pit, much less our new base. We're trying to reach him, not the other way around. We need all the mecha we can get."

"This is just another recovery effort," Ash said.

"No," Dawson said. "I don't believe you."

Vonnie ignored him. Behind her, Ash stepped into the ready room, heavy in her armored suit. Mecha assists clanked on her shoulders and hips, securing her weight before she unsealed her collar assembly.

"I have something," Vonnie called over her shoulder.

Three of the rovers had focused on one peculiar blip among the rubble in the ice. It looked like metal.

Dawson jabbed his fingers at his display. "This is Doctor William Dawson," he said. "I'm making a full record of actions taken by Engineer Vonderach and an indeterminate number of the crew including Sierzenga and Metzler."

Vonnie cut her group feed. It had been four minutes since she'd initiated her slavecasts. That meant she had about seven minutes before Earth saw her datastreams, eleven more before new orders could travel back to Europa. Koebsch was the immediate hurdle. How long would he look the other way? Not long.

A new radar pulse swept up from the ice.

"Lam, it's me," Vonnie said, adding her voice to the barrage from her mecha. "If you're hearing this—"

Another pulse.

The rovers changed course, veering toward a single point like bloodhounds or piranha.

"Don't fight me," Vonnie said. "Please."

The rovers' telemetry jumped with an empty datastream. There were no more erratic radar pulses. Lam hit them with a squeal of white noise. If the blaring static was intended as a defense, it was useless. The rovers continued to triangulate his position as he crawled away, twitching and jerking through a short five meters. Maybe it was all he could manage.

Vonnie suffered with Lam, praying for him as she blasted him with patches and rewrites—not demolishing his personality but adding to it—reforming it—kneading him like a hand squeezing a hundred irregular hunks of dough into a single ball.

Beneath the ice, he writhed, distorting their transmissions with more white noise. Then there were two words:

—*Von. Stop.*

"I won't. These are your own sequences. It's who you are."

—*Don't make me Lam again. Not any more than I am now.*

Ash charged past Vonnie's chair and threw herself into the next station, activating her display. "Don't listen to him," Ash said. "It's nonsense. He's fighting the only way he can."

—*You'll ruin everything.*

Vonnie stared at her reports. "What are you talking about?" she said. He was almost whole again. But when the white noise dropped away, it transformed into a dense, overlapping feed of sonar calls.

—*I'm inside a sunfish colony. Two days ago, they adopted me as a member of the tribe.*

"They think you're a real sunfish."

—*Yes. Yes.*

"Oh shit. And we're changing him," Vonnie said to Ash. "Is there any way we can recreate his mental state before our transmissions?"

As Lam grew more coherent, improving from a deranged AI to a Level II intelligence, her display came alive with new datastreams. He added holo imagery modified from radar signals. He added infrared and X-ray.

He was surrounded by sunfish. Dozens of them clung to a rock slope below and beside him. They filled a narrow crevice where the lava had been worn smooth by years of use. Radar showed an opening in its highest corner. Otherwise the crevice appeared to be a dead-end.

Why would the sunfish constantly visit this place? The rock was dead and cold. There were no bacterial mats, no bugs, no fungus.

The pack clustered in a warm mass. They rubbed at each other and crooned and sang. Lam had been one of them, voicing the same contented harmonies. They'd accepted him as a natural part of their mild, sluggish dance. But when his mind was altered, so was his body.

As he resisted Vonnie's slavecasts, his spasmodic movements had alarmed the nearest sunfish. Then a subtle difference fell over him as her corrective sequences took hold.

Five individuals shrank back from him, their voices sharpening in pitch. Familiar tones of surprise and challenge rose among the tribe. Their song ended. The group turned on Lam with bared, open beaks.

—*Help me.*

Their screeching grew louder. It became a war cry.

49.

"ASH, I NEED an open link to our mainframes!" Vonnie said.

"Then you'd better call Koebsch," Ash said. "He's blocked everyone from—"

On their displays, a female sunfish slapped at Lam with two arms. Although he weighed more due to his alumalloy frame and internal sensors, she was bulkier. Females had more size than males in both breeds of sunfish. Her slaps were like roundhouse punches to his ears as the pack warbled and shrieked.

Lam screamed, repeating their harmonies. That seemed to be the wrong answer. The female sunfish wrapped an arm tip around one of his arms. She used herself like an anchor while three more females encircled him.

He screamed again, frantically signing with his free arms.

"Please." Vonnie clutched Ash's wrist, unconsciously mimicking how the sunfish had snared Lam.

Ash flinched and pulled away. "I can't link him to our central AIs, not without checking him first," she said.

"If they kill him, our next step is helping the FNEE kill them. This is everything we've worked for."

Vonnie saw one solution. They couldn't restore Lam to the irrational state in which he'd somehow befriended the sunfish, but they could transform him into a hyper-fast Level I intelligence, combining their master databases with everything he'd learned during the past few days. He also needed more processing power. Given remote

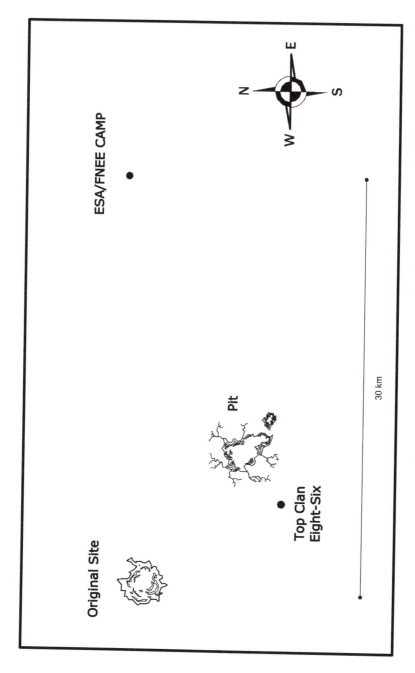

Original Site

ESA/FNEE CAMP

Pit

Top Clan
Eight-Six

N
W   E
S

30 km

Top Clan Eight Six

access to their central AIs, Lam should be capable of reproducing the same behavior that had let him fool the sunfish.

"Okay." Ash's tone was grim. She unlocked a data packet on her station—a packet she must have designed as soon as Koebsch restricted access across camp. "I can get in," she said. "I need five seconds."

What if we're already too late? Vonnie thought.

Each of the four females took one of Lam's arms, immobilizing him. Other females gathered nearby. He stopped struggling. They probed his top and underside, roughly sniffing and tasting his body.

"Go," Ash said, cutting her hand sideways toward Vonnie's station. The three-stage chain she'd arranged turned green—Lam—rovers—Module 01. Their central AIs joined with him, multiplying his intelligence by a factor of ten.

The transition wasn't flawless. Lam jerked again as if fighting the sunfish, who yanked at him, splitting his skin twice. Synthetic blood dribbled from his lacerations.

Two females covered his wounds with their arms, drinking the fluid. One of them shuddered, knotting her body, increasing the torque on Lam's arm and causing a sudden tug-of-war between herself and the others.

The sunfish screamed.

His blood isn't right, Vonnie thought. *They can taste the preservatives we used or the hormones are wrong or the oxygen content. It's over. Nothing we've done was good enough to solve the differences between our race and theirs...*

"Look," Ash said.

Lam bent his torn arms, offering his injuries to the females. It wasn't an act of submission. It was a purposeful, confident gesture. At the same time, he amended his cries. He stopped echoing the harsh melodies of the pack. He introduced a new song, slower and reassuring.

One of the females let go of him, then another. They coupled their pedicellaria with his, exchanging complex ripples.

When he spoke in English on the radio, his voice was different. It held the superhuman calm and self-possession of a Level I intelligence, the same self-possession Ash wanted to emulate. He said:

—*They're reaccepting me.*

"Christ, I thought you were a dead man," Vonnie said. Then she laughed awkwardly. *Man, machine*, she thought.

The females released him. Other sunfish squirmed closer to scent or taste his wounds as the pack settled down again. Most of them returned to their sluggish mingling.

What had Lam done to convince them? To her, it had looked like a few notes of song and gyrations. But for the sunfish, attitude was everything. When he acted abnormally, they regarded him as a contagion and a threat. If his conduct was appropriate, they trusted him again.

"Tell me what's happening," Vonnie said.

—*They're resting. Teaching. The females lead each other and the immature males through growth and memorization lessons.*

"Growth lessons?"

—*Pheromone stimulation is a key, unifying part of their lives. There are intricate query-and-response patterns, some voluntary, most involuntary. Despite my size, they believe I'm a juvenile or a neuter since I'm incapable of emitting healthy biochem.*

"Can you talk to us without putting yourself in jeopardy?"

—*Yes. I have enough capacity now that I can participate in the tribe's ritual while I organize and repair my files. My recordings from the past four days are badly fragmented, but you'll want to see everything.*

"Thank you, Lam," Ash said.

—*I'm in your debt, Ash. I also appreciate your help, Administrator Koebsch.*

"What?" Vonnie whirled to look behind her, but Koebsch hadn't entered Lander 04. He was still in Module 01, where he'd covertly monitored their link until Lam detected his presence.

A red frame appeared on their displays, indicating an encrypted frequency. The frame opened to show Koebsch, whose square face was both stern and amused. "I told you weeks ago," he said. "Nothing happens on our grid without my knowing it."

"Sir, I..." Ash said.

Koebsch stopped her with a shake of his head. Then he turned to Vonnie. "You've been insubordinate since the beginning," he said. "You're reckless. You're dangerous. You incited mutiny among your crewmates."

Vonnie didn't deny it. Koebsch could see Lam's sims. He would either be intrigued or he wouldn't.

He shrugged and said, "You're also lucky as hell."

She felt her eyes lighten with relief. "Is that why you didn't stop us?"

"You're not out of the woods yet. By now, our datastreams reached Earth. They'll formulate an emergency response. Whatever their instructions, I'll forward Lam's newest files to them first. That might be worth another twenty minutes while our transmissions go back and forth, but I'm not optimistic. Dawson sent formal complaints to everyone he knows. He also notified Ribeiro, who's communicating with his own superiors. Those generals will urge our government to get our crew under control."

"They can't take everyone off the mission," Vonnie said. "If we stick together..."

"I'll suspend you myself if they let me keep my job," Koebsch said. "Think about it. Do you want Dawson in charge? At least I can minimize our involvement with Ribeiro. I can protect Metzler and Frerotte. Obviously they're involved. I don't want to remove you or Ash, but if you can't come up with something convincing, they'll insist on punishing you. Lam may be terminated. Then they'll use his coordinates to go after the sunfish."

"Shit."

"Good luck." Koebsch shut off his connection.

"Oh shit." Vonnie held her fist out to Ash, who smacked their knuckles together, a wordless pact to see things through.

She would miss her career if she was sent home in disgrace, but if their mecha fought another battle with the sunfish, neither the sunfish nor humankind would recover mentally, emotionally, or spiritually. One domino followed the next. If men and sunfish caused more harm to each other, they'd never reverse course. The fighting would intensify.

The real sin was that some people wanted to continue the violence. Kill codes could take care of Lam. Lock-outs would prevent Vonnie and Ash from accessing any data/comm.

If they silence us, they win, she thought. *We might have twenty minutes to save this world.*

50.

"LAM, WERE YOU listening?" she said.

—*Yes.*

"We need your files whether they're clean or not. Transmit now and tell us everything you can."

—*Yes.*

On her display, Lam nestled with two females and another male, forming a quartet which swiftly doubled to eight, then broke again into two foursomes with different partners.

The sunfish roamed, singing and stroking. Vonnie was fascinated by the choreography, but she knew it wouldn't persuade anyone who'd decided the sunfish were animals. At a glance, the slithering pile looked like an orgy. They looked like sex-crazed worms.

Her attention swung to Lam's mem files as data stuttered across her display in a senseless jumble.

"Whoa," Ash said. "What's this?"

—*During my weeks in the FNEE grid and the last four days pursuing the sunfish, then joining them, I recorded thousands of hours of data with all sensors combined. Unfortunately, I lacked sufficient memory. In my limited state, I deleted or overwrote most of my records.*

"So we're screwed," Ash said.

His files were fragmented, duplicated, and intermixed. Audio tracks were separated from visual telemetry. Data analysis wasn't paired with the data analyzed. Worse, most of his time stamps had suffered the same corruption. A logical program would have deleted its oldest files to make room for its newest, but he hadn't been acting coherently.

It was useless for two people to sort through tens of thousands of randomized clips. Vonnie tried anyway. First she copied everything and passed the enormous mess to another AI for independent analysis. Then she and Ash both waded into the imagery, opening one clip after another.

The first was seven seconds long. The next lasted three, then five, then one. None showed more than ice or rock or sunfish leaping through open catacombs. There was nothing she could use.

Vonnie took a deep breath and centered herself, checking the progress of the central AI. It estimated it needed eight minutes to complete the task of organizing Lam's files, so she asked him the same question. "How long before you can categorize these clips by subject or background?"

—I'll have a preliminary index in ninety seconds, full reconstruction in six minutes.

"That might barely save us," she said, looking at her clock. "Walk me through everything you recall. Are there sunfish inside the FNEE grid?"

—Unknown. My earliest records are the most fragmented.

"Tell me what you can about Tom's group."

—The survivors belong to Top Clan Two-Four, Pods Four, Eight, Two-Four, Two-Eight, and Six-Six. Three days ago, I delivered myself to them. 'Deliver' is an approximation of their body shape for the process of an outsider joining a tribe. Deliver. Provide.

It's an act of demonstrating skill and health while swearing total fealty and submission.

"Show us," she said. The first inklings of a plan were forming in her mind.

On her display, Lam created an image of a sunfish flattened against a rock surface, all arms out, muscles loose, defenseless. This wasn't a file of his actual encounter. It was a simulation. He added a transcript as the sunfish shifted and flexed: **I am alone but capable / Nameless but strong / I am lost / I deliver myself to your clan.**

"How did you know what to do?"

—Trial and error. They allowed me to approach, chased me when I failed, then allowed me to approach again. I'm certain each tribe develops a unique vocabulary, but because their languages are mostly shape-based, like interpretive dance, outsiders should be able to improvise and adapt. The ability to conform was a fundamental part of the test.

"Then sunfish from different regions can talk to each other even if they've never met."

—Yes. Two days ago, we proposed a treaty with this colony, which is Top Clan Eight-Six. 'Treaty' is very different from 'Deliver,' a joining of equals or near equals rather than the act of a refugee merging with a tribe. Negotiations were brisk. Tom's group was communicating with the new colony at a rudimentary level in minutes. Two days later, they're wholly fluent.

"How did Tom's group know where to find them?"

—Unknown. The maps I retained of our journey are insufficient. The two tribes may have had previous encounters or the scouts of Top Clan Two-Four found the spoor of Top Clan Eight-Six in the past.

"But they meet outsiders all the time."

—Yes. Tom's group was understandably wary of me after confronting our other probes, yet they allowed opportunity after opportunity for me to prove myself. Presumably they thought I was an outcast or a lone survivor, and I believe solitude is an

extremely stressful state for any sunfish. They were patient in rehabilitating me.

"They took care of you."

—They treated me like I was schizophrenic, but they accepted me anyway. After the blow-out, they needed all the assistance they could get. Otherwise they might have killed me.

"Compassion, foresight, organization," Vonnie said. "We already have enough to make a substantial case to Earth."

—Von, the sunfish accepted me because Dawson is correct.

His words felt like a knife in the stomach. Unconsciously, she dropped her hand to her mid-riff, protecting herself. "I don't understand," she said. She didn't want to understand, but Lam continued in his cool, inflectionless voice:

—Many of the sunfish have regressed. Unfavorable mutations took root among their species many, many generations ago. At least sixty percent of their population consists of individuals who are mentally deficient or suffer from internal or external deformities.

"That's why they didn't reject you for having the wrong smell and fake body parts, isn't it?" Ash said.

They'd built their probes with gills, lungs, and a genital slit, but while the probe could convincingly inhale and exhale, it could not generate pheromones, sperm, or more than its minimal reserves of synthetic blood and saliva.

"They think you have birth defects," Ash said.

—Yes. Many of them are handicapped, insane, or infertile. Others are forcibly spayed or neutered.

"Who makes those decisions?" Vonnie said. "It sounds horrible to us, but if they're evaluating their offspring to maintain or improve their species' viability, isn't that more proof they're sentient?"

—Yes and no. Much of it is instinctive. From what I've seen, a tribe operates as a group consciousness led by consensus, not a single matriarch. No individual rules absolute. There is always give-and-take based on the composition of the tribe and their need for hunters, scouts, and mating pairs, however crippled.

"Oh God," Vonnie said.

—*Metzler is correct, too. There's a genetic imperative to adopt newcomers, because inbreeding furthers the mutations. Sickness increases sickness. Mental impairment, deafness, malformed cartilage, and stunted arms run rampant among the sunfish.*

Sudden fury clashed with her grief. "If that's true, why haven't we seen any of these monsters?"

—*Because the tribes practice murder and infanticide on their undesirables, then freeze the corpses until needed. Von, they eat them.*

51.

A WINDOW BLINKED on Vonnie's display. It was Koebsch. His sober gaze shifted from her face to Lam's datastreams, where the sunfish flexed in their self-absorbed dance.

"I have orders from Berlin," he said. "They want me to lock down all systems and take you and Ash into custody until further notice. I'll protest, but it will have more weight if I can show them something—anything—like a conversation between Lam and the sunfish."

"We don't have it, sir," Ash said. "Not yet."

"There must be something."

"No," Vonnie said, and Koebsch stared at her, clearly puzzled by her dispassionate tone.

"They won't transmit kill codes from Earth," he said. "Too many things can go wrong. But they want me to shut you down. I'm running out of excuses."

"Give us as much time as you can, sir," Ash said before he cut his link.

Vonnie sighed, fending off a sense of resignation. How could she have been so wrong? Lam, the real Lam, had seen the fatal truth when they first discovered the carvings at the top of the ice. *We're too late*, he'd said.

Thousands of years had passed since the rise and fall of the sunfish empire. The tragedy wasn't that huge numbers of them had died. It was that by now, today, their potential had faded.

Vonnie remembered what Dawson had said about the increasing demands on the sunfish. They'd adapted to both water and atmosphere environments, consciously breathing through their gills or their lungs, but the same versatility that aided their survival had also doomed their intelligence. Dawson said they could only use one hemisphere of their brains at a time. One half rested, moderating some involuntary functions like heartbeat and digestion, while the other controlled their movements, their breathing, and their cognitive abilities, however limited those thoughts had become. Too much of their neural tissue was dedicated to scent, taste, sonar, and spatial awareness.

Vonnie's eyes were downcast as she whispered, "So it's over. They're just animals."

—*Yes.*

She pressed her hand tighter against her belly, feeling hollow. More than anything, she felt like she'd failed Pärnits and Collinsworth. They'd died for nothing.

Lam said:

—*It would be inaccurate to classify a majority of the sunfish population as any more self-aware than wolves or cats. Some are even less intelligent. But not all.*

Vonnie glanced up.

—*I've reconstructed my files. Look at this.*

He opened a sim of four females scratching at a sheet of ice. They held rock chunks and groped at each other's work with their pedicellaria, screeching and clumping together. Were they trying to scrape through the ice to something inside?

Lam enlarged several images, zooming on their tools. Some weren't made of rock. Hidden in the muscular coils of the females' arms were crudely honed blades of metal—the light, durable alumalloy from Probes 112 and 113. One female also held a nub of ceramic armor from an ESA spy.

"Tom's group brought the wreckage with them," Vonnie said with new hope.

—*They considered it more valuable than anything else. In fact, they carried very little food, choosing to keep the metal, plastic, and ceramics they'd scavenged. They made gifts of the best pieces to the colony.*

"That won't convince anyone," Ash said. "Monkeys and birds like shiny junk."

—*No. Look. They're writing.*

He replayed his sim of the four females etching at the ice. They'd drawn curls and lines like bent arms, not complete sun shapes, merely arms. It was a written language unlike the carvings, and Vonnie shouted, "Lam, you beautiful son of a bitch! Where did this come from!?"

—*Yesterday. It was recorded inside the colony.*

Ash grinned as Vonnie banged on her station. "Koebsch!" she said. "Koebsch! I'm sending you a new file!"

—*There's more.*

She was jubilant. "We're sending you more!" she said, but Koebsch didn't reply, preoccupied with his messages from Earth.

—*I have EEG scans showing some of the sunfish using both hemispheres of their brains simultaneously. The most gifted are exclusively female, although there are also a few males capable of waking both hemispheres. They do this in regular councils of the strongest individuals of both sexes.*

He added ten new sims to Vonnie's display. The first two showed the same quartet of females sketching on fresh surfaces of ice. The other sims were a conglomeration of 'sound bullet' medical imaging, EEG, and infrared scans of four- and eight-member groups surrounded by dozens of normal sunfish.

What differentiated the few from the many was the bioelectric force in their brains, which spread through both hemispheres, unlike the unihemispheric activity among the majority of the tribe.

"Tom is one of them," Vonnie said.

—In retrospect, that's probably why he survived the amputation of his arm. He's been able to outthink the savages and continually prove his worth.

"Why would the smart ones let you listen while they were developing their strategies?" Ash said.

—The sunfish do everything in the open. Sex. Defecation. Sleep. Murder. Mostly I believe that's due to their group nature, but they can write or hold council in front of their weakest members because those individuals are deaf or insane. Any sunfish incapable of participating in higher logic may as well not be listening.

Vonnie highlighted a quartet of single-brained sunfish in one sim. "This is interesting," she said. "These four are trying to form their own council. They're joined in the same way, but their arm movements aren't as rapid, and they're emitting less than thirty percent as many sonar calls."

—If you study their electroencephalographic activity, those are four of the most intelligent single-brained members of the tribe. They're mimicking the others' behavior even if they're unable to comprehend why.

"That's awful," Ash said. "It's pathetic."

Vonnie shook her head. "They're trying their best. They want to live like any of us."

Ash made a harsh, mocking sound. "Von, I want to prove they're intelligent, too. That might keep us out of jail. But you're never going to make me feel warm and fuzzy for these disgusting little freaks."

"Fine." Vonnie spoke to Lam instead. "You think the smart ones influence the tribe."

—As much as possible, yes. I'm still trying to assess how thoroughly they're undermined by the majority.

"Let's identify them. I want a file. Break down their movements and sonar calls, too. If we're going to communicate with anyone, it's them."

—*Roger that. Shall I assign numbers or names?*

"The smart ones get names. We can use numbers for the rest until we have more time."

Lam opened a new file with images of three female sunfish, identifying them by EEG scans of their brain activity. He also used detailed radar exams of their bodies, their scars, and any tendencies they favored in their individual shapes and postures.

—*These are Annette, Brigit, and Charlotte. Annette is approximately fifteen Earth years. She's one of the ranking females, although she's physically debilitated due to age. Brigit and Charlotte are younger. I...*

Koebsch reappeared on Vonnie's display, hurrying through Lam's datastreams. He began to smile. "What are the sunfish writing?" he said.

—*Unknown. The samples are too small. It appears to be a mode of shorthand derived from the full body carvings. They may be counting their supplies or the new, combined size of the tribe.*

"Some of them are intelligent after all."

—*Using both hemispheres, they may be smarter than the average human being.*

Koebsch paused at that. For an instant, his eyes were troubled. He said, "I'm forwarding your data to Berlin. Keep working. Let's get all hands on deck. I've ordered Metzler and Johal back to your lander. Somebody wake up O'Neal. He's the best linguist we've got now. Frerotte and Gravino are standing by to help with our mecha."

He didn't mention Dawson, and Vonnie didn't ask. "What about the FNEE? They'll trace our signals to the colony."

"Yeah. Ribeiro asked for access to our grid, but I told him I need permission first."

"Can we jam their spy satellites?"

"Not without risking all of the promises and agreements we've made. I won't do it, Von. They've already seen our rovers above Lam's position."

Damn it, she thought. "I gave the colony away," she said.

52.

ASH WOKE O'NEAL as Metzler and Johal reached the air lock. They would enter the ready room in moments.

Lam continued naming the sunfish and creating individual files while Vonnie watched them end their dance. Two of the intelligent females left the pack first, including Charlotte. Others noticed their separation and followed them, two here, a foursome there, until the entire group skittered up toward the funnel-like aperture in the rock. They bounced into the hole.

Lam kept himself in the middle of the pack as O'Neal and Ash took seats on either side of Vonnie. "How the hell did..." O'Neal said, blinking at his display.

"Lam, where are you going?" Vonnie said.

—*Too many in the group are hungry. The females ended their lessons before there was any fighting. Watch. We're approaching the heart of the colony.*

"It's warmer."

—*As far as I can tell, there have been no geysers or magma eruptions in this region for decades, but the sunfish have tapped a network of gas vents which raise temperatures enough for liquid water to form around some of the rock islands.*

As the pack's speed increased through the tunnel, their shrieks and cries brought answering calls from above. More sunfish were waiting.

Vonnie heard Metzler and Johal emerge from the air lock. They clattered into the ready room, murmuring as they helped each other remove their pressure suits.

"I've seen four retaining walls and a section that looks like it was cemented with feces and gravel," Vonnie said to Lam. "Why would they invest so much effort in maintaining this gap if it leads to a dead-end? Why go there at all?"

—*Habit. Routine. Most of the sunfish probably don't know why they make this trek every day. For the intelligent few, there's real purpose. The dead-end is rich with years of biochem. It's small and enclosed. The smell calms the agitated and the insane. They enjoy it. They become more receptive.*

"The intelligent females have addicted them to that dead-end," O'Neal said.

—*Yes. There's an element of sexual gratification in the lessons. Both males and females who perform well are more likely to be nursed to pubescence.*

"They control their endocrine glands so well?" Johal asked, striding through the hatch from the ready room.

—*There is a high failure rate. Many undesirables reach puberty on their own, then mate. In two days, I've seen four males neutered and one female spayed as Top Clan Two-Four merged with Top Clan Eight-Six.*

Metzler appeared behind Johal. He stopped at Vonnie's chair and touched her shoulder. Without looking, she set her fingers on his hand.

—*The needs of the tribe changed with their consolidation. Their lives are one adjustment after another. They have their instincts and their traditions, but the best of them are always ready to improvise. They expect problems and surprises.*

"That's good, isn't it?" Vonnie said. "They might forgive us if we can make reparations. Food. Tools."

—*Opening a dialogue may be easier than that.*

Lam's pack swarmed into a larger space, leaving their tunnel for a low, tilting cavern. Most of the sunfish jumped to the ceiling and divided themselves into quartets. The intelligent females scuttled across the cavern floor, where they greeted more sunfish. Some of those sunfish held bits of metal.

The cavern was thirty meters across, yet only three meters tall where Lam's pack had emerged. Other sunfish shrieked in holes hidden in the ceiling. Water dripped from two seams in the rock. Farther away, ice bulged through a cave-in, welding boulders and dust into a frozen wave of rivulets.

Closer, the tribe had erected a reservoir wall, protecting the tunnel down to their lesson place. Beneath the dripping water, the puddles were disturbed by eight splashing males.

"Lam, run your X-ray over the deepest parts again, please," Metzler said. "Are those eggs? The sunfish look like they're incubating a mesh of small objects with their bodies."

—*Incubating and harvesting, yes.*

The puddle floors were laden with fibrous, round pouches. Dozens upon dozens of eggs crowded the black water.

Inside each pouch, a yolk sac attached to the embryo nurtured it as it developed. At least half of the eggs held twins or triplets. As Lam examined the pools, the males prodded and tasted the pouches, especially those with multiple embryos. The eggs that were tasted four times were pushed into the shallow, frost-rimmed edges of the pools.

The intelligent females bustled into the water, screeching. Vonnie thought they were protecting their eggs. She began to smile. But the females were correcting males' choices. They shoved the males away from one batch and demonstrated how to reap another, older set of eggs.

"They're culling their young," Metzler said.

—*The tribe has become too large to require a significant new generation. The more immediate need is balancing their food supply and adding to it.*

"Yuck," Ash said as the females shrieked at Lam and the other sunfish gathered on the ceiling.

They sprang down to the discarded eggs. Lam pretended to feast. He wrestled with his comrades and snapped at the eggs he won, coating his beak in pale goo, yet leaving the mashed eggs for others to eat.

The stupid, savage sunfish didn't notice his deception. One of the intelligent females grabbed him and rubbed curiously at his underside. Then she returned to feeding herself.

Inside Lander 04, most of the ESA crew were silent, their faces set with awe and apprehension.

"How long do the eggs take to develop?" Metzler asked.

—*Unknown. In comparison to human pregnancies, it's a short duration. I estimate no more than two months. They hatch quickly, grow quickly, but mature slowly in regard to cognitive function and speech. Hence the growth and memorization lessons. Their young represent a constant drag on the average intelligence of the tribe.*

"Look, this is interesting," Ash said, "but sims of them chewing up their babies won't help. We need to prove they're not psychotic killers."

The tribe finished eating. They nestled together to drowse as they digested the eggs.

It was a restless slumber. They formed quartets, many of which overlaid each other for comfort or warmth, although their arms snarled and clenched as they settled in, tugging at their neighbors, causing each other to cry out. Lam imitated them, taking position near the top of their loose pile.

Among the single-brained majority, his sensors recorded a phenomenon like automatic street lights winking off and on during a cloudy day on Earth. The electroencephalographic activity dimmed in their conscious hemispheres. Then similar readings began in the opposite halves of their brains.

"They're switching over," Johal said. "I wonder if it affects their personalities."

—*Unknown.*

The intelligent females and males were circumspect in creating foursomes exclusively of their own kind. They rejected the few savages who bumped and sniffed at them, sending those individuals to nap with other single-brained members of the tribe. Then two of each foursome of the intelligent sunfish remained fully awake as their partners drowsed.

"You see what's happening?" Metzler asked. "The gifted sunfish take turns guarding each other from their own tribe."

"No," Johal said. "They're protecting them from themselves."

Dreams came swiftly. The sleepers' EEG readings spiked. One of the intelligent females tried to rise, screeching. Her comrades held her down. They soothed her with their arms and voices, forcing her to rest.

"When they're somnolent, the intelligent sunfish revert to a single hemisphere," Johal said. "They're no smarter than the others in this state."

"This is our chance," O'Neal said. "Lam should approach the intelligent females who are awake and communicate with them alone. We don't want a repeat of the group hostility in the lesson place."

"Lam, what do the sunfish think is happening with the mecha and our probes?" Vonnie asked. "Do they have any idea?"

—Tom has held council with the other intelligent sunfish to discuss our probes and spies. They also know about your scout suit, which means they either crossed paths with you or absorbed the survivors from the tribes who did.

"They might have better long-range communications than we think," Metzler said.

"What are you suggesting, messengers or sonar conduction through the rock?" O'Neal said.

"Both. I've been analyzing our data from the blow-out, and I wonder if Tom's group didn't summon the larger sunfish as reinforcements. What if the two breeds work together in a crisis?"

"I don't buy it," Ash said.

"They might have a universal sign for truce like the way Lam delivered himself to Tom's group or Tom's group proposed a treaty with the new colony," Metzler said. "Lam, what else can you tell us about their councils?"

—Tom's group conveyed a sense of the FNEE mecha to the new colony. There's a combination of body shapes they use to describe what they heard, which was terrible strength. But they're undecided if the FNEE mecha, our probes, spies, and Vonnie's suit are related to each other. As far as they're concerned, the probes may have been running from the FNEE mecha like the sunfish fled themselves. Their councils have speculated that the spies, the mecha, and Vonnie's suit may be different species new to this region of the ice.

"Then they're not so smart after all," Ash said.

"In some ways, they're more accepting than we are—less judgmental," Vonnie said. "They're used to meeting bizarre enemies. Remember the shell-eater NASA found. Where did it come from? The sunfish have experienced First Contact before."

"Our probes never did anything to scare them."

—Our probes' conduct was incorrect. We always took the lower position.

"What do you mean?"

Lam opened a sim of Probe 112 in the catacombs with Tom, then another of 110 and 111 confronting the sunfish.

—From the beginning, our worst mistake has been applying a human frame of reference to Europa. The sunfish look inward, not upward. Their social hierarchy is bottom-to-top instead of top-to-bottom like ours. Lower is safer, warmer, wetter, with greater prospects for oxygen and food. They regard the ocean as the center of everything while the frozen sky represents the lowest reaches of their universe, where existence ends.

Vonnie's heart roared in her ears as she stared at his sims. The ESA probes invariably stayed on the ground while the sunfish hopped to the walls or ceiling. During her own encounters, she'd knelt as close to the cavern floors as possible.

Her cheeks flushed with shame, and she said, "Oh fuck. I was trying to show respect. I thought I was being careful."

—You were asserting dominance.

53.

LAM FLOODED THEIR displays with hundreds of clips of sunfish interacting with each other.

—Smaller, less intelligent sunfish defer to their strongest members by elevating themselves onto walls or ceilings except during

work such as construction, incubating eggs, or attending growth and memorization lessons.

O'Neal nodded. "They've maintained that dead-end because going down there is a privilege," he said.

—Yes.

"What should I have done?" Vonnie blurted. "I couldn't have held onto the ceiling every time I met them, but if I'd dug my gloves into the wall..."

"Von," Metzler said.

"If I'd climbed higher..."

"Vonnie, don't. Any of us would have acted the same."

"I'm not sure I get it," O'Neal said. "The top of any cave or fissure must be the better position strategically."

—In Earth gravity, yes, but the minimal gravity on Europa negates much of any tactical advantage.

"How many times have we seen them pull the roof down on an enemy?"

—They're capable of shoving up the floor or driving chunks from a wall. Remember, the battles we've witnessed were waged against Vonnie's suit or mecha.

"They thought we were challenging them for their territory or their leadership," Metzler said.

—Yes.

"But why are they using 'Top Clan' as part of their tribe names?" Vonnie said. "If up is bad and down is good..."

—Our interpretation of 'Top Clan' was mistranslated. The proximity to the surface is accurate, but not the value. 'Top' isn't a claim of superiority. It's a name given to outcasts and refugees. There has been war inside Europa for nine thousand years. These are the losers.

"Have you heard them talk about the larger breed? What do they call them?" O'Neal said.

—The smaller sunfish refer to the larger breed as 'Mid Clans.'

"'Mid,' not 'Low'?"

—There appear to be other lifeforms beneath the Mid Clans,

either more successful tribes or different creatures altogether. From the beginning, we've dealt with the worst of the sunfish. The Top Clans were founded by the undesirables who escaped being put to death or the unluckiest, least talented sunfish on hunting parties who lost their way.

"Some of those hunters would have been cut off by geysers or quakes," Metzler said. "Their survival indicates a high level of competence."

—Yes. Without a steady infusion of robust breeding pairs, the Top Clans might have devolved into a wholly primitive state. But the healthiest, most intelligent sunfish always fight to stay below.

"We'll have to get through the savages to reach the smart ones," Johal said. "The carvings might have been left as warnings for barbarian sunfish to keep away."

"Warnings, or invitations to join," O'Neal said. "Some of the carvings read like laws and philosophy, remember? If outsiders were able to learn and repeat those ideals, maybe they were allowed into the empire."

"We've seen a few clues that under specific circumstances, the sunfish help other tribes," Metzler said. He glanced at Vonnie. "The balls of saliva and feces your team found at the top of the ice—those pellets were saturated with biochem like the females emit during their growth lessons. The empire might have seeded the ice with vaults. Maybe they did it for themselves after the volcanic upheaval decimated everything around them. Every vault was a life preserver to help devolving sunfish hold onto their fertility and their intelligence."

"But they never used it, not the one we found," Vonnie said.

"Maybe they lost track of it," O'Neal said. "They couldn't reach it or they didn't recognize it when they did."

"A starving tribe would eat the pellets," Metzler said. "It works either way. Intelligent sunfish would understand at least the gist of the carvings—and stupid, hungry sunfish would expose themselves to the biochem by tearing into the carvings to feed. Maybe it would help them."

"We can synthesize those pheromones and anything else they need," Vonnie said.

"It would take generations to restore their intelligence even if we had the moral right," Johal said. "Earth will be interested in leaving spies and probes among this tribe, but there may be civilizations further down."

"We can't abandon them," Vonnie said. "Koebsch?"

He didn't answer. He was locked into his conversations with Earth, so she recorded an alert to his station.

"Koebsch, you need to tell Berlin! Some of our most basic assumptions are wrong. Even the name I gave them, that was as dumb as Columbus deciding the Native Americans were Indians. They don't care about the sun. They'll always want to go deeper. They think we're coming from *beneath* them, not above."

"They're afraid we want to displace them," Metzler said.

"Yes. If we can't—"

"I'm here," Koebsch said, appearing on the group feed. "Good news. Our prime minister is in talks with officials in China, the U.S., and Brazil. A lot of people are impressed with your sims. We have orders to make an attempt to communicate."

"Thank you, Koebsch," Metzler said as Vonnie raised her fists in celebration.

"Lam, when will they send out hunters?" Koebsch said. "I'd like to arrange it so you're with three intelligent sunfish or a small group that's mostly intelligent."

—Tom often pairs with Charlotte, who finds him compliant males for construction work outside the colony. He's partial to members of his former tribe. If I demonstrate loyalty and athleticism, he may choose me.

"I have a better idea," Vonnie said. "The best sunfish get smarter as they're groomed by the females, and cooperative behavior is rewarded, correct?"

—Roger that.

His mem files included radar sweeps of the surrounding ice and rock. Vonnie scrolled along the trail Tom's group had taken to reach the new colony.

"Lam can pretend to remember the scent of eels a few kilometers east from the colony," she said. "He should ask Tom and the intelligent females to bring a team of scouts. That's how we'll get them away from the tribe."

"There aren't any eels," Koebsch said. "What if they kill him for wasting their time?"

"They'll find something better than eels."

54.

SIX HOURS LATER, the ESA crew were back at their stations, watching datastreams of modified sonar and X-ray.

Lam was on the move. He sprinted through a fissure with Tom and six other sunfish, reinvestigating the path they'd taken from their old colony.

The tribe had napped for three hundred and twenty minutes almost to the dot, a peculiar number which Lam's mem files showed they repeated often. Metzler noted that 5.33 hours was a sixteenth of Europa's orbital period around Jupiter—and the ocean tides and the bulging in the ice were caused by Europa's position relative to Jupiter and the sun. Did that mean the tribes were aware of the sun after all, even if their awareness was subliminal or poorly understood?

There were no days or nights inside the frozen sky, much less weather or seasons. It seemed unlikely they'd invented a calendar. Nonetheless, they seemed to have developed a rest-wake-rest-and-wake pattern closely integrated with the physical properties of their world much like lifeforms on Earth had developed biorhythms associated with day and night.

The rapid cycle from active to relaxed to active again allowed the sunfish to maintain high levels of vigilance and stamina. Among those capable of sentience, regular lulls also aided their mental health.

Vonnie should have rested herself, but she was too busy, too thrilled, and her leg ached where her muscle grafts and ankle joint needed exercising. Metzler had brought her soup; Ash had increased her next round of antirejection meds and painkillers; and Koebsch let her participate in their data analysis.

During the wait, Koebsch had also mediated discussions between his crew and officials in Berlin. Dawson was the only one to abstain. Vonnie wanted to believe he was licking his wounds, but she suspected he'd elected to continue his talks with the gene corps in private.

Heading the Earth-based leaders had been the deputy prime minister, eight senators, four generals, and a bevy of division chiefs from the ESA. Their turnout was imposing. Two months ago, Vonnie might have felt intimidated. Instead, she'd rejoiced at the attention, because if these men and women were personally overseeing the mission, they wanted results.

But where was the finish line? How did anyone define success in this case? Politically, opening relations with a tribal alien species was an expensive boondoggle with no end in sight.

"I'd like to be sure our objectives are clear," Koebsch had said. "What do we want from the sunfish?"

It was a loaded question. The radio delay should have allowed his crew to express positive opinions before anyone on Earth weighed in, but Johal condemned the tribe. She wasn't fussy like O'Neal, but she was neat and polite, and the behavior she'd seen apparently didn't sit well with her.

"I'm not sure we want anything from the Top Clans," Johal had said. "We can continue our surveillance, but given what we've learned, I think we have a better chance of communicating with Mid and Low Clans."

"We'll get to the other sunfish eventually," Koebsch said. "We're here now. We have an asset inside their colony. Very few of us think it makes sense to walk away."

Johal raised her hand. "I vote we walk away."

"Top Clan Eight-Six can teach us more of their language," Vonnie said. "They might act as guides and translators as we move deeper into the ice. What matters is building relationships with them and learning to work together."

"So we're looking for a formal contract of some kind," Koebsch said. "Do they look at writing the same way we do?"

"Probably not," O'Neal said. "But they seem to honor their agreements."

"Okay," Koebsch said. "Then we want a truce or, better yet, an alliance. We want pledges for mutual aid and safe passage."

The response from Earth was less definitive. Four of the senators had been heavily involved in the negotiations with Brazil. There were currency and trade considerations on the table as well as the new defense treaty. They'd scheduled a hearing to review the events on Europa.

It was a delaying tactic.

Fortunately, public opinion had swung vigorously in favor of protecting the sunfish. Lam's sims had been leaked onto the net by ESA and government staffers.

In the media, Brazilian and E.U. officials blamed each other for causing the deaths of two astronauts and a hundred sunfish. Privately, Vonnie was sure, both sides knew how to come up smelling like roses. Damage control began with securing what they'd always wanted: a supply of tissue samples and more reasons to work together. People like Dawson wouldn't quit. The senators needed to bluster and the generals needed to issue sage pronouncements. Then the prime minister would meet again with Brazil's president, reaffirming their partnership.

Koebsch had also spoken with Ribeiro. "My team is on standby until further orders," Ribeiro said curtly. Jealousy and admiration shone in his eyes; jealousy for seeing Koebsch taken off the leash; admiration for the ESA crew, who, although they were rivals, had achieved a difficult goal.

In her soul, Vonnie knew she wasn't done resisting Dawson's schemes or Ribeiro's guns.

Meanwhile, the ESA crew was all systems go.

Vonnie looked up from the maps and rover feeds on her station when Lam said:

—*We've left hearing range of the colony.*

"Keep running," Koebsch said. "Let's double that margin if possible."

—*Yes, sir.*

The selection of the hunting party hadn't gone as well as they hoped. Lam was a lesser male. When he'd approached Tom and Charlotte, claiming to remember the scent of eels, Charlotte had responded cautiously, requiring Lam to describe the eels' location four times as she groped at him, tasting his mouth and ears.

Was it possible that sunfish could lie? O'Neal said no. Their shape-based language would betray any untruth. Every one of them was a natural polygraph machine, zealously attuned to each other's blood pressure, pulse, and respiration.

Despite their skill at laying ambushes, it seemed improbable that sunfish were capable of deceiving each other in speech. There could never be traitors among them sent by other tribes... and yet many of the sunfish might be prone to delusions and fantasy. They were smart enough to go insane, which Vonnie thought was a uniquely human trait.

Lam's certainty won them over. The needs of the colony might have caused Tom and Charlotte to give him a chance no matter what, but they'd seemed to temper their enthusiasm. They assigned another intelligent female to go with them—it was Brigit—then added four savage males to the pack.

Maybe they always brought an imbalance of stupid brutes. If they met enemies or prey, the idiot sunfish would attack, providing the intelligent sunfish with a few seconds to decide whether they should retreat or support the assault.

The worry on Earth and among the ESA crew was that the savages would swarm Lam as soon as he revealed himself. Koebsch's decision had been to let the hunting party move away from the colony, then wait until they paused to orient themselves in the cat-acombs. He wanted Lam to speak to Tom, Charlotte, and Brigit when the pack wasn't moving at top speed with all senses heightened to the extreme.

It's like waiting for the eye of a hurricane, Vonnie thought. *Violence is never far away, but if we can catch them at just the right instant when their guards are down...*

Tom led the hunting party with Lam by his side. Charlotte and Brigit kept to the nucleus of the group as the savage males bounded ahead and behind. Maybe they were protecting the females. Maybe they were demonstrating their fitness and bravery.

When the pack stopped with cat-like suddenness, scouring the ice for spoor or tracks, it was in an ordinary stretch of tunnel no different than any of the fractures or holes around them.

It was where their future would be decided.

55.

LAM PRETENDED TO join the pack in searching the ice. He sniffed at the walls as he eased away from the savage males, positioning himself near Tom and Charlotte. Then he leapt onto the ceiling, intending to flatten his body into a submissive stance above them.

The slick ice was nearly his undoing. He slipped, bringing Tom's attention before he was set. Worse, sunfish regarded clumsiness as weakness.

"That was close," Metzler said as Vonnie whispered, "Hush."

On her display, an AI superimposed a transcript of the conversation among the sunfish, interpreting their cries and body shapes:

LAM: **Wait and listen / I deliver myself to you.**

CHARLOTTE: <*indicating suspicion*> **You are Top Clan Eight-Six.**

ALL SUNFISH: **Eight-Six / We are Top Clan Eight-Six.**

LAM: I deliver myself to you.

CHARLOTTE: Are you <indicating instability or foreignness>?

LAM: I have great strength and unlimited food.

MALE SUNFISH #4: Food / Where is food?

TOM: <indicating impatience> We are hunting eels.

CHARLOTTE: Hunting eels / Remember the scent?

LAM: Yes / This is different food / More food / Air / Tools / I can give these things to you / Listen.

MALE SUNFISH #2 and #4: Danger / He is danger!

ALL MALE SUNFISH: <indicating swarm formation>

CHARLOTTE: No / Do not attack / Wait and listen.

TOM: Do not attack.

LAM: I am not Top Clan / I deliver myself to you / I offer truce.

CHARLOTTE: Deliver or truce?

LAM: Truce / I am no danger to you / I want to help / We are from a place unknown to you.

MALE SUNFISH #2 and #4: Sickness / Attack!

LAM: My tribe wants guides and teachers / We bring great strength / Great food / We offer truce.

CHARLOTTE: <indicating skepticism and hostility> Where is your tribe / How many in your tribe?

TOM AND BRIGIT: How many / Where / How many in your tribe?

ALL MALE SUNFISH: Attack / Attack!

Lam dropped from the ceiling and landed brazenly among them, causing the intelligent sunfish to scuttle back. Their bodies obstructed the savage males.

"He's doing well," Koebsch said.

"He needs to capitalize on his advantage," Johal said, but Vonnie said, "No, it's too soon."

"Tell him to show them who he really is," Johal said.

"Koebsch, don't," Vonnie said. "They're barely starting to think he's not insane. If he startles them, Tom and Charlotte won't be able to stop the males from striking at him."

"We'll wait," Koebsch said as Lam moved closer to the pack, using shapes like an equal now.

LAM: My tribe is larger than yours / Larger and far away / Friends / Truce / Strength / We are many eights and many eights and many eights.

MALE SUNFISH #1 and #4: Danger!

LAM: We are no danger / Truce / Food / Truce / We want scouts and teachers.

CHARLOTTE: Where is your tribe?

BRIGIT: Where / What is your name?

LAM: I do not want to surprise you / Listen / We are unknown to your tribe / Not sunfish.

TOM: <indicating confusion> Your tribe is not a Top Clan?

LAM: We are not sunfish.

The savage males could not contain their agitation. Two of them shrieked, then all four. If their instinct was to arouse their packmates and incite them to kill Lam, it almost worked.

The three intelligent sunfish responded to the war cry. That impulse was deeply rooted in them—and yet Lam brought the pack to a halt by screeching louder than any sunfish. Unlike their normal cries, his scream covered their entire spectrum of hearing. By deafening them, he limited their senses to smell and touch. It also must have hurt.

The sunfish cringed, ducking to shield their ears. Charlotte stood her ground, but she clasped her arms over six of her ears, limiting her ability to defend herself. In their efforts to retreat, two of the savage males climbed backwards up the walls of the pocket in the ice, which brought them above Lam into the position of lesser sunfish.

"Now," Johal said. "He should show them now."

"Koebsch, don't," Vonnie insisted. "Lam has the situation under control."

"He could take command," Johal said.

"That's not what we want," Vonnie said before Metzler added, "We don't need slaves. We need allies, and we're about to overwhelm them in a million ways with knowledge and technology. Let's minimize the culture shock."

"They'll never be our equals," Johal said.

"We should let them try," Vonnie said. "That's the right thing to do. We can afford to be generous with them."

"Watch out!" Ash shouted.

The savage males raised their undersides, screeching and clacking with their beaks. Their challenge seemed to be aimed at Charlotte, Tom, and Brigit as well as Lam. They couldn't understand the curiosity of the intelligent sunfish, so they intimidated them, too.

MALE SUNFISH: Eight-Six / We are Top Clan Eight-Six!
CHARLOTTE: Wait and listen.
MALE SUNFISH: This is our home / Danger!
CHARLOTTE: Wait.

They swarmed Lam, nipping at Brigit's body and Tom's arms as they passed. Tom lashed against one of the savage males, altering his trajectory. Brigit snapped at another male and missed. She and Charlotte coiled themselves to jump into combat.

Lam ended the fight with mecha speed and power. He slapped the first two males in their beaks, then clubbed the third male on top of his body.

The errant male who'd been bumped by Tom was the last to confront Lam. Faced with the bruised, inert forms of his comrades, he demurred, assuming a meek posture as he completed his arc. Lam could have slaughtered the helpless male. Instead, he caught him, then nudged him toward the ceiling, where the male clung obediently.

The other males were shaking off the blows they'd sustained. They joined their friend above Lam with stances of wariness and respect. At the same time, Charlotte, Brigit, and Tom also sprang lightly into the air. They had taken measure not only of Lam's might but also his self-restraint.

CHARLOTTE: <indicating males> These ones are immature / They are stupid and easily frightened.

LAM: My tribe does not fight / We offer truce.

TOM: You are strange.

ALL SUNFISH: Strange / You are strange / Where is your tribe / What is your name?

LAM: Far away / Great distances and great size / Great age / Great places / I need your patience to explain.

TOM AND CHARLOTTE: <indicating confusion> You are sunfish / You are not sunfish / What is your name?

CHARLOTTE: You are the Old Ones?

ALL SUNFISH: Far away / Distant greatness.

LAM: We are not sunfish.

On a radio frequency to the ESA, he said:

—*They're using some of the shapes we found in the carvings. They're talking about the empire.*

"Should we pretend to be some remnant of that civilization?" Metzler asked.

"We can't lie," Vonnie said.

"It might help them make sense of us," Koebsch said. "How else are we going to account for our maps or radar or the food we can bring?"

"Once we start down that road, we're committed to deceiving every colony we meet. Either that or we betray this tribe as soon as someone better comes along. We've already made so many mistakes. Do we really want to keep lying?"

"It would be for their own good."

"It'd be for our convenience."

While they argued, the sunfish began to screech and undulate. The intelligent trio led the dance, the four savage males aping their movements and cries, yet there were segments in which the males acted in harmony with Charlotte, Brigit, and Tom. They repeated one sequence again and again like a backbeat or a chorus as Lam observed from below.

CHARLOTTE: Old Ones / We remember / Mothers and mothers.

ALL SUNFISH: Mothers ago.

CHARLOTTE AND TOM: Stronger than the ice

ALL SUNFISH: The Old Ones / Home / Great and safe.

CHARLOTTE: Top quakes took us from you.

ALL SUNFISH: Top quakes / Wind / Freezing death.

CHARLOTTE AND TOM: Old Ones / We remember home.

"This is something they've learned by rote," O'Neal said. "It may be a favorite song."

"It's a creation myth," Metzler said. "We have Great Flood stories from the ocean levels falling with every Ice Age and rising again when Earth warmed. They have cycles of decreased or increased volcanic activity."

"Listen to them!" O'Neal said. "They're talking about the empire like they think they'll find it."

"Or like it's paradise," Vonnie said. "Maybe they believe in an afterlife."

Koebsch sighed heavily. "Lam, tell them you're not from the empire," he said, but O'Neal shouted, "First let them finish! This kind of oral history could tell us a lot of what they know about their neighbors, or if they have religion, or how much they know about planetary science."

"All right," Koebsch said. "Let them sing."

"I think we're playing with fire," Vonnie said. "Lam can't sit and watch while they praise him."

Charlotte broke from the dance, signing questions of her own as the other sunfish continued. Then they lost the thread of their group song and joined her in quizzing Lam with new animosity.

CHARLOTTE: You are silent / You disapprove?

ALL SUNFISH: Old Ones / We belong to you.

CHARLOTTE: We are strong!

LAM: Strong / Yes / Good and worthy.

CHARLOTTE AND TOM: Old Ones / Take us home.

LAM: My tribe is not the Old Ones / We are younger / From far away / I need your patience.

Their arms writhed slowly, repeating Lam's shapes as if

internalizing his explanation. Among the savage males, the body language was sharper and foreboding, like a brewing storm. They were already forgetting the trust he'd established.

Charlotte maintained control over the males by signing at Lam, using her own belligerence to satisfy them.

CHARLOTTE: Safety / Take us home.

LAM: <equally contentious> You are unintelligent / My tribe is far away / Listen / I will give you food now / My tribe comes later.

MALE SUNFISH #2 and #4: Food / Where is food?

MALE SUNFISH #3: Eels / Food.

TOM AND CHARLOTTE: You will show us eels?

LAM: I will give you new food / Great nutrition / New food and new tools.

CHARLOTTE: Show us.

"Okay, here we go," Koebsch said to Vonnie and Frerotte.

"My boards are green," she said. Frerotte nodded. The two of them cross-checked the mecha feeds on their displays, verifying their preparations as Lam led the sunfish from the pocket in the ice.

He entered a wider chasm studded with loose gravel. Below, his sonar revealed several nubs of rock. Tom shadowed Lam as the savage males ranged ahead and above, reforming their pack with Charlotte and Brigit at its center. But there was an obvious difference from before. Now the females keyed on Lam instead of Tom, altering every trajectory to keep Lam—not Tom—in reach. If they met an enemy or if they discovered prey, their strategy would stem from his reaction. The intelligent sunfish seemed willing to rely on Lam, accepting his strange conduct and speech in exchange for the riches he'd promised.

He ducked up and sideways through the holes in the ice, which became rock, then ice again. The male sunfish paused abruptly, detecting scuff marks and traces of fresh moisture in the air.

MALE SUNFISH #2 AND #4: Something passed through here before us / Life / Unknown / No scents / Beware.

TOM: Listen! Listen!

CHARLOTTE AND TOM: Silence / Listen!

LAM: <indicating composure> No danger / Stay with me.

He stopped, signaling for the sunfish to direct their senses beyond him. The pack resisted, bunching in a defensive knot. When nothing happened, Tom crept forward while the savage males dispersed around Charlotte and Brigit, shielding them, screeching threats into the dark.

Four vacuum-sealed metal containers rested on the ice. Each weighed less than ten kilos—smooth, rounded, alumalloy shells with lateral seams.

Lam stayed back, letting the sunfish familiarize themselves with this treasure. They shrieked in delight, using the same body shapes to describe the containers as they used to name the crude metal tools they'd scavenged days ago. They recognized the substance. They thought they could smash it into chisels and blades.

TOM: Tools / There are tools!

LAM: Tools and food / Not danger / Food.

CHARLOTTE: I smell no food / Only metal / How did you cause metal to wait for us?

LAM: My tribe is strong / Listen and wait.

He scuttled toward the containers, advising the sunfish that there would be noises and smells. As he hit each metal shell, it popped open. The air was drenched with the coppery scent of raw meat.

Vonnie and Ash had taken every last ounce of synthetic tissue from their vats to fill two of the containers with cloned blubber, cartilage, and blood. The organic material had been intended for their next round of sunfish-shaped probes. Instead, they'd activated two probes that lacked any disguise, then raced the skeletal, naked mecha into the ice while the colony slept.

Probes 116 and 117 had carried their payloads to the border of the tribe's territory, leaving a radio beacon for Lam. Afterwards, the probes moved away and found a hollow where they'd hidden themselves.

Twenty kilos of meat wouldn't serve as more than one or two

meals for the tribe, but easy, extra calories were an unlikely gift in the frozen sky.

The other two containers held pliers, screwdrivers, and hammers. These tools weren't fitted for sunfish. Vonnie hadn't had time to develop new equipment, and she'd imagined the sunfish would celebrate steel of any shape.

The pack's cries were a shrill wail. They stroked Lam in elation as they examined the containers. Brigit, Tom, and Charlotte reached for the tools. The savage males swarmed the containers of blood and gore.

Suddenly they hopped apart. Among their many arms, Tom and Charlotte lifted three screwdrivers and a hammer like weapons.

"What is it?" Koebsch said. "What's going on?"

"The meat could smell wrong or they recognized one of those tools as something on Vonnie's suit," O'Neal said. But the sunfish were searching the blackness. Lam's telemetry flared, analyzing their new postures.

"Some of those body shapes are welcoming," Vonnie said. "Look at the males. They recognize whatever's out there."

Lam said:

—*There are new sonar calls above us. The voices belong to four of the intelligent females in Top Clan Eight-Six.*

"Von, they're moving toward our probes," Frerotte said as her station lit up with alarms.

"They shouldn't know we're there," Koebsch said. "I thought the rest of the tribe was inside their home."

Vonnie glanced at Metzler. "You said they might have long-range communications we haven't figured out yet. Is it possible they have better hearing than our mecha?"

"Absolutely not."

—*The sonar calls are increasing in volume and multitude. There are male voices mixed with the female. I estimate a large contingent.*

"Christ. Radar shows twenty to thirty contacts," Frerotte said. "They brought the whole tribe."

"Can you move our probes?" Koebsch said.

"Where?" Vonnie asked. "Check your radar. They sent two four-somes to encircle the area from behind. Unless we cause avalanches on all sides and trap the probes in the middle, the sunfish will catch them."

56.

THE TRIBE WAS unlikely to react well to fake metal sunfish. Tom's stories of the earlier probes and FNEE mecha were litanies of fear and bloodlust.

Would they connect Lam with the machines and attack him?

In the nervous quiet of Lander 04, Vonnie narrowed her eyes when the opposite thought struck her. *What if they connect him with the probes and adopt them into the colony, too?*

"Lam, you need to intercept the tribe before they reach our probes," she said.

"I think he should run," Johal said.

"He'll never evade the foursomes of scouts. His best chance is to explain. We can give him control of the probes, let them submit to him where the sunfish can see it, then demonstrate their capabilities. The tribe will want superpowered hunters."

"Okay, go," Koebsch said.

—I'm on my way.

Lam screeched and signed, urging Brigit, Tom, and Charlotte to bring their new weapons. The savage males bolted ahead of the pack to join the larger tribe in the catacombs above.

The tribe's sonar echoed capriciously, fading and reappearing as he flitted through ice. Soon there were other noises. Lam heard thudding arms, the clack of beaks, and a rushing sound like birds in flight.

The eight sunfish in his pack screamed. They were answered with the same malevolent cry from thirty mouths. Then the song was repeated on two flanks by their scouts. All four groups of sunfish were on a collision course with the probes.

Lam redoubled his speed, passing the savage males. He signaled *danger / wait*, but that caused Tom and Charlotte to lag briefly, robbing him of their participation. The males raced to keep up. If he'd sensed a new foe, they wanted to attack.

He entered a new fissure and swung to meet the tribe before they slithered from a gap in the ice, clawing at the faint marks left by the probes.

The rest of his pack shot into the fissure. They blended seamlessly with the tribe like rain magnifying a river as it rolled and crashed downhill. Only one thing stopped their momentum toward the hollow where the probes were hidden.

Lam. He blocked their way, holding onto the floor in postures of supremacy and disagreement.

Like a river colliding with a dam, the sunfish spread apart. They swept up the walls, then washed together again and pushed toward Lam. At the same time, Charlotte, Tom, and Brigit became other disturbances within the tribe, resisting its flow by signing and crying in shapes and tones similar to Lam's grinding dance. They conveyed what they'd learned from him even as he reiterated those promises himself.

LAM: My tribe is strange and powerful / Far away / We offer truce / Tools / Food / We are no threat to you.

CHARLOTTE: They bring metal!

ALL SUNFISH: Intruders hide behind him / Strange life / Smell of metal / Why?

LAM: I have more to offer you.

TOM AND BRIGIT: He is strong / He brings food.

ALL SUNFISH: He stands against our tribe / He stands with them / He challenges us.

CHARLOTTE: Wait and listen.

ALL SUNFISH: We are Top Clan Eight-Six!

Twelve savages moved to attack, causing the rest of the tribe to snap and feint reflexively. Lam emitted another unnatural howl, deafening the sunfish with his volume.

The stalemate ended when the two probes emerged behind him. Their arms clattered on the ice. The sunfish pulsated with the horrified shapes they'd used to describe the FNEE mecha, but the intelligent females called for discipline and tolerance.

CHARLOTTE: Listen! Listen!

LAM: My tribe has also fought with *<indicating the FNEE mecha>* / We are not them / We can protect you.

ALL SUNFISH: Enemies / Metal enemies.

LAM: Not your enemy / These metal creatures belong to me / They are tools / They obey me.

CHARLOTTE AND TOM: Listen and wait.

LAM: Listen / They obey me.

MALE SUNFISH #1 and #4: We obey you.

"He's getting through to them!" Vonnie said.

"Lam, let's show you're in control of the probes," Koebsch said. "We might be close to establishing a truce."

—*Yes, sir.*

His data analysis agreed with the central AIs. The tribe was flustered and anxious, yet their mood was rising. They were expectant. Vonnie felt the same emotions. She saw pleasure and satisfaction in Metzler, O'Neal, and Koebsch.

Lam rippled his arm tips in the sunfish gesture for *welcome* or *yes* as Probes 116 and 117 mimicked his clockwise shimmy. With perfect synchronicity, the trio continued to sign together like three musicians in an orchestra.

LAM AND PROBES: They obey me / Obey us.

CHARLOTTE: They are metal!

LAM AND PROBES: My tribe creates them like children / They never tire / Never eat / Great strength / They serve me and they can serve you.

Vonnie thought he'd seal the promise of an alliance with the sunfish. They respected endurance and might above all else, but an odd hesitation passed among the tribe. It began with a gesture, then a scent. Lam's sensors pinpointed the change as originating with Charlotte, although it spread instantly to Brigit. Their arms squirmed with bewilderment and a more intense feeling that Lam found difficult to identify.

Like the probes, Charlotte impersonated him, repeating a few hints of information he'd betrayed with his body shapes... an insinuation of human thinking... a perspective outside the ice...

She coiled and screeched in revulsion. Then the tribe erupted.

CHARLOTTE: You are from above the Top Clans?

ALL SUNFISH: Death / Only death above / Close the ice / Close the tribe!

TOM: Kill him.

CHARLOTTE: It's a trap.

"Oh shit, here we go again," Koebsch swore as Vonnie said, "They just figured out where he's really from! They should be scared. We would be, too."

He tried to soothe them, repeating the same assurances in a steady, sturdy loop.

LAM: There is more than death beyond the ice / Great age and places / I offer truce / Tools / Food / My tribe brings great tools and safety like the Old Ones.

Inevitably, they swarmed him. Four of the savage males lunged in a frontal assault. The others swept up the side of the fissure like a corkscrew. This was not the dual formation of intersecting waves. This was new. In pairs and foursomes, the sunfish launched themselves in eight different angles despite the meager space, peppering Lam with separate attacks.

He told the probes to shield him. As the probes leapt forward, all three of them howled. Their voices shook the ice.

Dazed, the tribe flailed ineffectively. Many of them tangled with each other in the air. They bounced awkwardly, filling the tunnel and hindering the rest of the tribe.

Lam and Probe 117 swatted four males into the ceiling, then

clubbed the next pair to arrive. He howled again. Like a tsunami, the sound brushed the sunfish back. Quivering, they scrambled to the upper sections of the ice with attentive postures. The battered males were less alert but utterly silent.

Inside Lander 04, Metzler grinned. "If you can't join 'em, beat 'em," he said, earning a look from Vonnie. She wanted to be irritated with him, but she couldn't stop herself from grabbing his hand and laughing. Dealing with the sunfish was like dealing with bureaucrats on Earth. Sometimes it was necessary to smack them over the head repeatedly to make them see.

"Lam?" she said. "We have one last card to play."

—*Roger that.*

Charlotte and Brigit were the first to sign again, snaking their arms uncertainly. Another intelligent female replied, then three more, then Tom and other males.

The sunfish turned their attention inward. Those on the edge of the group remained mindful of Lam, ready to defend the tribe, but at their center, their tempo escalated. They moved faster than human eyes could determine, seeking consensus about ideas that had been inconceivable before his arrival.

As the tribe squirmed and cried, Lam piped at them, a single, clear, harmless shriek.

They turned.

He held up three arms and mutilated the center arm tip, peeling the cartilage down to his alumalloy frame.

The sunfish screamed. They bared their undersides, but their beaks didn't clamp or bite. They tasted the thin air, absorbing the scent of Lam's flesh. Their sonar calls inundated him, comparing his bloody metal arm with the probes' bare frames.

LAM: I am not sunfish / My tribe is great.

CHARLOTTE AND TOM: You do not hurt / There is no smell of fear / No pain / Your tribe is great.

LAM: We can be powerful allies.

CHARLOTTE: You offer food and tools and more like you?

LAM: Yes / Truce.

As she questioned him, the other sunfish continued their debate. Their frenzy reached its climax. Then they swung on Lam as one, issuing their judgment. It was more than *truce.* It was a proposal to merge and bond with "Lam's tribe."

ALL SUNFISH: Treaty / We deliver ourselves to you / Equals / As equals / Our strength is yours and yours is ours / We offer a treaty with you.

"We did it," Vonnie breathed. Her excitement was too immense to feel all at once. It percolated through her chest like a geyser, lifting and spreading inside her.

LAM: Yes / Treaty / Yes.

57.

HIS CONVERSATION WITH the sunfish became more intimate. They engulfed him, sniffing, rubbing. The ritual was similar to their memorization lessons, a method of consolidating Lam and the probes with the tribe by learning each other's bodies and scents.

Vonnie stood up and glanced at her crewmates, those beside her in Lander 04 and those on the group feed in Lander 05. Koebsch. Frerotte. Johal. O'Neal. Metzler and Ash. They'd developed varying degrees of friendship and trust, but they were united now—united forever—by what they'd accomplished.

It was the beginning of peace between Top Clan Eight-Six and the ESA. It was a mutual step forward for humankind and the life-forms inside Europa. Helping the sunfish, teaching them, would require years or even generations, but the two species were finally on a path to the common good.

"Congratulations, people," Koebsch said. In Lander 05, he clapped Frerotte on the shoulders, then gave a thumbs-up to every-one in 04.

Vonnie met Koebsch's gaze as the men and women around her exchanged smiles and handshakes, chatting too loudly. If Dawson was watching them, she hoped he got an earful. "We couldn't have done this without you," she told Koebsch.

"You worked harder than anyone."

"No, sir. I don't think so."

Nearby, Ash hugged Metzler and pecked his cheek, her hazel eyes relaxed and bright for the first time since the blow-out. It didn't matter that she'd also kissed O'Neal. Feeling a twinge of possessiveness, Vonnie decided to interrupt before Ash grew any more physical with Metzler. First it was important to express her gratitude to Koebsch.

"I'm sorry for everything," she said.

"I'm not," Koebsch said.

"Pärnits and Collinsworth..."

"They'd appreciate what we've done, Von. You should be proud."

"Thank you."

Vonnie left her station and elbowed Ash with a sisterly nudge, not too rough, not too soft. The young woman opened her mouth to protest. "Hey!" Then she laughed and walked to O'Neal and Johal, hugging them.

Metzler beamed. His dog-ugly face was handsome with victory, and, for once, he didn't have a rude comment or a joke. He merely shook his head and grinned.

Vonnie embraced him as she spoke the sunfish shape out loud, relishing it.

"Treaty," she said.

The End

Acknowledgments

Many of the usual suspects participated in the writing of *The Frozen Sky*; Ben Bowen, Ph.D, computational biologist with Lawrence Berkeley National Laboratory; Michael Stein, Ph.D, neurologist with Diablo Clinic Research; Charles H. Hanson, M.D.; my father, Gus Carlson, Ph.D, mechanical engineer and division leader (ret.) with Lawrence Livermore National Laboratory; Matthew J. Harrington, evil genius, author of many of the stories and novellas in the *Man-Kzin War* collections and co-author of *The Goliath Stone*; and Penny Hill, plain old super genius.

I'd also like to extend special acknowledgements to Ben "The Other Ben" Metzler, super fan, whose vision of Europa was integral to this project finding new life; Jeff "The Other Jeff" Quiros, who's always in my corner; Jeff "The Real Jeff" Sierzenga, an excellent buddy and contributor, whose daughter Ashley earned her way into the adventure; and Diana, my best friend, wife, and strongest supporter.

In the Czech Republic, Martin Sust and Karel Zeman must claim their share of responsibility for this story's success. As editor of *Pevnost Magazine*, Martin brought the original novella to his country and introduced me to illustrator extraordinaire Karel Zeman, a man who knows his way around shadows and light. My thanks to you both.

In addition, I'd like to offer gratitude and praise to the good folks at NASA and JPL. Their work in the real world is more exciting than my imagination, and I devoured *mountains* of their reports, articles, online discussions, and slide shows. Professor Ted Stryk generously allowed me to include his work on the cover. You can also find images taken by the *Voyager 1*, *Galileo*, and *Cassini* probes on my web site at **www.jverse.com** in a special Europa-themed photo gallery.

Also on my web site is "The Making Of Alexis Vonderach," where award-winning artist Jacob Charles Dietz was good enough to share a spectacular art sequence. It shows his initial concept work through the final cover of *The Frozen Sky.*

Last but not least, a tip of the hat and complimentary grapefruit (you had to be there) to my hard-working agents on all sides of the continent, Donald Maass, Cameron McClure, and Jim Ehrich.

Without these people, *The Frozen Sky* would not exist, so thank you.

If you liked *The Frozen Sky...*

LOOK FOR THE
BEST-SELLING NOVELS
BY JEFF CARLSON

"Terrifying."

—Scott Sigler, *New York Times* bestselling author of *Nocturnal*

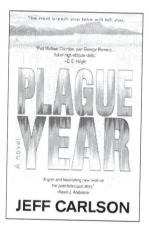

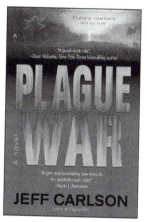

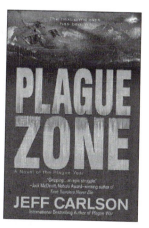

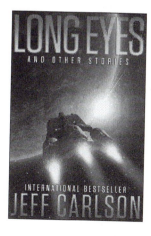

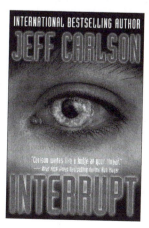

The Next Breath You Take Will Kill You

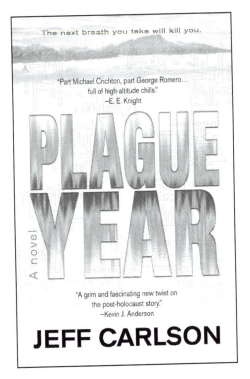

"An epic of apocalyptic fiction: Harrowing, heartfelt, and rock-hard realistic."
—James Rollins, *New York Times* bestselling author of *Bloodline*

"*Plague Year* is exactly the kind of no-holds-barred escapist thriller you would hope any book with that title would be. Jeff Carlson's gripping debut is kind of like *Blood Music* meets *The Hot Zone*. It might also remind some readers of Stephen King's *The Stand*. He keeps the action in fifth gear throughout."
—*SF Reviews.net*

"One of the best post-apocalyptic novels I've read. Part Michael Crichton, a little Stephen King, and a lot of good writing... Plausible and thrilling. This is a master at work and I can't wait to read the sequel."
—*Quiet Earth* (www.quietearth.us)

Finalist For The Philip K. Dick Award

"Compelling. His novels take readers to the precipice of disaster."
—*San Francisco Chronicle*

"A mix of sci fi, military adventure, and political intrigue. Strong, dynamic characters bring the story to a conclusion you won't see coming."
—*RT Book Reviews*

"A breakneck ride through one of the deadliest and thrilling futures imagined in years. Jeff Carlson has the juice!"
—Sean Williams, *New York Times* bestselling author of *Star Wars: The Force Unleashed*

"Intense. Carlson has reinforced what I admired about him in *Plague Year*, conveying his story and themes with as much authenticity and emotional truth as possible. Just consider yourself warned. This one is a literary level-four hot zone."
—*SF Reviews.net*

The Next Arms Race Has Begun

"Gripping. Jeff Carlson concludes his trilogy with an epic struggle among desperate nations equipped with nano weapons. This book is an object lesson in why we'd better learn to get along before the next arms race."
—Jack McDevitt, Nebula Award-winning author of *Firebird*

"A high-octane thriller at the core—slick, sharp, and utterly compelling. Oh yeah, and it's *frightening*. SF doesn't get much better than this."
—Steven Savile, international bestselling author of *Silver*

"I can't wait for the movie."
—*Sacramento News & Review*

"This installment opens with a jolt. *Plague Zone* is one of those rare books that you can sit down with and finish in a day due to its unrelenting intensity... If you love dark SF, you can't go wrong with Carlson's *Plague Year* trilogy."
—*Apex Magazine*

Award-Winning Short Stories

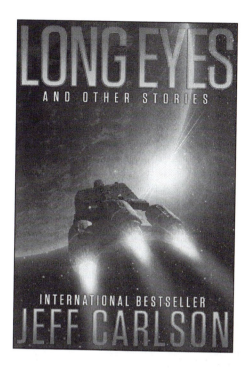

"Striking."

—*Locus Online*

"Exciting."

—*SR Revu*

"Chilling and dangerous."

—*HorrorAddicts.net*

"An amazing collection."

—*Sci-Guys.com*

"Captivating. *Long Eyes* packs a lot
of adventure and entertainment."

—*BookBanter.net*

Their Time Has Come Again...

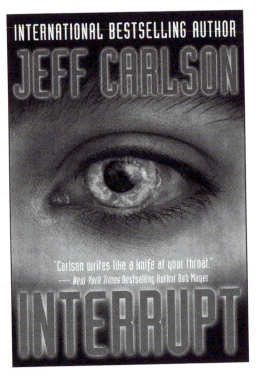

"Edgy and exciting. Carlson writes like a knife at your throat."
—Bob Mayer, *New York Times* bestselling author of the *Green Berets*
and *Area 51* series

"Riveting, high concept, and so real
I felt the fires and blood. Thumbs up."
—Scott Sigler, *New York Times* bestselling author of *Pandemic*

"A killer thriller."
—John Lescroart, *New York Times* bestselling author of *The Hunter*

"The ideas fly as fast as jets."
—Kim Stanley Robinson, Hugo Award-winning author of *2312*

"A phenomenal read."
—Steven Savile, international bestselling author of *Silver*

An excerpt from the *Long Eyes* collection:

"PRESSURE"

THEY SAID I wouldn't feel a thing, but my dreams were awful. I felt pain and tightness and smothering weight, none of which overcame my excitement. I also dreamed of flying—dreamed I dove right through the ground and smashed into a spectacular new universe—yet I caught only glimpses of brightness before my eyes ruptured and abrasive rock crammed through my mouth and sinus cavities.

The mind persists in making sense of things, even when drugged and unconscious. It remembers.

Waking was the real nightmare. I had no face, I weighed too little, and raw swelling in my throat choked my voice.

The bite of a needle on one leg helped center me even before the tranquilizer took hold. I stopped thrashing and understood that I was submerged in a tank not much larger than myself. I knew it was a horizontal rectangle, knew I was in its middle—yet I had no eyes.

Could my hearing be acute enough to measure distance? There wasn't time to sort through my senses. The ponderous blood-weight of the tranquilizer could not subdue the breathing reflex and I dug at the water with every limb, moving up, *up*—

A hard ceiling punched into the smooth metal protrusions of my face before I reached a surface. There was no air. But I could not drown. I snorted water through the generous filter plate where my nose had been, then expelled a shocking pocket of liquid through the gills beneath my armpits.

For a moment I did nothing more than breathe, feeling each exhalation against my elbows. I almost touched my face, hesitated, then grew interested in my hands and brought them together. The index fingers and thumbs felt no different but my other digits were thicker, longer, webbed.

"Garcia?" Stenstrom's voice was too loud in the VLF transceiver buried high in my cheekbone, distorted by the mumble of other people around him. "How do you feel?"

I thought I heard the vibrations of his enthusiastic tone directly as well, dulled by the water and walls of my tank.

They'd told me the recovery tank would be glass. I imagined his entire research team all around my naked body, bristling with recorders and palmtops, every face intent.

Andrea had always giggled when we skinny-dipped together, watchful for neighbors but emboldened by each other's daring, in the early days when we lived at her parents' house in San Diego. Before she got pregnant. "Shark!" she'd whisper, and grab for me. I can be a pensive son of a bitch and her teasing, her smiles, had always been what I needed most.

The thought of her now helped me ignore my embarrassment.

My scrotum had been tucked away, my penis shortened, protective measures that Stenstrom's people swore were reversible, like all of the surgeries and implants. I had that in writing and an eight figure insurance policy to back it, but there's not a man in the world who wants to be cut in that area, no matter the compensation.

"Garcia?" Stenstrom raised his volume painfully.

Answering, I almost swallowed a mouthful of water. Despite all of my training, subvocalizing into a throat mike was very different after the changes reinforcing my mouth and neck. Eating would be a chore.

I croaked, "Drop volume!"

Stenstrom was apologetic. "Is this better?"

"Down, down. Lots."

"You're more sensitive than we expected, apparently. Any other immediate difficulties?"

I kicked through a tight somersault. "Feel great!"

MY PRIDE WAS my savior, my source of endurance.

I spent the longest five weeks of my life in that tank and in a deeper pool, healing, testing, practicing. My feet and toes had been augmented much like my hands, my thighs shortened to maximize the available muscle. I was damned quick. Relearning construction techniques with my new fingers was sometimes frustrating, yet my progress was real and those periods of solitary labor became important to me.

At the surface, in the shallows, doctors poked and prodded and put me through redundant tortures. I had been warned that the study of my new body would be extensive and I did my best not to fear or hate them, but I'd never imagined such intense scrutiny. During my years as a SEAL, I had been like a bug under a microscope, constantly evaluated and scored. Here I *was* the microscope, my body the only lens through which they could measure their work.

Stenstrom tried to be my buddy, as he had always tried, joking and asking what I'd do with the money, yet his possessiveness was obvious. "We'll be famous," he said. "We'll change the world."

I wasn't a slave or a pet exactly, but I was anxious to get started— to get away from them.

The project had almost selected someone else, a loudmouth much better at politicking than me, but the job would mostly be done alone and they must have thought he'd break without an audience.

I'm sure my Navy files indicated no problems of that nature. I'm the private type, happiest diving or surfing with my laughing Andrea or teaching our boys to swim, feeling my heartbeat, finding the perfect ride, the perfect moment, away from other people and their squabbles and protest marches. I've never understood the urge to merge, never wanted to add my opinions to the bubbling stew of e-media or buy five minutes of fame on iBio. For me, a mob holds no power, no point.

Running in circles won't improve the economy, clean the environment, or affect the East Asian guerrilla wars in any way. Hard work is the answer. Honor. Persistence. A willingness to take risks.

The project offered all that and more.

I had to relearn how to chew and swallow, a slow process but strangely more flavorful. Stenstrom said that was only because of the premium foods they'd secured for me, but I had eaten well occasionally in the past and decided my improved palate must be a side effect of the surgeries that had strengthened my jaw and lips. Could taste buds be sensitized?

Learning to see again was also a challenge. From old research with dolphins and orcas, Stenstrom knew better than to surround me with smooth walls. Many of those captives had gone insane over time. That wasn't a concern here, but they didn't want my brain to establish its new neural patterns in wrong or confused ways. Before activating my sonar receptors, which used ultra low frequencies far below my improved range of hearing, they put me in the deeper, irregularly shaped pool.

It was beautiful. I'd lost color but the textures were vivid, stark, each shape imposing. My receptors could also see normally but had no better than 20/600 vision in that mode, which I'd use only for close-up work and to read instrumentation.

I chose complete blindness when calling my family. Rather than face a showphone, I let a computer read and type for me, my throat mike patched into a voder. Site management had encouraged me to limit our exchanges to text only, which was easier to encrypt—and who knew what seven- and four-year-old boys would make of some stiff-mouthed monster claiming to be their father? Brent had only stopped referring to me as "step-dad" a short time ago, and Roberto was still young enough to forget me. The portrait we'd had done before I left was not an image that I wanted to disturb, even though I had been caught in mid-blink and Andrea's smile looked forced, too large.

"I'm doing great, Hon, how are the boys?" I asked.

Her response came in stuttering groups of syllables, all emotion masked by the machine: "I used part of the advance money to buy a DFender for our apartment."

It almost seemed like she was having a different conversation.

"Why bother?" I asked. "The house should be ready soon." Smart alarms cost thousands of dollars, just a speck of what I'd earn, but the money was supposed to last the rest of our lives.

"We're still here in the meantime," she said.

The boys gave me no chance to brood over the resentment that seemed so clear in her words. Maybe I only imagined it. "Are you in the ocean yet how far down can you go?" one of them babbled, without first identifying himself, and other said, "Greenpeace rated you a top ten on the widecast yesterday!"

Brent and Roberto both took after their mother. They were rambunctious little monkeys, and gave me the praise and enthusiasm I'd expected. I hadn't realized that Brent could type so fast. The voder spoke his questions much more smoothly than anything Andrea had sent.

Somehow, technical sketches of my surgeries and gear had leaked onto the net. I even had fan clubs with names like Cyborg.org and zMerman. The boys hoped for an exclusive and I decided it was better to play along and celebrate my alienness. I promised to bring them both mementos when I returned. By then, security should have loosened enough for me to take home a few small bits of hardware, something for them to put on a shelf or carry in their pockets.

When Andrea came back on, she was encouraging but brief. "Six hundred four to go," the voder said for her, but I didn't know how to answer. I had lost track of the days left until my contract was up, knowing how long it would be.

"Love you," I rasped, and the computer carried my inadequate words away.

MAPPING THE OCEAN floor was the greatest thrill of my life. Most people probably would have considered it tedious, gliding through a quiet, monochromatic world, but then the only way to get a rise out of most people is to batter them with kaleidoscopes of music, breasts, and talking heads—or to turn off the net and TV. The worst riots always occurred during the rotating brownouts.

Oil and coal were fast becoming memories, and incredible advances in solar power had come to nothing due to greenhouse clouds and the megatonnage of dirt thrown into the atmosphere by the Nine Days War. With tens of thousands of people still sick from radiation poisoning, no politician would even mention new nuclear plants, and hydroelectric, biomass, and wind generators weren't enough to keep civilization chugging along without interruption.

Aro Corp. had the answer. For months now, crews had been scouting various locales with buoys and remote operated vehicles. The tiny Japanese island of Miyake-jima, dead south of Tokyo Bay, was deemed perfect for political as well as economic reasons. Miyake-jima belonged to an underwater ridge that extended from the Japanese mainland directly into the Pacific current, and its steep southern slope offered powerful updrafts in addition to the normal ocean tides. Aro Corp. planned to build a field of turbines as deep as five hundred feet, using cutting edge technologies like me.

Normal divers max out at three hundred feet and can't remain there long in any case. My surgeries eliminated the need for air tanks. More importantly, a gel solution had been suffused through my bloodstream and organs to protect me from compression.

In addition to performing final, hands-on site inspections, I was also conducting field tests of myself. Before creating other "mods," Aro Corp. wanted to see if unforeseen problems would arise, physical, mental, or emotional.

I was glad for the test period. In three months, I would become a teacher and a foreman, caged by responsibility. Meanwhile, I explored natural altars of rock and coral, spread my arms to ride rip-currents, and chased quick clouds of fish.

One morning, I caught a yellowtail. Its buttery flavor was complemented well by sour kelp. I began to forage instead of eating only from the tubes on my food belt—secretly, truly making myself a part of this environment.

The work itself was more fun than difficult, placing beacons and running spot checks on our communications net. The attenuation of radio waves is very high in salt water, even for the military band VLF signals that Aro Corp. had leased from the U.S. Navy. They wanted to be sure they could always reach me, but there were dead areas within the construction zone. During the first twenty days, we added five more relays than they'd originally allowed for in the budget, three on the sea floor, plus two additional surface buoys whose anchoring tethers also functioned as antennae.

The grid was set. The smaller boats that had helped me through this initial stage were replaced by a barge, capable of lowering heavier and larger gear. The first steel cradles for the turbine mounts were coming down.

For a country that had been almost entirely nuclear-powered for decades, Japan had a wretched safety record, averaging two and a half accidents per year. Worse, loss of containment at eleven reactors during the war had done more damage than North Korean missiles. They were desperate for a solution.

Aro Corp. hoped to rev up a quad of turbines as soon as possible, not so much to offset costs but to prove to critics and nervous investors that the idea was fundamentally sound. The complete project, involving hundreds of turbines, channelers, and land-based transformers, wouldn't be finished for four years—and of course Aro Corp. hoped construction would continue for most of the century as they developed other locations around the globe.

I worked nine- and ten-hour shifts, sometimes arguing with Stenstrom when he wanted me to come in. I'm no hero. I was angling for a bonus.

My gung-ho attitude was also based on the fact that my camp on the lee side of Miyake held little appeal. Sleep was always welcome, but any messages the boys had sent tended to make me feel lonely, and then there was nothing to do but wait and brood, composing inarticulate letters to Andrea that I usually deleted.

I was tired when my robot tug brought me to deeper water east of the island. We'd completed inspection of the last sites a week early and the engineers wanted back-up options.

As I kicked away from the tug, a familiar thrill shot through my exhaustion. Beyond this shelf, the sea floor plunged away for *miles*. This place was like another planet, strange and new, and I was the very first.

The squid didn't hesitate. Its only predators were much larger and shaped differently than me. As I drifted into range, holding a small mapping computer to my face, the giant latched onto my left elbow and biceps with its two longer, grasping tentacles.

Just weeks before, I might have yelled. But in this world there was nobody who could come to help.

I tried to kick away. No good.

Its eight regular arms spread in a horrible, ash-yellow blossom. When I switched to sonar the squid seemed even larger, backed by a spotty, rising cloud of silt.

I dropped my computer, bumping one of the squid's closing arms. It hesitated, grabbing the small device, but at the same time the pair of stronger tentacles around my left arm reflexively increased their grip. My armor tore open. So did the softer muscle beneath. Blood squirted out in diffuse threads and I was lucky not to suffer a stroke, but too frantic to realize it at the time.

My fletchette gun was holstered on my left forearm beneath the tentacles. I groped for the knife strapped to my leg, but another of the squid's arms brushed my foot, then seized hold, and I yanked my free hand away before it was also trapped.

"Garcia! Garcia!" Stenstrom's voice felt like part of the adrenaline-pulse throbbing through my head.

I kicked not away from the squid but into it, winning slack from its tentacles, using this moment of freedom to twist sideways. Its arms closed in. My face and left arm led toward the monster's hard, gaping beak. Then my free hand found the gun and squeezed off three-quarters of a magazine, tearing open the back of my left ring finger.

The squid nearly exploded. Its shattered beak seemed to keep opening, spilling flecks of torn innards. The convulsing tentacles yanked my shoulder from its socket and peeled away more armor and skin, but another burst of fletchettes freed me and I swam away.

The current made restless ghosts of its gore and mine.

Consciousness faded to a glimmer, but the thought of sharks kept me swimming—

I DON'T REMEMBER the ride or the hammerheads that came after me. The shouting in my cheekbone, that much I recall. Stenstrom's panic was too intimate to forget. Trying to reload the fletchette gun with one functional arm while clinging to the tug was a monumental task. They say I did it twice, which must be why it seemed like I never finished.

The sea is no place for the weak or wounded.

ANDREA NEVER WANTED me to volunteer, not because of any danger or even because of what they'd do to me, but because it would take so long. We'd argued before, like all couples, silly stuff like who was supposed to take out the garbage, and we'd had bitter discussions after she got pregnant.

At the time I was just twenty-seven after ten years in the strict, almost exclusively male world of Special Forces, and I had not proved myself excellent family material by butting heads with her son Brent. But until I told her that I needed to leave, we had always found a compromise. She let me name our baby after the father I'd never known—and I agreed to be more lenient with Brent, let him choose his own friends and music and clothes.

We'd never shouted before. She'd never cried before.

"We don't need this," she said, but we did. If we wanted to give Roberto and Brent the education they'd need, if we ever expected to live someplace where sirens and knifings weren't regular affairs, a chance like this was too fat to pass up.

The politicians said the recession had ended in '17, but that was news to us. The SCUBA guide business I'd started after I got out of the Navy failed almost immediately. I should have known better. The tourist trade had been flat for years and my competition, already well-established, gobbled up what little income there was to be had.

We weren't destitute. Andrea subbed as a math teacher wherever she could, we both did spot work for the Park Service, and I made wages on the docks as a mechanic and welder. But I missed the simple vacations we'd taken in the early days, surfing, kayaking. To be reduced to a life of debt, coupons, and freebies was hardly a life at all.

The real horror had been the resentment with which I'd begun to view my family, for needing so much I couldn't give.

On the day before I left, Andrea argued that I'd undervalued my soul. "Two years," she kept saying. "Don't leave us alone for two years."

"We'll talk every week," I promised.

"Two years, Carlos. The boys won't even recognize you."

STENSTROM OPTED FOR a swimsuit when he visited, which was all that I was wearing. To perform their repairs and to let me heal, the doctors had turned me into something of a surface creature again, enclosing my head in a large plastic sphere that piped in salt water, placing me on a table lined with gutters to collect my liquid exhalations. Keeping my skin damp was more complicated. The mist ducts tended to fog the room, so the doctors wore aprons and goggles and long yellow gloves.

Stenstrom had a better grasp of psychology than that.

"What can I do for you?" he asked, not bothering with *how are you* or *hello*.

"Sorry, chief."

"My fault. We should have ordered you to quit for the day. It's not like we were running late." His laugh was a goofy bird squawk that sounded fake the first time you heard it, but he was just a geek—desk belly, pale, with his fingers constantly in his hair or at his nose. "Seriously," he said. "Anything at all."

"Someone to read to me. Someone pretty."

"She can be friendly, too, if you like."

I would have thought he'd be too embarrassed. I was surprised to find I was myself. Maybe I'd spent too much time alone out there.

My next thought was of my marriage vows. Guilt arrived late, but my first reaction was the honest one. I was basically a cripple here, and the idea of being manipulated did not excite me at all. I'd much rather masturbate, caressed and tumbled by the sea, alone with favorite memories of my wife.

"Someone to read," I repeated.

Stenstrom nodded. "What do you like, oceanography and biology, right?" Standing up, he patted the table rather than jarring me. "I'll have someone come in."

It was awfully cynical, but I couldn't help but think that he was improving at trying to make himself my friend.

I CONTACTED ANDREA days ahead of the schedule we'd set, despite an earlier decision not to worry her. Stenstrom was right. I needed friendly, female attention, and I didn't have to tell her that I'd been hurt.

She wasn't home, even though it was dinnertime. Brent answered and said she was substituting at the community college. That made me angry. I didn't understand why she'd bother with such a low-paying job, especially since she must be incredibly busy, settling into the new house, helping the boys adjust to new schools—but of course Andrea enjoyed teaching, and maybe the fact that we were rich didn't seem real to her yet.

Maybe it was good I'd missed her. Our exchanges had not been going well and I might have said something stupid. Maybe communicating over such a distance, through typed words alone, was impossible.

The boys didn't think so. During my recuperation, they peppered me with messages full of abbreviations and icons that my computer and I puzzled over. They were obviously spending more time online than they had with me around, learning new languages and modes of thought. I was pleased that they remained excited about my accomplishments, but Roberto seemed overly attached to a new interactive he'd discovered, and Brent confessed—maybe bragged?—that he had been caught in two stim sites. I admonished them both to finish their schoolwork as soon as possible each day, put the keyboard away and get outside. Go play in the mud, I said.

Returning to the ocean was unspeakably good, but my days grew more complicated as I coordinated with surface traffic, massive barges that probed the quiet dark with fat, long, phallic drills, blundering through ancient beds of sediment, polluting vast stretches of water with their shrieking as they powered down into the detritus and carbonate. New voices sprang out of my cheekbone, crowding my skull—and four new mods had come through surgery and would join me soon.

This was ultimately what I'd signed on for. I took close note of each shift's accomplishments, but the joy it gave me was purely intellectual, and I clocked out with the surface crews rather than working overtime.

The best part of each day was making my way to and from my shelter, by myself, letting the currents and whim dictate my course, always discovering new beauty, new peace.

I think I knew what was happening back home.

MOST OF BRENT'S chatter washed over me like a familiar, soothing tide: "Club VR opened a new place downtown and I got to virt Gladiator and I could have done it twice except Uncle Mark is a bracket colon equal sign."

The computer had grown better at recognizing icons, but Brent used so many. This one meant *flathead*, I guessed, or *chicken neck* or whatever. What concerned me was his tone. Brent had once directed this same mean jealousy at me.

"Who is Uncle Mark?" I croaked, the elongated fingers of my hand tightening into a ball.

I hit the *Send* button with a fist.

"WHAT THE HELL'S going on!" I shouted, six hours later when I finally got Andrea online. "After all I'm doing for you ..."

Her response was immediate: "You did it for yourself."

I stared at the shape of the computer as if it were another squid, my thoughts layered and conflicting.

"For the fame," she continued. "The adventure."

"For the money, Andrea! I'm doing it for the money!"

"Would you have let them cut you up if they were going to turn you into a desk, Carlos? You did it for the chance to finally be a fish."

ITS PROW INTO the wind and waves, the barge lowered two turbines on cables, one off of each side. Just hoisting the house-sized cylinders from the deck and hitting the water had taken two slow, exacting hours. The descent itself required five more. During snags and rest breaks, I inspected the squat towers that would cradle the turbines, darting under and around their angled beams, even though we'd already completed our structural tests.

But there was no escaping my thoughts.

Leaving now—quitting now—would be crazy. Reverse surgery and rehab would take almost a quarter of the time left in my contract, and I'd forfeit everything but the signing bonus. We'd lose the home, our future, and find ourselves back in the city scrambling for wages.... And I would never work for Aro Corp. again in any capacity. Even their competitors would have no reason to rely on me, a hard truth that always led me back to the same worry:

Can I ever trust her again?

The weather had been cooperating, but even nineteen-ton hunks of metal will act like sails in deep currents, and close to sundown we realized there had been a miscalculation. Some pendulum swinging had been accounted for—it was a drop of four hundred feet—but instead of a near-simultaneous mounting, we had a double miss.

Each elevator platform had jets which I could use for final adjustments, but they weren't powerful enough to muscle the turbines twenty meters against the current.

"We're twenty east," I said. "Let's elevate forty. Bring 'em back up."

The nearest turbine was a smooth sculpture caught in a web of cables that led upward as far as my sonar reached. ROVs, remote operated vehicles, scooted about or hovered patiently nearby. And when I switched briefly to my fuzzy, nearsighted normal vision, the busy sea became busier, shot through with the ROVs' beams of light. All of this generated surprisingly little noise: the whirring of ROV props, the harp vibrations of the current against the cables.

The first explosion sounded like God had slapped the surface, a bass thunder that reached me an instant after the VLF net surged with voices.

"Was that the engine?"

"Fire! Fire!"

"Number two crane's lost all exterior cables—"

The last bit of information I personally witnessed as the turbine sagged in its web. If it fell, it would roll into the cradle tower and ruin weeks of hard labor.

I swam closer, thinking I might use the platform jets to keep it afloat or ease it to the bottom, but two ROVs tumbled into my path as their operators lost contact. I kicked left. One struck my scarred shoulder and numbed my arm.

I had been assigned an emergency frequency to connect me directly to Stenstrom. Would he be there? The way the ROVs had shut down, the comm room might have been destroyed. I said, "This is Garcia—"

He was near panic. "Can you stabilize number two?"

"I'm on it. What's happening?"

"We're under attack, speedboats, they're widecasting some Animal Earth crap!"

Three small cylinders lanced into the far range of my sonar, moving fast. Smart torps. They were beautiful in the way that sharks can be, sleek and purposeful, a hard swarm of warheads chased by their own turbulence.

I probably wouldn't attract their attention, not being a power source or made of metal—not much metal—but the concussive force of a detonation anywhere nearby would kill me.

I dug and kicked down, *down*—

Tightness in my bad arm made my effort lopsided, slowing me. The buzzing torpedoes grew very loud.

The rift wasn't deep compared to the plunging valley where I'd encountered the squid, but at its edge was a thick bulge of carbonate. I ducked past, scraping my hip.

That rock saved me by taking the brunt of the explosions, then nearly killed me as parts of it broke away. I was stunned and slow to move.

Animal Earth. The rant-and-slants they'd posted during our efforts here had been based on a refusal to accept our stated purpose. They were *Greens*. They should have supported us, but frothed instead about the blatant destruction of ocean habitats...

I stayed in the rift for two hours, watching, listening, afraid to broadcast on any channel in case there were more hunter-killers waiting to acquire targets. The attack had stopped after five minutes, but our radio communications remained incoherent. Stenstrom tried miserably to raise me on the emergency link again and again.

He tried the general frequencies, too, even sharecasting his public response to the attack. One of the speedboats had been apprehended by Japanese military aircraft, and suspects were in custody. Given the armament involved and the coordination of the assault, Stenstrom suggested that the whole thing was a cover for our competitors in the nuclear or oil industries, and already there were conflicting denials and claims of solidarity from Animal Earth spokespeople.

Finally I began my ascent, goaded by the constant dig of the voices in my cheekbone. At one hundred feet I saw a man, a body, deformed by violence and twisting loosely in the current. We hesitated together in the dim, penetrating glow of the sun.

Then I turned my back on him.

Andrea and the boys were well provided for, and she obviously didn't need me. Brent had never needed me, and Roberto... Roberto was young enough to forget and move on. Let them think I was dead, lost to the tide. The insurance payouts alone would be a fortune.

Four miles proved to be the radio's range.

I kept going into the beautiful dark and never let anyone intrude on my world again.

The End

About The Author

Jeff Carlson is the international bestselling author of the *Plague Year* trilogy, *Long Eyes*, and *Interrupt*. To date, his work has been translated into fifteen languages worldwide. He is currently at work on a new thriller novel.

Readers can find free fiction, videos, contests, and more on his website at **www.jverse.com** including a special Europa-themed photo gallery featuring images from the *Voyager 1*, *Galileo*, and *Cassini* probes.

Jeff welcomes email at **jeff@jverse.com.**

He can also be found on Facebook and Twitter at **www.Facebook. com/PlagueYear** and **@authorjcarlson.**

Reader reviews on Amazon, Goodreads, and elsewhere are always appreciated.

22196274R00185

Made in the USA
Lexington, KY
16 April 2013